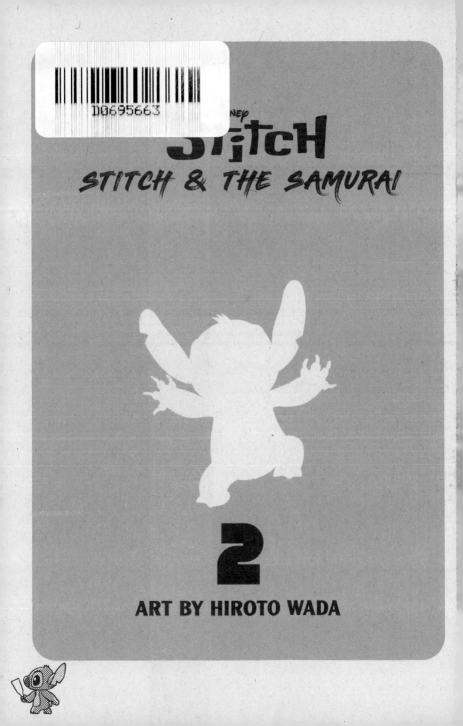

Disney Stitch

STITCH & THE SAMURAI

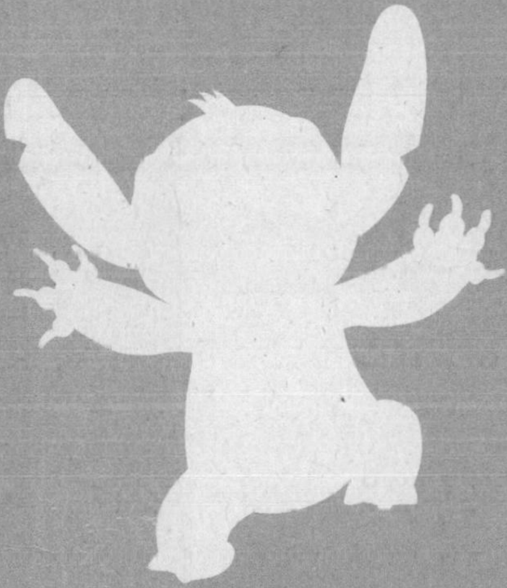

2

ART BY HIROTO WADA

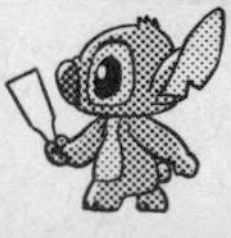

CONTENTS

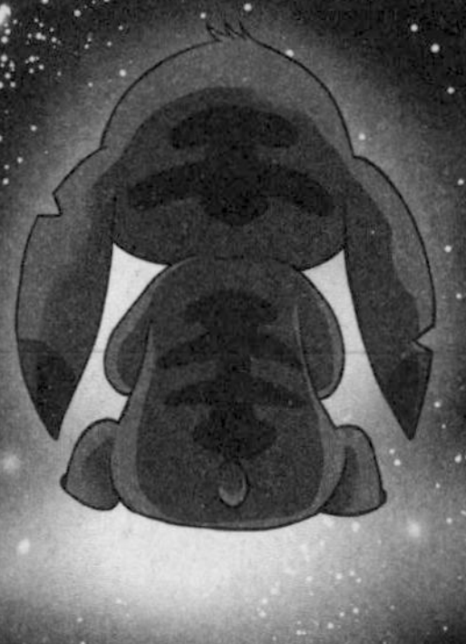

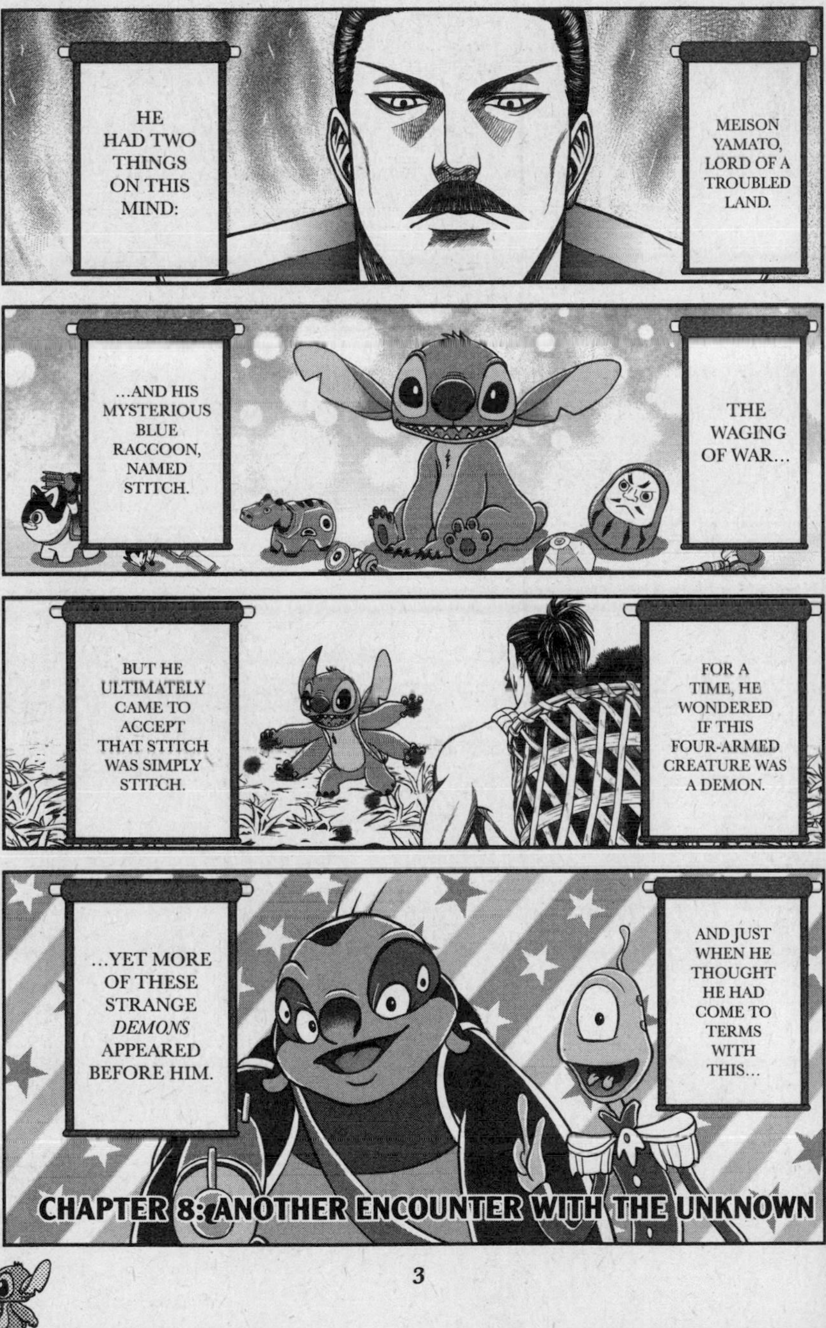
MEISON YAMATO, LORD OF A TROUBLED LAND.
HE HAD TWO THINGS ON THIS MIND:
THE WAGING OF WAR...
...AND HIS MYSTERIOUS BLUE RACCOON, NAMED STITCH.
FOR A TIME, HE WONDERED IF THIS FOUR-ARMED CREATURE WAS A DEMON.
BUT HE ULTIMATELY CAME TO ACCEPT THAT STITCH WAS SIMPLY STITCH.
AND JUST WHEN HE THOUGHT HE HAD COME TO TERMS WITH THIS...
...YET MORE OF THESE STRANGE *DEMONS* APPEARED BEFORE HIM.
CHAPTER 8: ANOTHER ENCOUNTER WITH THE UNKNOWN

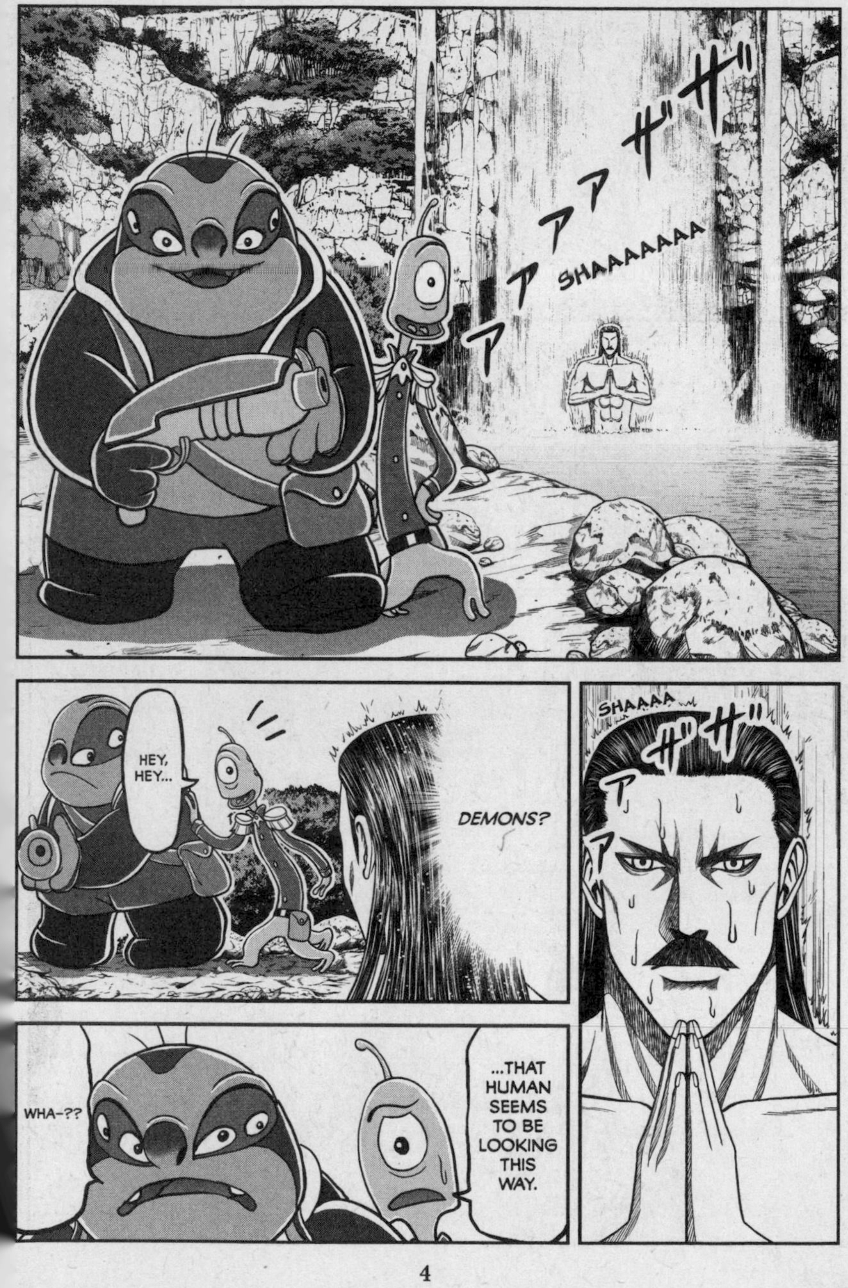
アアアアザザ
SHAAAAAAA
SHAAAA
アアザザ
DEMONS?
HEY, HEY...
...THAT HUMAN SEEMS TO BE LOOKING THIS WAY.
WHA-??

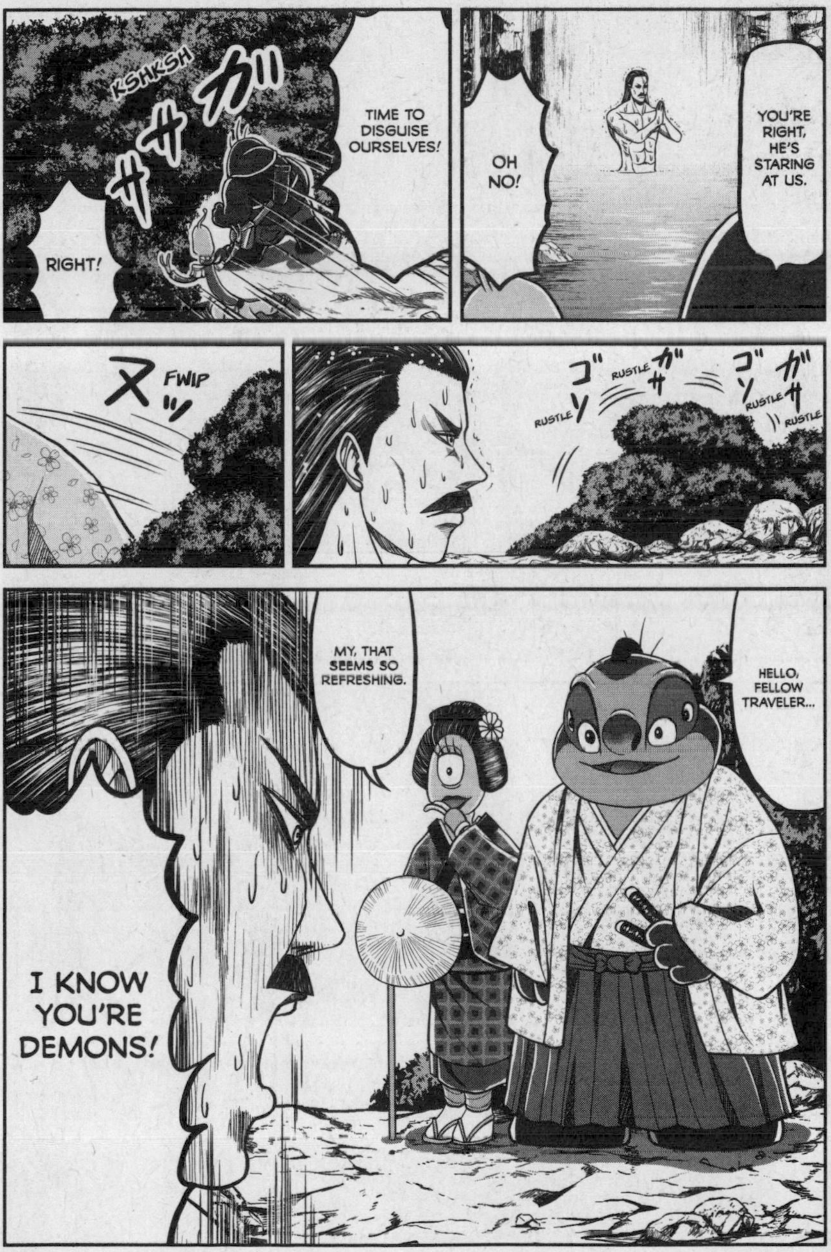
YOU'RE RIGHT, HE'S STARING AT US.
OH NO!
TIME TO DISGUISE OURSELVES!
KSHKSH
RIGHT!
ゴソ
ガサ
RUSTLE
RUSTLE
RUSTLE
RUSTLE
FWIP
ヌッ
HELLO, FELLOW TRAVELER...
MY, THAT SEEMS SO REFRESHING.
I KNOW YOU'RE DEMONS!

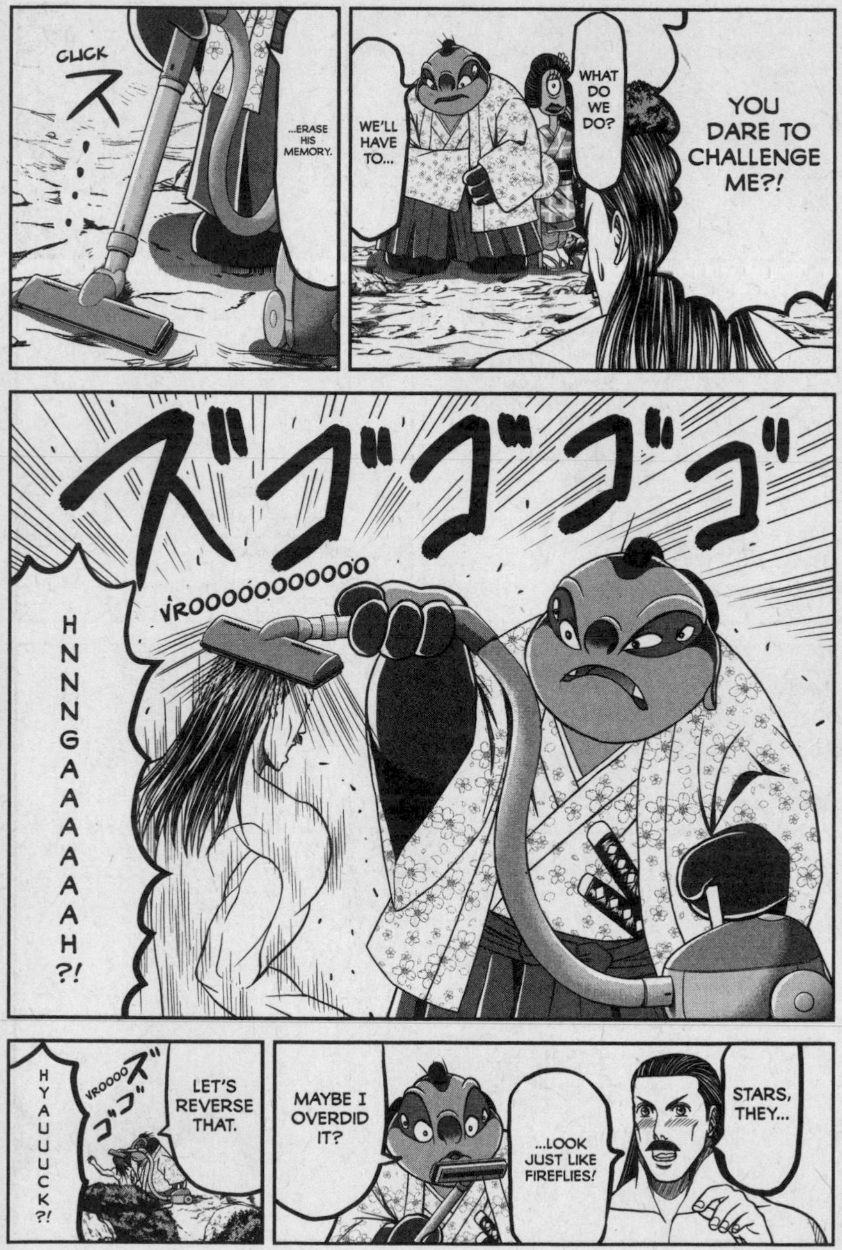
YOU DARE TO CHALLENGE ME?!
WHAT DO WE DO?
WE'LL HAVE TO...
...ERASE HIS MEMORY.
CLICK
ス
ズゴゴゴ
VROOOOOOOOOOOO
HNNNGAAAAAAH?!
STARS, THEY...
...LOOK JUST LIKE FIREFLIES!
MAYBE I OVERDID IT?
LET'S REVERSE THAT.
VROOOO
ズゴゴ
HYAUUUCK?!

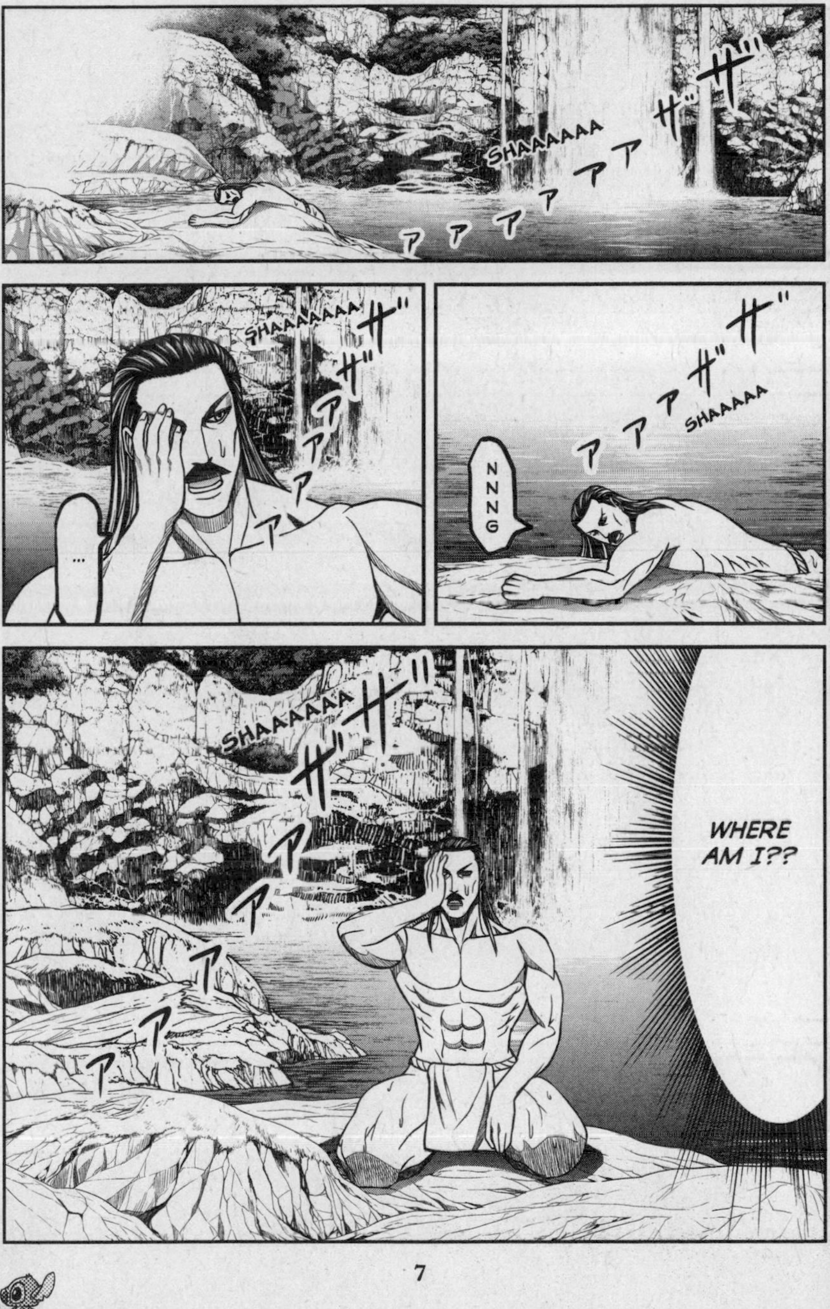
SHAAAAAA
NNNG
SHAAAAA
SHAAAAAAA
...
SHAAAAAA
WHERE AM I??

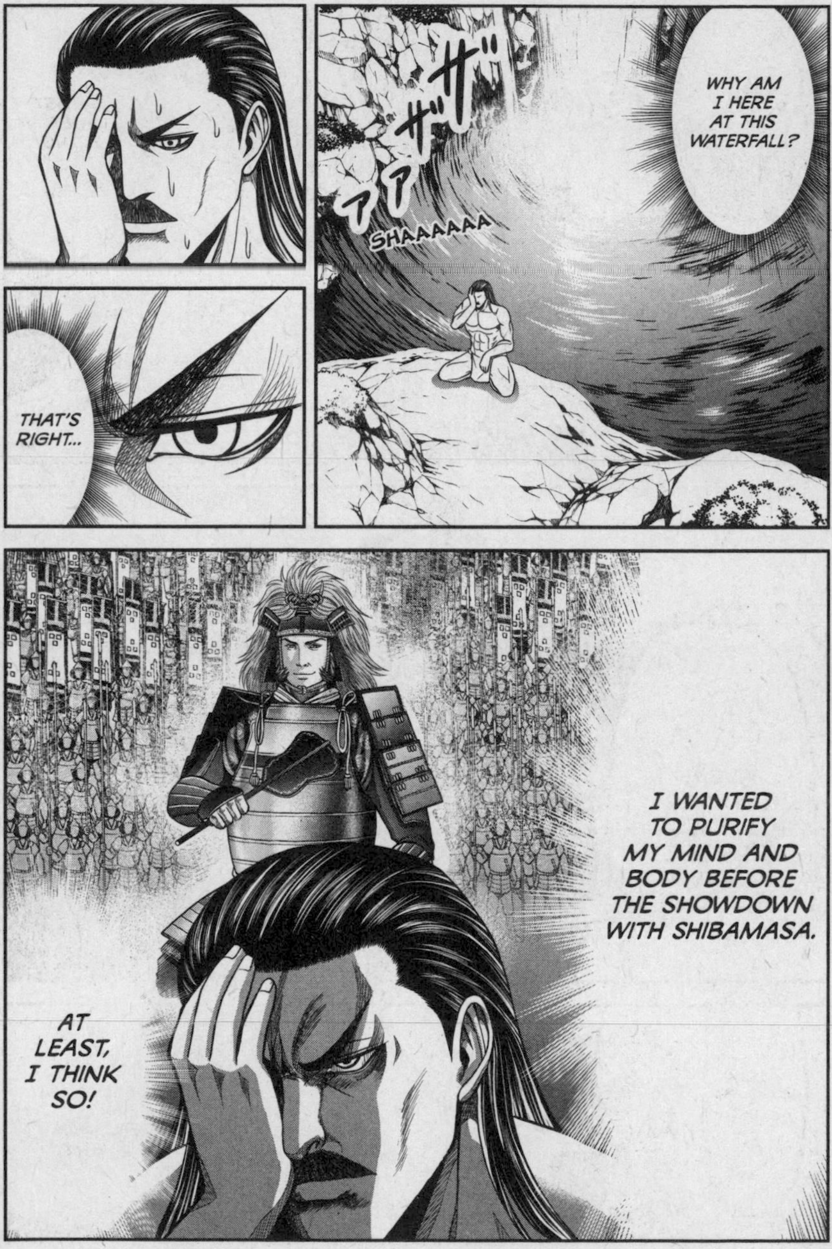
WHY AM I HERE AT THIS WATERFALL?
ザザアア
SHAAAAAA
THAT'S RIGHT...
I WANTED TO PURIFY MY MIND AND BODY BEFORE THE SHOWDOWN WITH SHIBAMASA.
AT LEAST, I THINK SO!

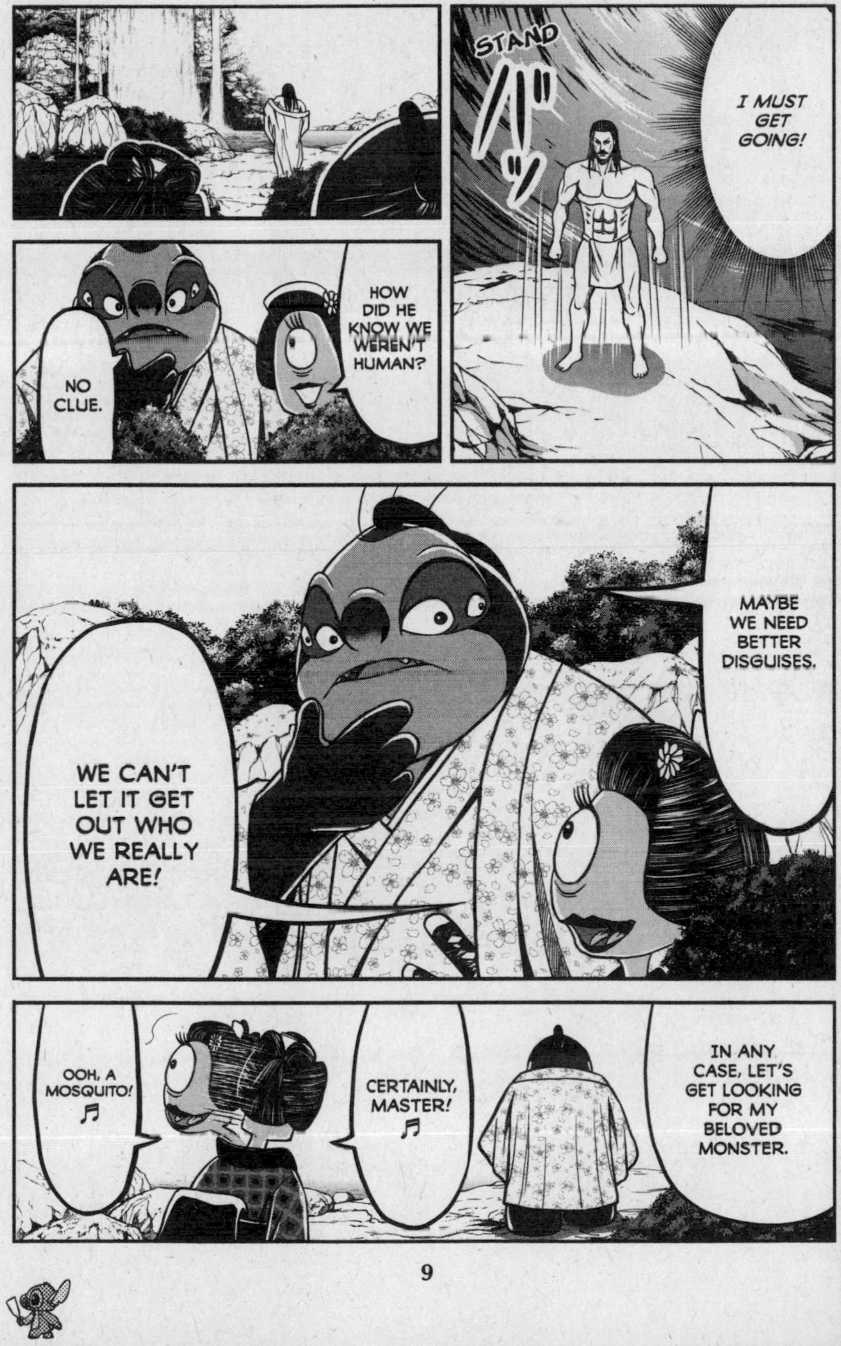
STAND
I MUST GET GOING!
HOW DID HE KNOW WE WEREN'T HUMAN?
NO CLUE.
MAYBE WE NEED BETTER DISGUISES.
WE CAN'T LET IT GET OUT WHO WE REALLY ARE!
IN ANY CASE, LET'S GET LOOKING FOR MY BELOVED MONSTER.
CERTAINLY, MASTER! ♬
OOH, A MOSQUITO! ♬

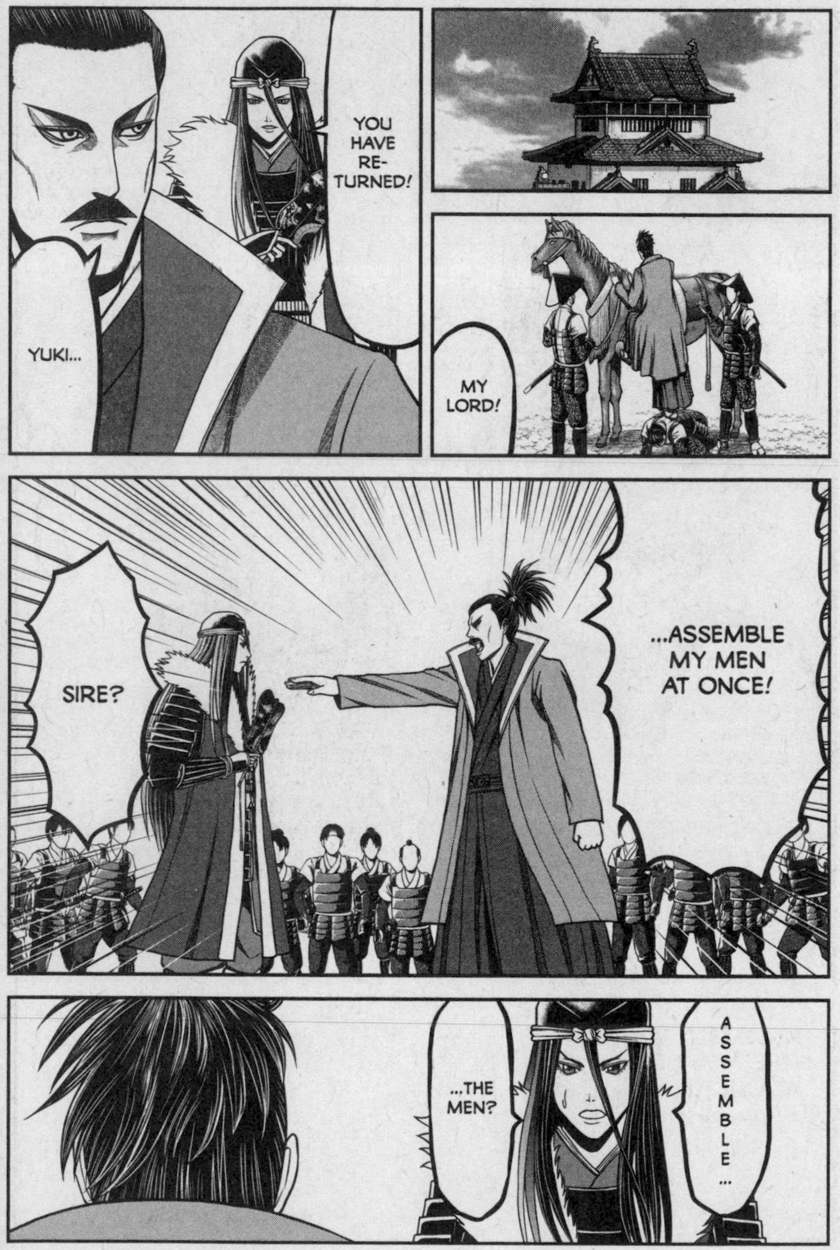
MY LORD!
YOU HAVE RE-TURNED!
YUKI...
...ASSEMBLE MY MEN AT ONCE!
SIRE?
ASSEMBLE...
...THE MEN?

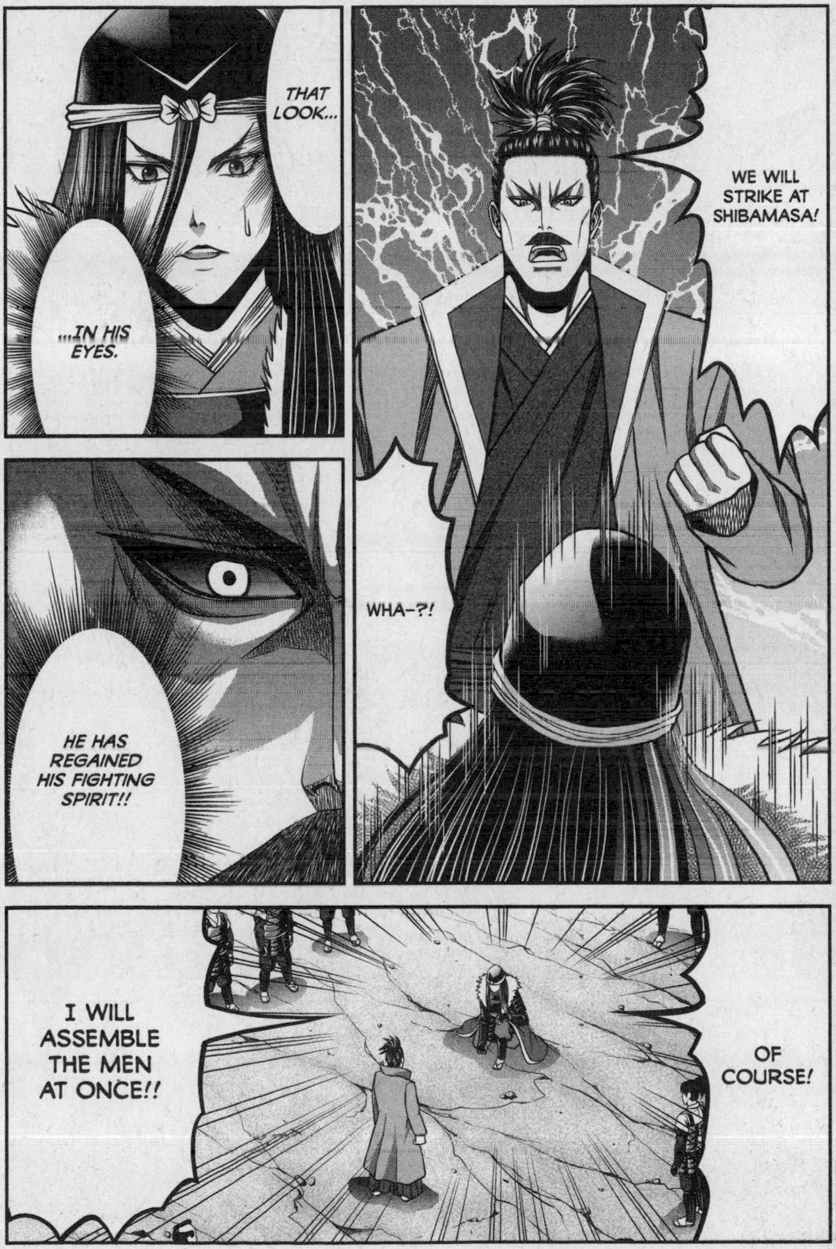
WE WILL STRIKE AT SHIBAMASA!
WHA-?!
THAT LOOK...
...IN HIS EYES.
HE HAS REGAINED HIS FIGHTING SPIRIT!!
OF COURSE!
I WILL ASSEMBLE THE MEN AT ONCE!!

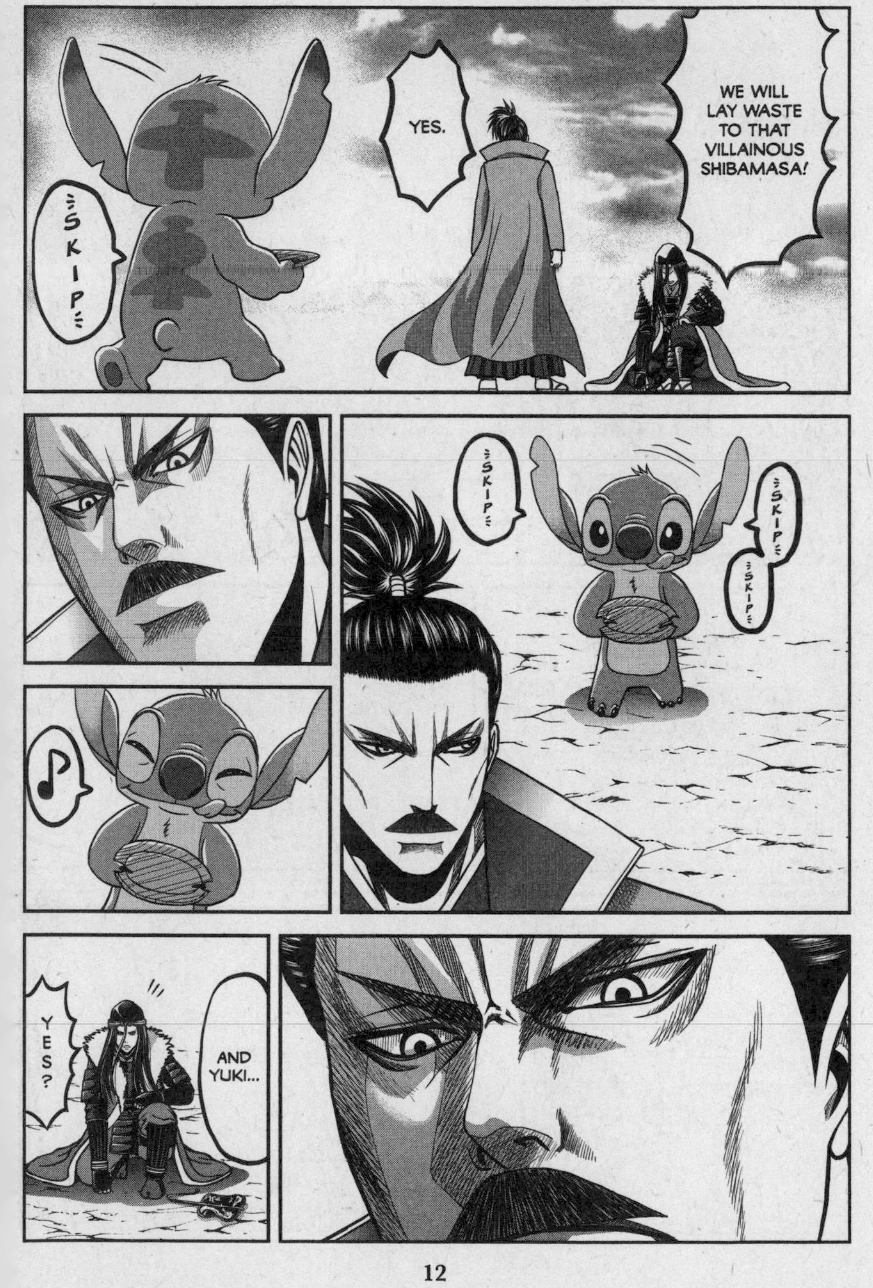
WE WILL LAY WASTE TO THAT VILLAINOUS SHIBAMASA!
YES.
SKIP
SKIP
SKIP
SKIP
♪
AND YUKI...
YES?

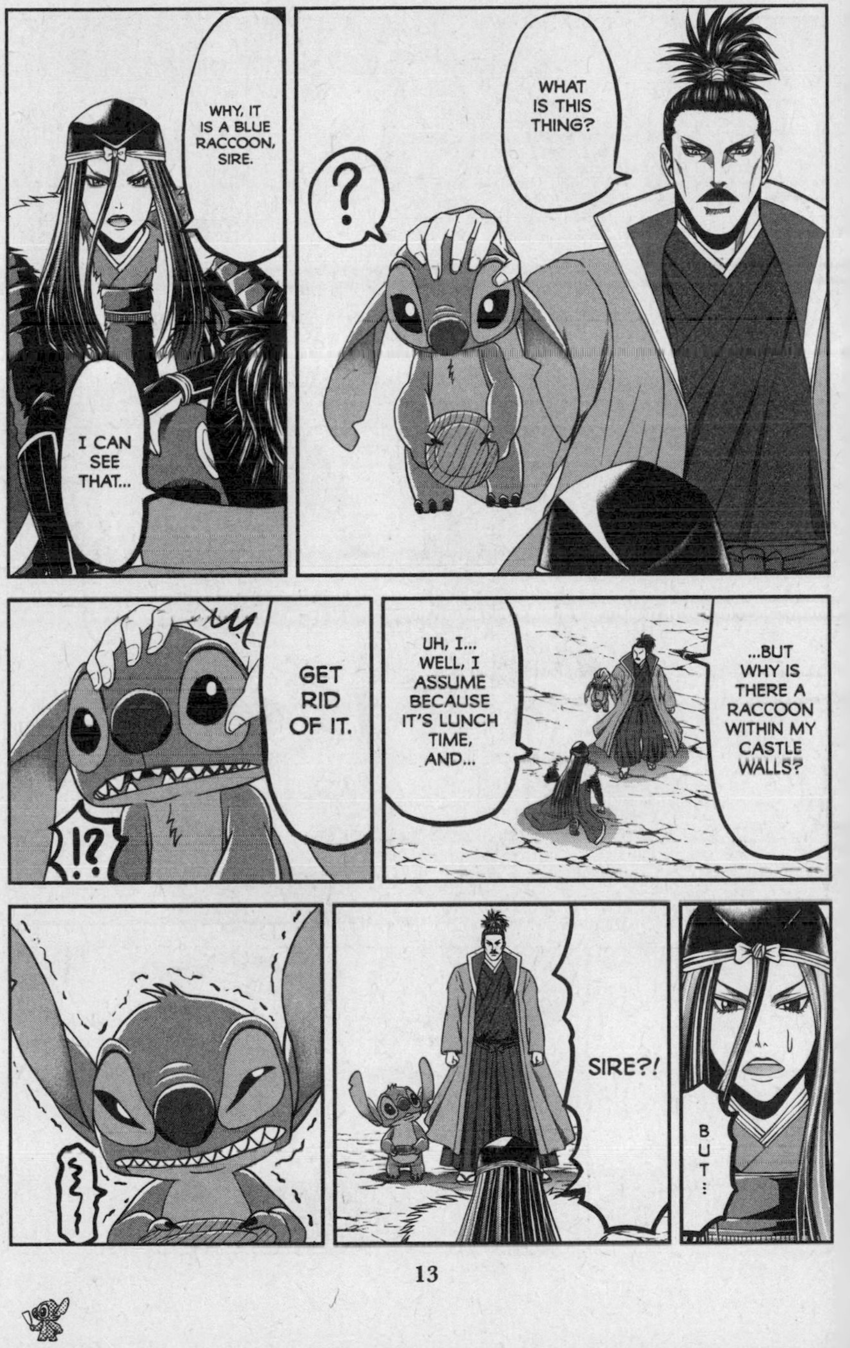
WHAT IS THIS THING?
?
WHY, IT IS A BLUE RACCOON, SIRE.
I CAN SEE THAT...
...BUT WHY IS THERE A RACCOON WITHIN MY CASTLE WALLS?
UH, I... WELL, I ASSUME BECAUSE IT'S LUNCH TIME, AND...
GET RID OF IT.
!?
BUT...
SIRE?!

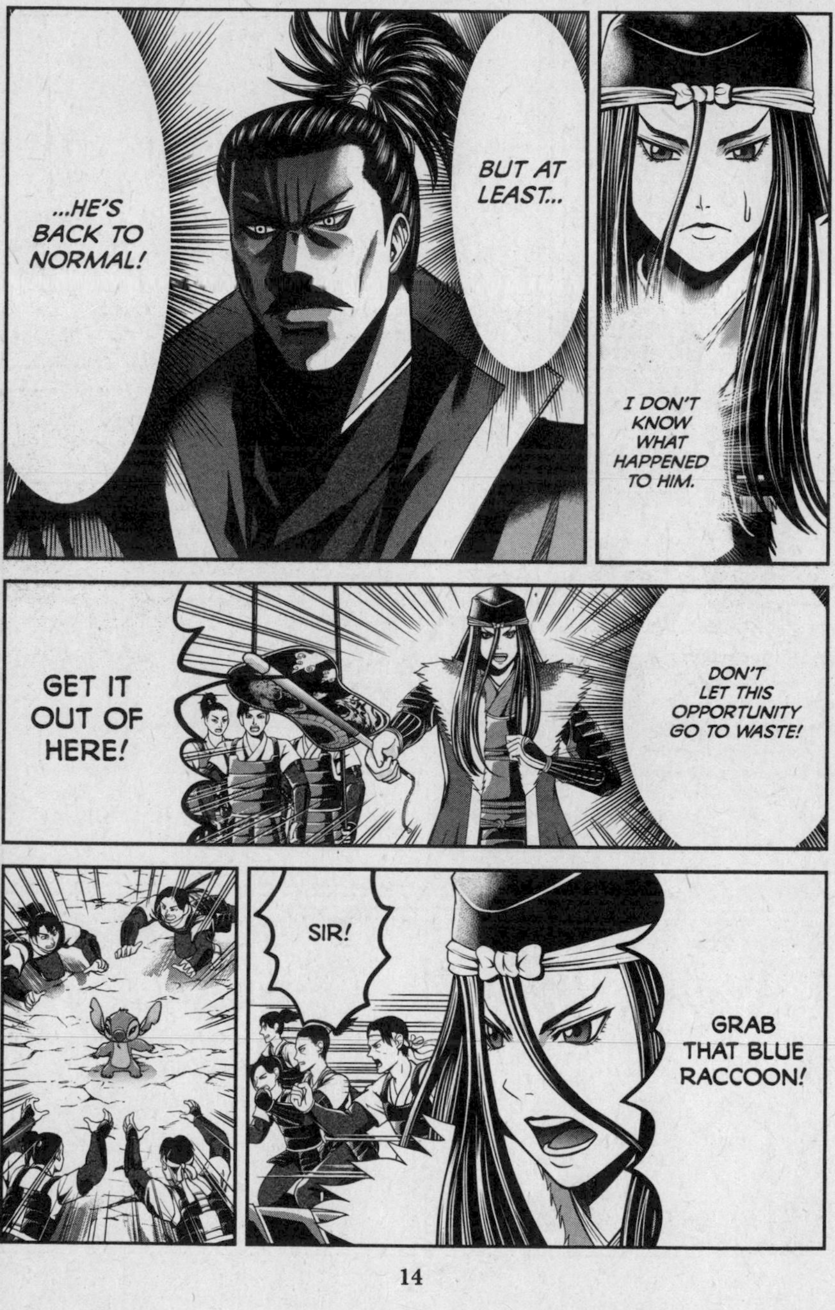
I DON'T KNOW WHAT HAPPENED TO HIM.
BUT AT LEAST...
...HE'S BACK TO NORMAL!
DON'T LET THIS OPPORTUNITY GO TO WASTE!
GET IT OUT OF HERE!
GRAB THAT BLUE RACCOON!
SIR!

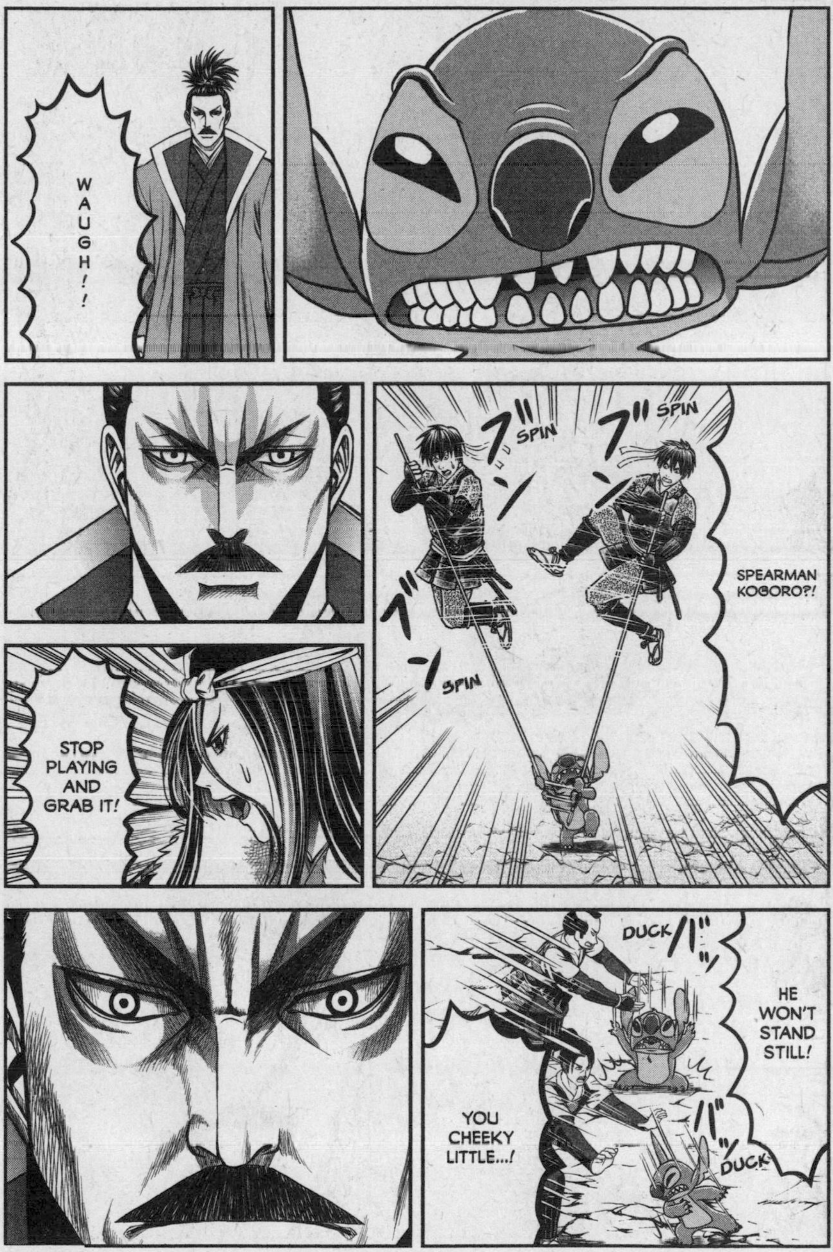
WAUGH!!
SPIN
SPIN
SPEARMAN KOGORO?!
SPIN
STOP PLAYING AND GRAB IT!
DUCK
HE WON'T STAND STILL!
YOU CHEEKY LITTLE...!
DUCK

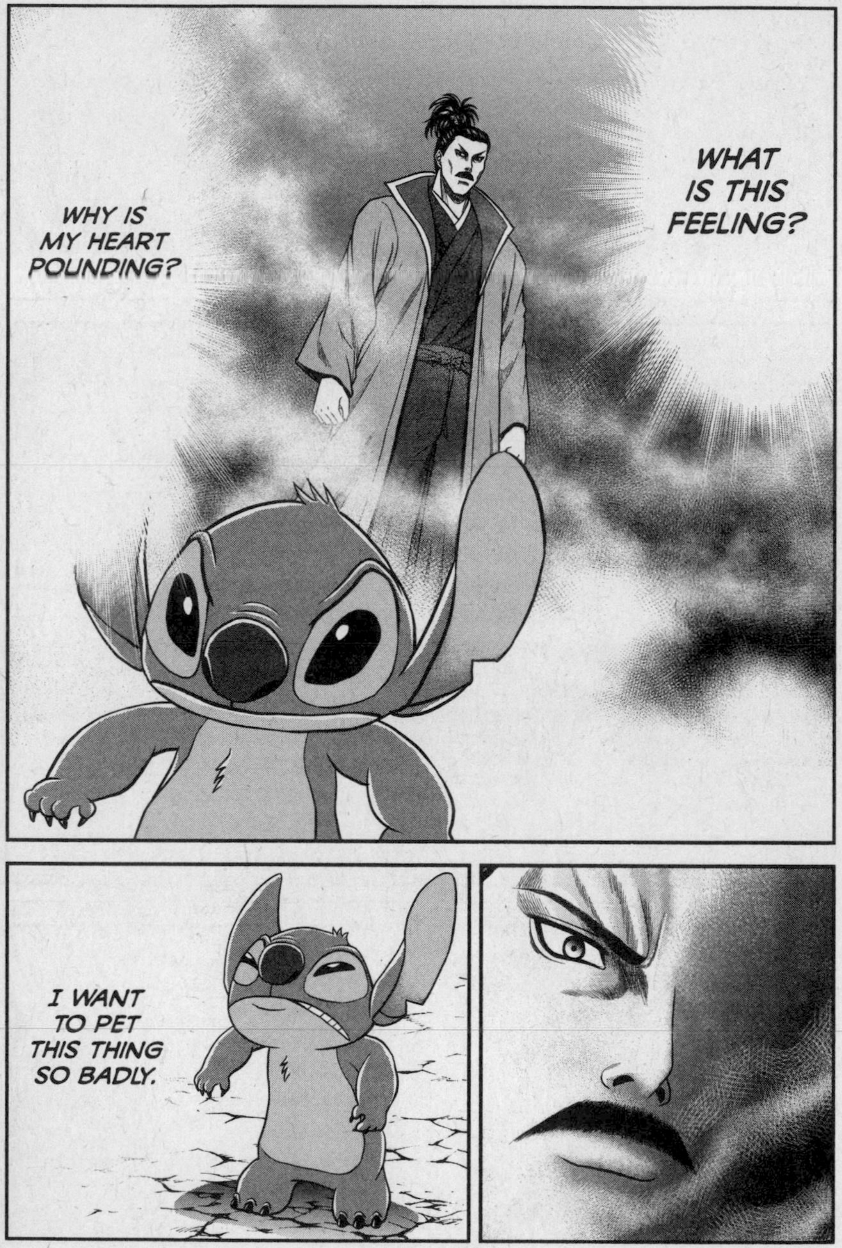
WHAT IS THIS FEELING?
WHY IS MY HEART POUNDING?
I WANT TO PET THIS THING SO BADLY.

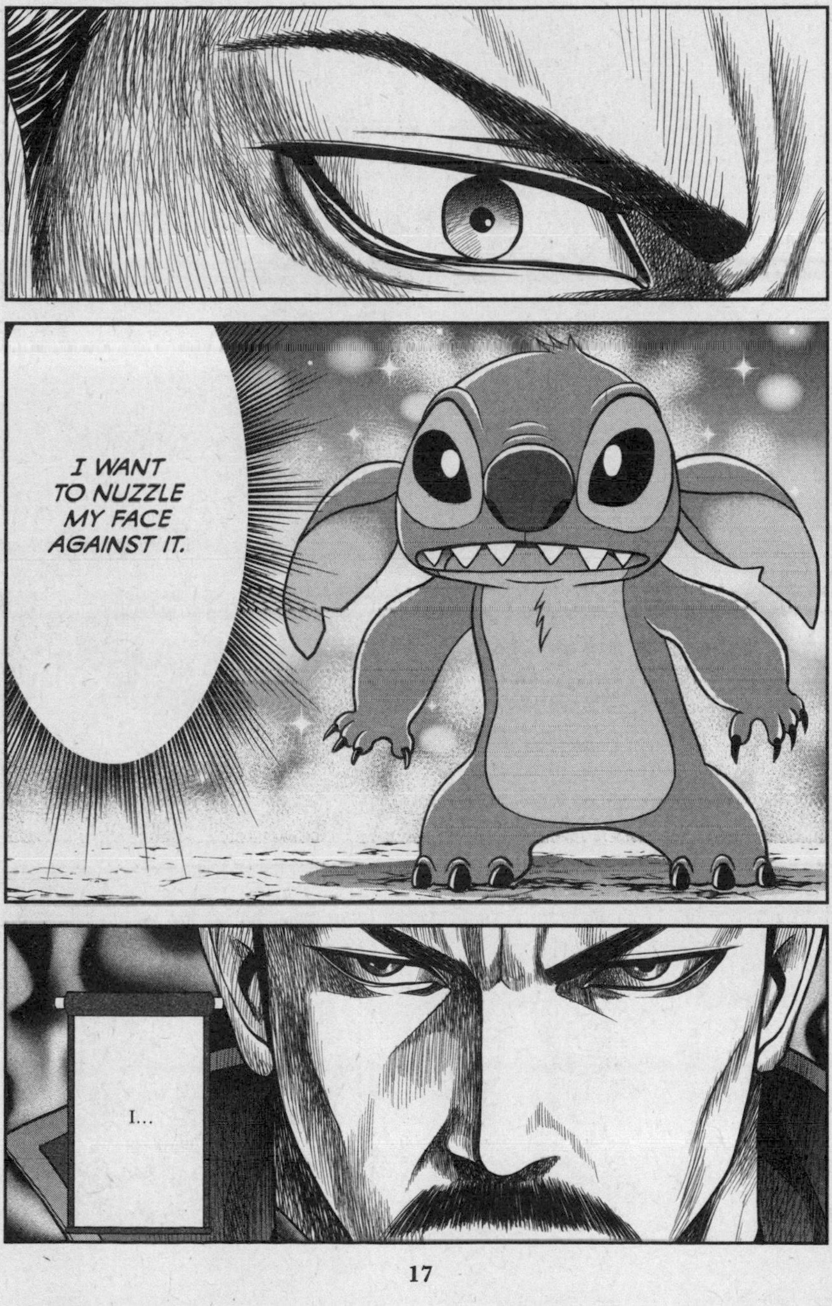
I WANT TO NUZZLE MY FACE AGAINST IT.
I...

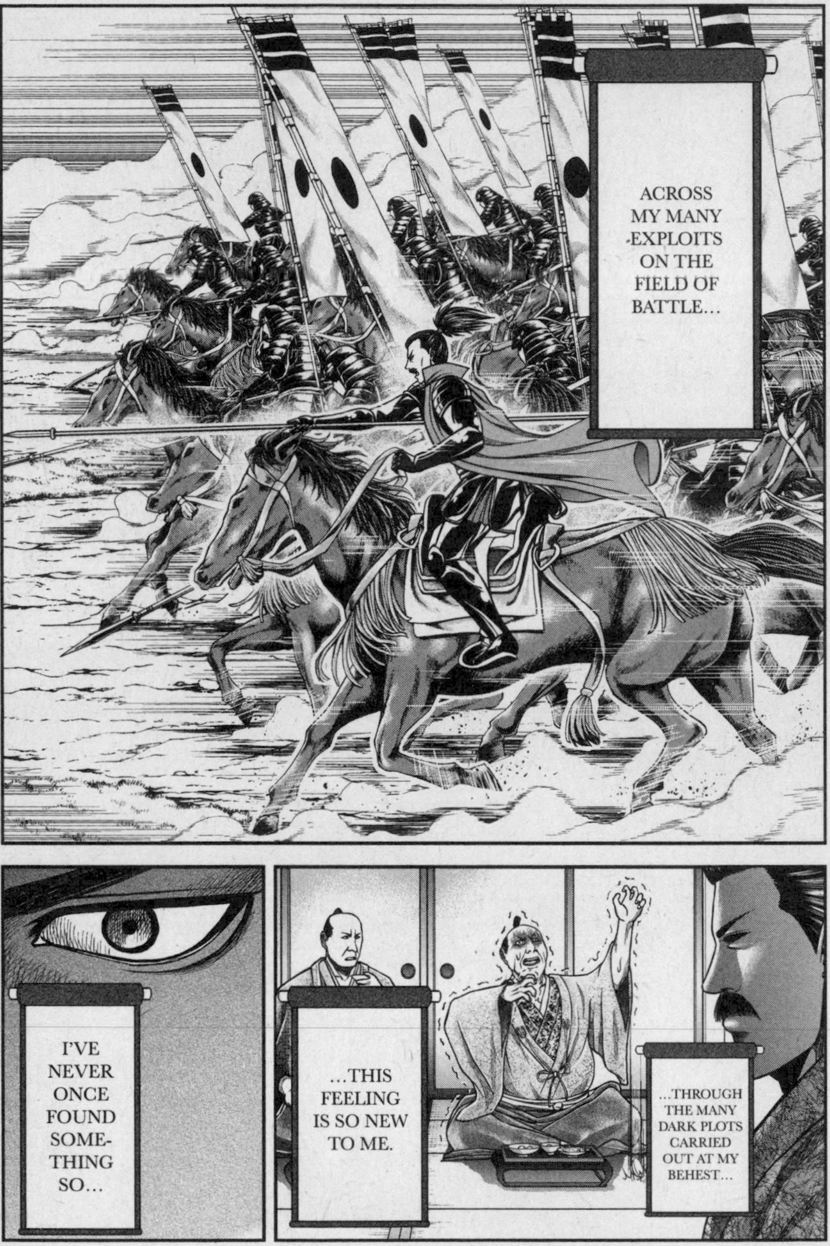
ACROSS MY MANY EXPLOITS ON THE FIELD OF BATTLE…
…THROUGH THE MANY DARK PLOTS CARRIED OUT AT MY BEHEST…
…THIS FEELING IS SO NEW TO ME.
I'VE NEVER ONCE FOUND SOME-THING SO…

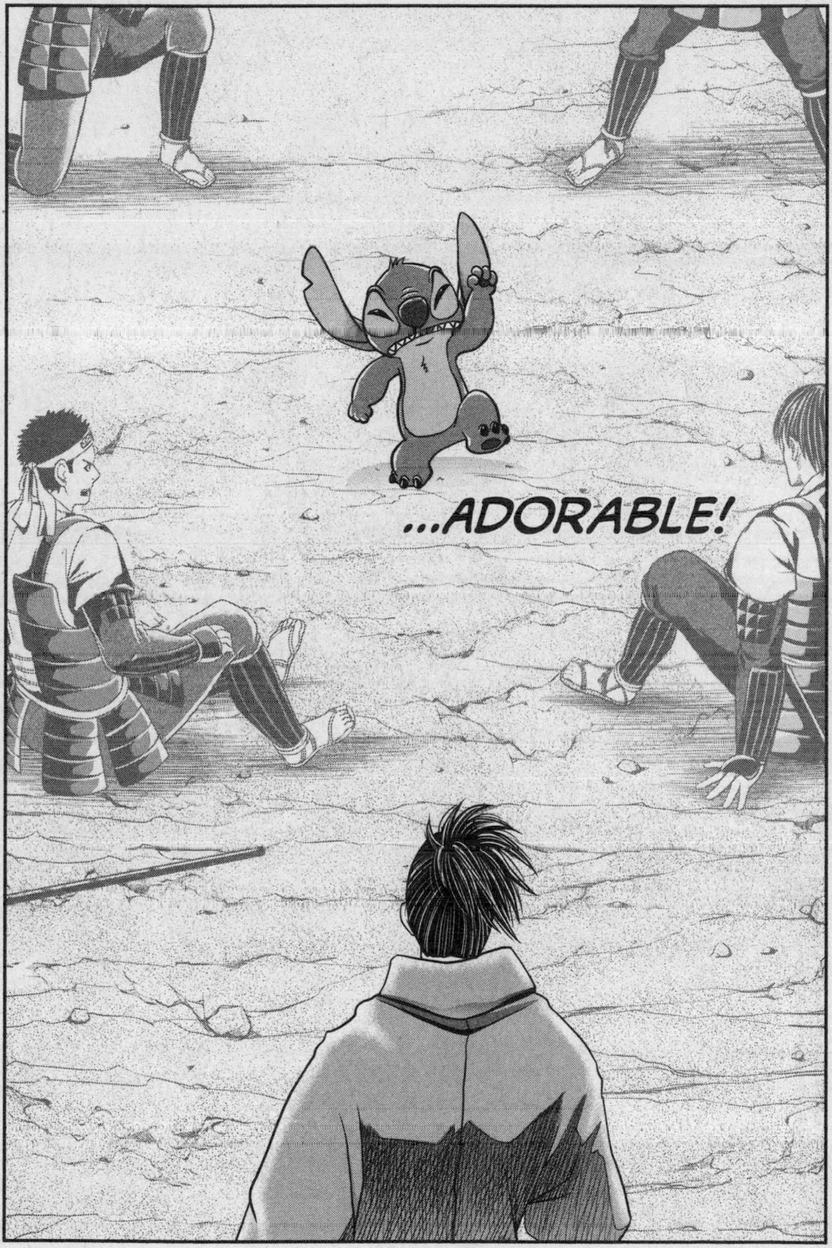
...ADORABLE!

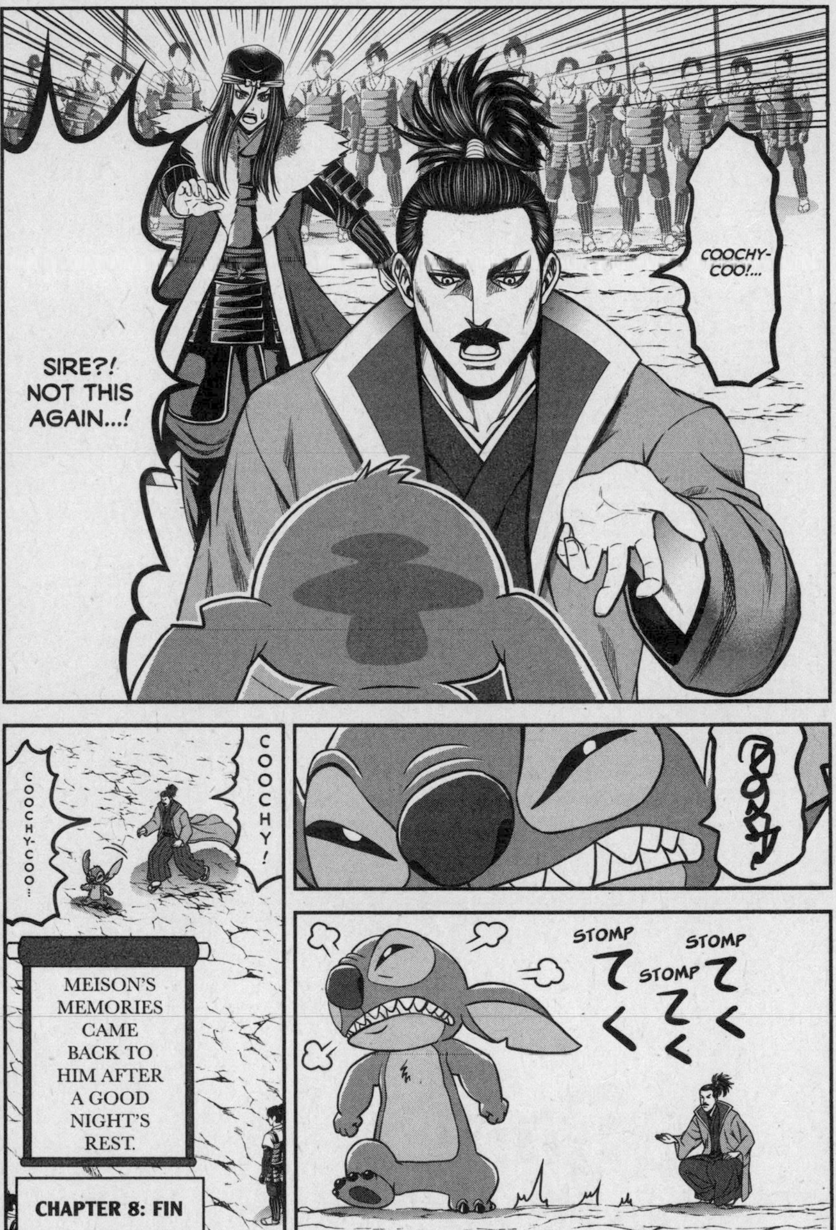
COOCHY-COO!...
SIRE?! NOT THIS AGAIN...!
STOMP
STOMP
STOMP
COOCHY!
COOCHY-COO...
MEISON'S MEMORIES CAME BACK TO HIM AFTER A GOOD NIGHT'S REST.
CHAPTER 8: FIN

DISNEP
STITCH

STITCH & THE SAMURAI

Disney

Stitch

STITCH & THE SAMURAI

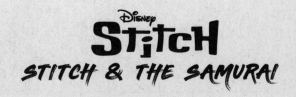

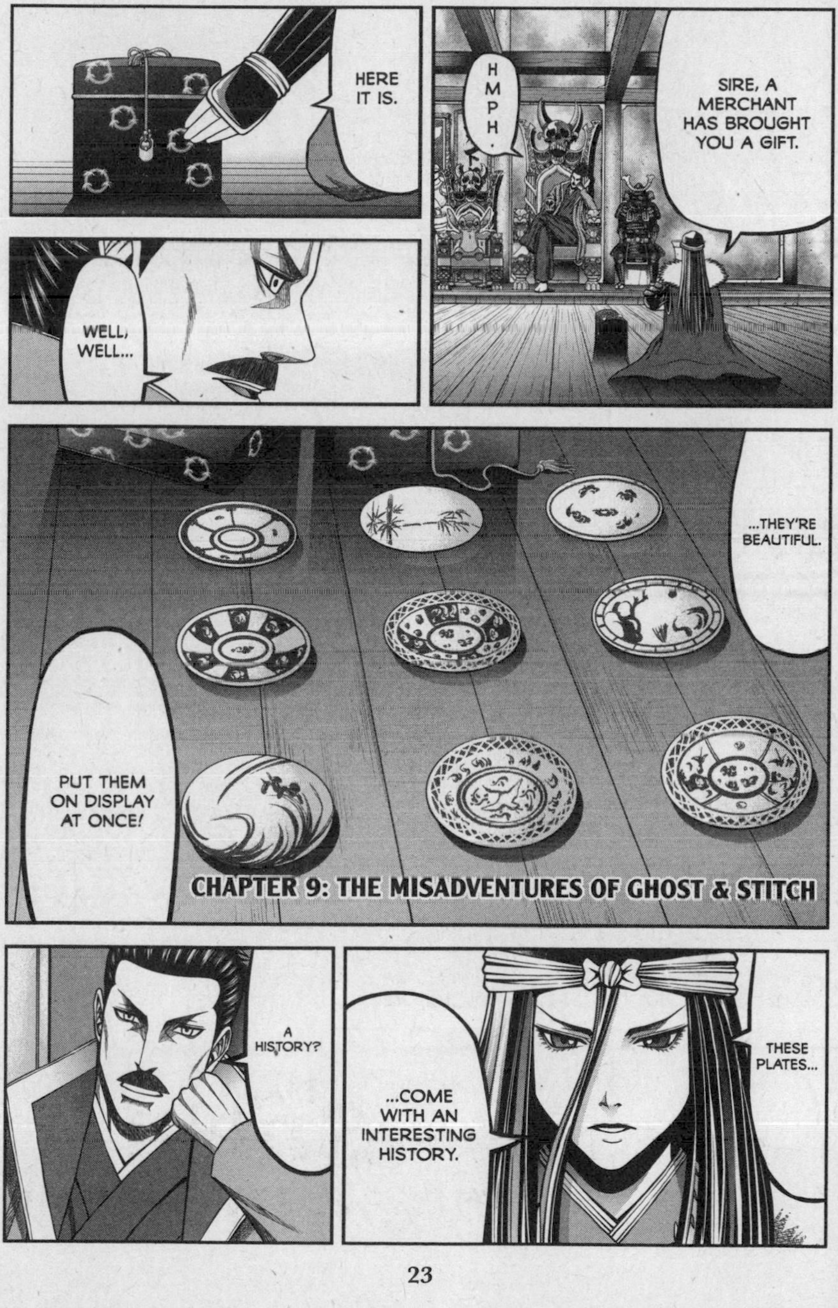
SIRE, A MERCHANT HAS BROUGHT YOU A GIFT.
HMPH.
HERE IT IS.
WELL, WELL...
...THEY'RE BEAUTIFUL.
PUT THEM ON DISPLAY AT ONCE!
CHAPTER 9: THE MISADVENTURES OF GHOST & STITCH
THESE PLATES...
...COME WITH AN INTERESTING HISTORY.
A HISTORY?

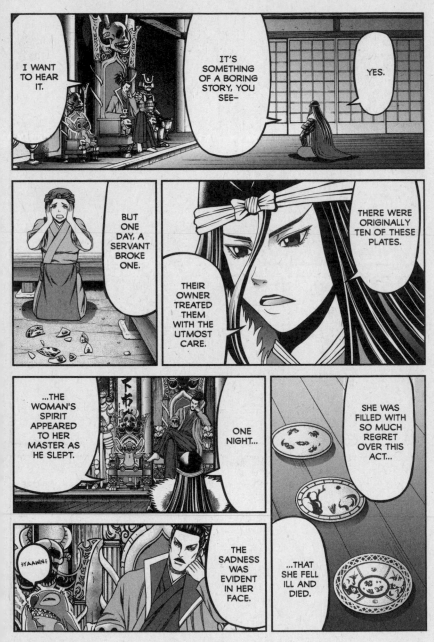

YES.
IT'S SOMETHING OF A BORING STORY, YOU SEE–
I WANT TO HEAR IT.
THERE WERE ORIGINALLY TEN OF THESE PLATES.
THEIR OWNER TREATED THEM WITH THE UTMOST CARE.
BUT ONE DAY, A SERVANT BROKE ONE.
SHE WAS FILLED WITH SO MUCH REGRET OVER THIS ACT...
...THAT SHE FELL ILL AND DIED.
ONE NIGHT...
...THE WOMAN'S SPIRIT APPEARED TO HER MASTER AS HE SLEPT.
THE SADNESS WAS EVIDENT IN HER FACE.
YAAWN

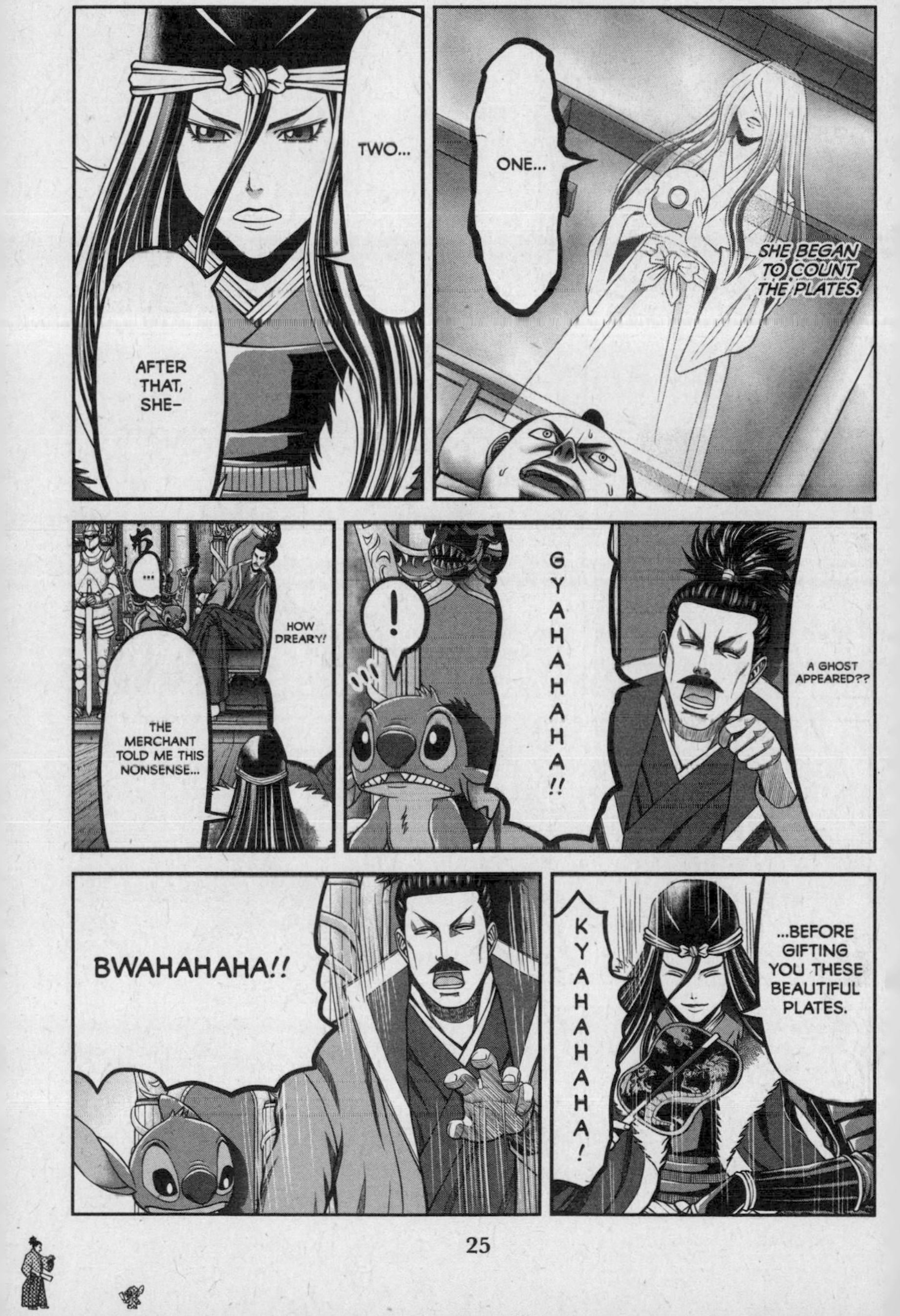

SHE BEGAN TO COUNT THE PLATES.
ONE...
TWO...
AFTER THAT, SHE–
A GHOST APPEARED??
GYAHAHAHAHA!!
!
HOW DREARY!
...
THE MERCHANT TOLD ME THIS NONSENSE...
...BEFORE GIFTING YOU THESE BEAUTIFUL PLATES.
KYAHAHAHAHA!
BWAHAHAHA!!

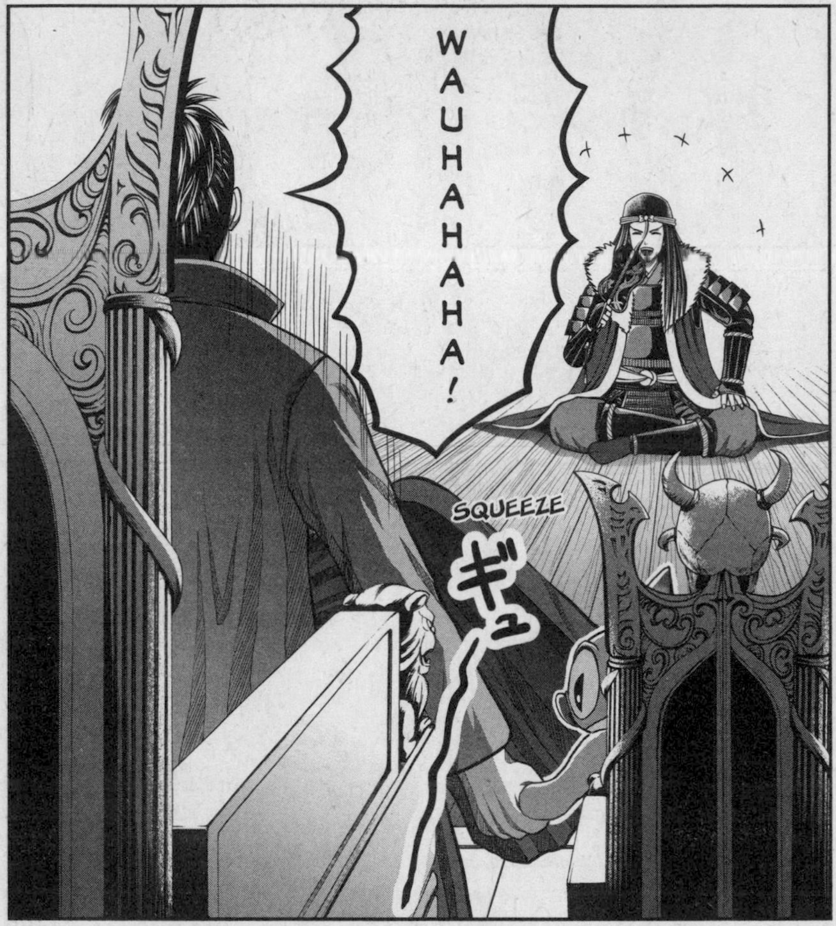
WAUHAHAHA!
SQUEEZE
ギュ

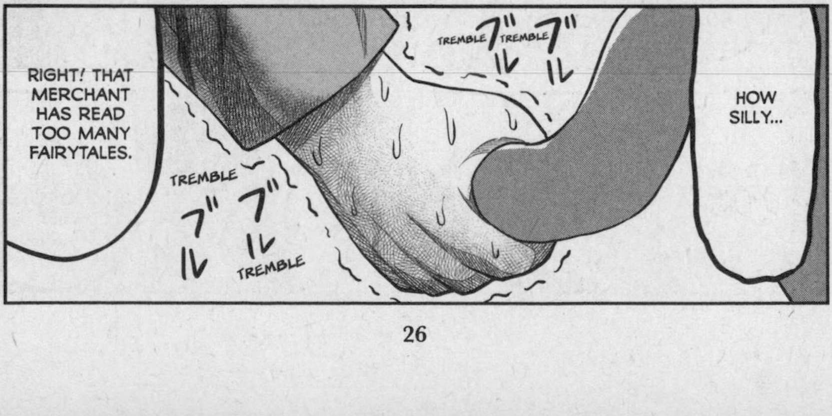
HOW SILLY...
TREMBLE ブル TREMBLE ブル
RIGHT! THAT MERCHANT HAS READ TOO MANY FAIRYTALES.
TREMBLE ブル ブル TREMBLE

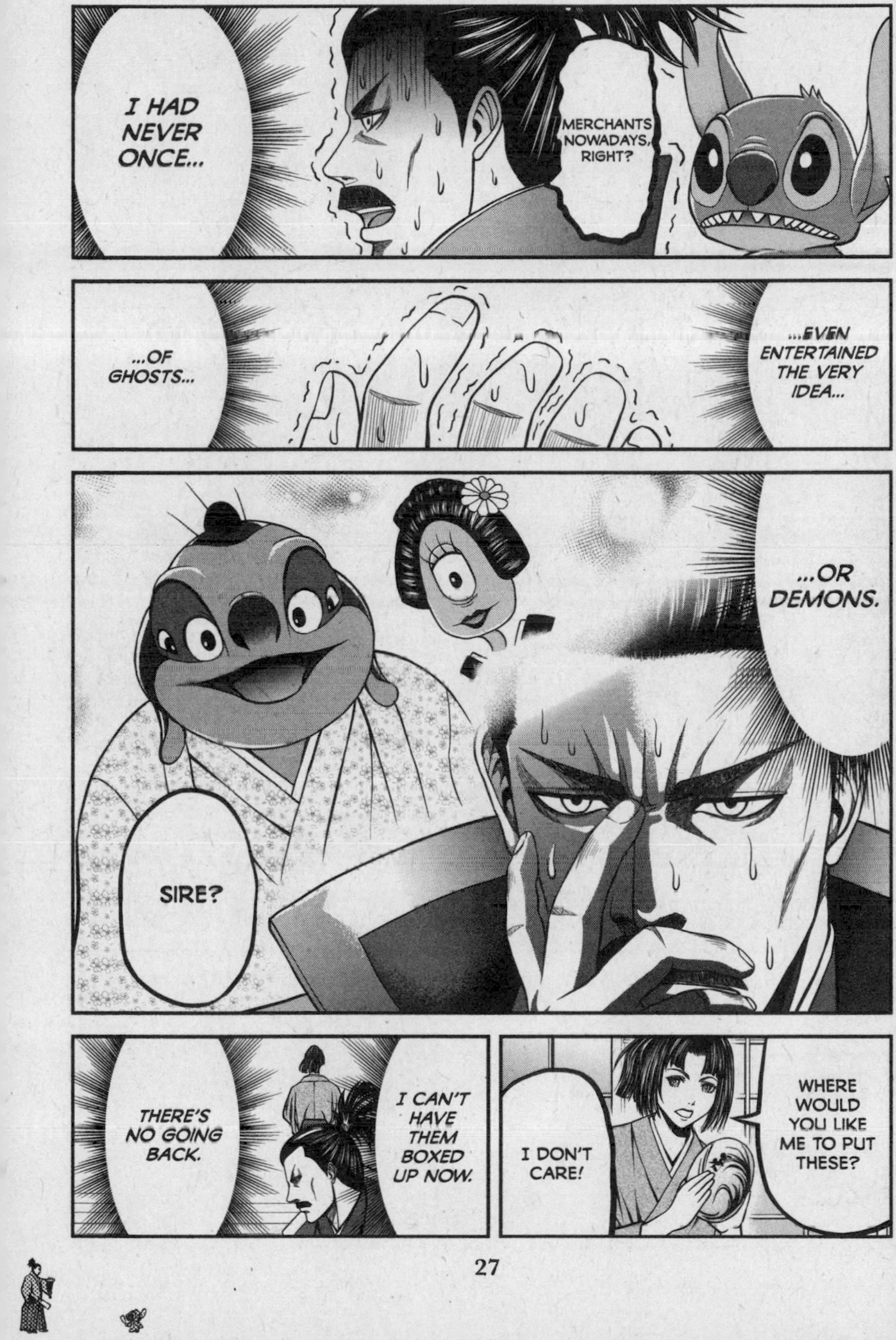
MERCHANTS NOWADAYS, RIGHT?
I HAD NEVER ONCE...
...EVEN ENTERTAINED THE VERY IDEA...
...OF GHOSTS...
...OR DEMONS.
SIRE?
WHERE WOULD YOU LIKE ME TO PUT THESE?
I DON'T CARE!
I CAN'T HAVE THEM BOXED UP NOW.
THERE'S NO GOING BACK.

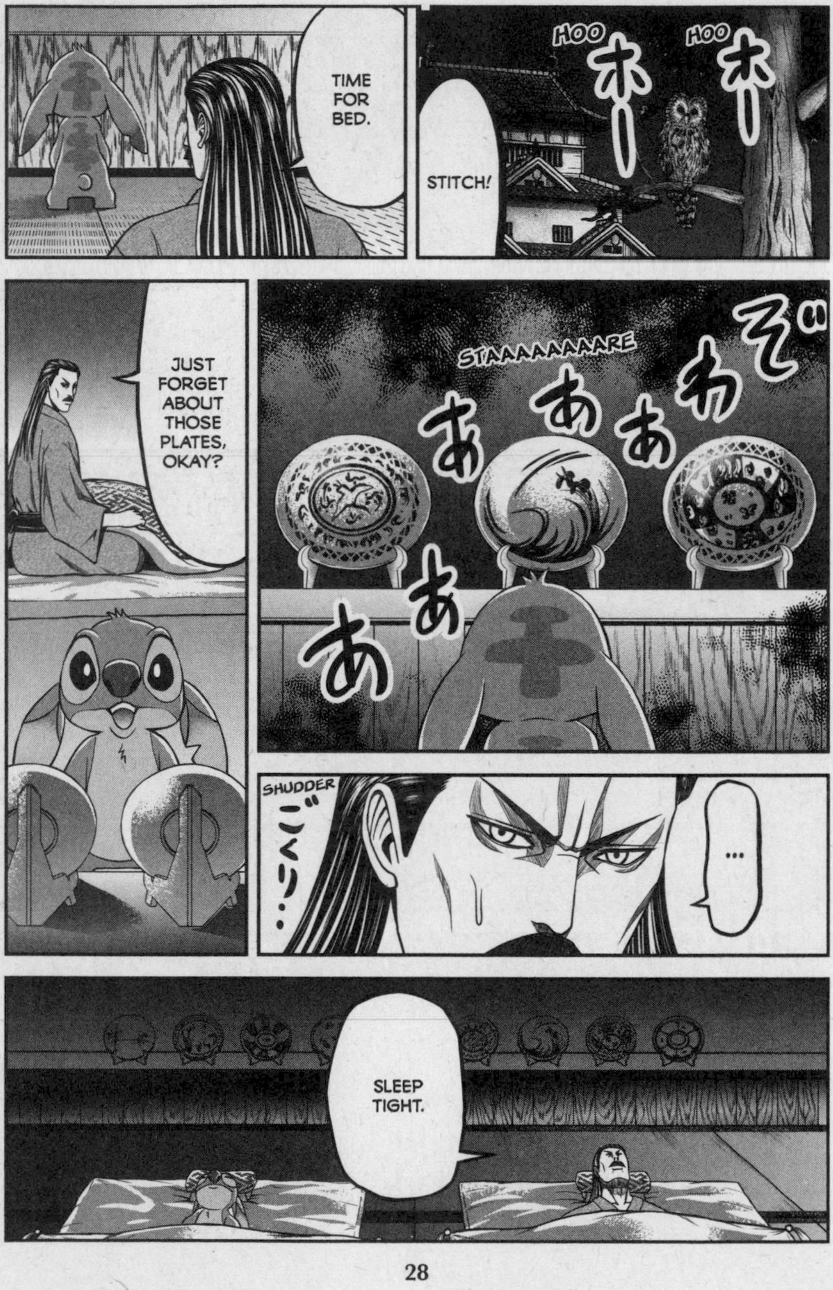
HOO
ホー
HOO
ホー
STITCH!
TIME FOR BED.
STAAAAAAAARE
ぞわあああああ
SHUDDER
ごくり‥
...
JUST FORGET ABOUT THOSE PLATES, OKAY?
SLEEP TIGHT.

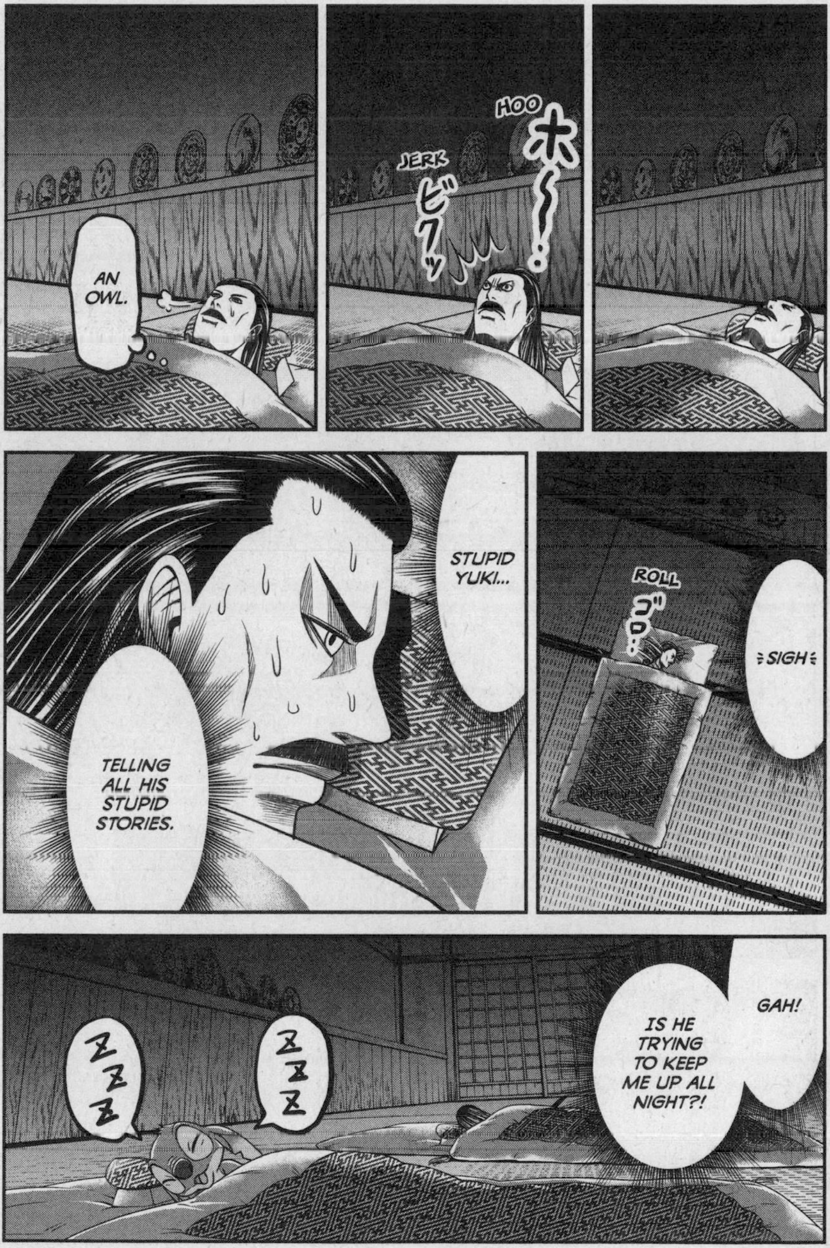
HOO
ホ～！
JERK
ビクッ
AN OWL.
ROLL
ゴロ…
≷SIGH≶
STUPID YUKI...
TELLING ALL HIS STUPID STORIES.
GAH!
IS HE TRYING TO KEEP ME UP ALL NIGHT?!
Z Z Z
Z Z Z

Z
Z
Z
Z
Z
Z
HE'D USUALLY BE PRETTY ANNOYED...
...BUT HE'S SLEEPING.
MAYBE I'LL JUST...
...CLIMB UNDER THE COVERS WITH HIM.
ALL RIGHT...
RUSTLE
...
LET'S GO!
HUH?

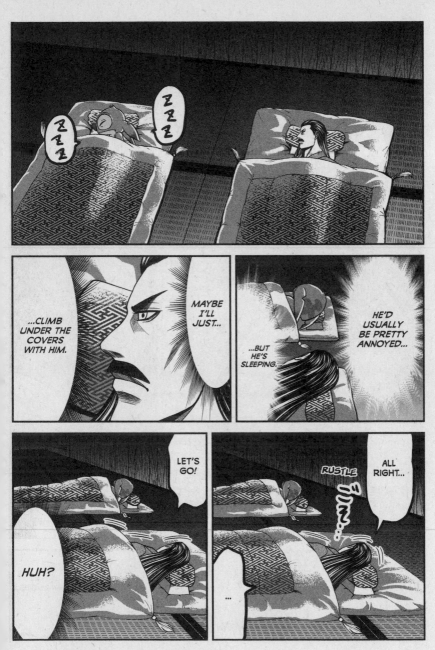

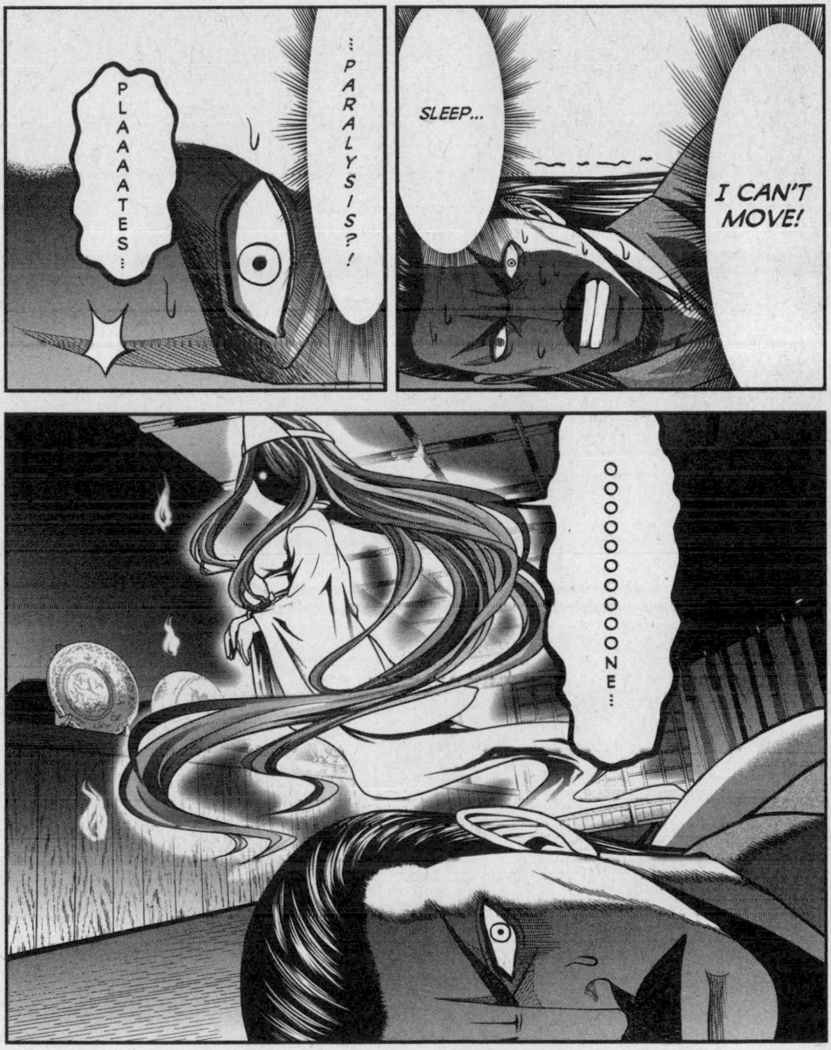
I CAN'T MOVE!
SLEEP...
...PARALYSIS?!
PLAAAATES...
OOOOOOOOOOONE...
THREE PLAAAAATES...
SWEAT
FOUR PLAAAAATES...

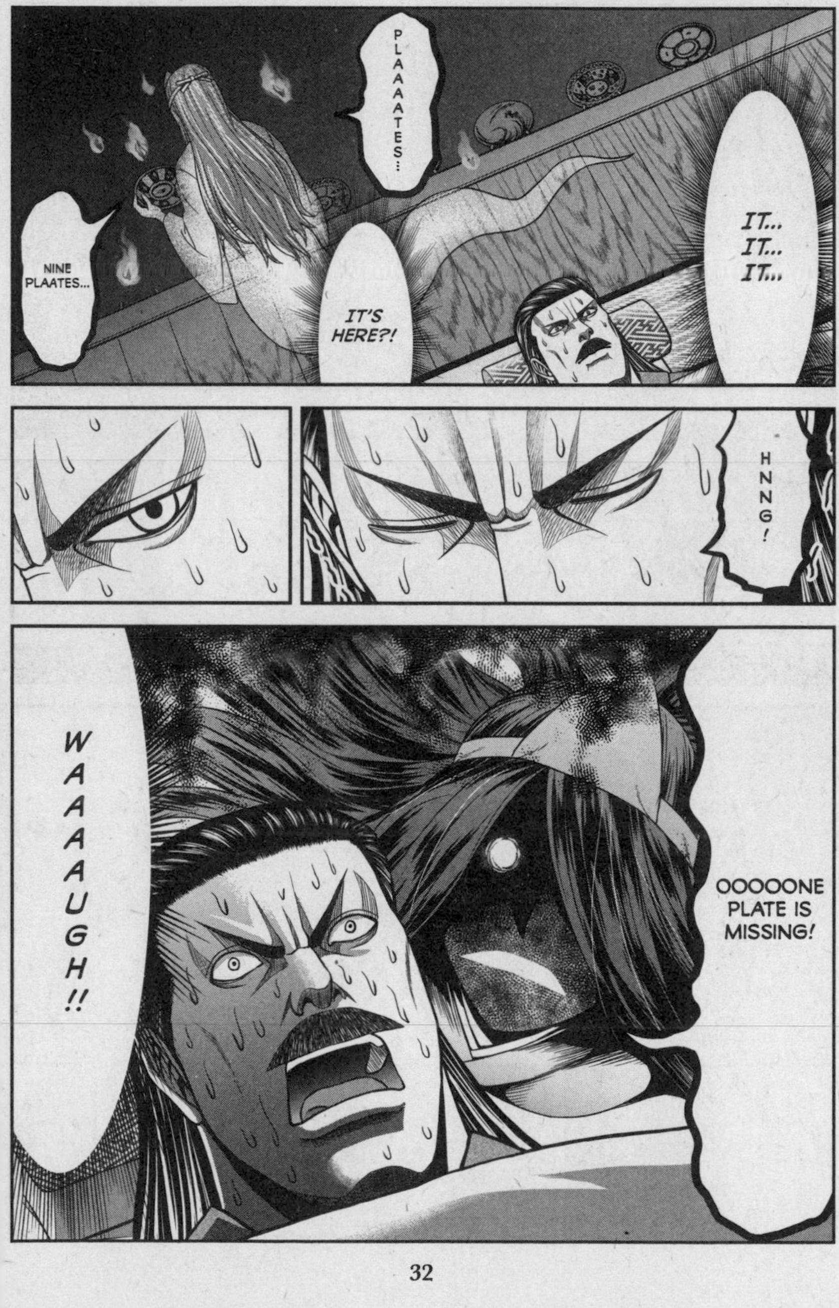

IT... IT... IT...
PLAAAATES...
IT'S HERE?!
NINE PLAATES...
HNNG!
OOOOONE PLATE IS MISSING!
WAAAAAUGH!!

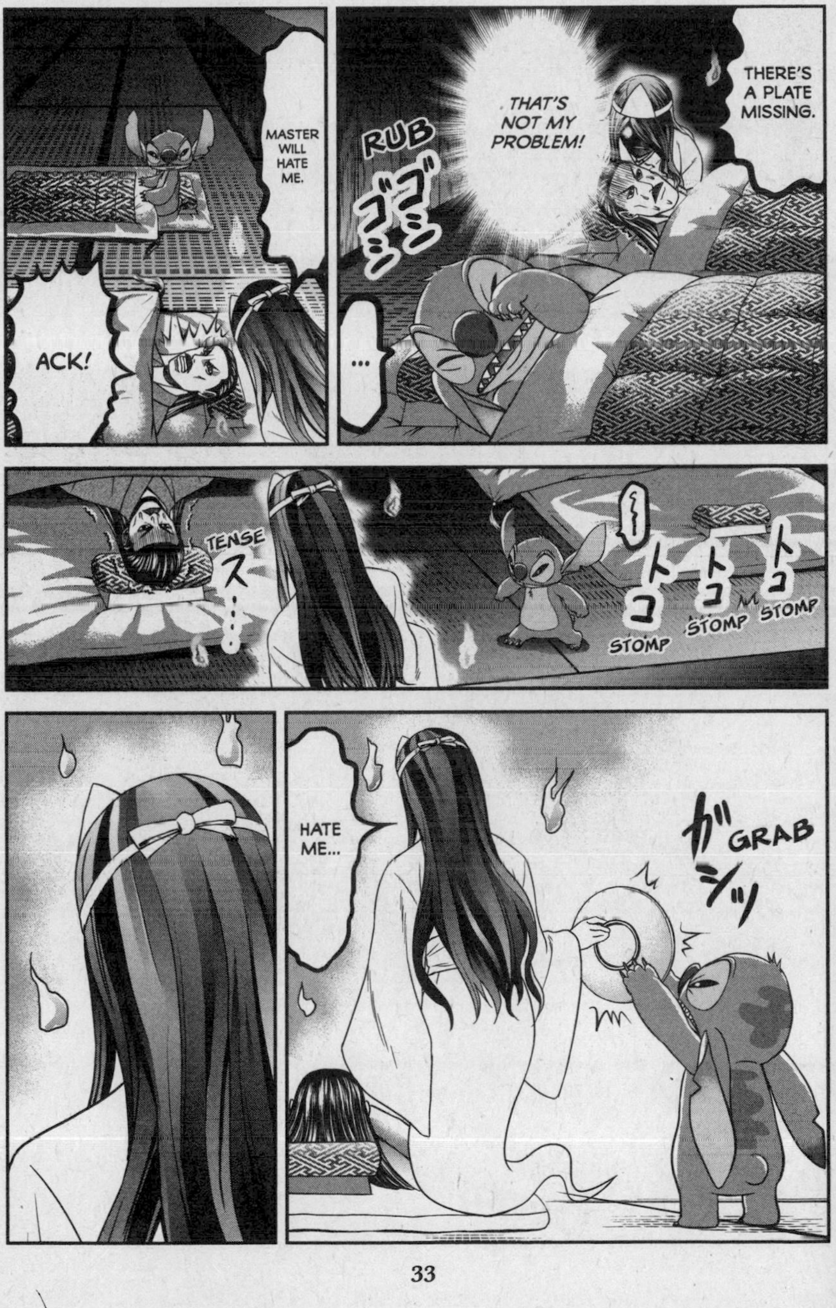
THERE'S A PLATE MISSING.
THAT'S NOT MY PROBLEM!
RUB
ゴシゴシ
...
MASTER WILL HATE ME.
ACK!
トコ トコ トコ
STOMP STOMP STOMP
TENSE
ス…
ガシッ
GRAB
HATE ME...

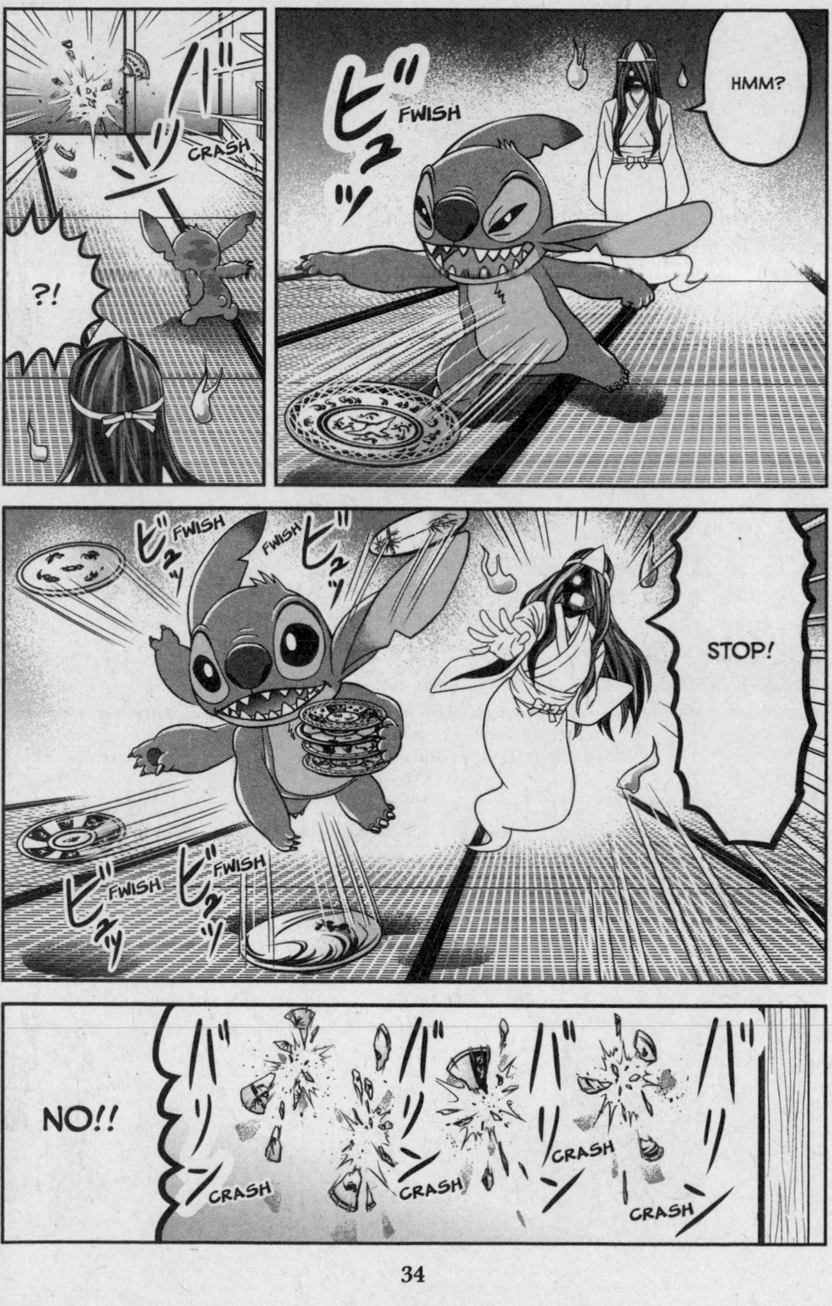
HMM?
ビュッ
FWISH
バリッ
CRASH
?!
STOP!
ビュッ
FWISH
ビュッ
FWISH
ビュッ
FWISH
ビュッ
FWISH
バリーン
CRASH
バリーン
CRASH
バリーン
CRASH
バリーン
CRASH
NO!!

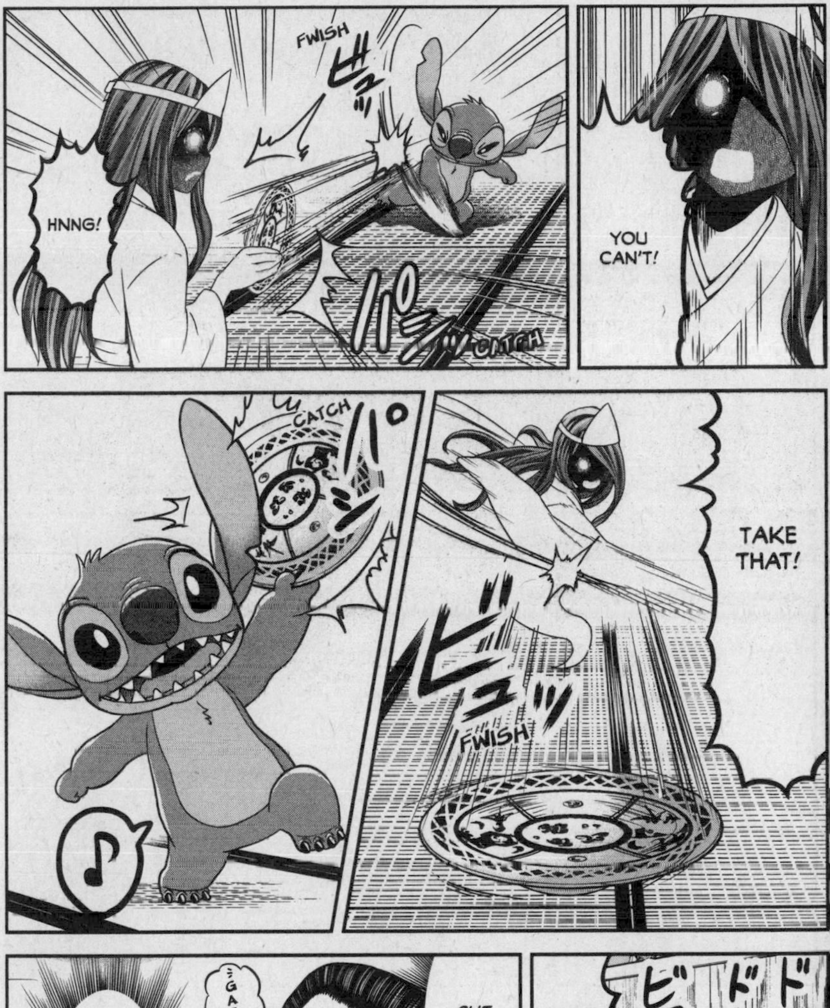
YOU CAN'T!
FWISH
HNNG!
CATCH
TAKE THAT!
FWISH
CATCH
♪
DON'T THROW THESE!!
THUMP
THUMP
THUMP
GASP
GASP
CUT IT OUT, STITCH!
GASP
YOU'RE GOING TO MAKE HER MAD!
GASP

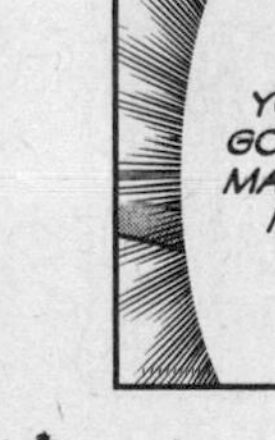

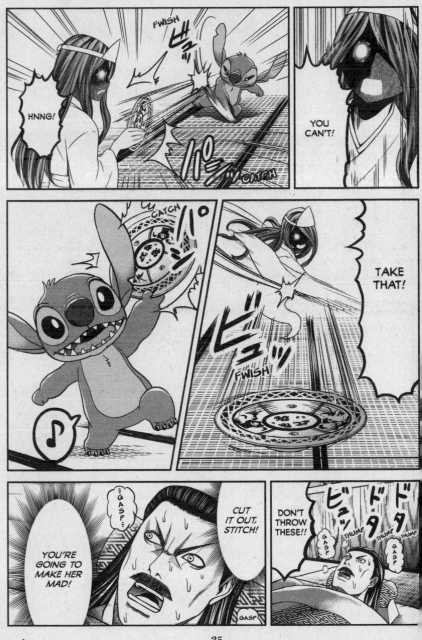

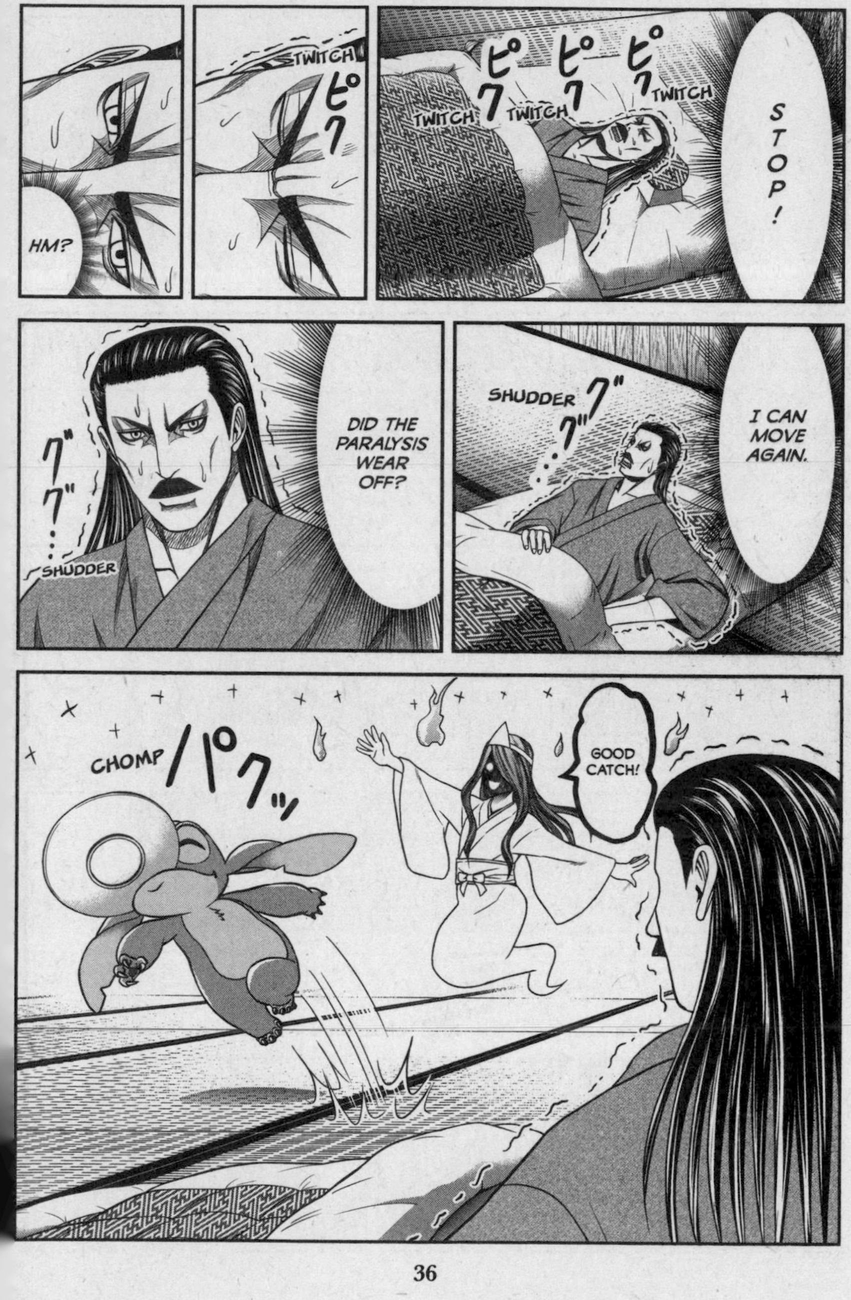
STOP!
ピク
TWITCH
ピク
TWITCH
ピク
TWITCH
TWITCH
ピク
HM?
I CAN MOVE AGAIN.
SHUDDER
グ
グ
DID THE PARALYSIS WEAR OFF?
グ
グ
SHUDDER
GOOD CATCH!
CHOMP
パクッ

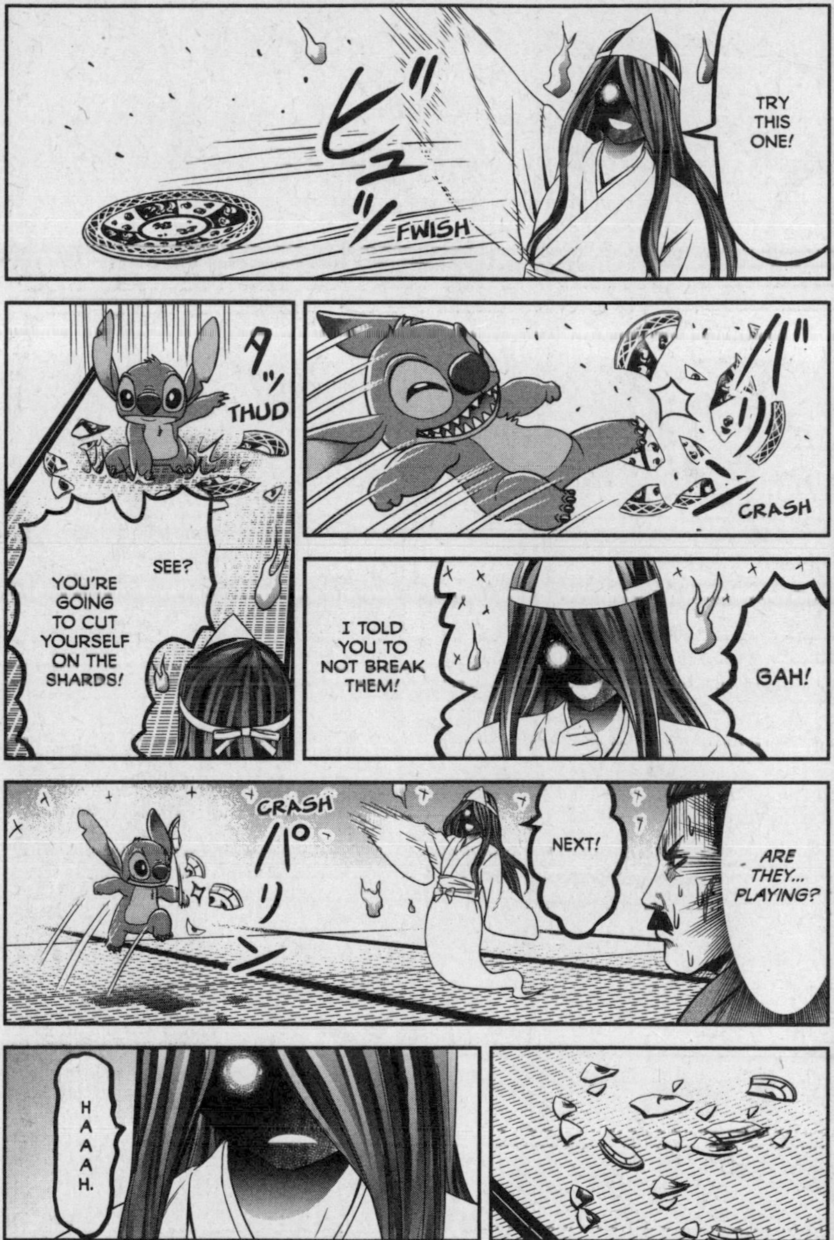
TRY THIS ONE!
FWISH
CRASH
GAH!
I TOLD YOU TO NOT BREAK THEM!
THUD
SEE?
YOU'RE GOING TO CUT YOURSELF ON THE SHARDS!
ARE THEY... PLAYING?
NEXT!
CRASH
HAAAH.

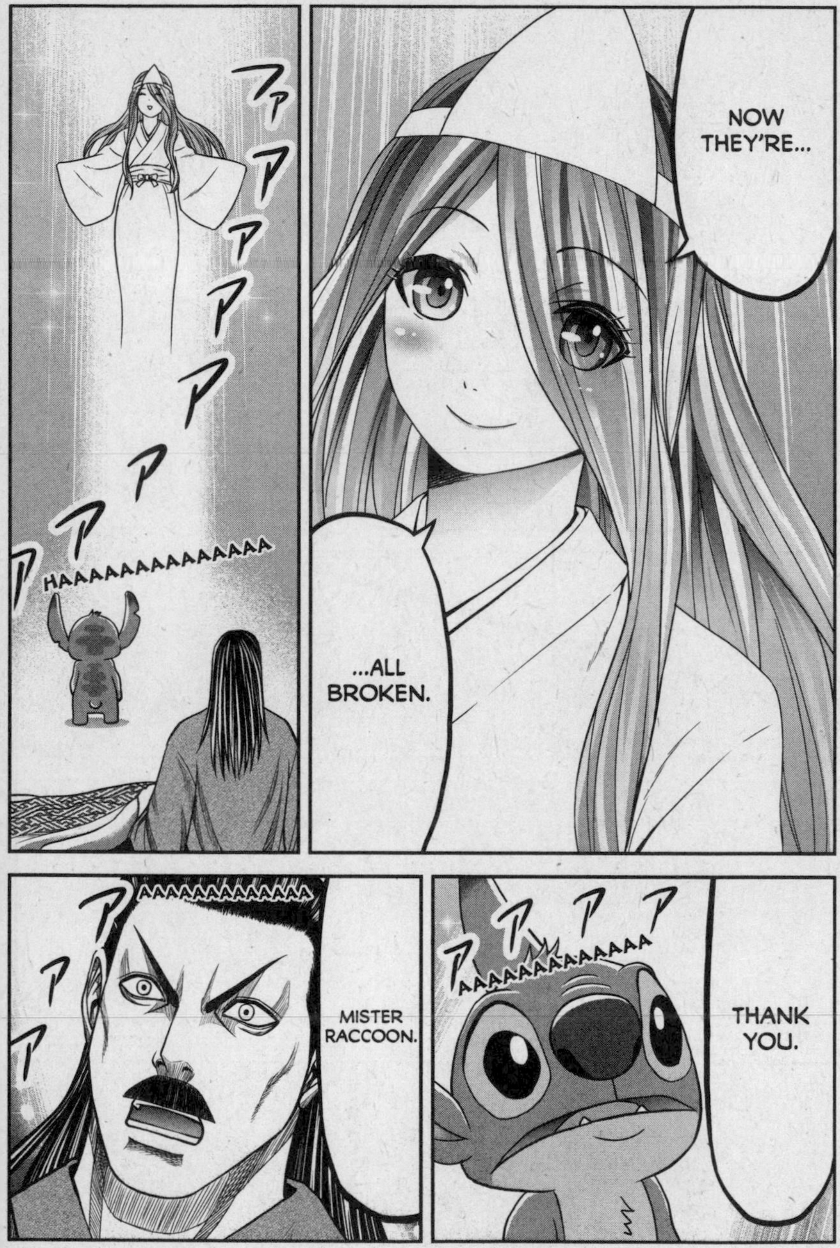
NOW THEY'RE...
...ALL BROKEN.
HAAAAAAAAAAAAA
THANK YOU.
AAAAAAAAAAAAA
MISTER RACCOON.
AAAAAAAAAAAAA

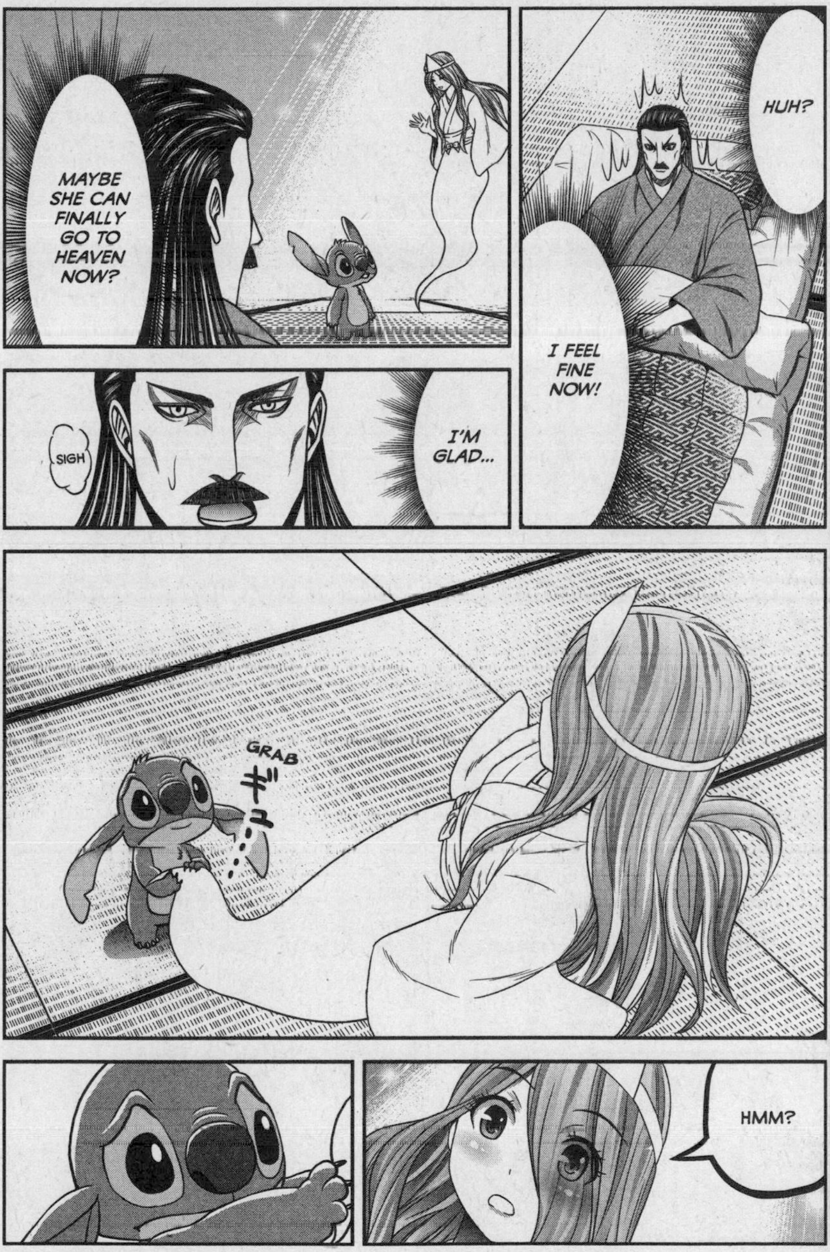
HUH?
I FEEL FINE NOW!
MAYBE SHE CAN FINALLY GO TO HEAVEN NOW?
I'M GLAD...
SIGH
GRAB
ギュ…
HMM?

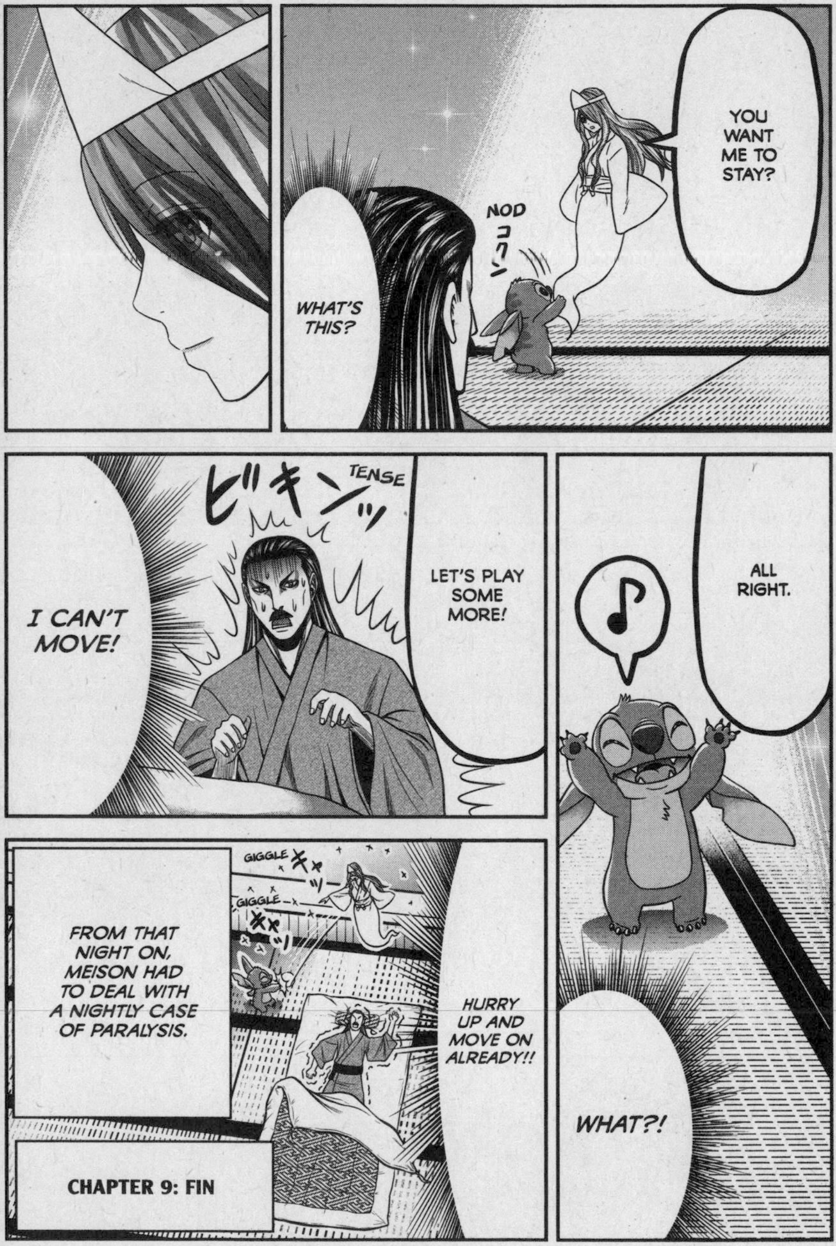
YOU WANT ME TO STAY?
NOD
コクン
WHAT'S THIS?
ALL RIGHT.
♪
WHAT?!
LET'S PLAY SOME MORE!
ビキンッ
TENSE
I CAN'T MOVE!
HURRY UP AND MOVE ON ALREADY!!
GIGGLE
キャッ
GIGGLE
キャッ
FROM THAT NIGHT ON, MEISON HAD TO DEAL WITH A NIGHTLY CASE OF PARALYSIS.
CHAPTER 9: FIN

Disney
Stitch
STITCH & THE SAMURAI

Disney

Stitch

STITCH & THE SAMURAI

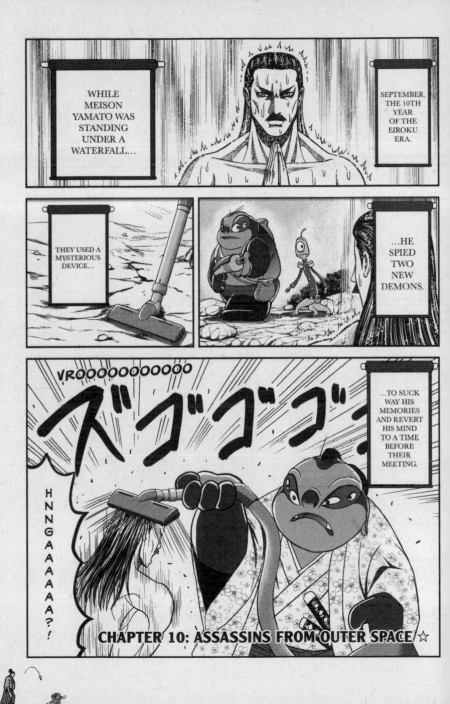

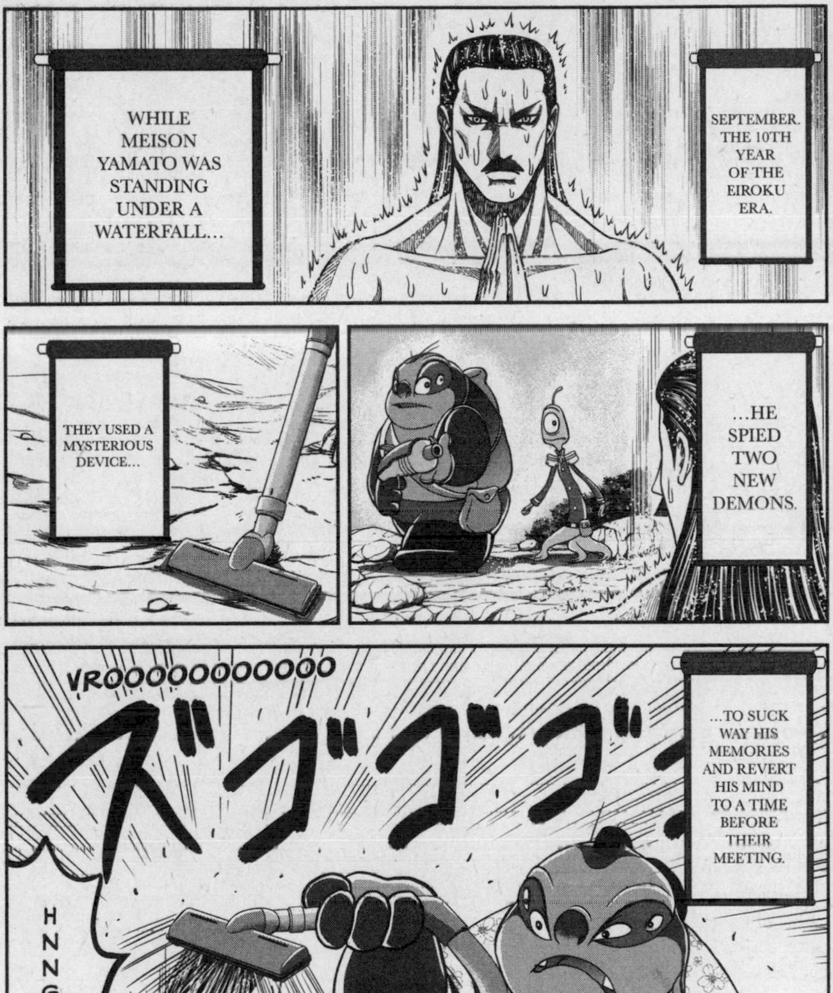
SEPTEMBER. THE 10TH YEAR OF THE EIROKU ERA.
WHILE MEISON YAMATO WAS STANDING UNDER A WATERFALL…
…HE SPIED TWO NEW DEMONS.
THEY USED A MYSTERIOUS DEVICE…
…TO SUCK WAY HIS MEMORIES AND REVERT HIS MIND TO A TIME BEFORE THEIR MEETING.
VROOOOOOOOOOO
ズゴゴゴ
HNNGAAAAAAAA?!
CHAPTER 10: ASSASSINS FROM OUTER SPACE ☆

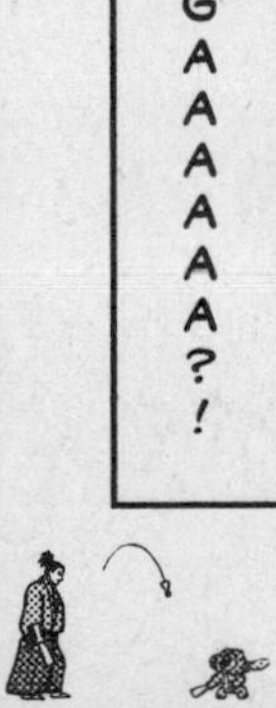

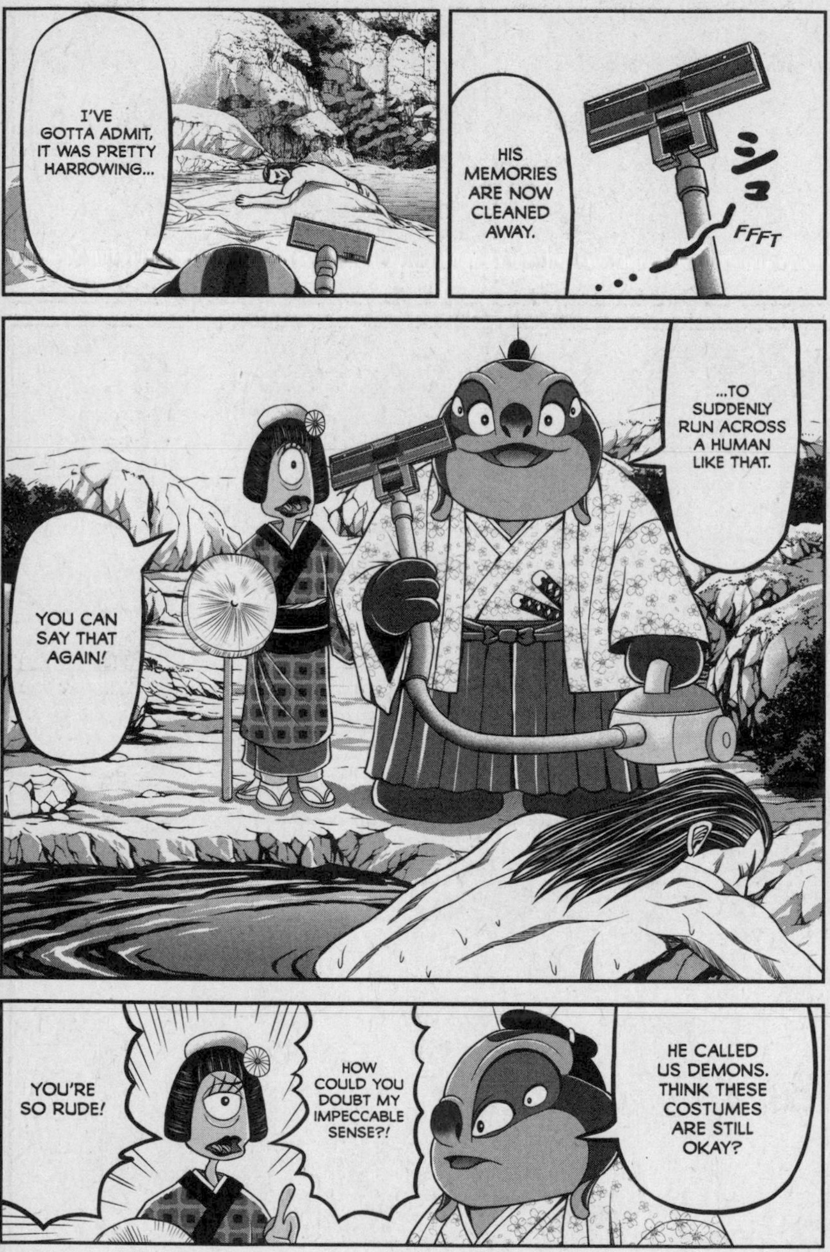
シュ
FFFT
HIS MEMORIES ARE NOW CLEANED AWAY.
I'VE GOTTA ADMIT, IT WAS PRETTY HARROWING...
...TO SUDDENLY RUN ACROSS A HUMAN LIKE THAT.
YOU CAN SAY THAT AGAIN!
HE CALLED US DEMONS. THINK THESE COSTUMES ARE STILL OKAY?
HOW COULD YOU DOUBT MY IMPECCABLE SENSE?!
YOU'RE SO RUDE!

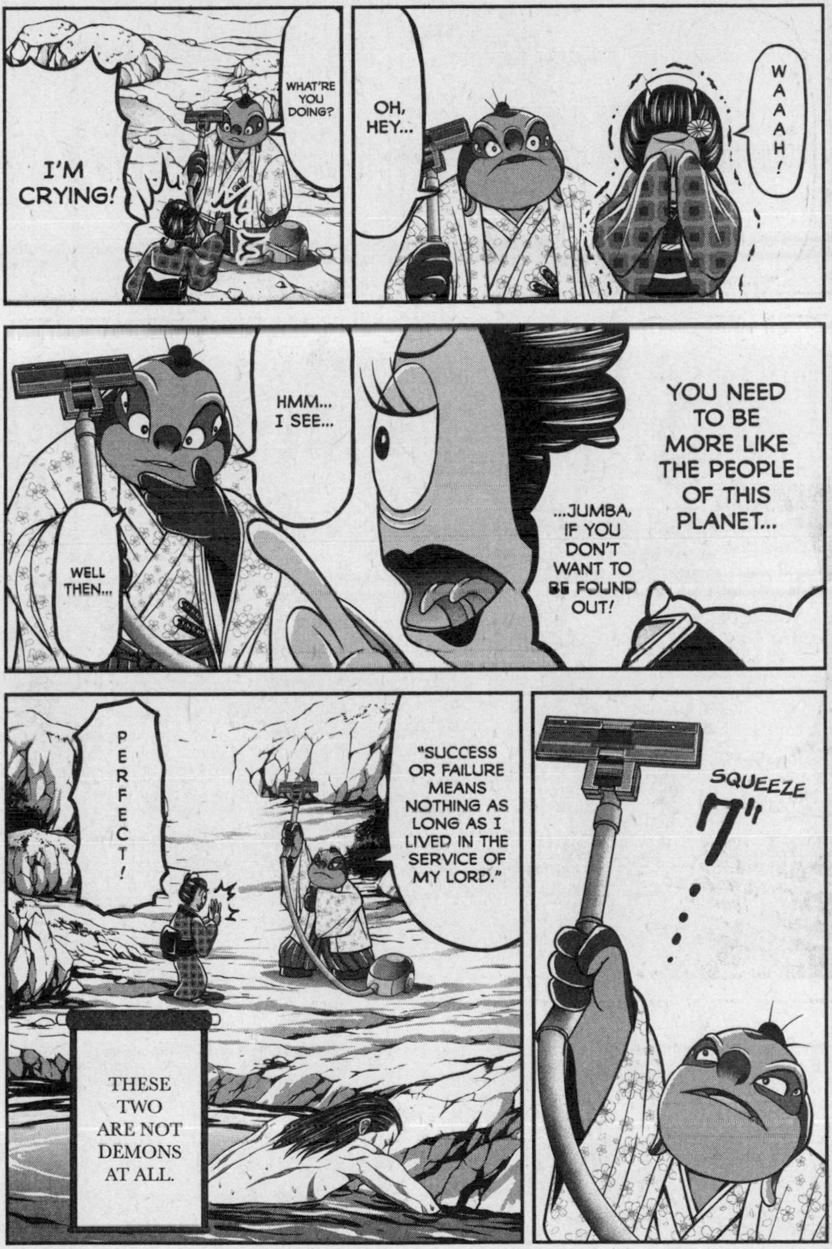
WAAAH!
OH, HEY...
WHAT'RE YOU DOING?
I'M CRYING!
YOU NEED TO BE MORE LIKE THE PEOPLE OF THIS PLANET...
...JUMBA, IF YOU DON'T WANT TO BE FOUND OUT!
HMM... I SEE...
WELL THEN...
SQUEEZE
"SUCCESS OR FAILURE MEANS NOTHING AS LONG AS I LIVED IN THE SERVICE OF MY LORD."
PERFECT!
THESE TWO ARE NOT DEMONS AT ALL.

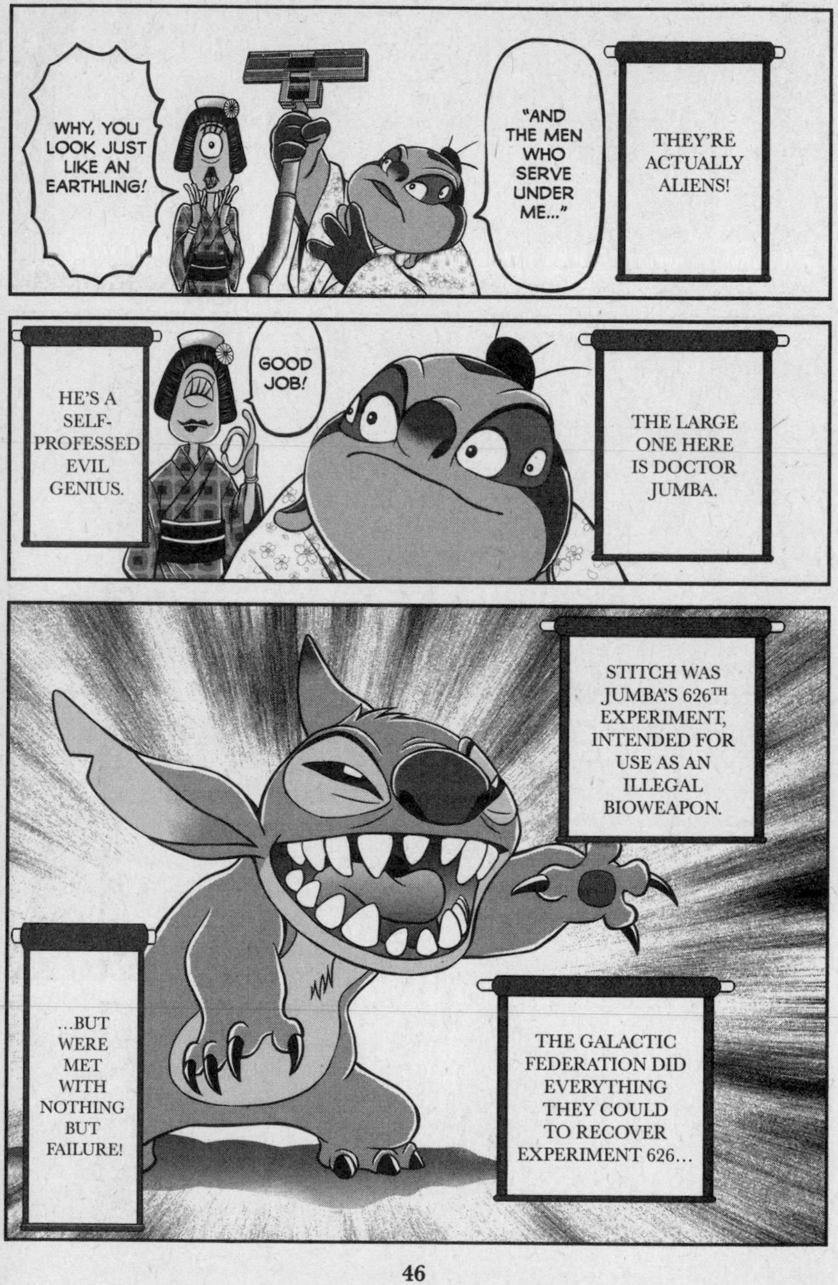
THEY'RE ACTUALLY ALIENS!
"AND THE MEN WHO SERVE UNDER ME..."
WHY, YOU LOOK JUST LIKE AN EARTHLING!
THE LARGE ONE HERE IS DOCTOR JUMBA.
GOOD JOB!
HE'S A SELF-PROFESSED EVIL GENIUS.
STITCH WAS JUMBA'S 626TH EXPERIMENT, INTENDED FOR USE AS AN ILLEGAL BIOWEAPON.
THE GALACTIC FEDERATION DID EVERYTHING THEY COULD TO RECOVER EXPERIMENT 626...
...BUT WERE MET WITH NOTHING BUT FAILURE!

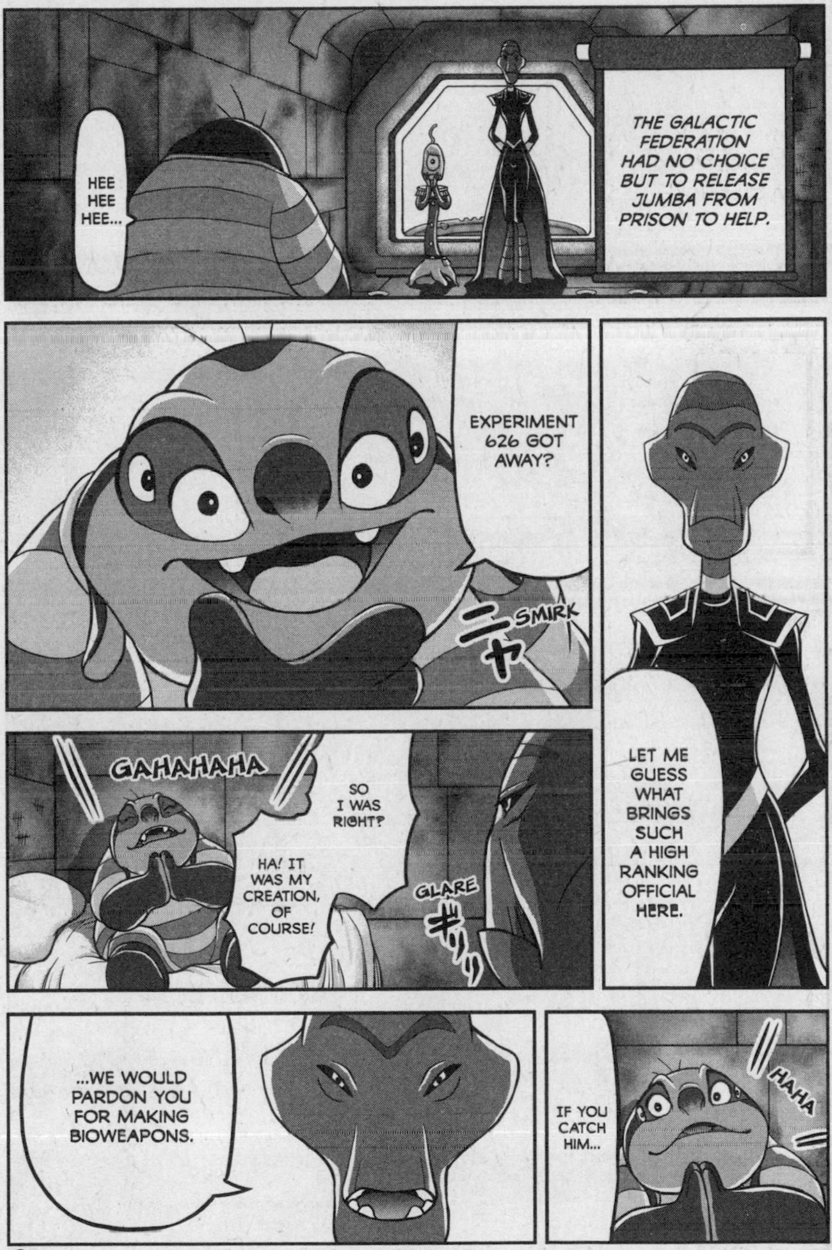
THE GALACTIC FEDERATION HAD NO CHOICE BUT TO RELEASE JUMBA FROM PRISON TO HELP.
HEE HEE HEE...
LET ME GUESS WHAT BRINGS SUCH A HIGH RANKING OFFICIAL HERE.
EXPERIMENT 626 GOT AWAY?
SMIRK
SO I WAS RIGHT?
HA! IT WAS MY CREATION, OF COURSE!
GAHAHAHA
GLARE
HAHA
IF YOU CATCH HIM...
...WE WOULD PARDON YOU FOR MAKING BIOWEAPONS.

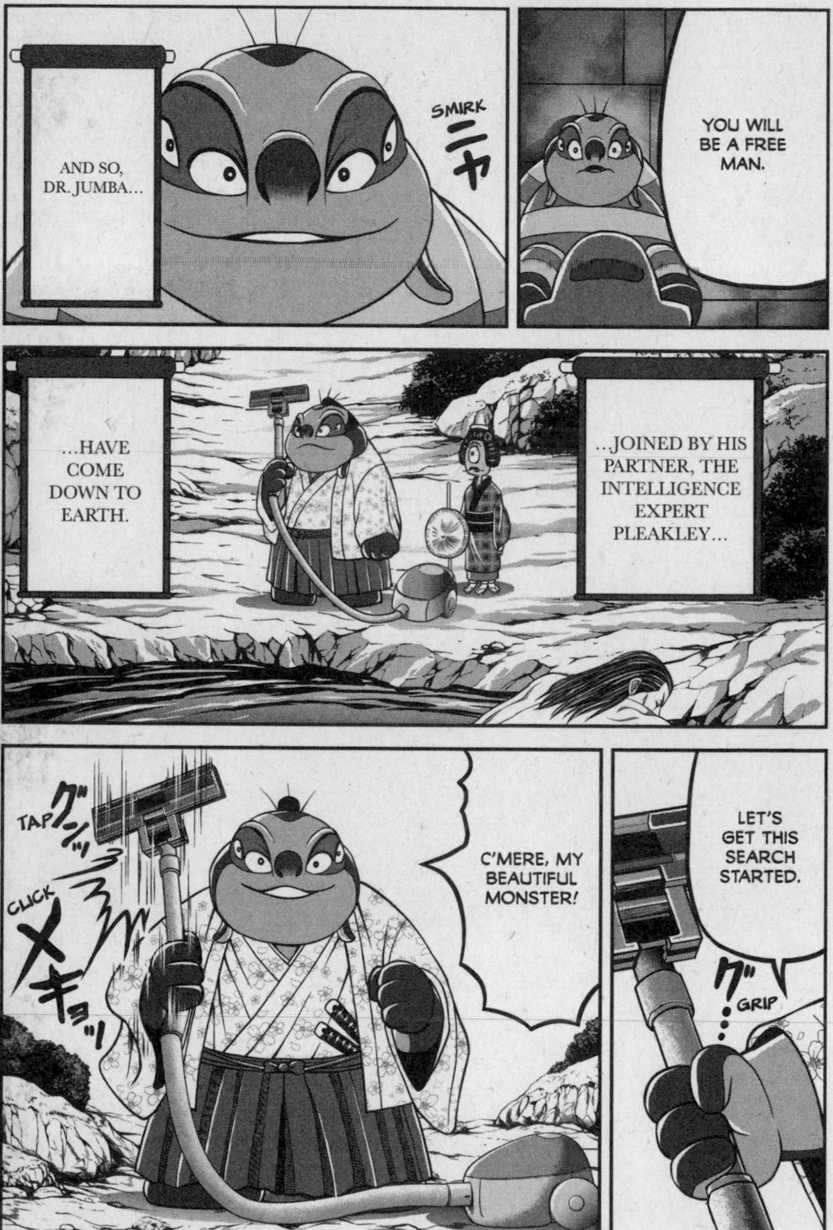
YOU WILL BE A FREE MAN.
AND SO, DR. JUMBA…
SMIRK
ニヤ
…JOINED BY HIS PARTNER, THE INTELLIGENCE EXPERT PLEAKLEY…
…HAVE COME DOWN TO EARTH.
LET'S GET THIS SEARCH STARTED.
グ
GRIP
C'MERE, MY BEAUTIFUL MONSTER!
TAP
グッ
CLICK
メキョッ

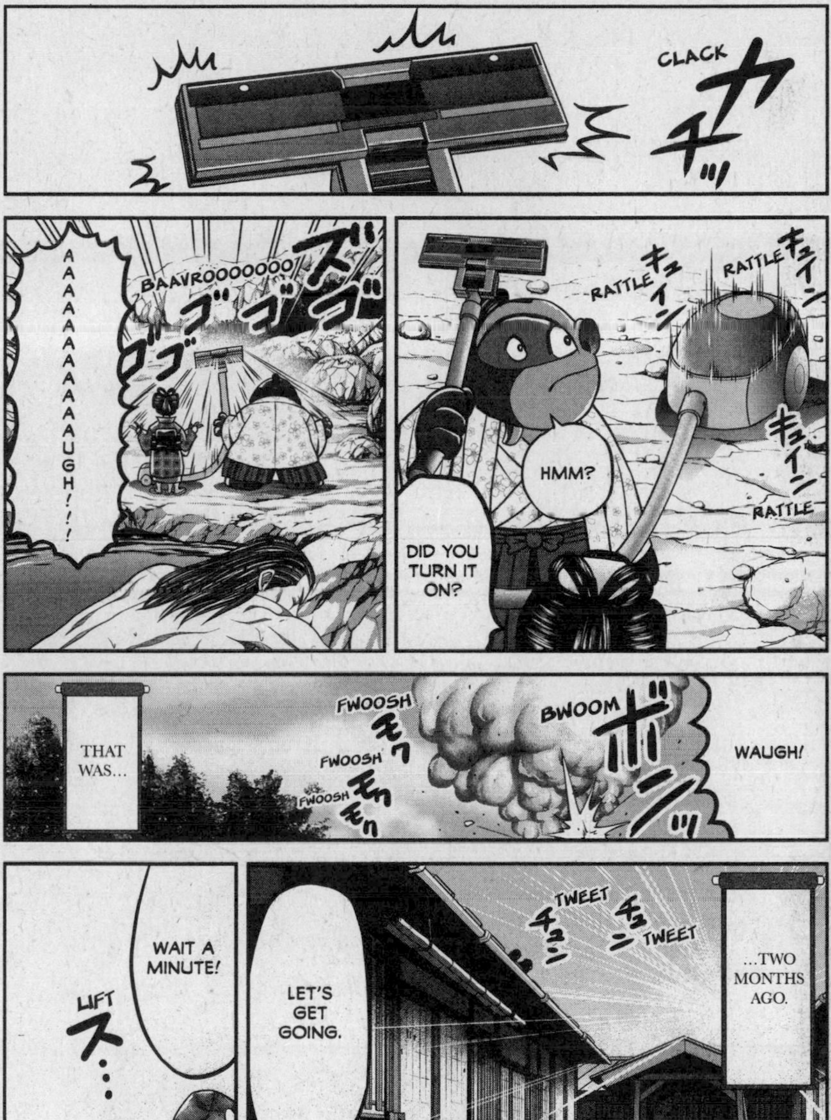
CLACK
RATTLE
RATTLE
HMM?
DID YOU TURN IT ON?
RATTLE
BAAVROOOOOOO
AAAAAAAAAAAAAAUGH!!!
WAUGH!
BWOOM
FWOOSH
FWOOSH
FWOOSH
THAT WAS…
…TWO MONTHS AGO.
TWEET
TWEET
LET'S GET GOING.
CLACK
CLACK
WAIT A MINUTE!
LIFT

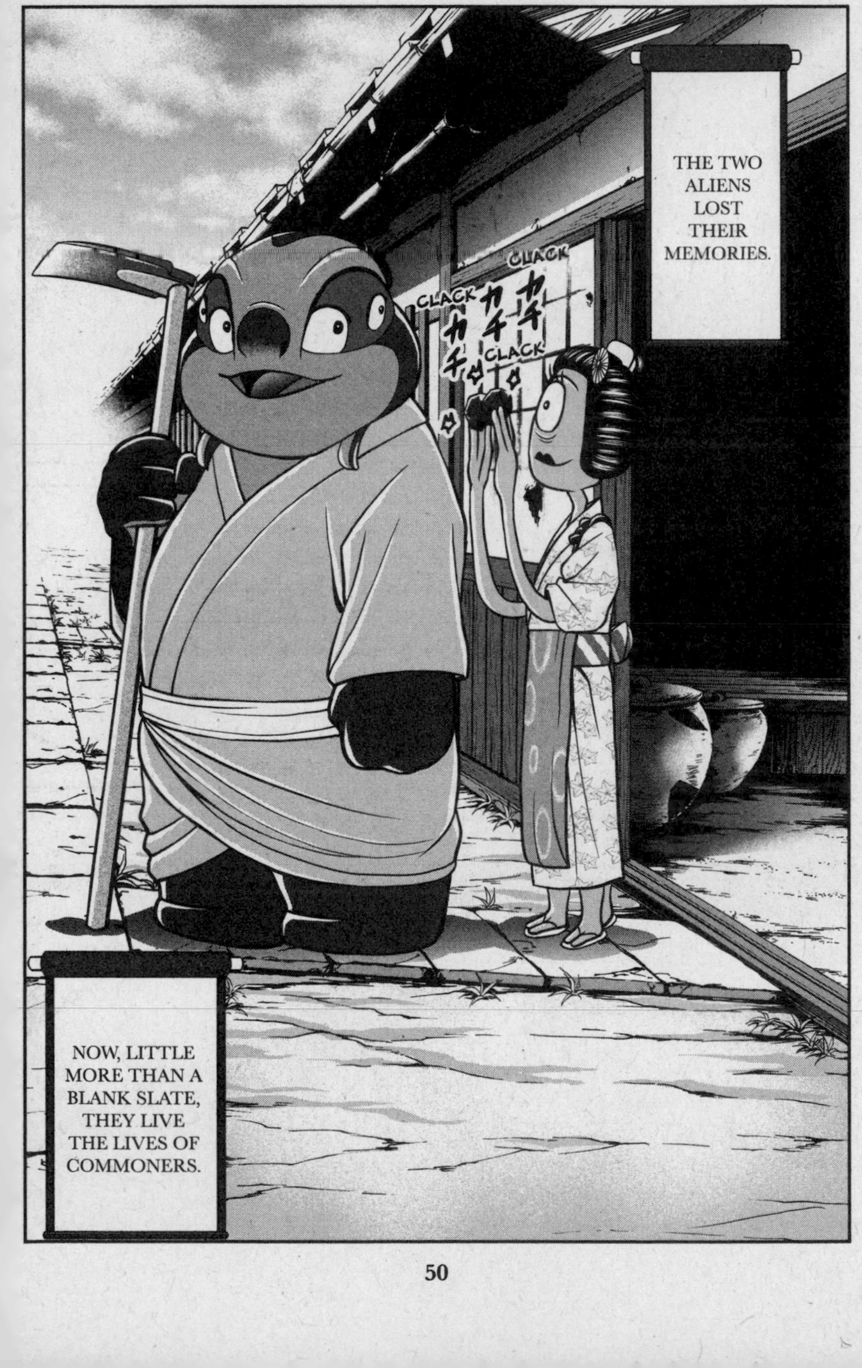
THE TWO ALIENS LOST THEIR MEMORIES.
CLACK
カチ
CLACK
カチ
CLACK
カチ
NOW, LITTLE MORE THAN A BLANK SLATE, THEY LIVE THE LIVES OF COMMONERS.

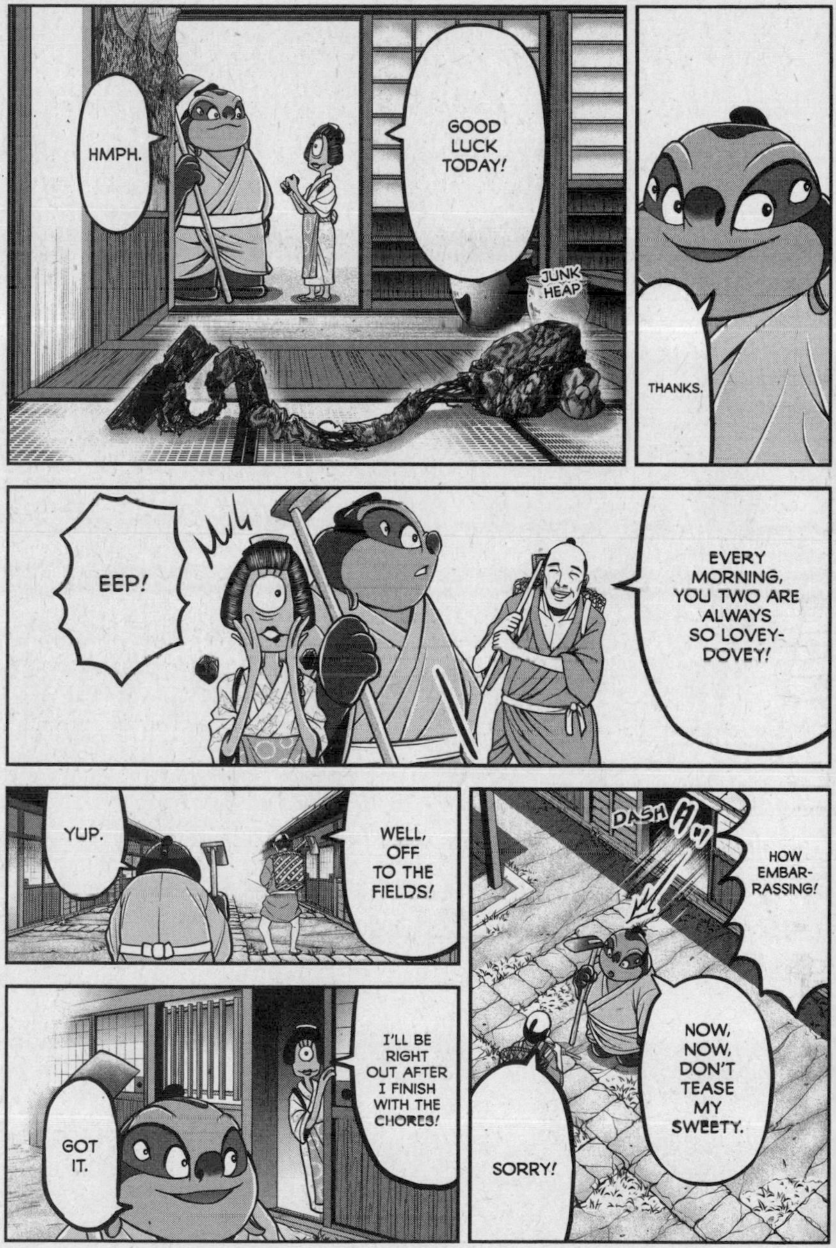
THANKS.
GOOD LUCK TODAY!
HMPH.
JUNK HEAP
EVERY MORNING, YOU TWO ARE ALWAYS SO LOVEY-DOVEY!
EEP!
DASH
HOW EMBARRASSING!
NOW, NOW, DON'T TEASE MY SWEETY.
SORRY!
WELL, OFF TO THE FIELDS!
YUP.
I'LL BE RIGHT OUT AFTER I FINISH WITH THE CHORES!
GOT IT.

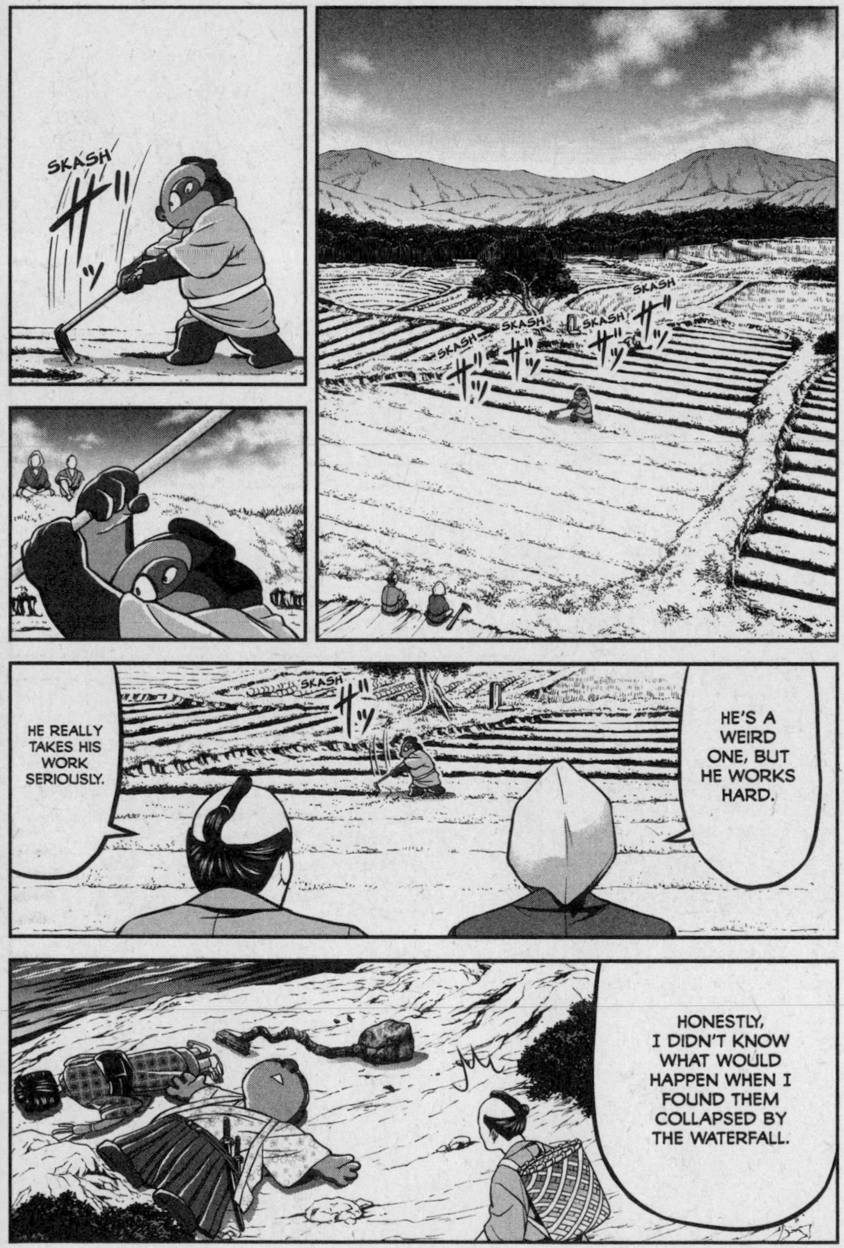
SKASH
SKASH
SKASH
SKASH
SKASH
SKASH
HE'S A WEIRD ONE, BUT HE WORKS HARD.
HE REALLY TAKES HIS WORK SERIOUSLY.
HONESTLY, I DIDN'T KNOW WHAT WOULD HAPPEN WHEN I FOUND THEM COLLAPSED BY THE WATERFALL.

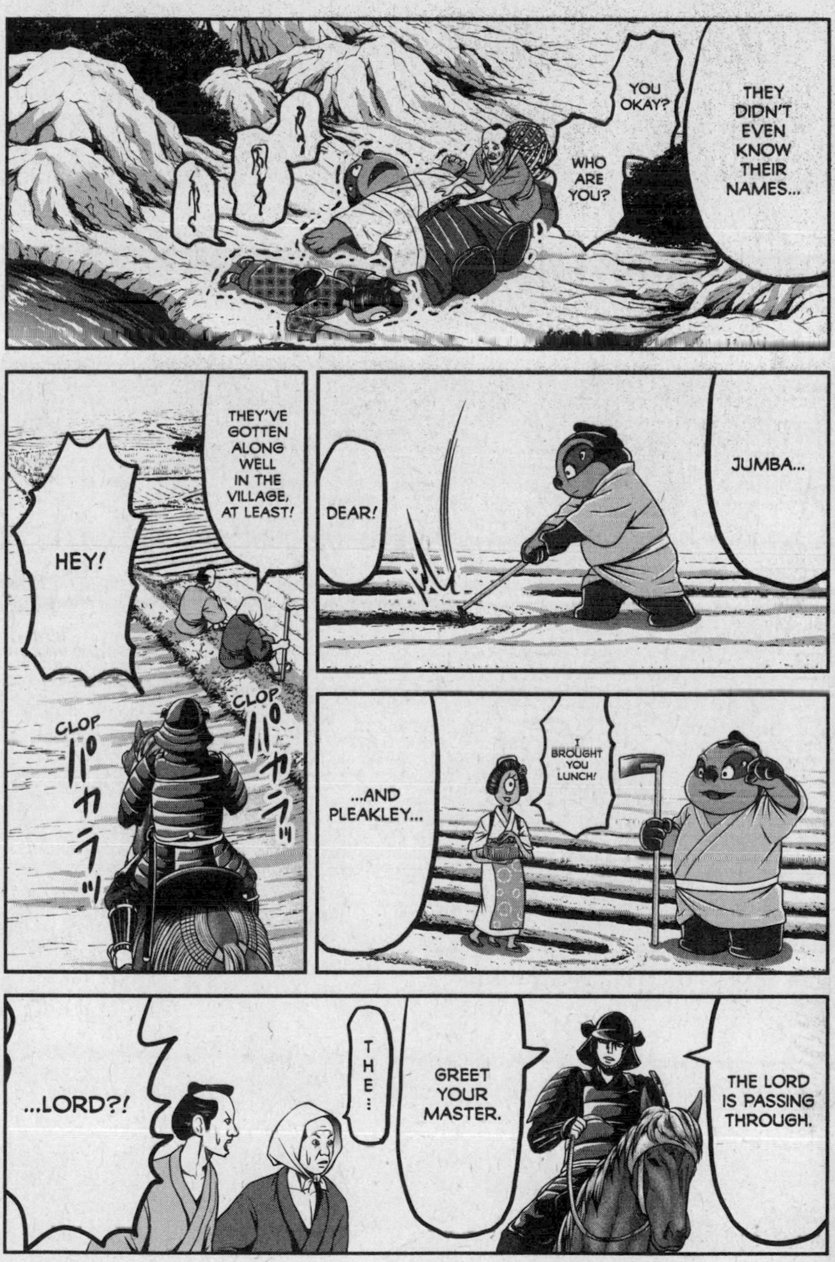
THEY DIDN'T EVEN KNOW THEIR NAMES...
YOU OKAY?
WHO ARE YOU?
JUMBA...
DEAR!
...AND PLEAKLEY...
I BROUGHT YOU LUNCH!
THEY'VE GOTTEN ALONG WELL IN THE VILLAGE, AT LEAST!
HEY!
CLOP
パカラッ
CLOP
パカラッ
THE LORD IS PASSING THROUGH.
GREET YOUR MASTER.
THE...
...LORD?!

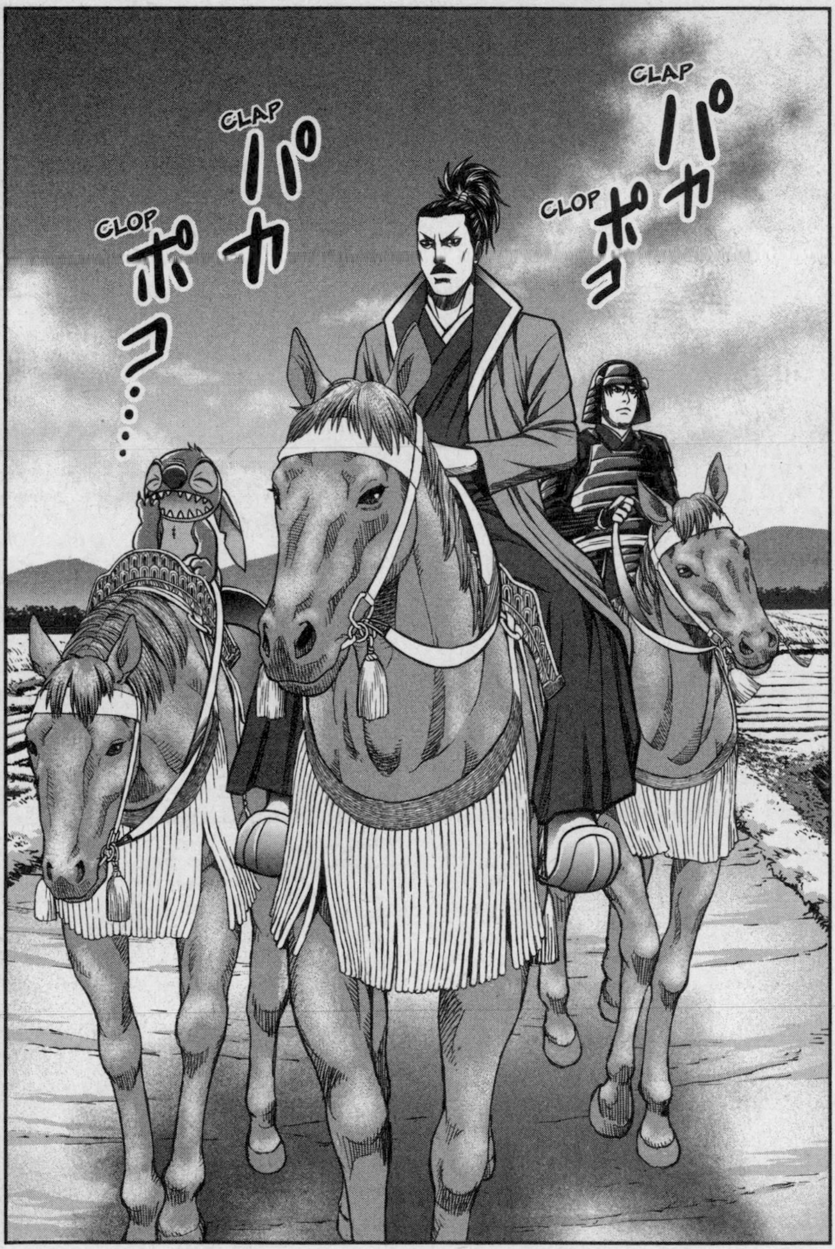

CLAP
パカ
CLOP
ポコ
CLAP
パカ
CLOP
ポコ?…

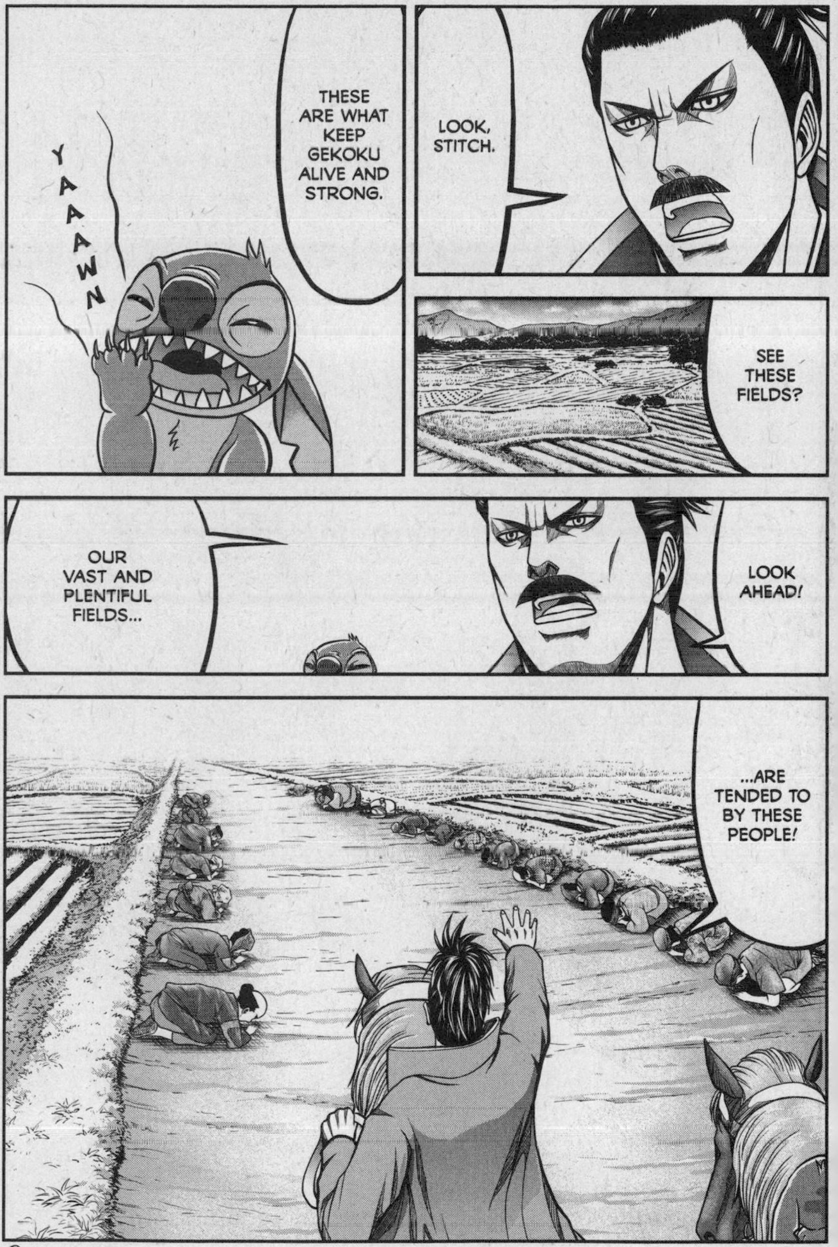
LOOK, STITCH.
SEE THESE FIELDS?
THESE ARE WHAT KEEP GEKOKU ALIVE AND STRONG.
YAAAWN
LOOK AHEAD!
OUR VAST AND PLENTIFUL FIELDS...
...ARE TENDED TO BY THESE PEOPLE!

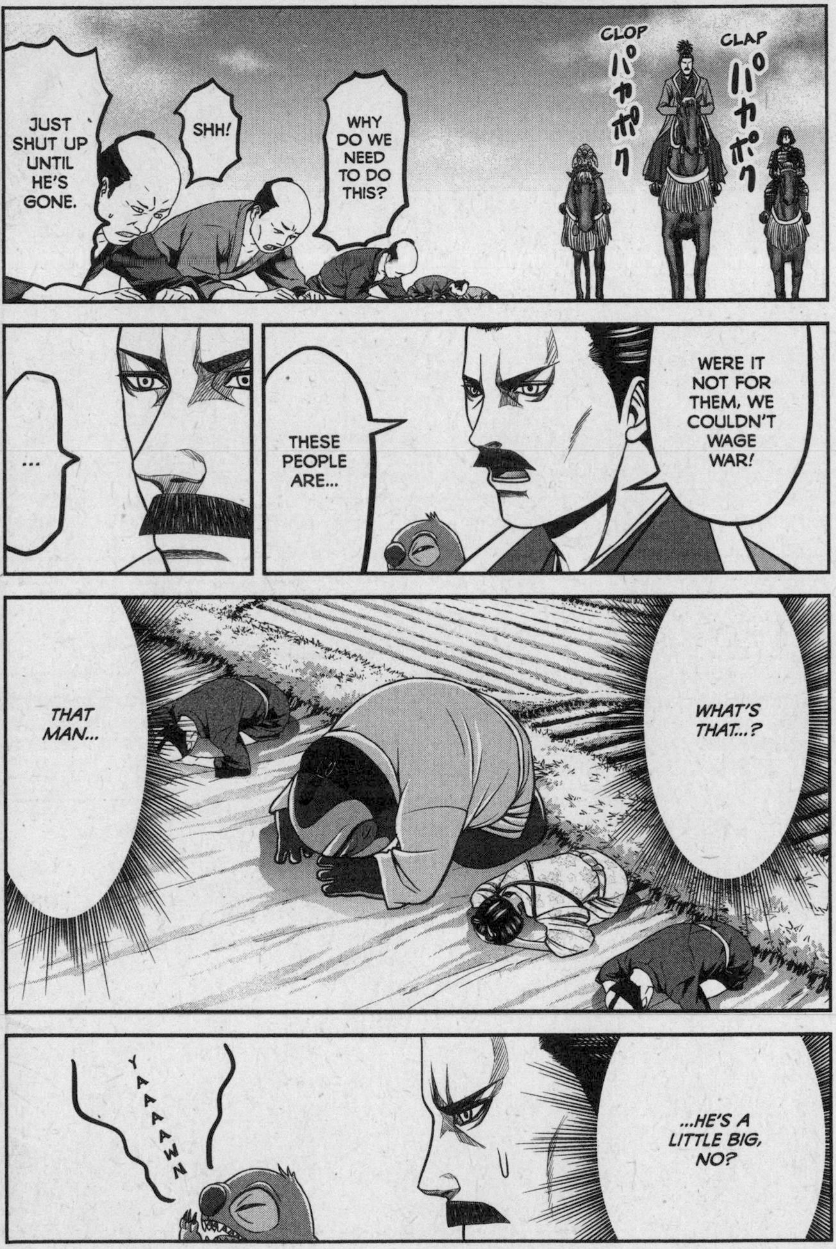
CLAP
パカポク
CLOP
パカポク
WHY DO WE NEED TO DO THIS?
SHH!
JUST SHUT UP UNTIL HE'S GONE.
WERE IT NOT FOR THEM, WE COULDN'T WAGE WAR!
THESE PEOPLE ARE...
...
WHAT'S THAT...?
THAT MAN...
...HE'S A LITTLE BIG, NO?
YAAAAWN

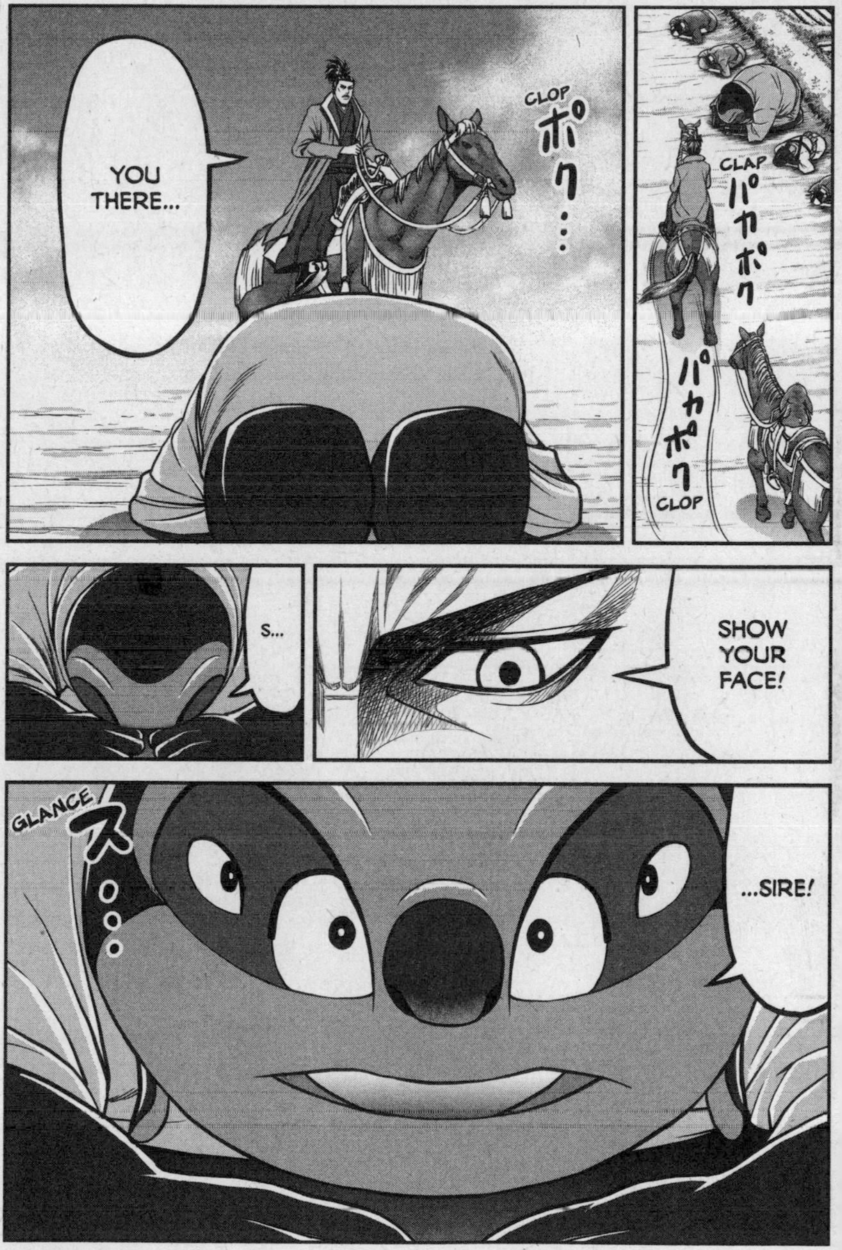
CLAP
パカポク
パカポク
CLOP
CLOP
ポク…
YOU THERE...
SHOW YOUR FACE!
S...
...SIRE!
GLANCE
ス…

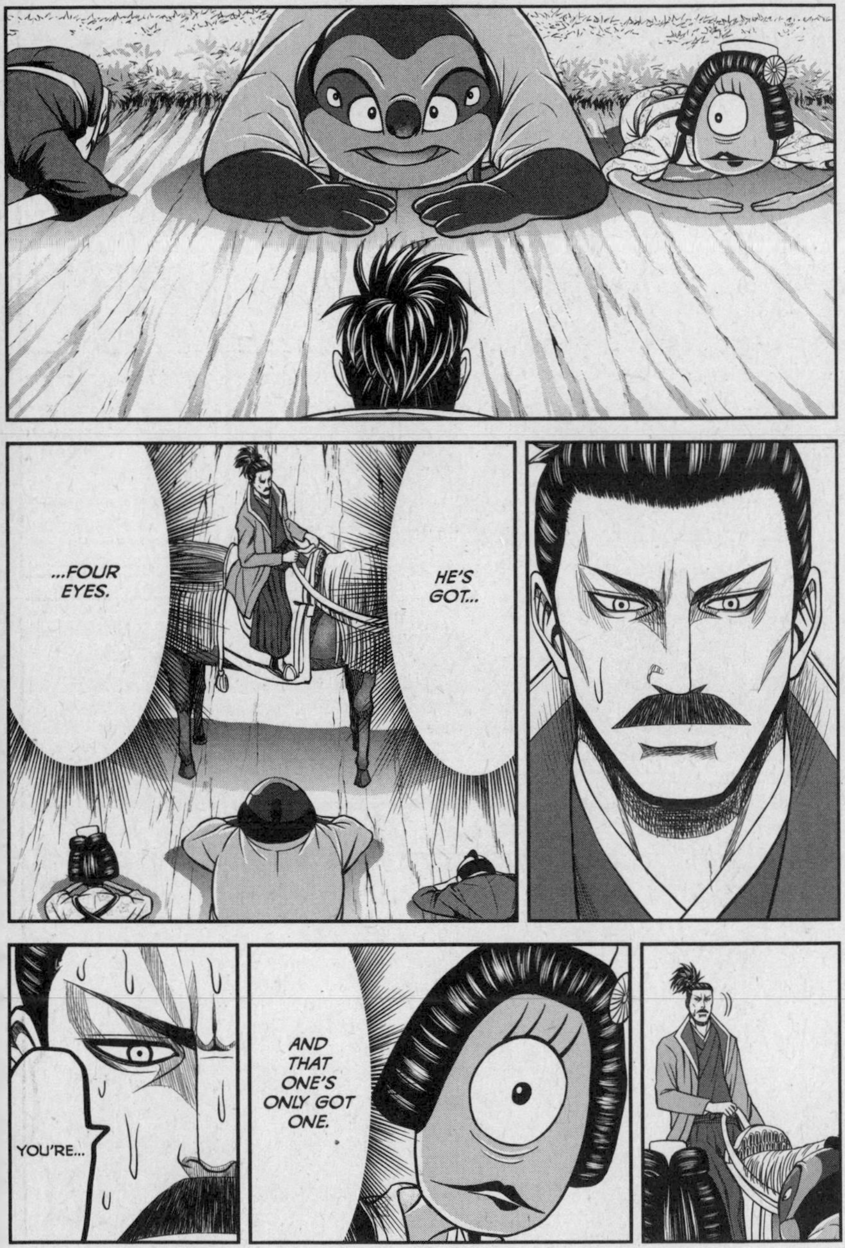
HE'S GOT...
...FOUR EYES.
AND THAT ONE'S ONLY GOT ONE.
YOU'RE...

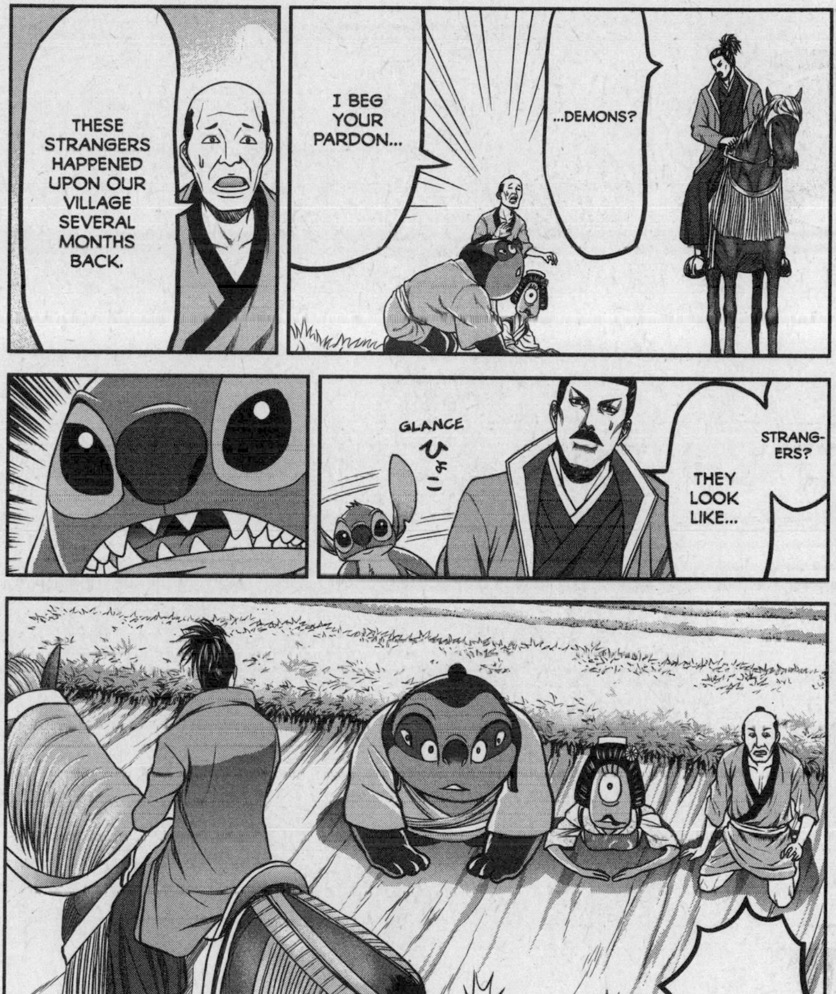
...DEMONS?
I BEG YOUR PARDON...
THESE STRANGERS HAPPENED UPON OUR VILLAGE SEVERAL MONTHS BACK.
STRANGERS?
THEY LOOK LIKE...
GLANCE
ひょこ
JUMBA!

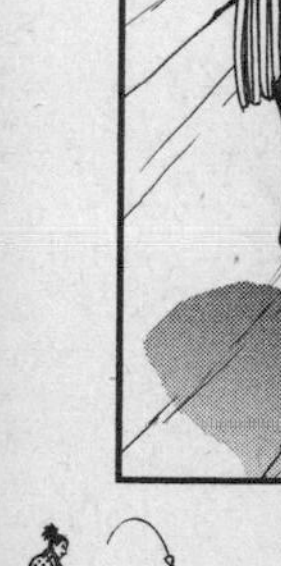

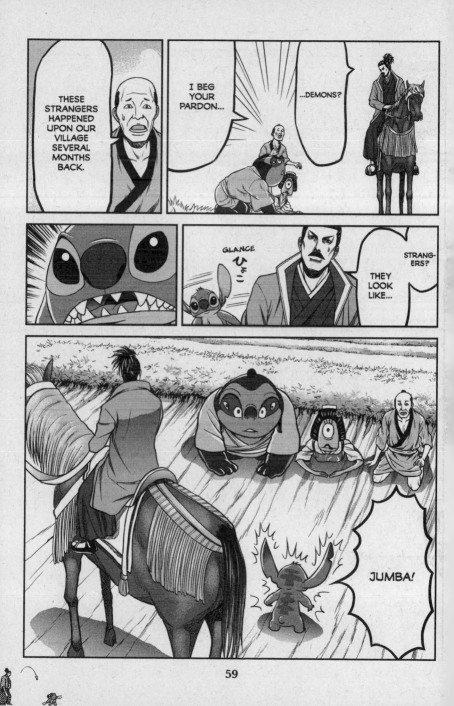

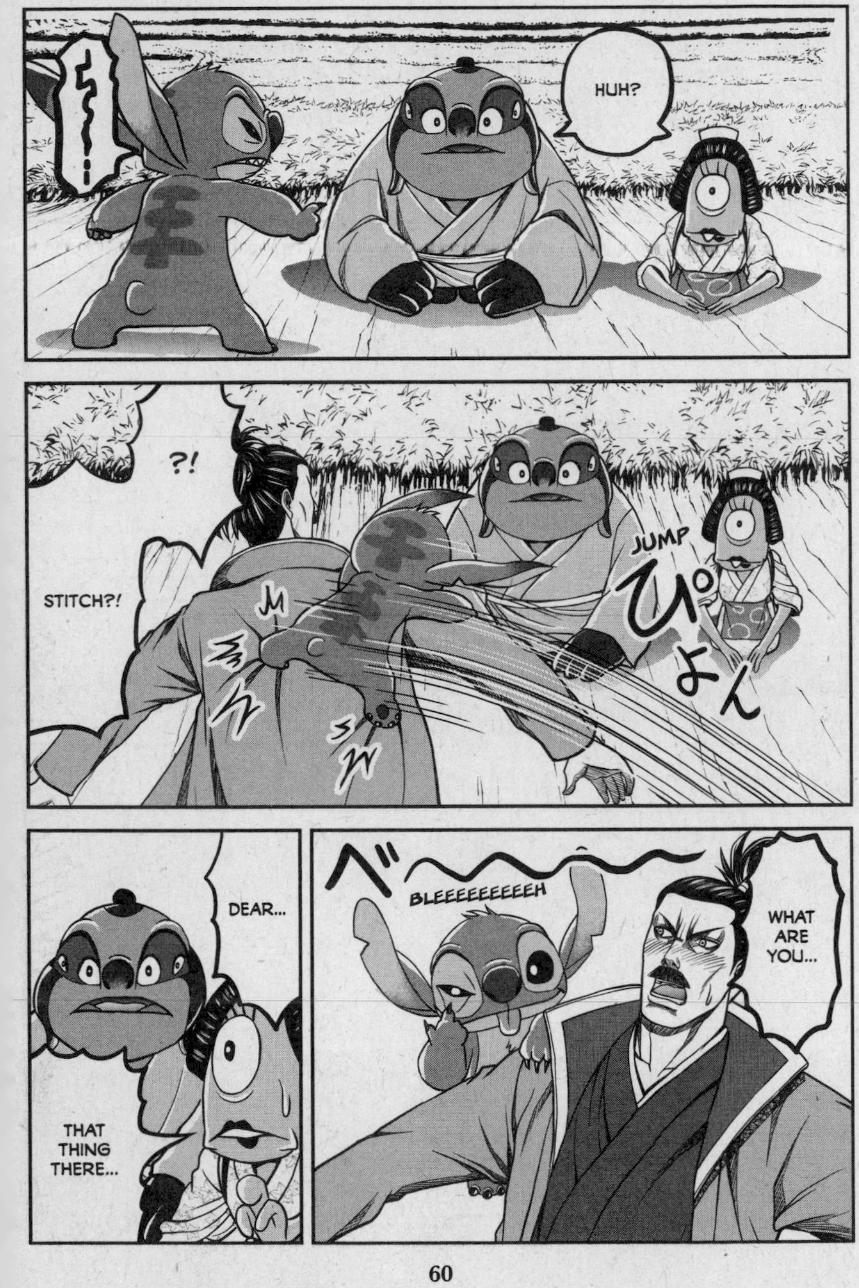
HUH?
JUMP
ぴょん
?!
STITCH?!
WHAT ARE YOU...
べ〜〜〜
BLEEEEEEEEEH
DEAR...
THAT THING THERE...

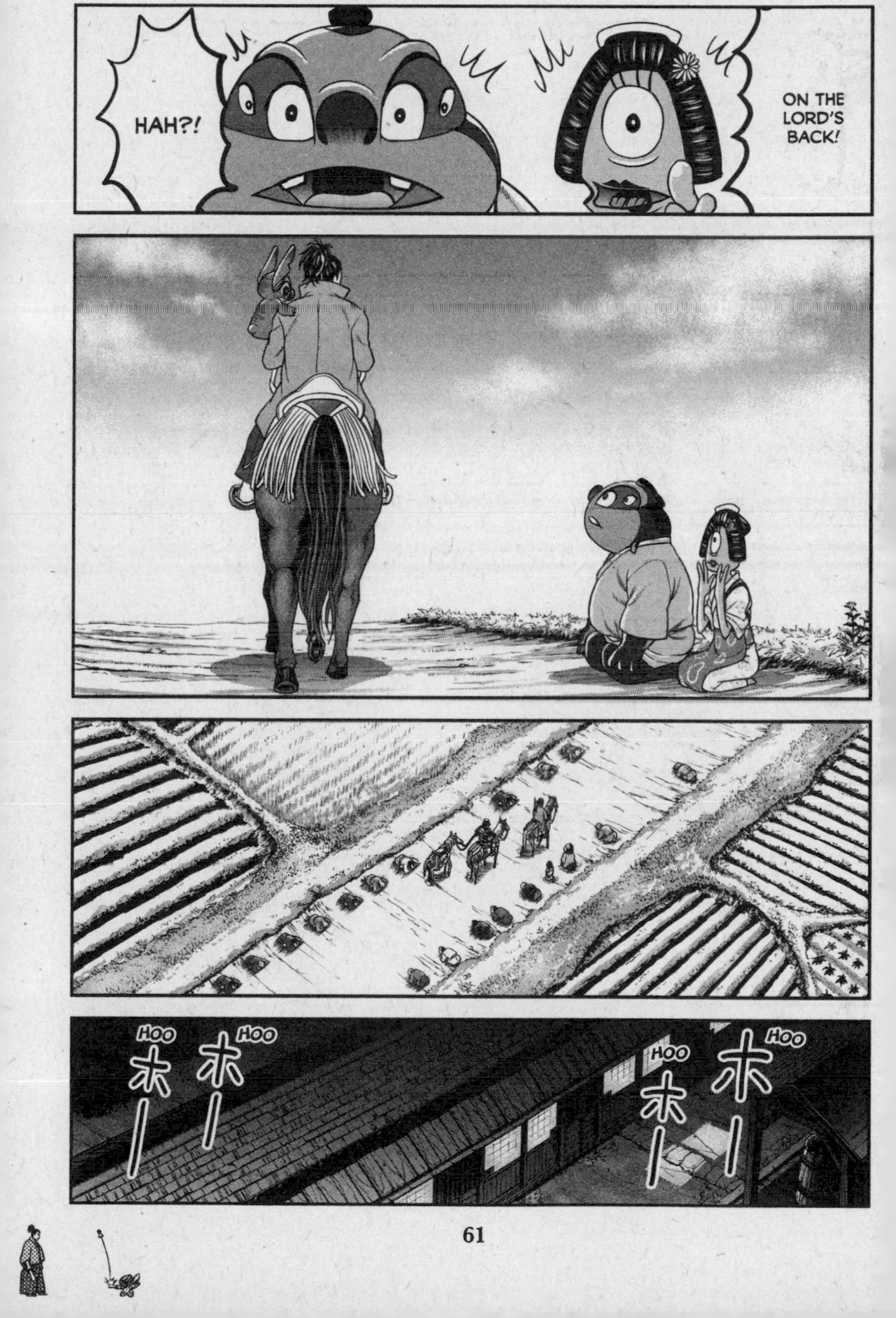
ON THE LORD'S BACK!
HAH?!
HOO
ホー
HOO
ホー
HOO
ホー
HOO
ホー

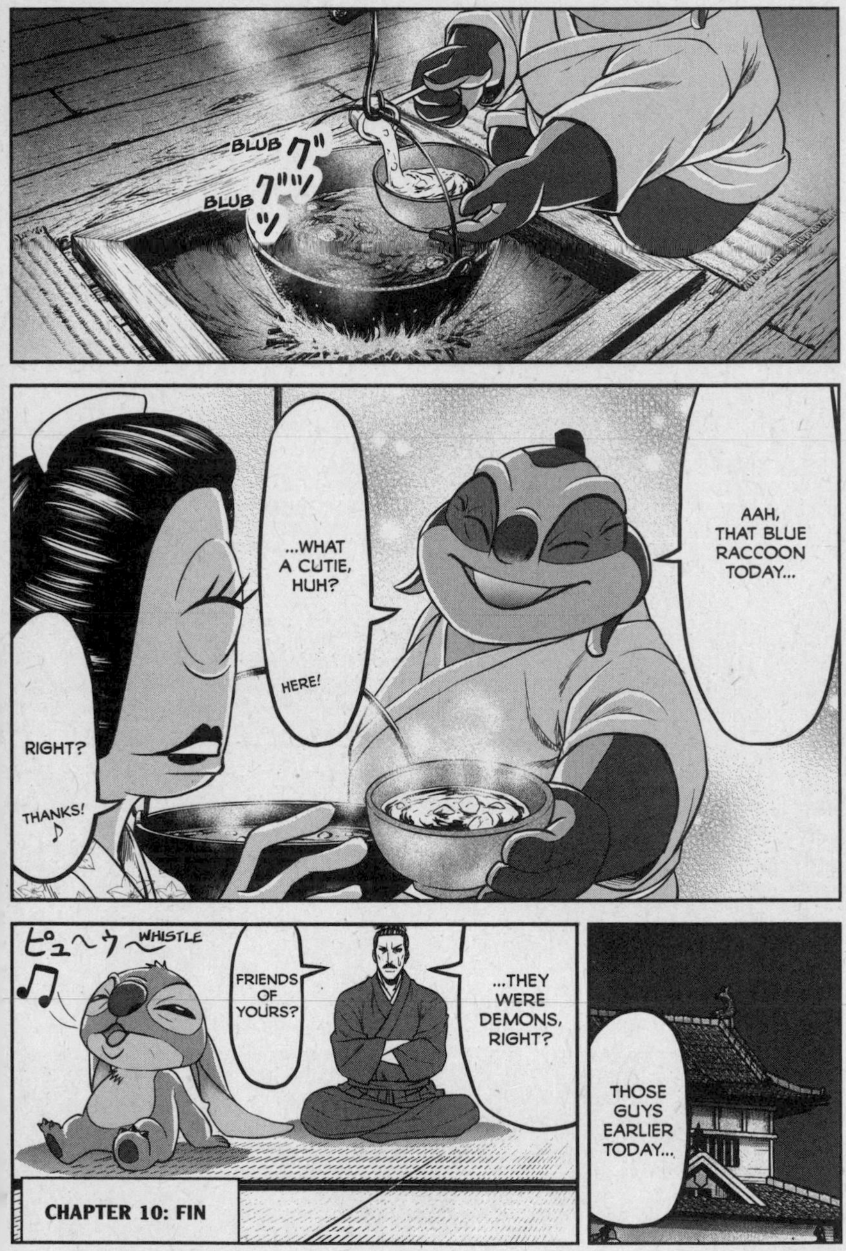
BLUB グ
BLUB グツ
ツ
AAH, THAT BLUE RACCOON TODAY...
...WHAT A CUTIE, HUH?
HERE!
RIGHT?
THANKS! ♪
THOSE GUYS EARLIER TODAY...
...THEY WERE DEMONS, RIGHT?
FRIENDS OF YOURS?
ピュ〜ウ〜 WHISTLE
CHAPTER 10: FIN

Disney
STiTCH
STITCH & THE SAMURAI

Disney

Stitch

STITCH & THE SAMURAI

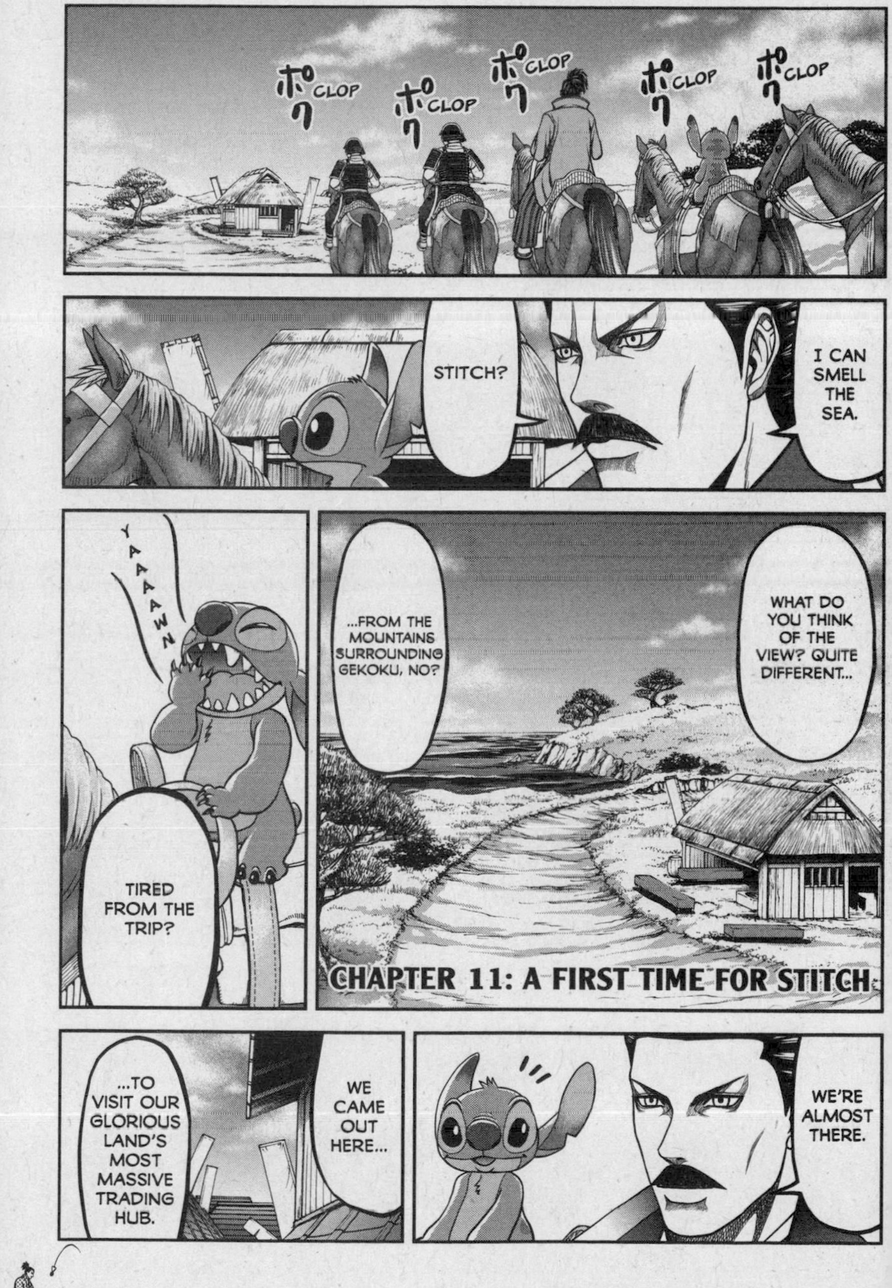
ポク CLOP
ポク CLOP
ポク CLOP
ポク CLOP
ポク CLOP
I CAN SMELL THE SEA.
STITCH?
WHAT DO YOU THINK OF THE VIEW? QUITE DIFFERENT...
...FROM THE MOUNTAINS SURROUNDING GEKOKU, NO?
CHAPTER 11: A FIRST TIME FOR STITCH
YAAAAWN
TIRED FROM THE TRIP?
WE'RE ALMOST THERE.
WE CAME OUT HERE...
...TO VISIT OUR GLORIOUS LAND'S MOST MASSIVE TRADING HUB.

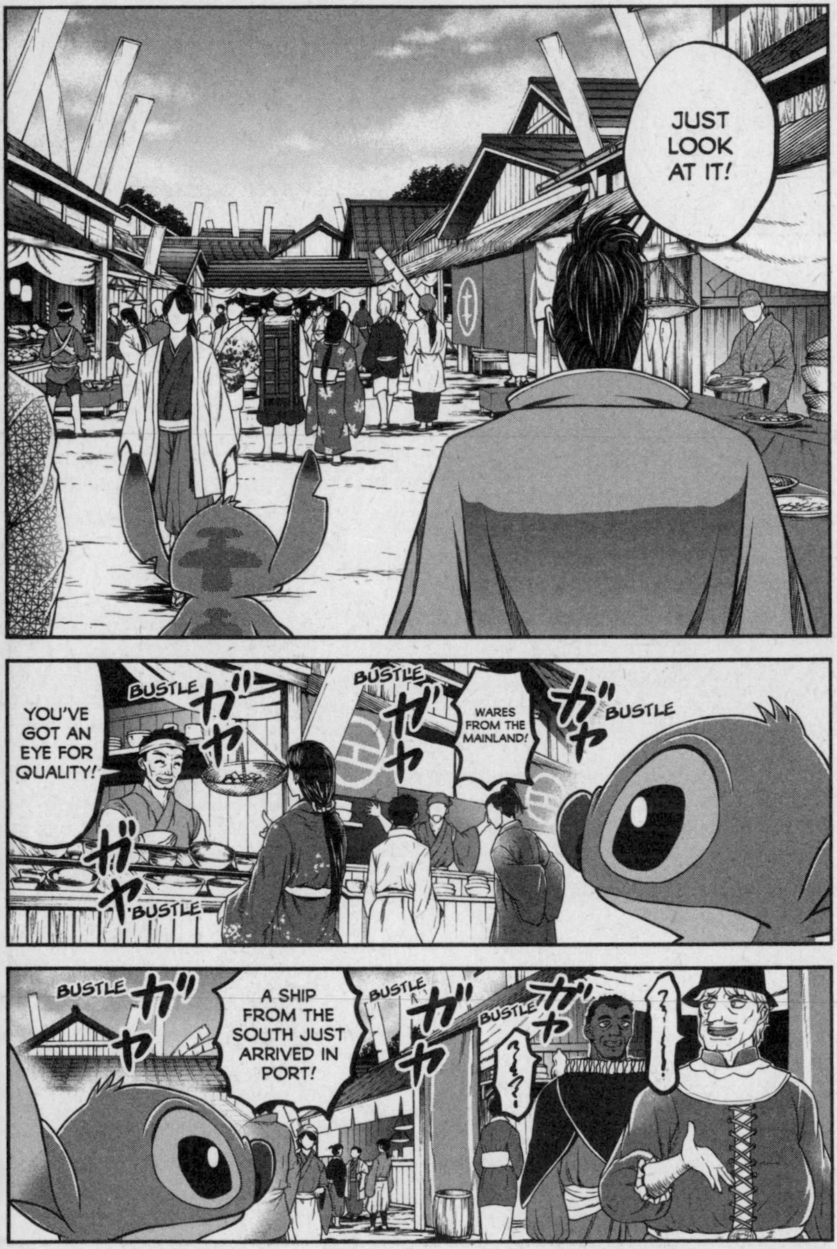
JUST LOOK AT IT!
ガヤ BUSTLE
WARES FROM THE MAINLAND!
BUSTLE ガヤ
BUSTLE ガヤ
YOU'VE GOT AN EYE FOR QUALITY!
ガヤ BUSTLE
BUSTLE ガヤ
BUSTLE ガヤ
A SHIP FROM THE SOUTH JUST ARRIVED IN PORT!
BUSTLE ガヤ

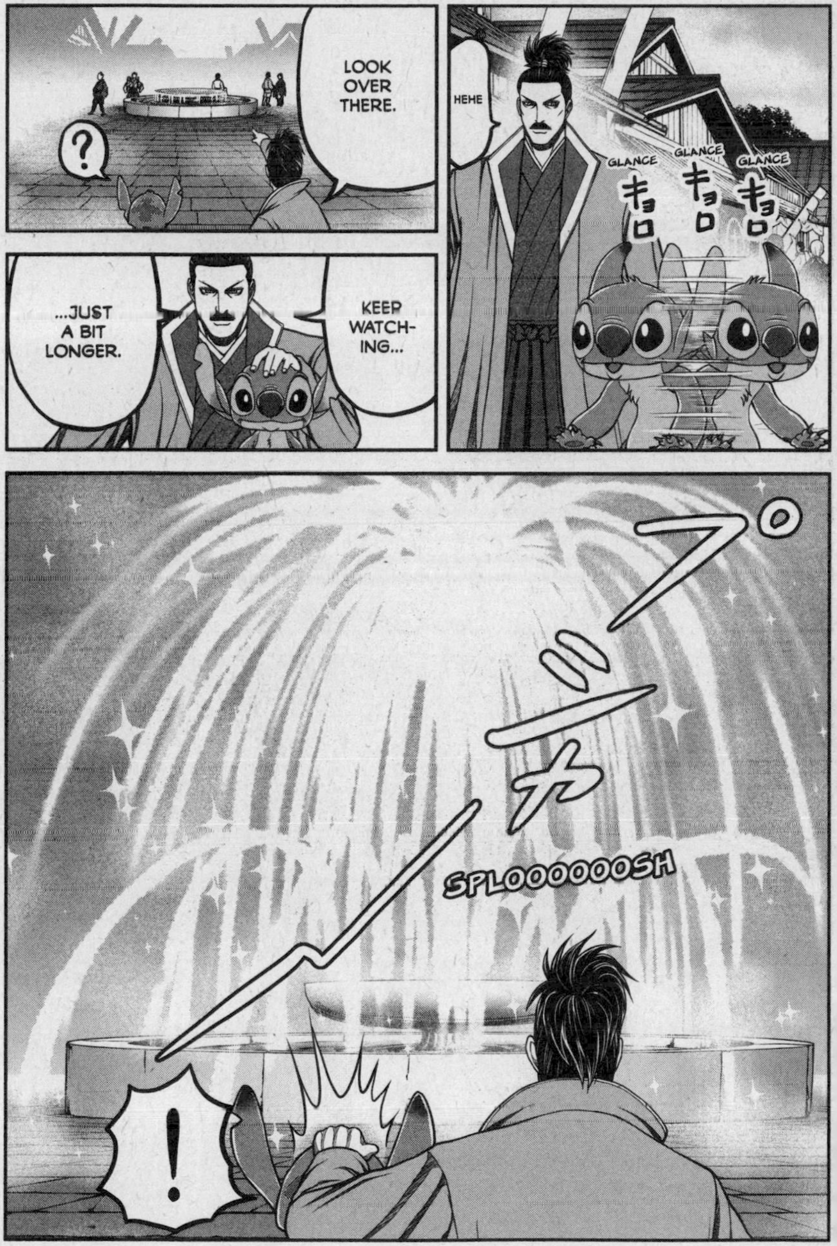
HEHE
GLANCE
キョロ
GLANCE
キョロ
GLANCE
キョロ
LOOK OVER THERE.
?
KEEP WATCHING...
...JUST A BIT LONGER.
SPLOOOOOOSH
!

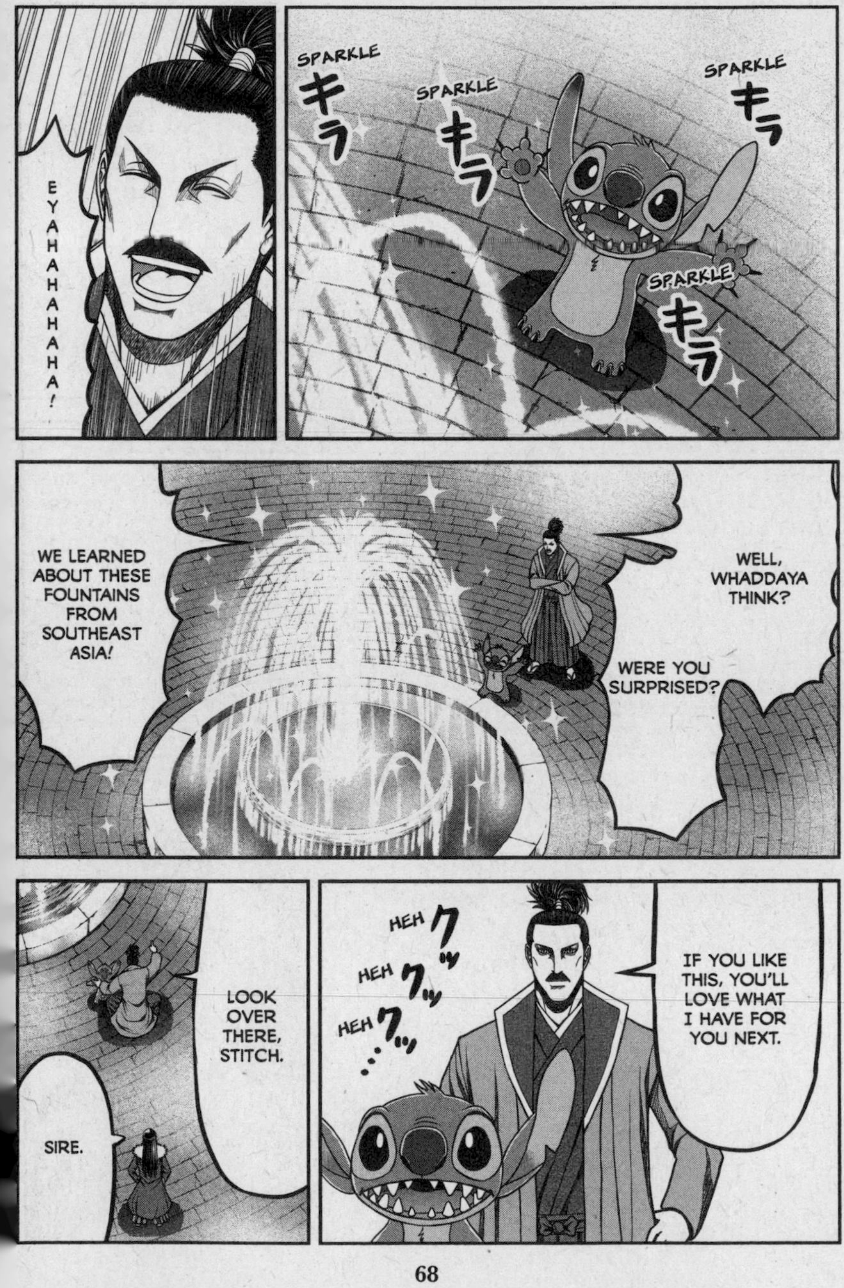
SPARKLE キラ
SPARKLE キラ
SPARKLE キラ
SPARKLE キラ
EYAHAHAHAHAHA!
WELL, WHADDAYA THINK?
WERE YOU SURPRISED?
WE LEARNED ABOUT THESE FOUNTAINS FROM SOUTHEAST ASIA!
IF YOU LIKE THIS, YOU'LL LOVE WHAT I HAVE FOR YOU NEXT.
HEH クッ
HEH クッ
HEH クッ
...
LOOK OVER THERE, STITCH.
SIRE.

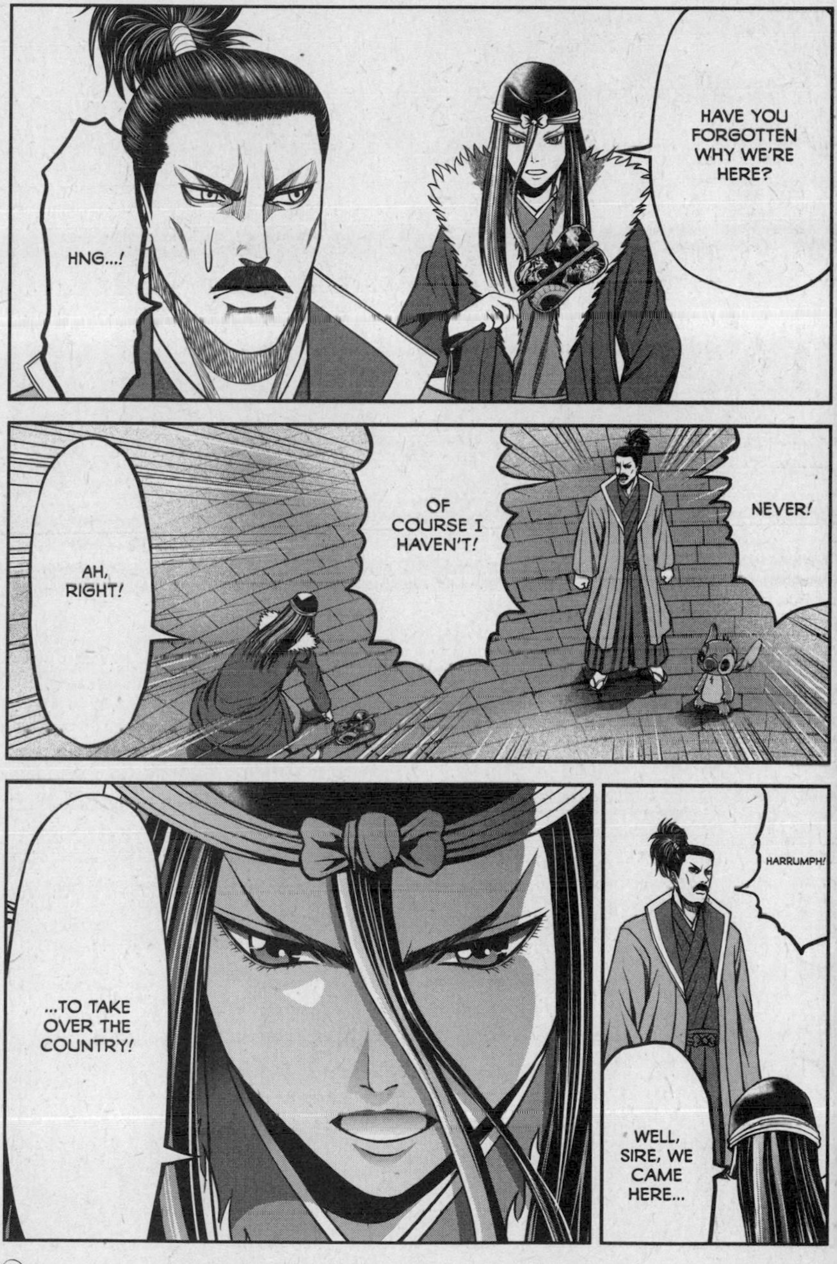
HAVE YOU FORGOTTEN WHY WE'RE HERE?
HNG...!
NEVER!
OF COURSE I HAVEN'T!
AH, RIGHT!
HARRUMPH!
WELL, SIRE, WE CAME HERE...
...TO TAKE OVER THE COUNTRY!

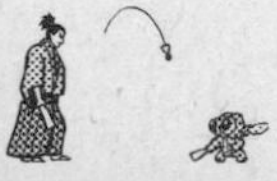

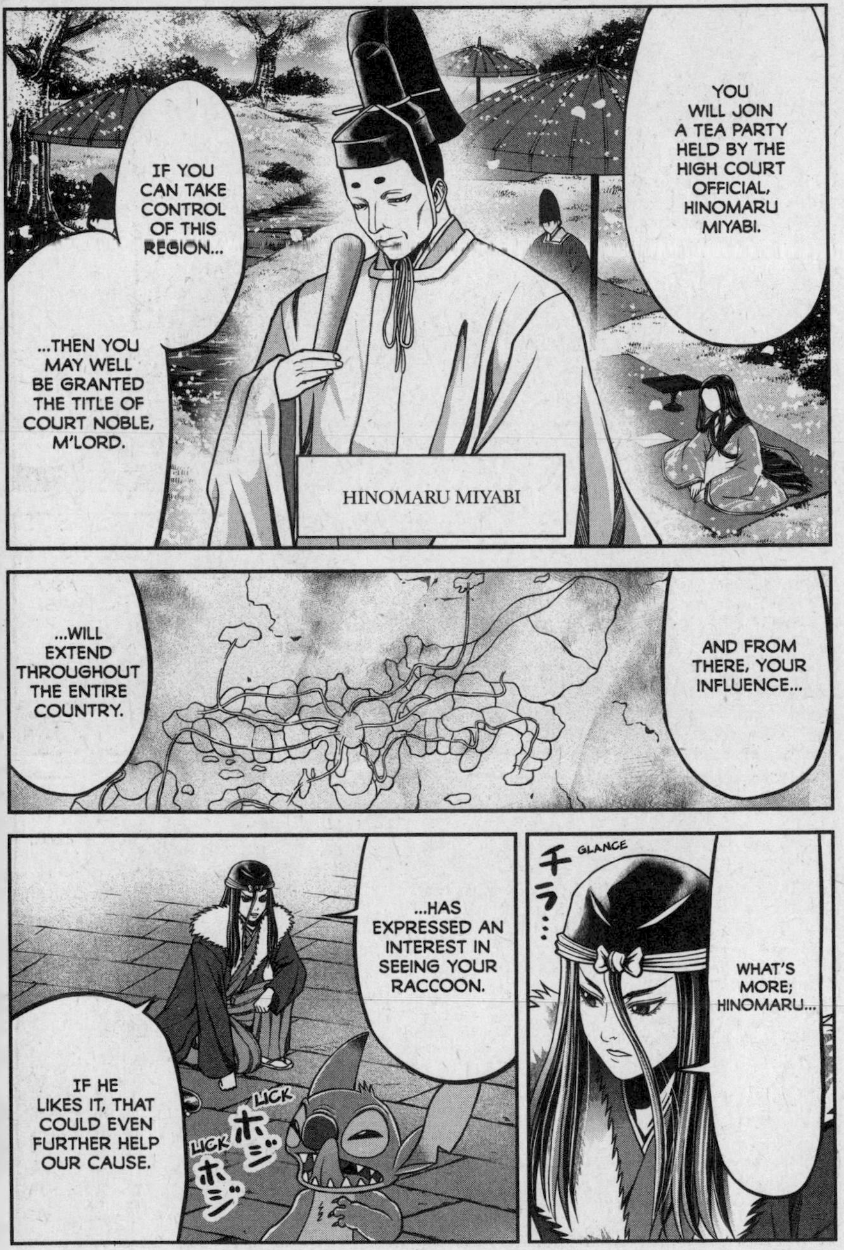
YOU WILL JOIN A TEA PARTY HELD BY THE HIGH COURT OFFICIAL, HINOMARU MIYABI.
IF YOU CAN TAKE CONTROL OF THIS REGION...
...THEN YOU MAY WELL BE GRANTED THE TITLE OF COURT NOBLE, M'LORD.
HINOMARU MIYABI
AND FROM THERE, YOUR INFLUENCE...
...WILL EXTEND THROUGHOUT THE ENTIRE COUNTRY.
チラ…
GLANCE
WHAT'S MORE; HINOMARU...
...HAS EXPRESSED AN INTEREST IN SEEING YOUR RACCOON.
IF HE LIKES IT, THAT COULD EVEN FURTHER HELP OUR CAUSE.
ホジ
LICK
ホジ
LICK

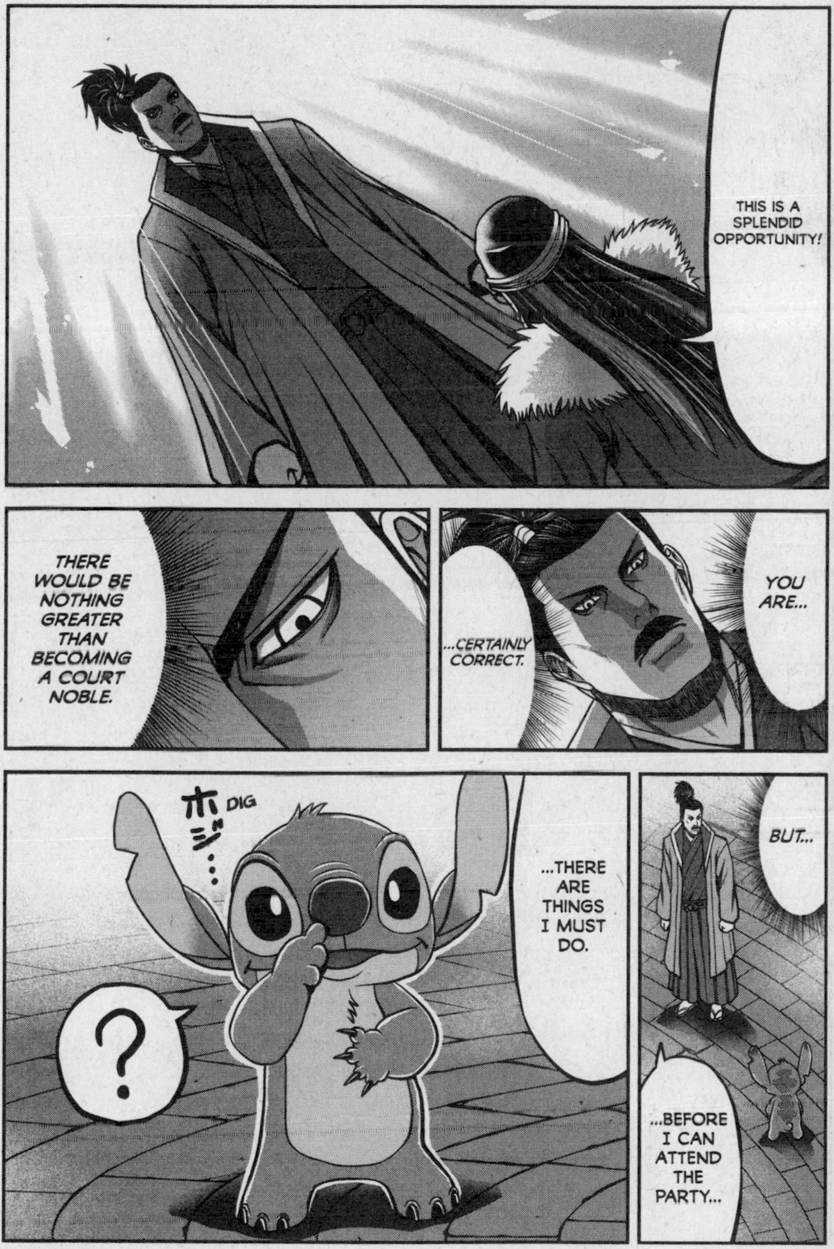
THIS IS A SPLENDID OPPORTUNITY!
YOU ARE...
...CERTAINLY CORRECT.
THERE WOULD BE NOTHING GREATER THAN BECOMING A COURT NOBLE.
BUT...
...BEFORE I CAN ATTEND THE PARTY...
...THERE ARE THINGS I MUST DO.
ホジ DIG
?

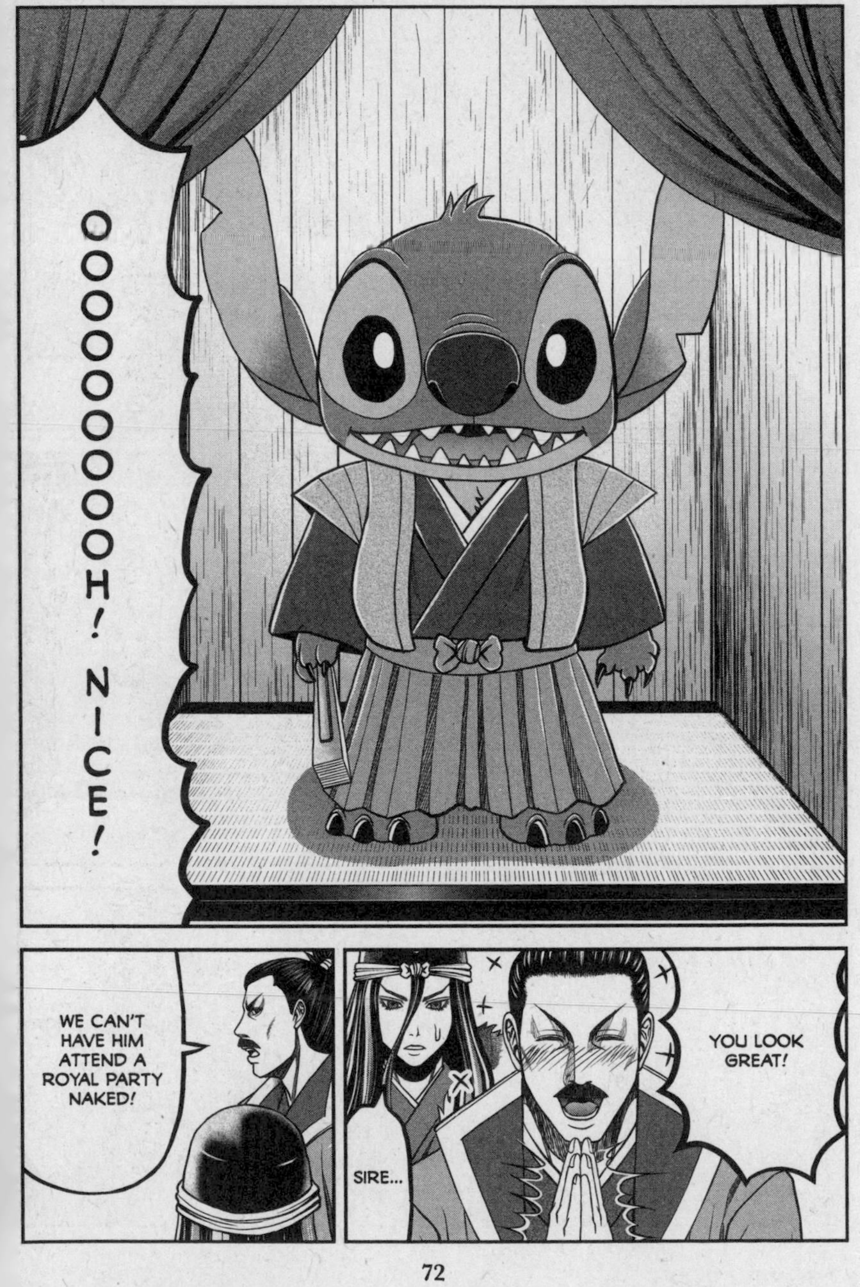
OOOOOOOOOH! NICE!
YOU LOOK GREAT!
SIRE...
WE CAN'T HAVE HIM ATTEND A ROYAL PARTY NAKED!

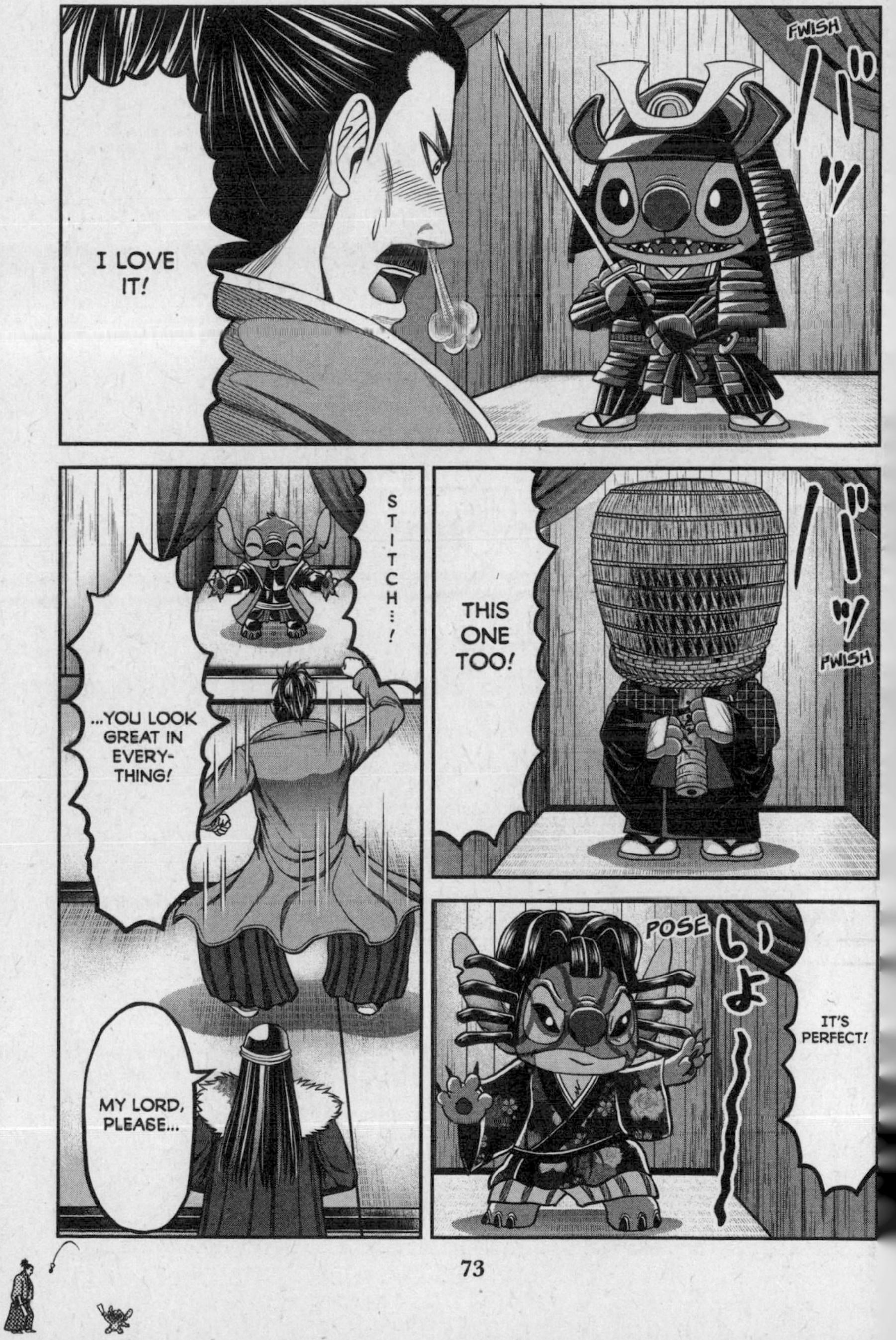
FWISH
バッ
I LOVE IT!
バーッ
FWISH
THIS ONE TOO!
POSE
いよ～
IT'S PERFECT!
STITCH...!
...YOU LOOK GREAT IN EVERYTHING!
MY LORD, PLEASE...

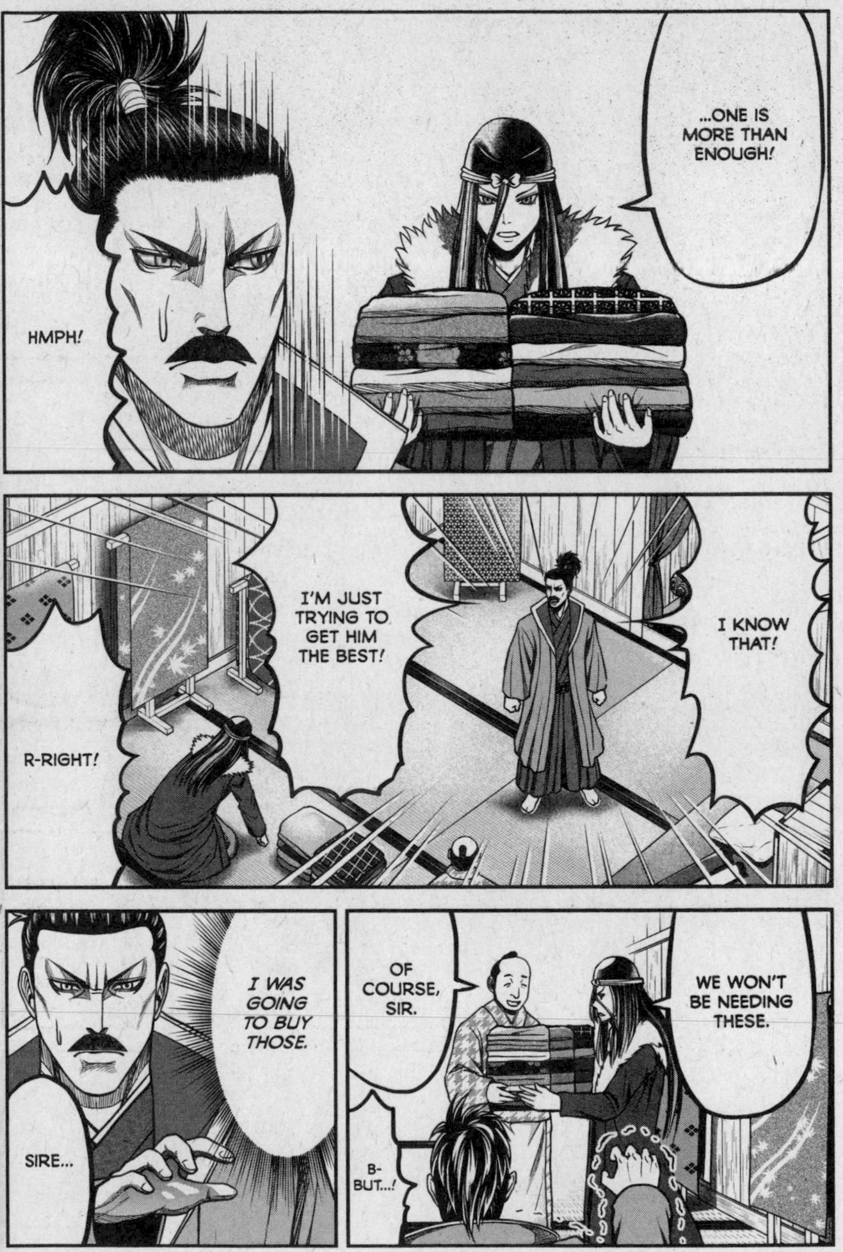
...ONE IS MORE THAN ENOUGH!
HMPH!
I KNOW THAT!
I'M JUST TRYING TO GET HIM THE BEST!
R-RIGHT!
WE WON'T BE NEEDING THESE.
OF COURSE, SIR.
B-BUT...!
I WAS GOING TO BUY THOSE.
SIRE...

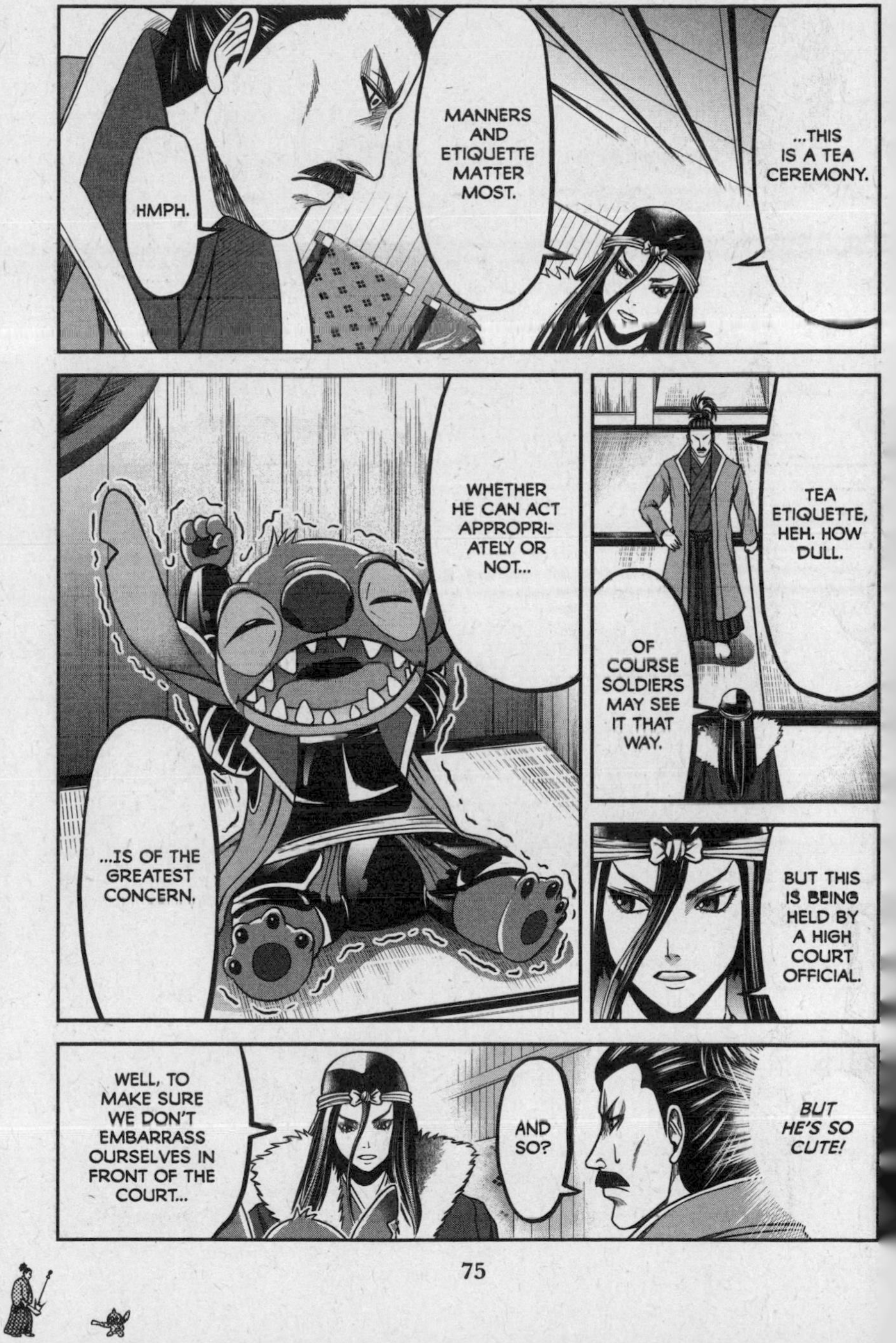
...THIS IS A TEA CEREMONY.
MANNERS AND ETIQUETTE MATTER MOST.
HMPH.
TEA ETIQUETTE, HEH. HOW DULL.
OF COURSE SOLDIERS MAY SEE IT THAT WAY.
BUT THIS IS BEING HELD BY A HIGH COURT OFFICIAL.
WHETHER HE CAN ACT APPROPRIATELY OR NOT...
...IS OF THE GREATEST CONCERN.
BUT HE'S SO CUTE!
AND SO?
WELL, TO MAKE SURE WE DON'T EMBARRASS OURSELVES IN FRONT OF THE COURT...

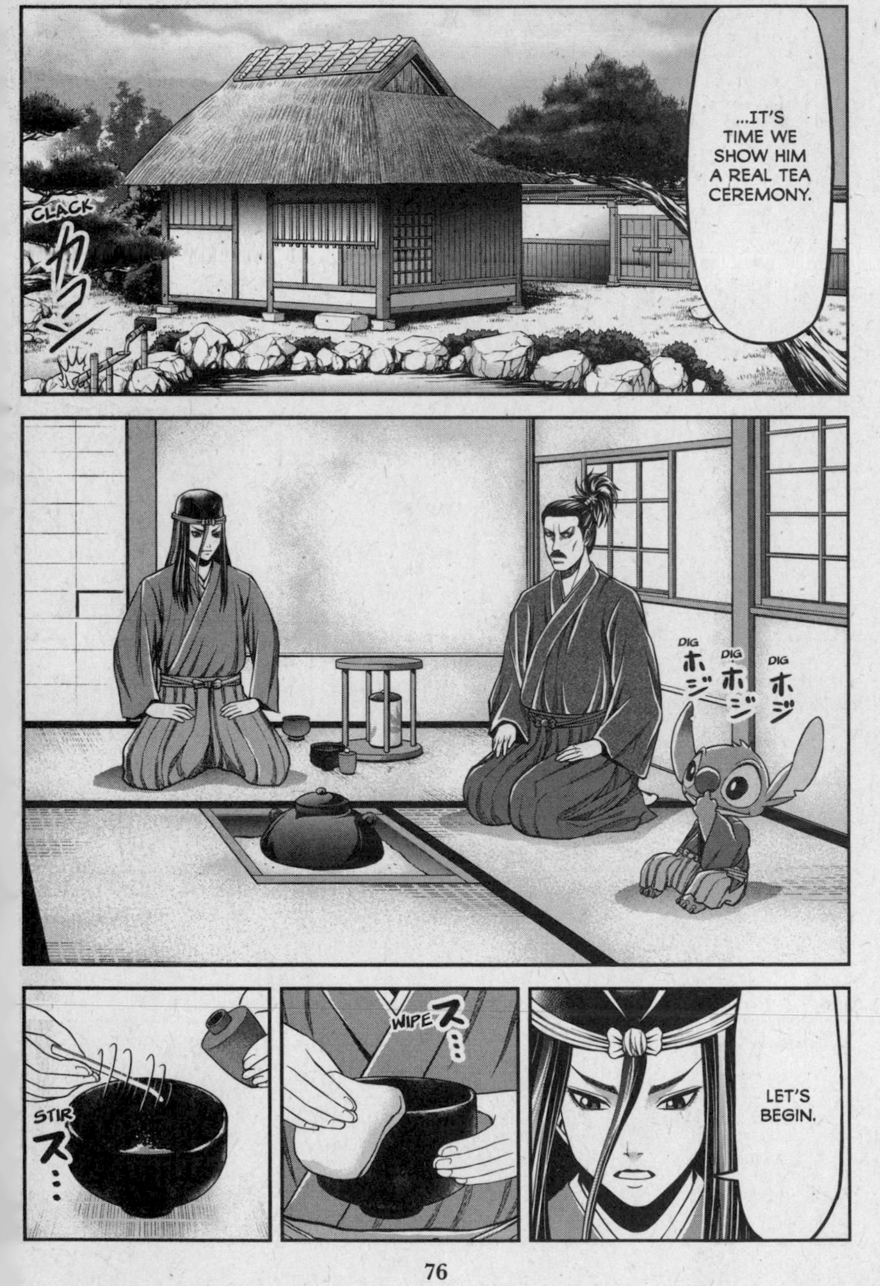
...IT'S TIME WE SHOW HIM A REAL TEA CEREMONY.
CLACK
DIG ホジ
DIG ホジ
DIG ホジ
LET'S BEGIN.
WIPE ス…
STIR ス…

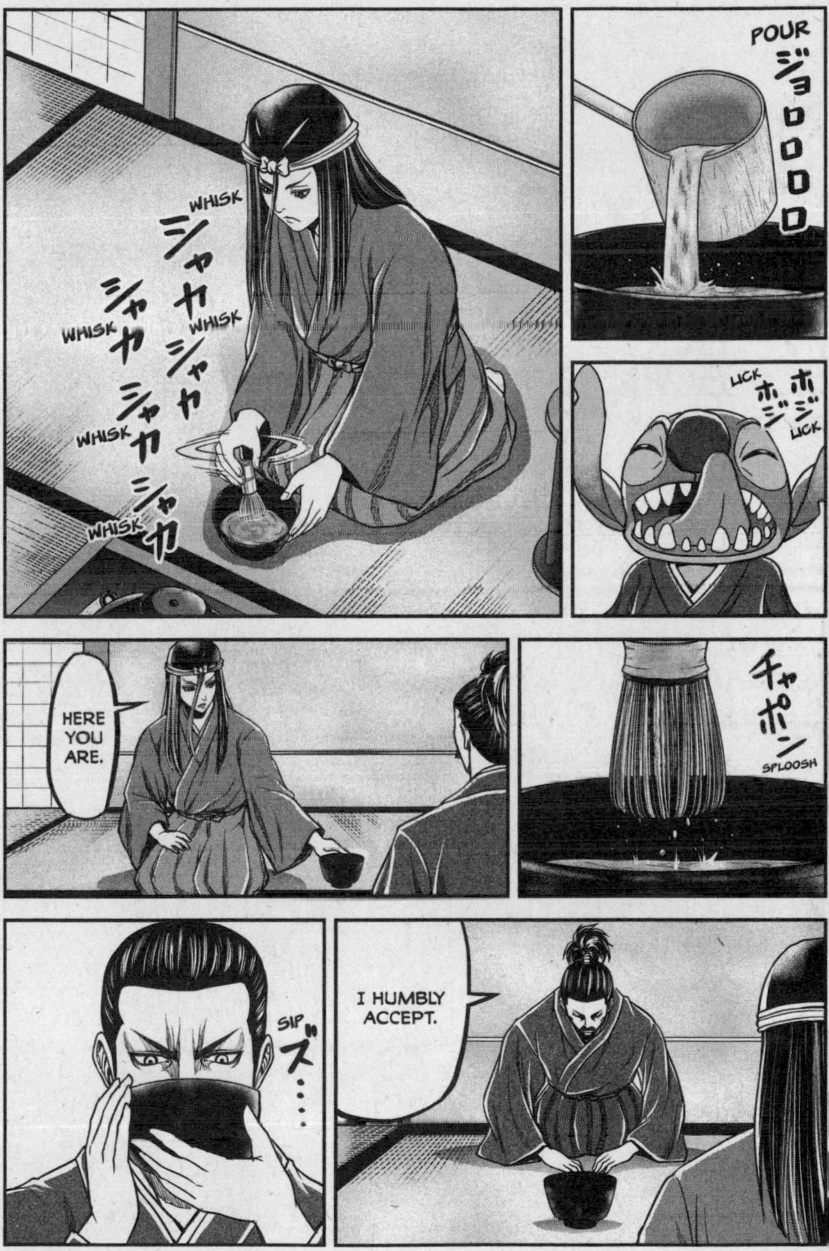
POUR
ジョロロロロ
ホジホジ
LICK
LICK
シャカシャカシャカシャカシャカ
WHISK
WHISK
WHISK
WHISK
WHISK
チャポン
SPLOOSH
HERE YOU ARE.
I HUMBLY ACCEPT.
SIP
ズ…

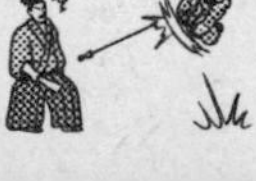

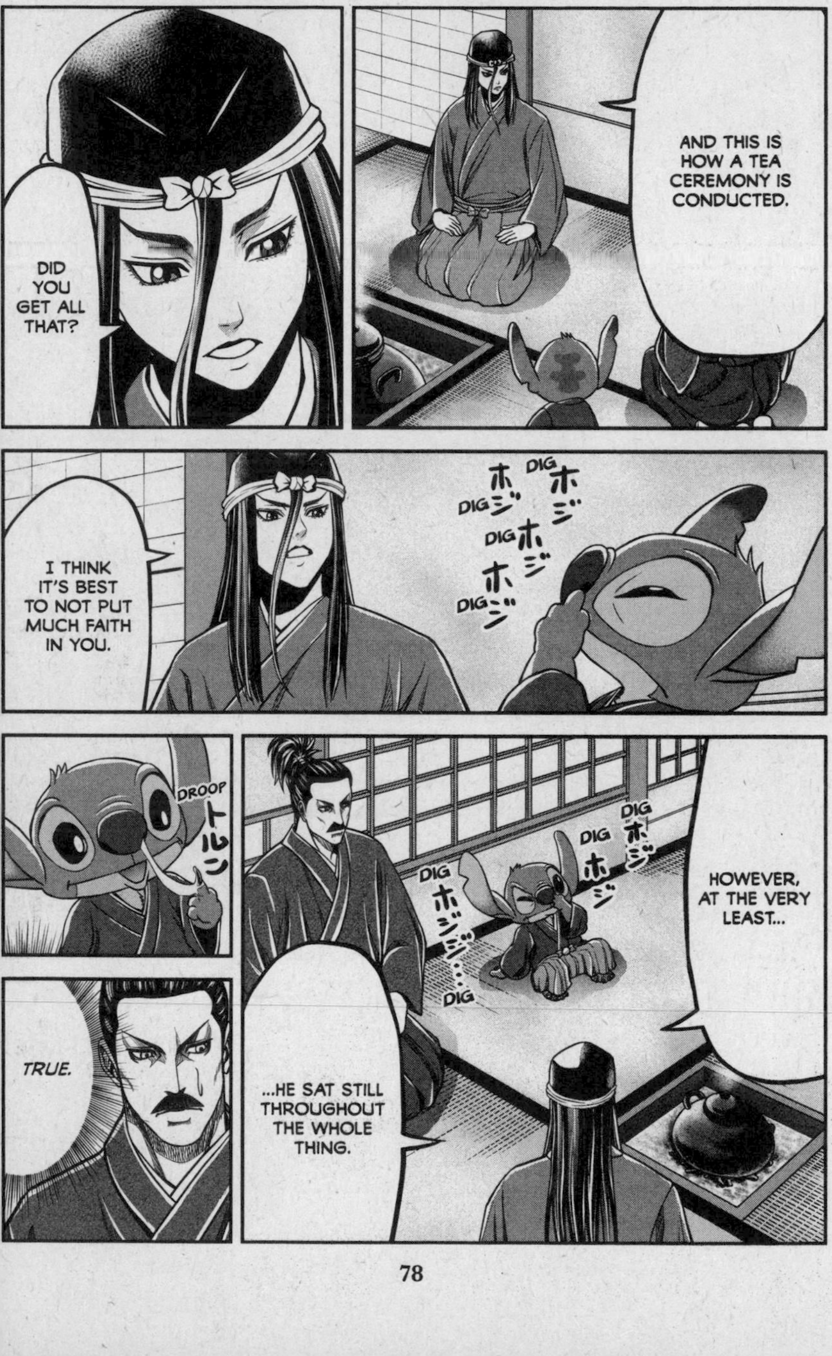
AND THIS IS HOW A TEA CEREMONY IS CONDUCTED.
DID YOU GET ALL THAT?
DIG ホジ
DIG ホジ
DIG ホジ
DIG ホジ
I THINK IT'S BEST TO NOT PUT MUCH FAITH IN YOU.
HOWEVER, AT THE VERY LEAST...
DIG ホジ
DIG ホジ
DIG ホジジ... DIG
...HE SAT STILL THROUGHOUT THE WHOLE THING.
DROOP トルン
TRUE.

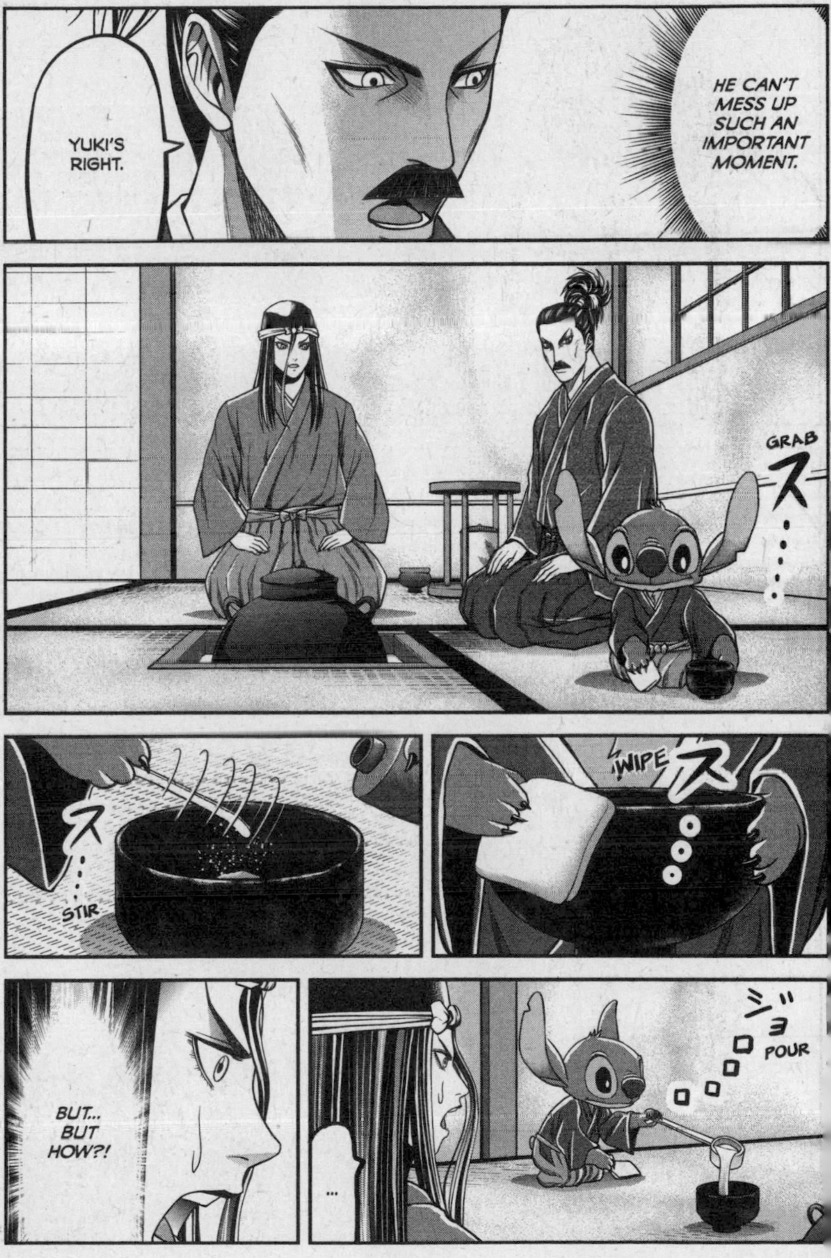
HE CAN'T MESS UP SUCH AN IMPORTANT MOMENT.
YUKI'S RIGHT.
GRAB
ス
WIPE
ス
ス
STIR
ジョ
POUR
...
BUT... BUT HOW?!

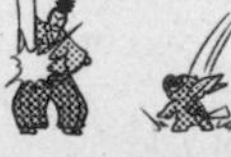

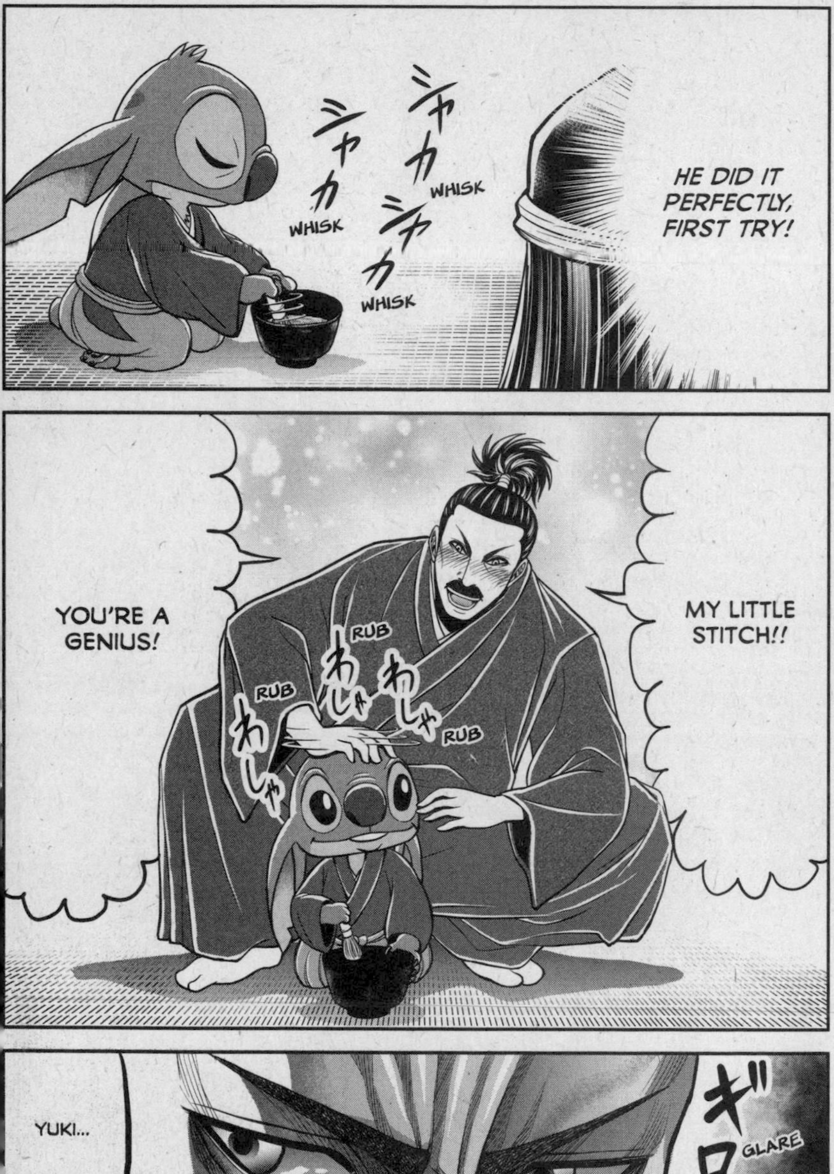

HE DID IT PERFECTLY, FIRST TRY!
シャカ
WHISK
シャカ
WHISK
シャカ
WHISK
MY LITTLE STITCH!!
YOU'RE A GENIUS!
わしゃ
RUB
わしゃ
RUB
わしゃ
RUB
ギロッ
GLARE
YUKI...

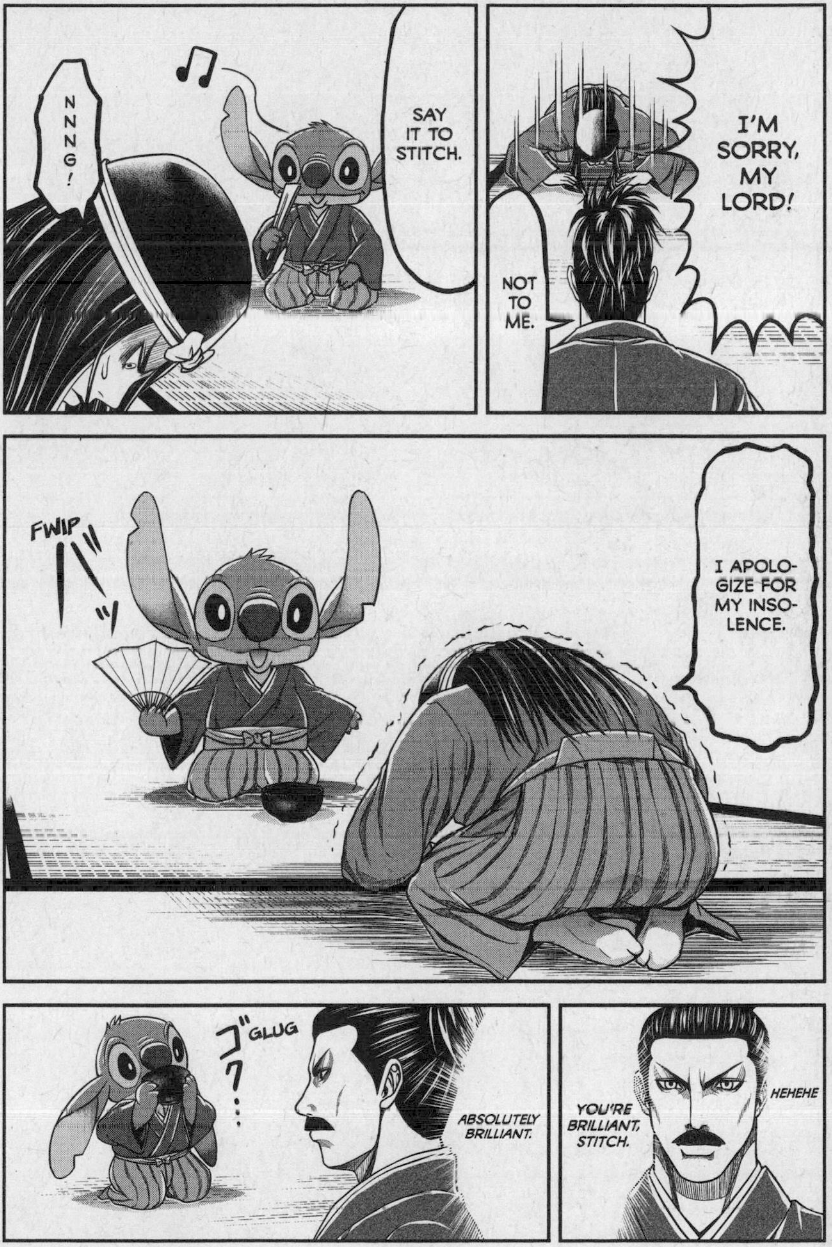

I'M SORRY, MY LORD!
NOT TO ME.
SAY IT TO STITCH.
NNNG!
I APOLOGIZE FOR MY INSOLENCE.
FWIP
HEHEHE
YOU'RE BRILLIANT, STITCH.
ABSOLUTELY BRILLIANT.
GLUG
ゴク…

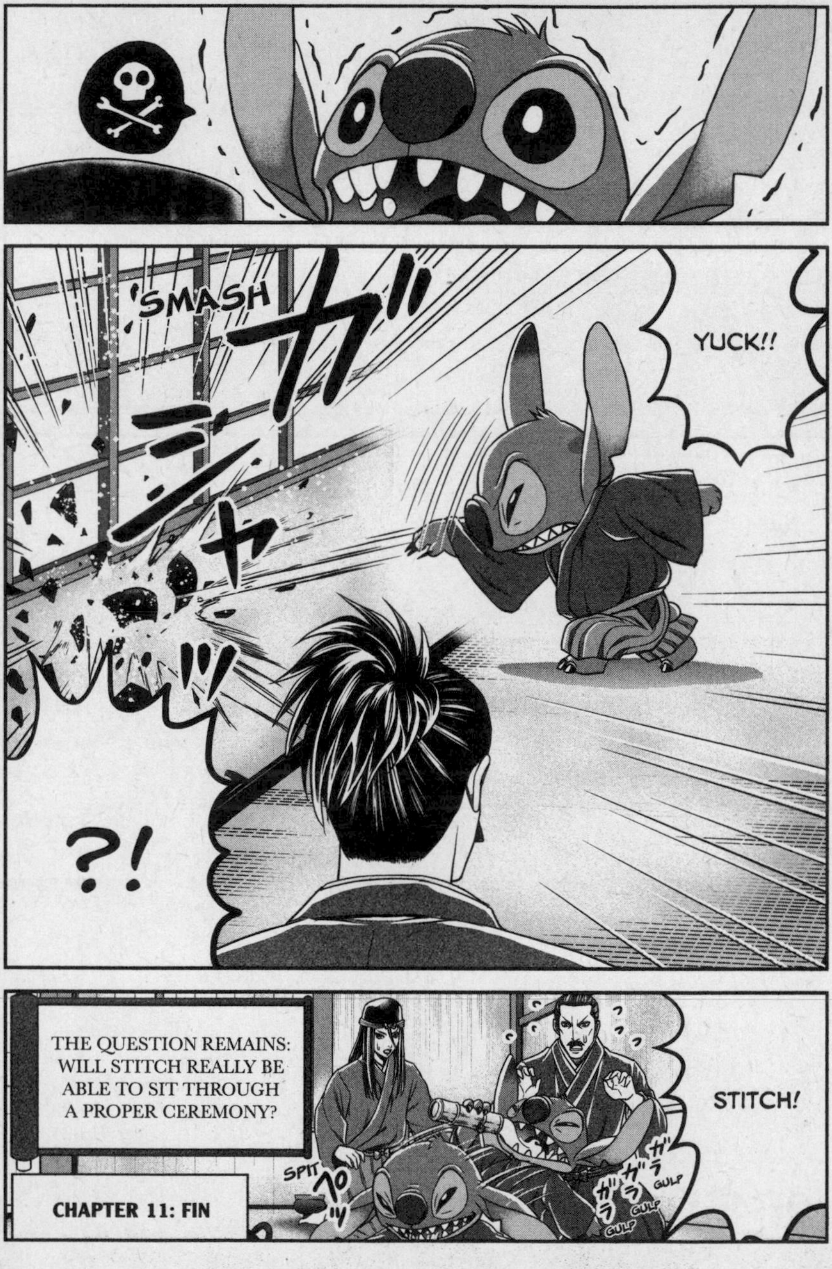
YUCK!!
SMASH
?!
STITCH!
ガラ ガラ ガラ
GULP GULP GULP
SPIT
THE QUESTION REMAINS: WILL STITCH REALLY BE ABLE TO SIT THROUGH A PROPER CEREMONY?
CHAPTER 11: FIN

DISNEY
STITCH
STITCH & THE SAMURAI

Disney
STiTCH
STITCH & THE SAMURAI

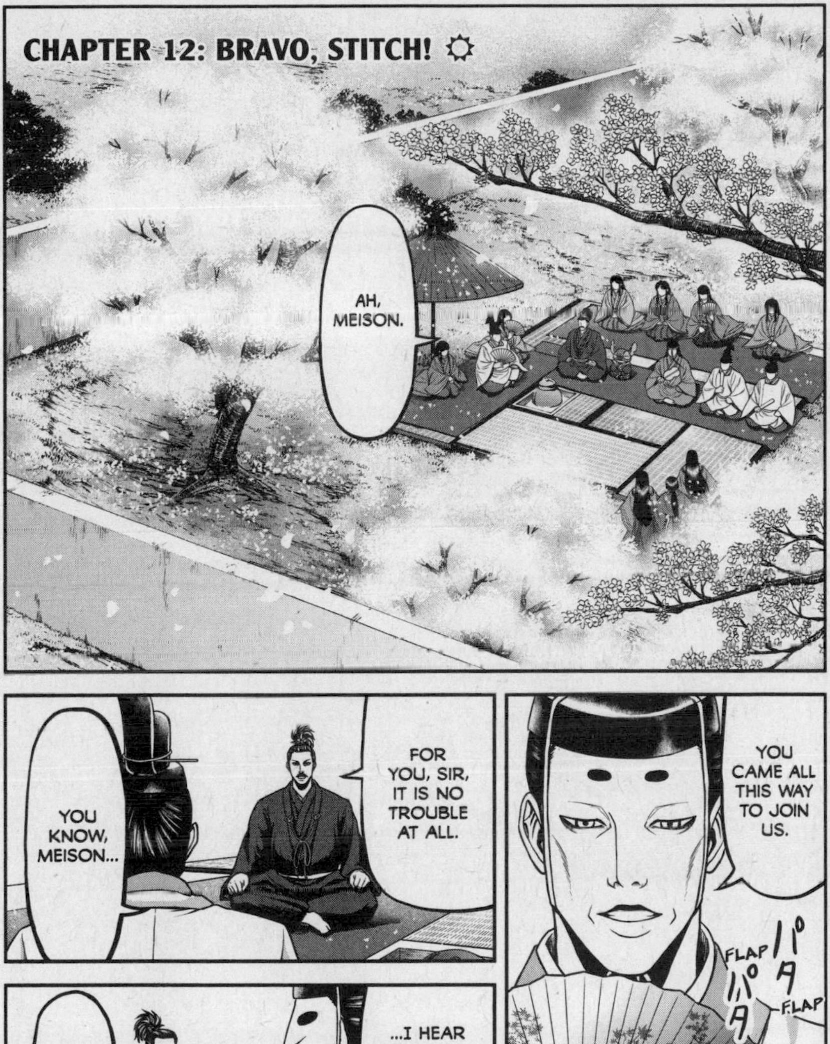
CHAPTER 12: BRAVO, STITCH!
AH, MEISON.
YOU CAME ALL THIS WAY TO JOIN US.
FLAP パタ
パタ FLAP
HIGH COURT OFFICIAL HINOMARU MIYABI
FOR YOU, SIR, IT IS NO TROUBLE AT ALL.
YOU KNOW, MEISON...
...I HEAR STORIES ABOUT YOU HAVING A BLUE RACCOON.
AH, YES!

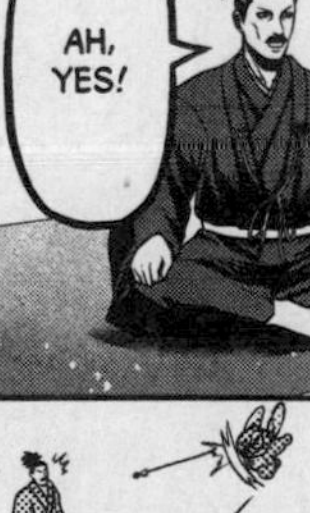

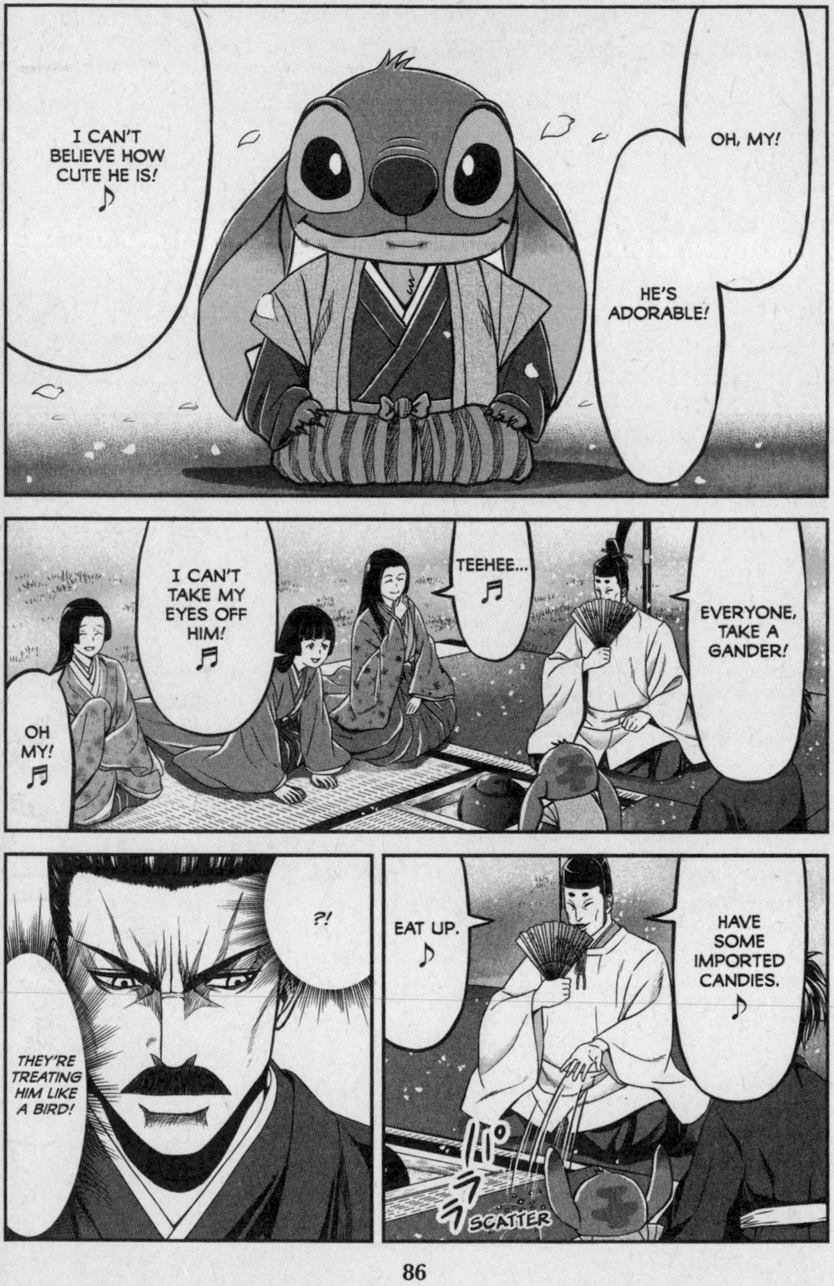
OH, MY!
HE'S ADORABLE!
I CAN'T BELIEVE HOW CUTE HE IS! ♪
EVERYONE, TAKE A GANDER!
TEEHEE... ♬
I CAN'T TAKE MY EYES OFF HIM! ♬
OH MY! ♬
HAVE SOME IMPORTED CANDIES. ♪
EAT UP. ♪
SCATTER
?!
THEY'RE TREATING HIM LIKE A BIRD!

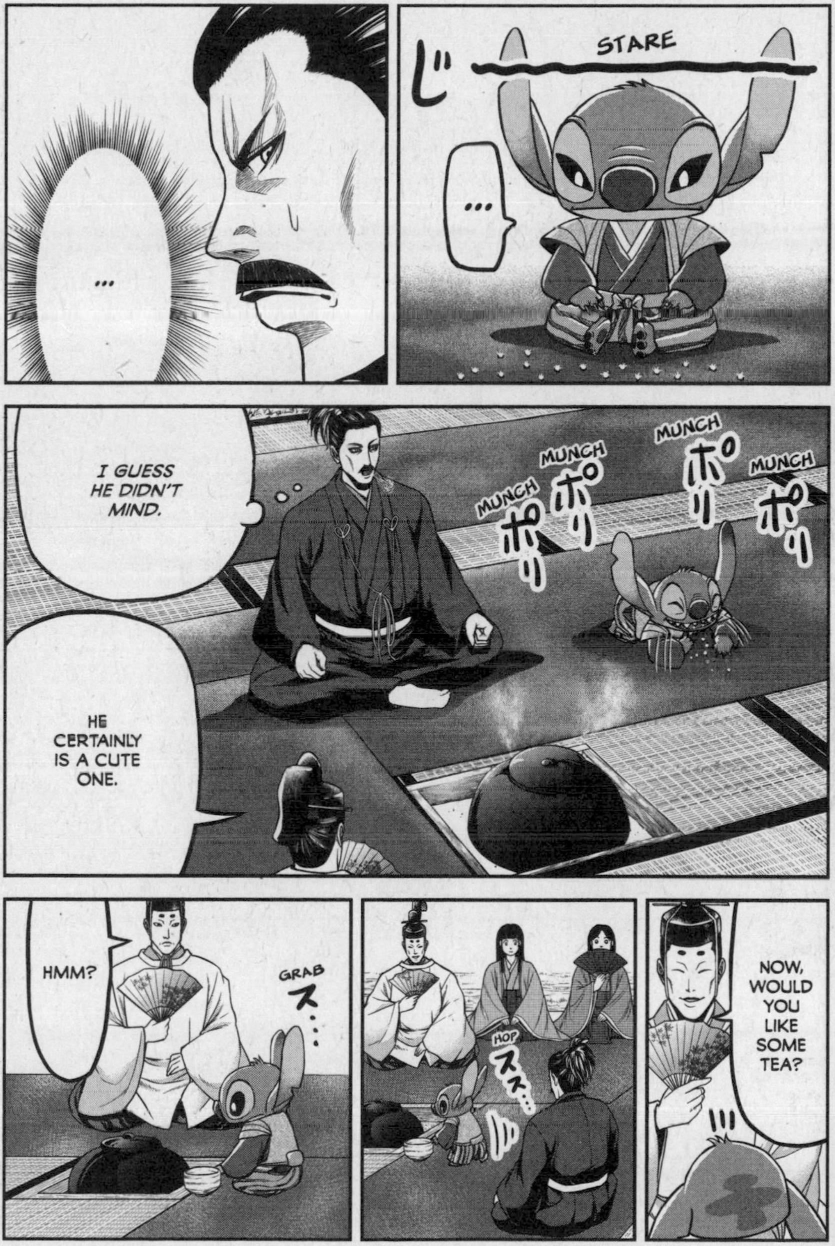

STARE
じ
...
...
MUNCH
ポリ
MUNCH
ポリ
MUNCH
ポリ
MUNCH
ポリ
I GUESS HE DIDN'T MIND.
HE CERTAINLY IS A CUTE ONE.
NOW, WOULD YOU LIKE SOME TEA?
HOP
スス…
GRAB
ス…
HMM?

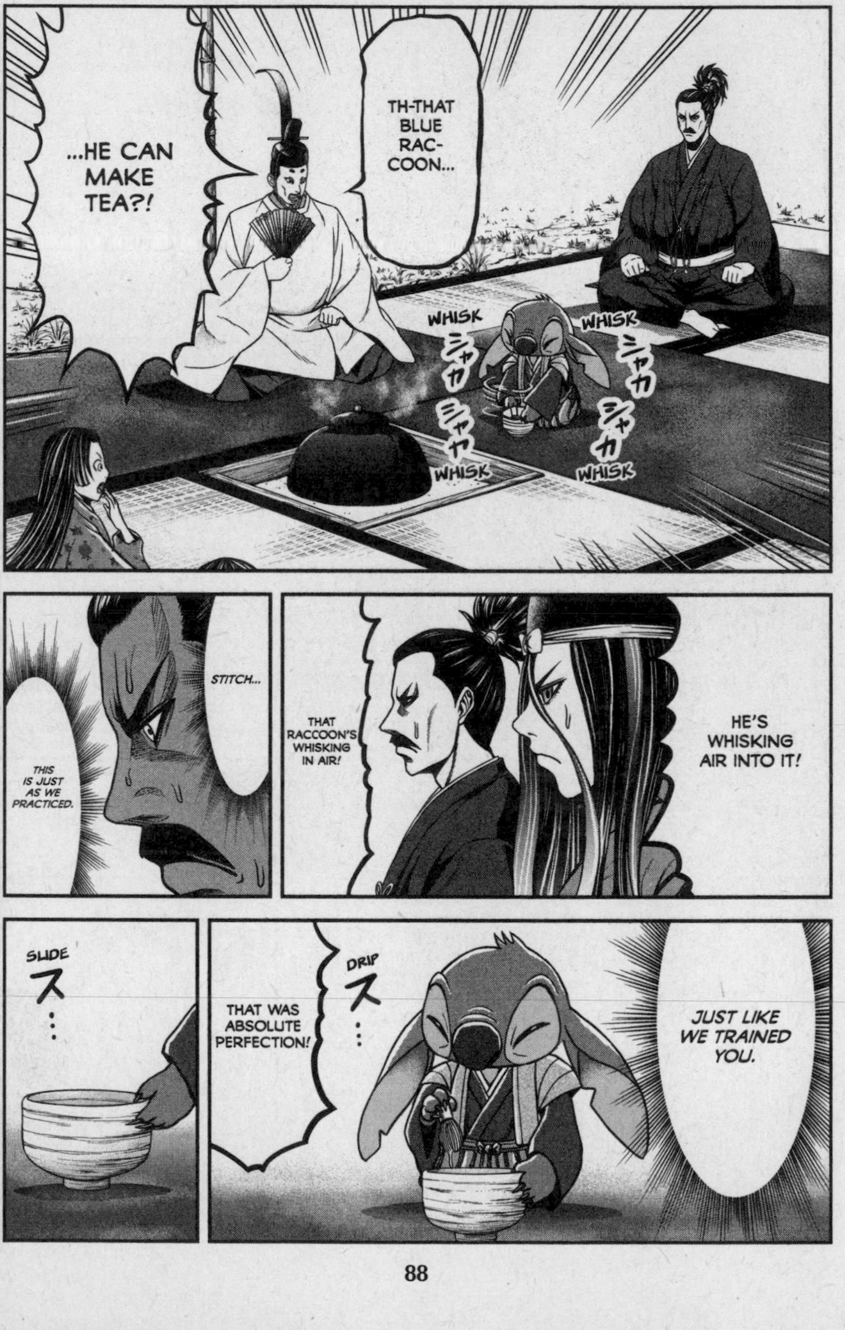
TH-THAT BLUE RAC-COON...
...HE CAN MAKE TEA?!
WHISK シャカ
シャカ WHISK
WHISK シャカ
シャカ WHISK
HE'S WHISKING AIR INTO IT!
THAT RACCOON'S WHISKING IN AIR!
STITCH...
THIS IS JUST AS WE PRACTICED.
JUST LIKE WE TRAINED YOU.
DRIP ス...
THAT WAS ABSOLUTE PERFECTION!
SLIDE ス...

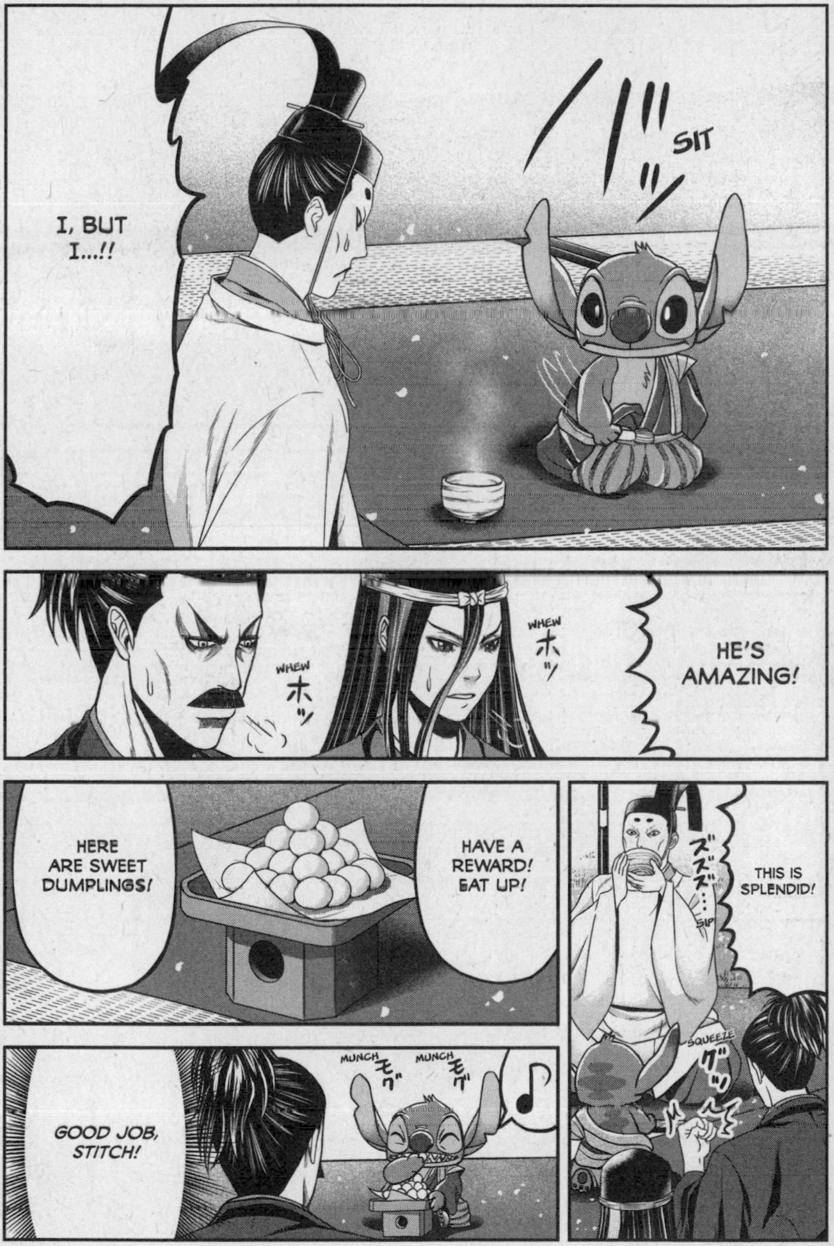
SIT
I, BUT I...!!
HE'S AMAZING!
WHEW ホッ
WHEW ホッ
THIS IS SPLENDID!
ズズズ… SIP
SQUEEZE グッ
HAVE A REWARD! EAT UP!
HERE ARE SWEET DUMPLINGS!
♪
MUNCH モグ
MUNCH モグ
GOOD JOB, STITCH!

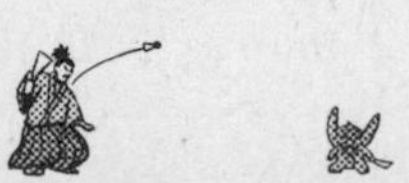

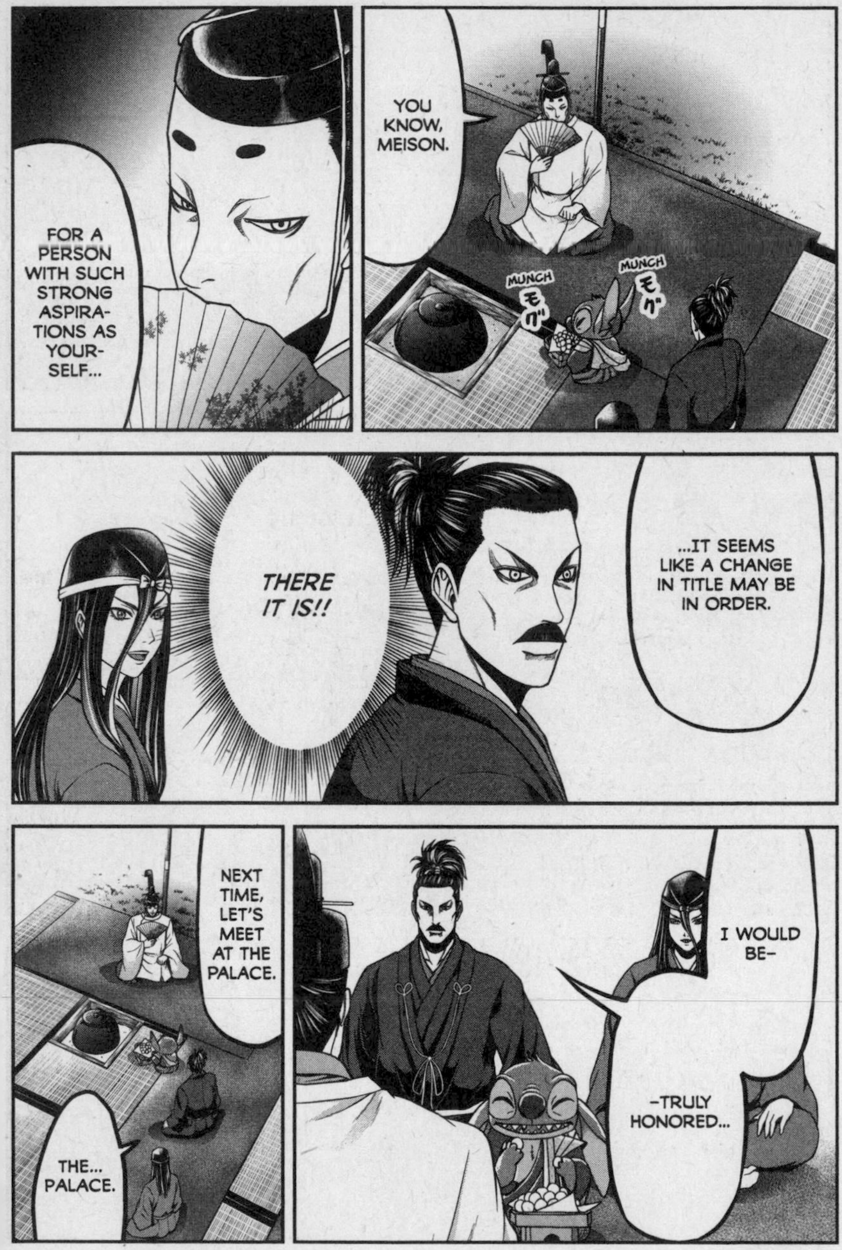
YOU KNOW, MEISON.
MUNCH
モグ
MUNCH
モグ
FOR A PERSON WITH SUCH STRONG ASPIRA- TIONS AS YOUR- SELF...
...IT SEEMS LIKE A CHANGE IN TITLE MAY BE IN ORDER.
THERE IT IS!!
I WOULD BE–
–TRULY HONORED...
NEXT TIME, LET'S MEET AT THE PALACE.
THE... PALACE.

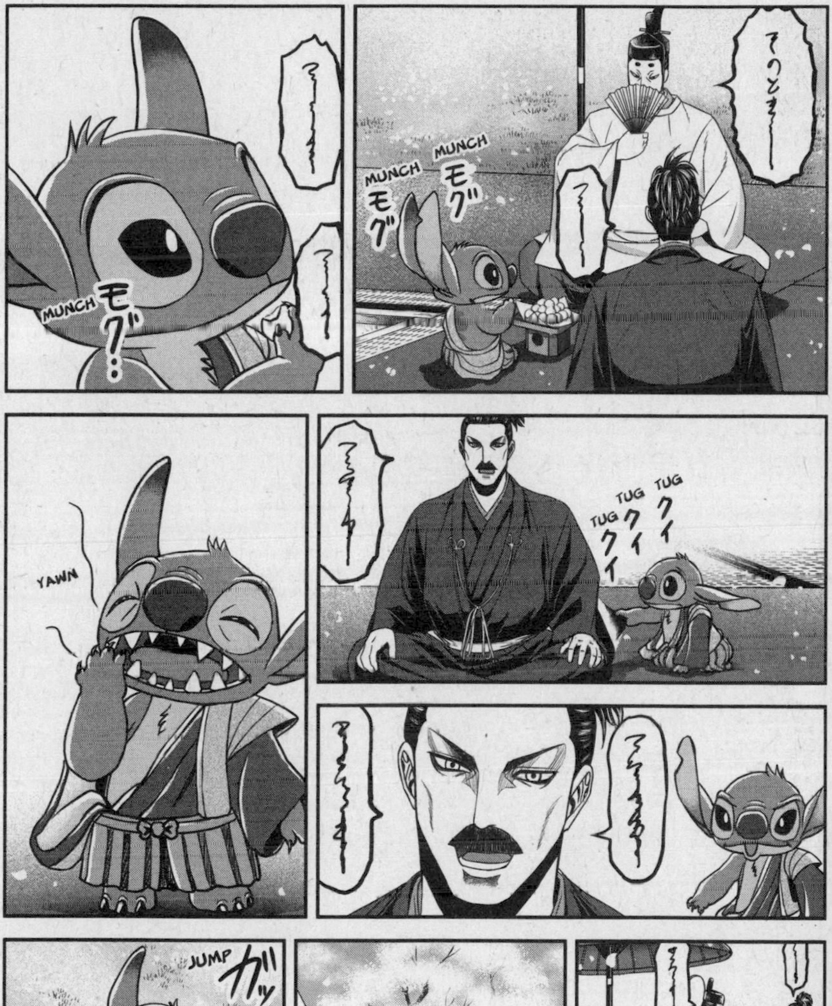
そのとき—
MUNCH モグ
MUNCH モグ
MUNCH モグ…
TUG クイ
TUG クイ
TUG クイ
YAWN
PWOP トコ
PWOP トコ
PWOP トコ
JUMP ガッ
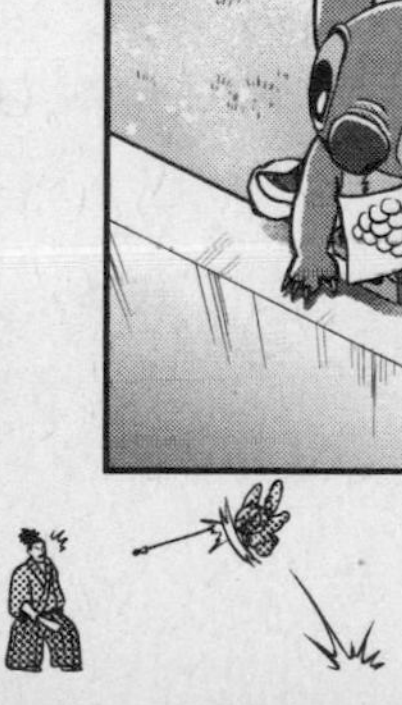

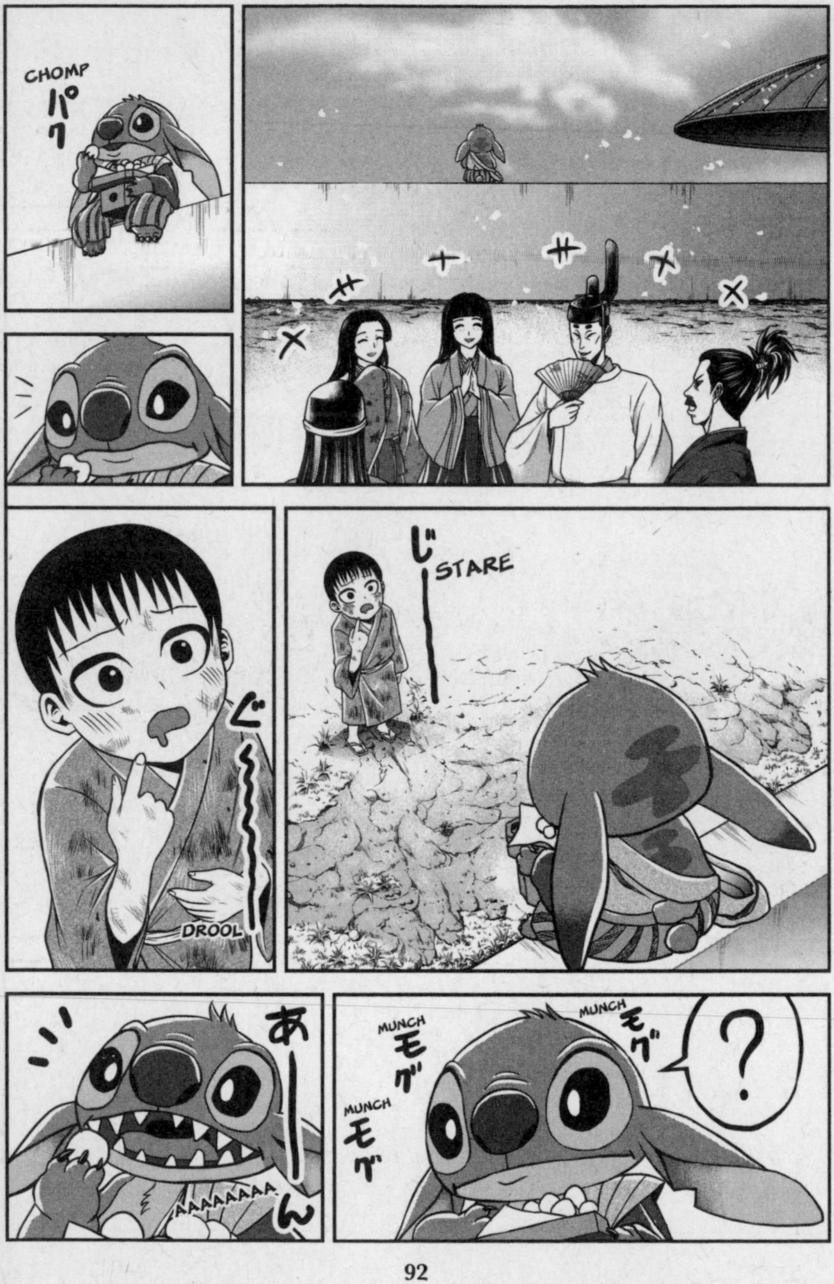
CHOMP
パク
じー
STARE
ぐ〜〜
DROOL
?
MUNCH
モグ
MUNCH
モグ
MUNCH
モグ
あーーん
AAAAAAAA

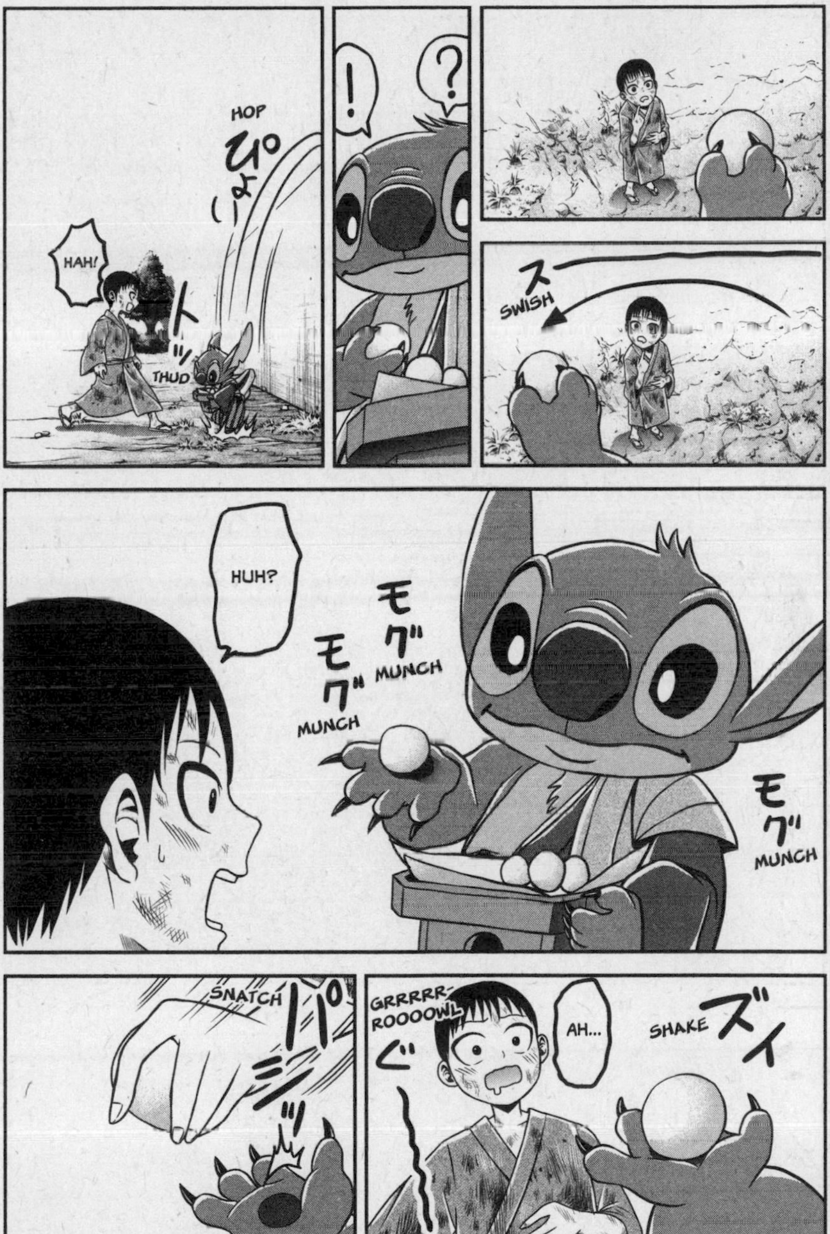

ス
SWISH
!
?
HAH!
HOP
ぴょ
トッ
THUD
モグ
MUNCH
モグ
MUNCH
モグ
MUNCH
HUH?
ズイ
SHAKE
AH...
GRRRRR-ROOOOWL
ぐ
パシッ
SNATCH

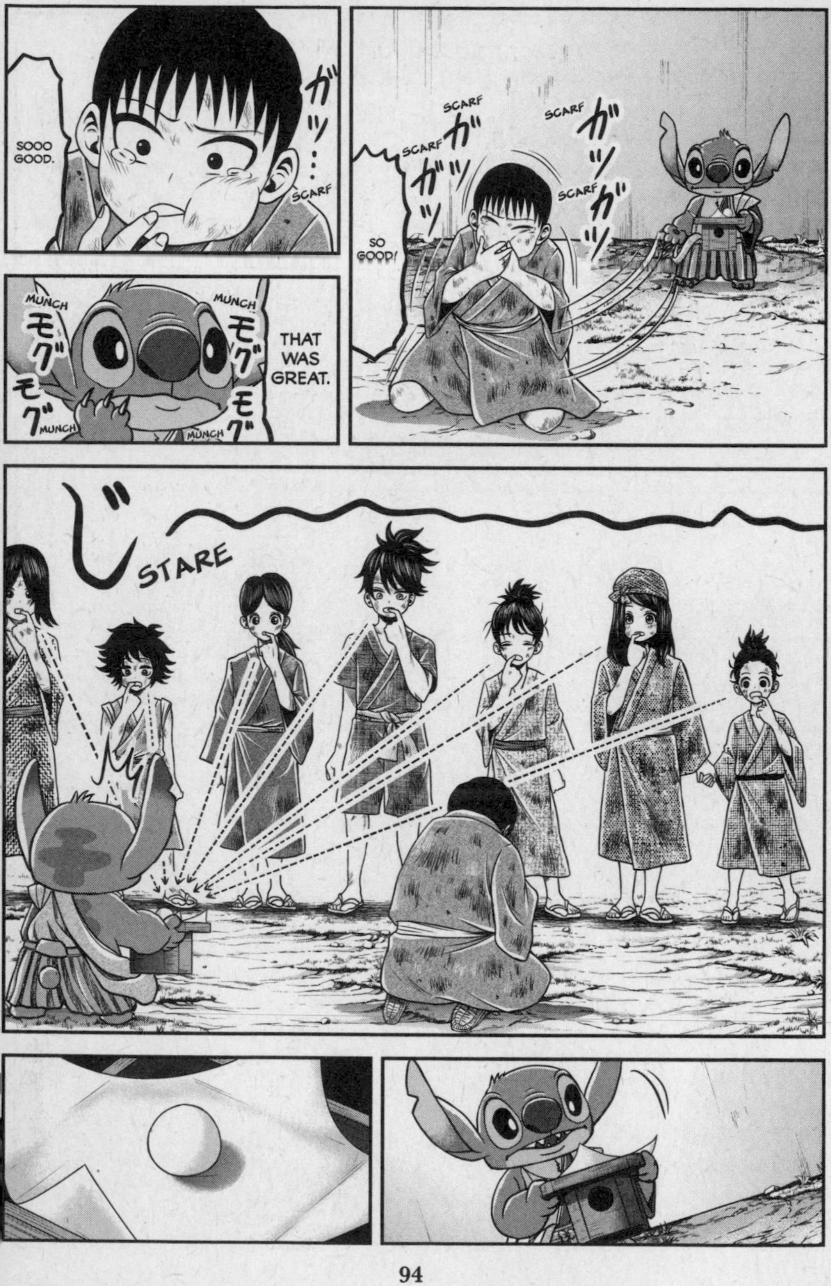
SCARF
ガッ
SCARF
ガッ
SCARF
ガッ
SCARF
ガッ
SO GOOD!
ガッ…
SCARF
SOOO GOOD.
THAT WAS GREAT.
MUNCH
モグ
モグ
MUNCH
MUNCH
モグ
モグ
MUNCH
じ
STARE

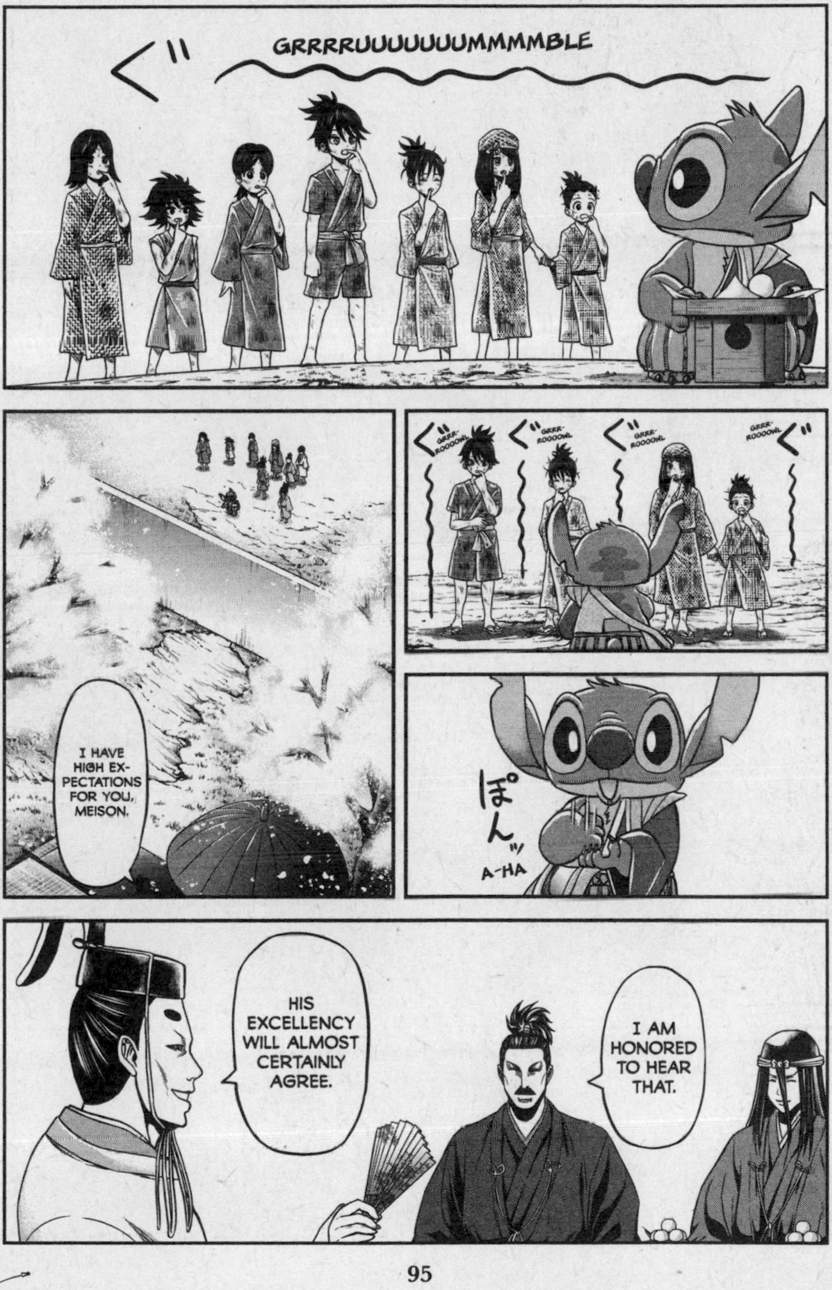
ぐ"
GRRRRUUUUUUUMMMMBLE
ぐ"
GRRR-ROOOOWL
ぐ"
GRRR-ROOOOWL
ぐ"
GRRR-ROOOOWL
ぐ"
GRRR-ROOOOWL
ぽん
A-HA
I HAVE HIGH EX-PECTATIONS FOR YOU, MEISON.
I AM HONORED TO HEAR THAT.
HIS EXCELLENCY WILL ALMOST CERTAINLY AGREE.

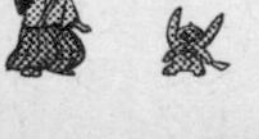

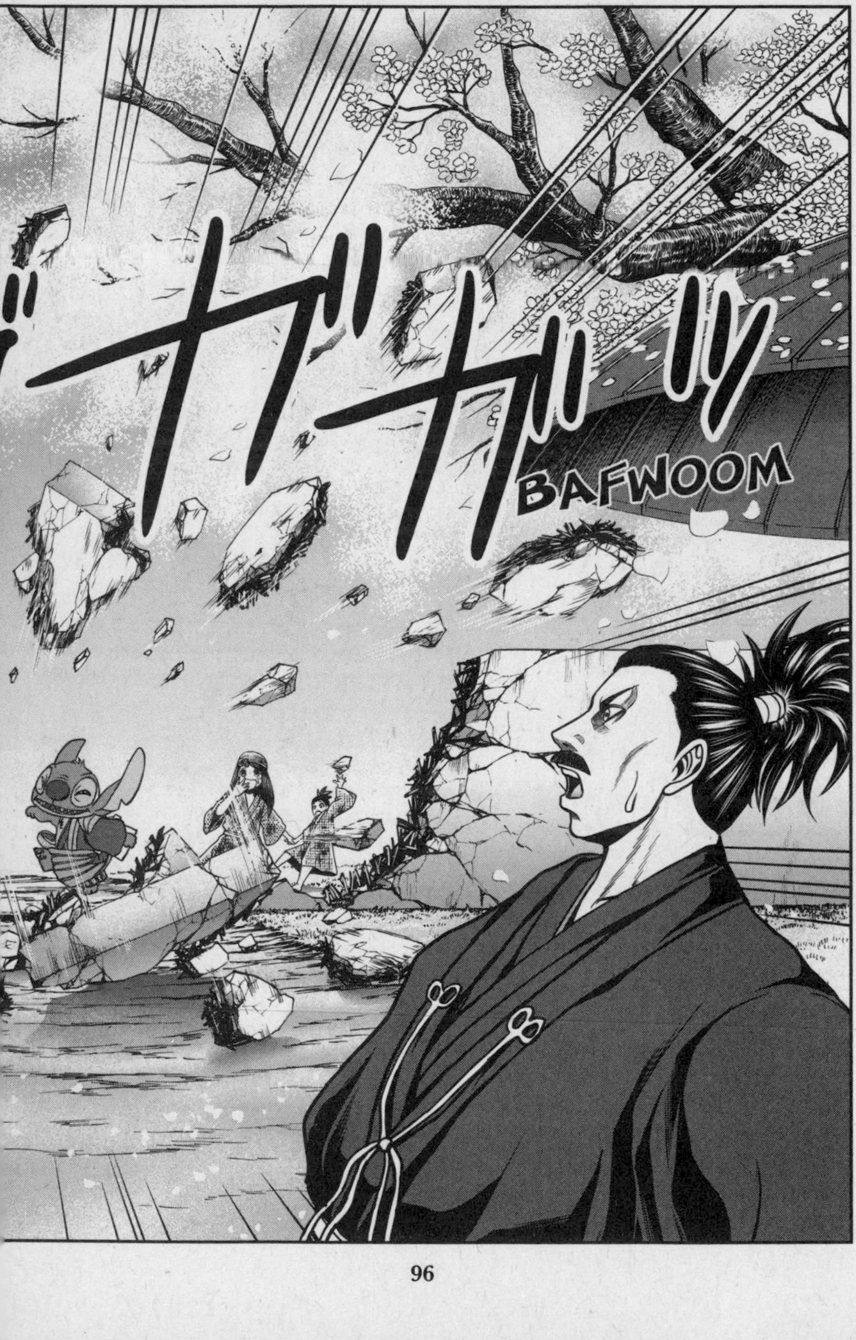
BAFWOOM

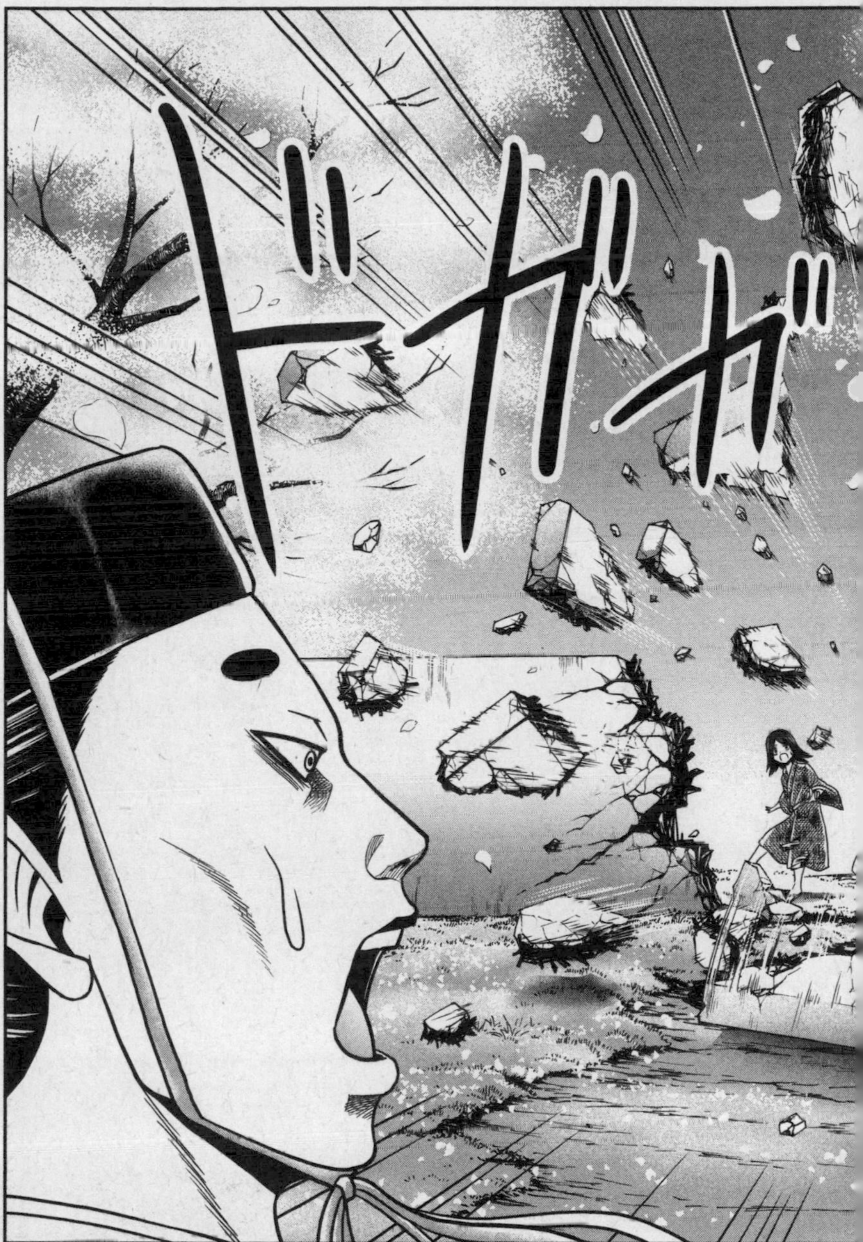
ドガガ

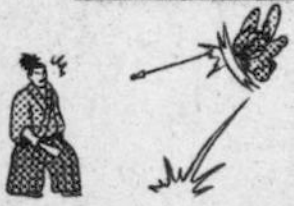

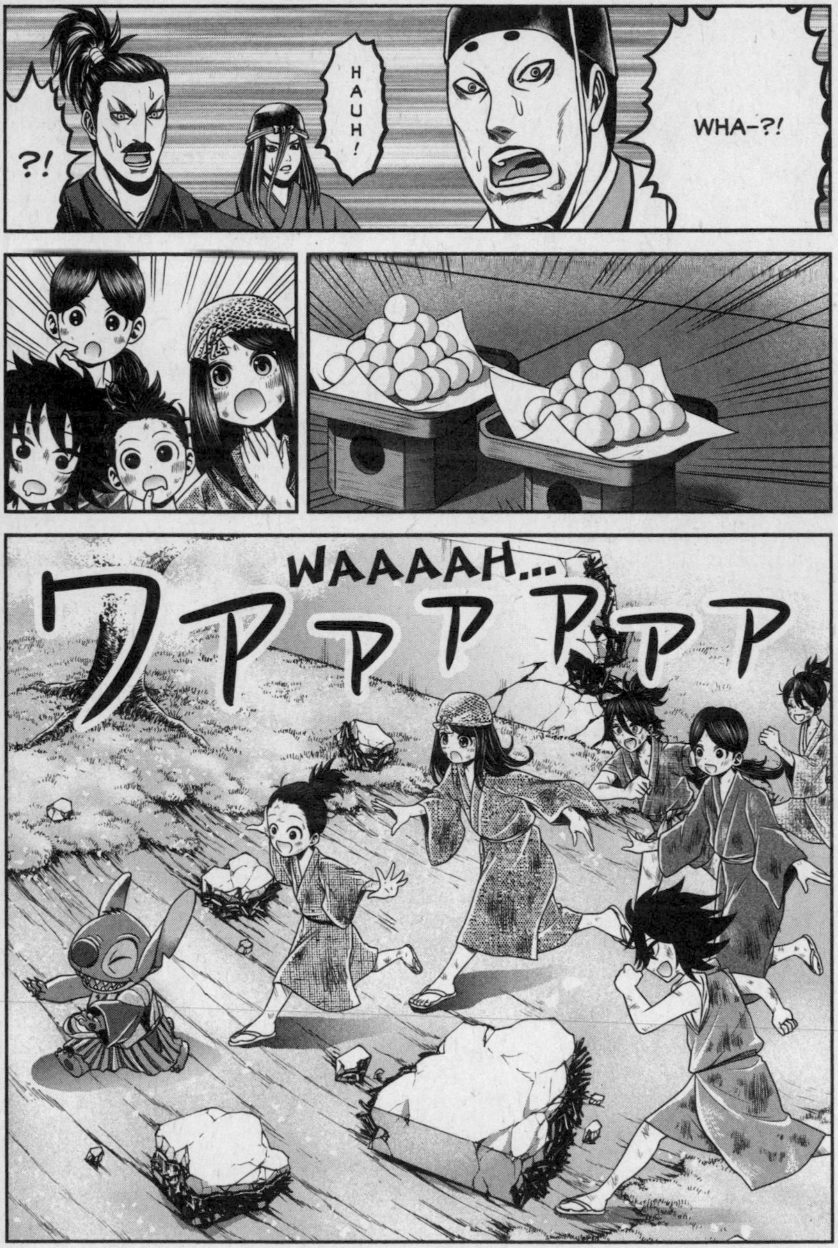
WHA-?!
HAUH!
?!
WAAAAH...
ワァァァァァァ

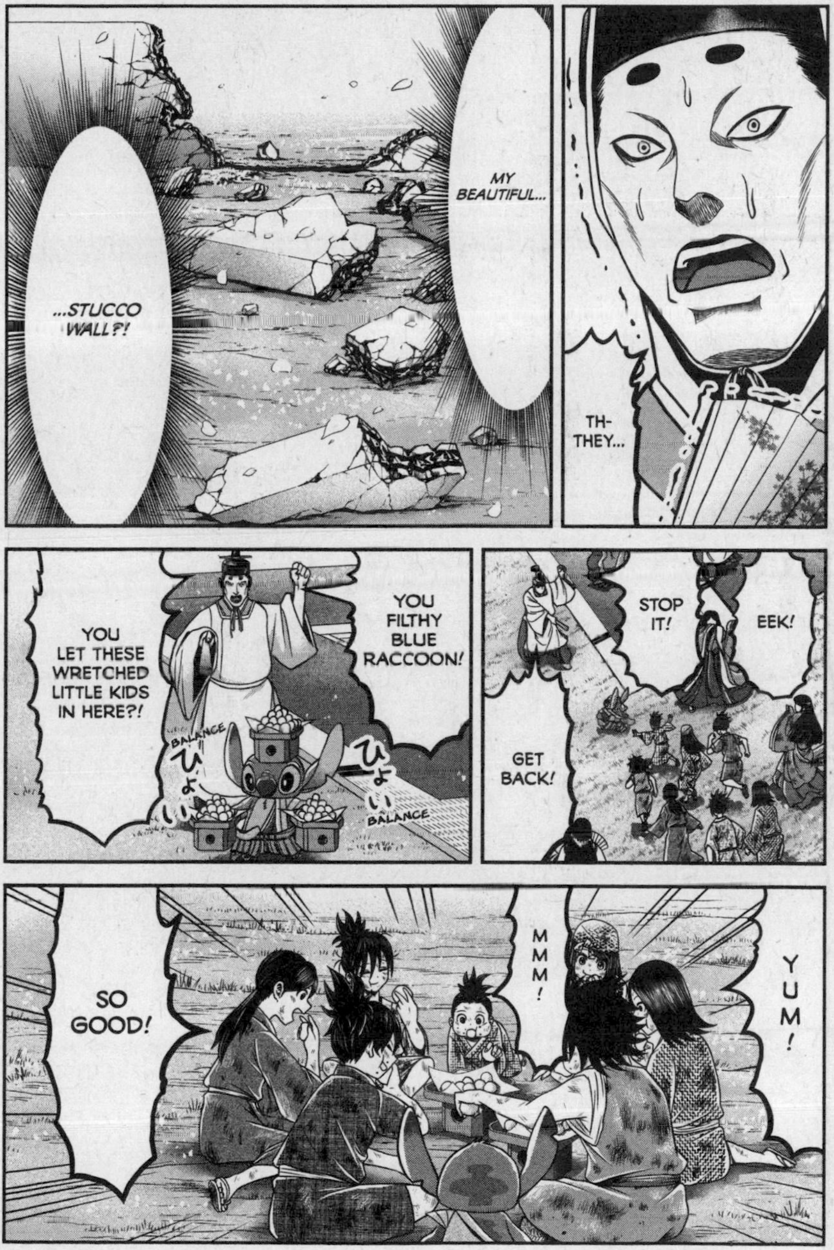
TH-
THEY...
MY BEAUTIFUL...
...STUCCO WALL?!
EEK!
STOP IT!
GET BACK!
YOU FILTHY BLUE RACCOON!
YOU LET THESE WRETCHED LITTLE KIDS IN HERE?!
ひょい
BALANCE
ひょい
BALANCE
YUM!
MMM!
SO GOOD!

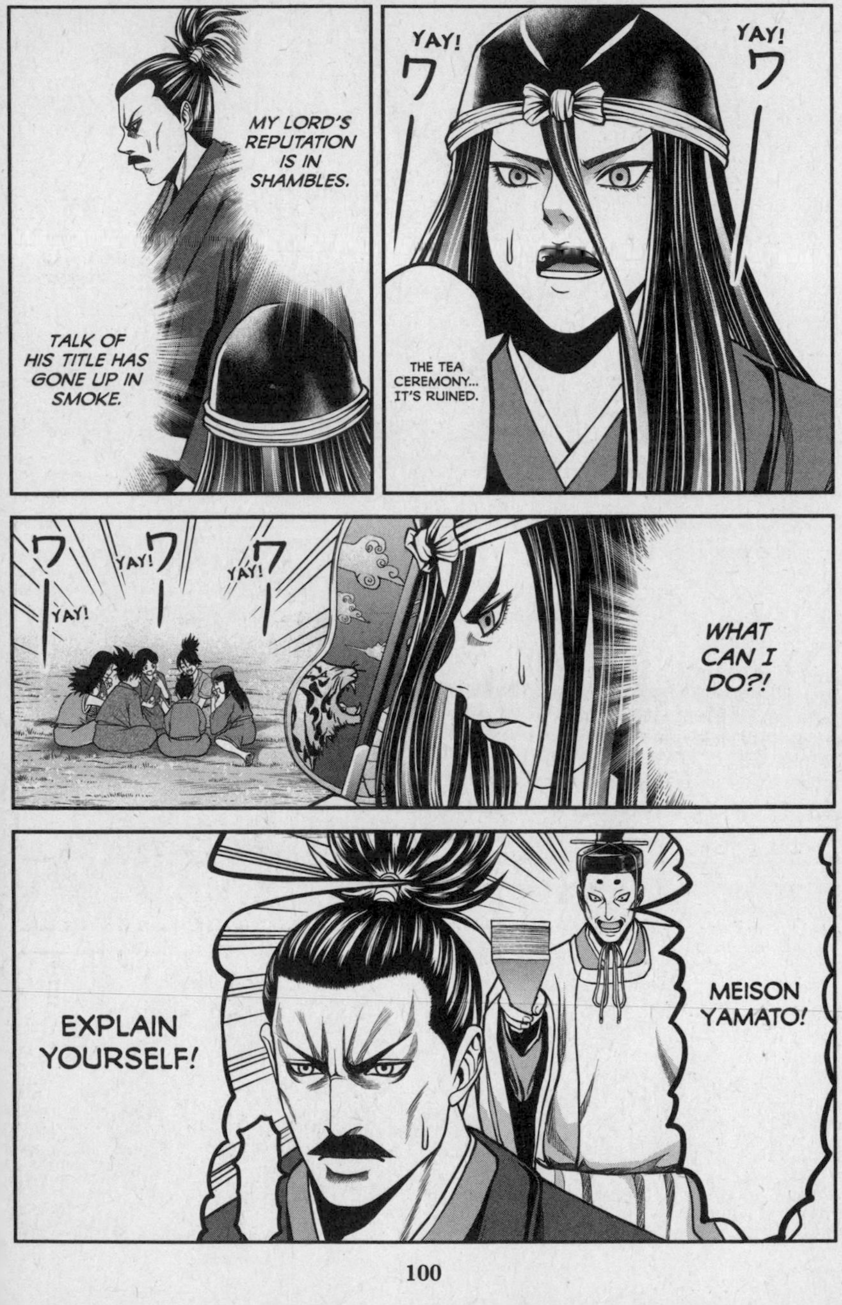
YAY!
ワ
YAY!
ワ
THE TEA CEREMONY... IT'S RUINED.
MY LORD'S REPUTATION IS IN SHAMBLES.
TALK OF HIS TITLE HAS GONE UP IN SMOKE.
WHAT CAN I DO?!
YAY!
ワ
YAY!
ワ
YAY!
ワ
MEISON YAMATO!
EXPLAIN YOURSELF!

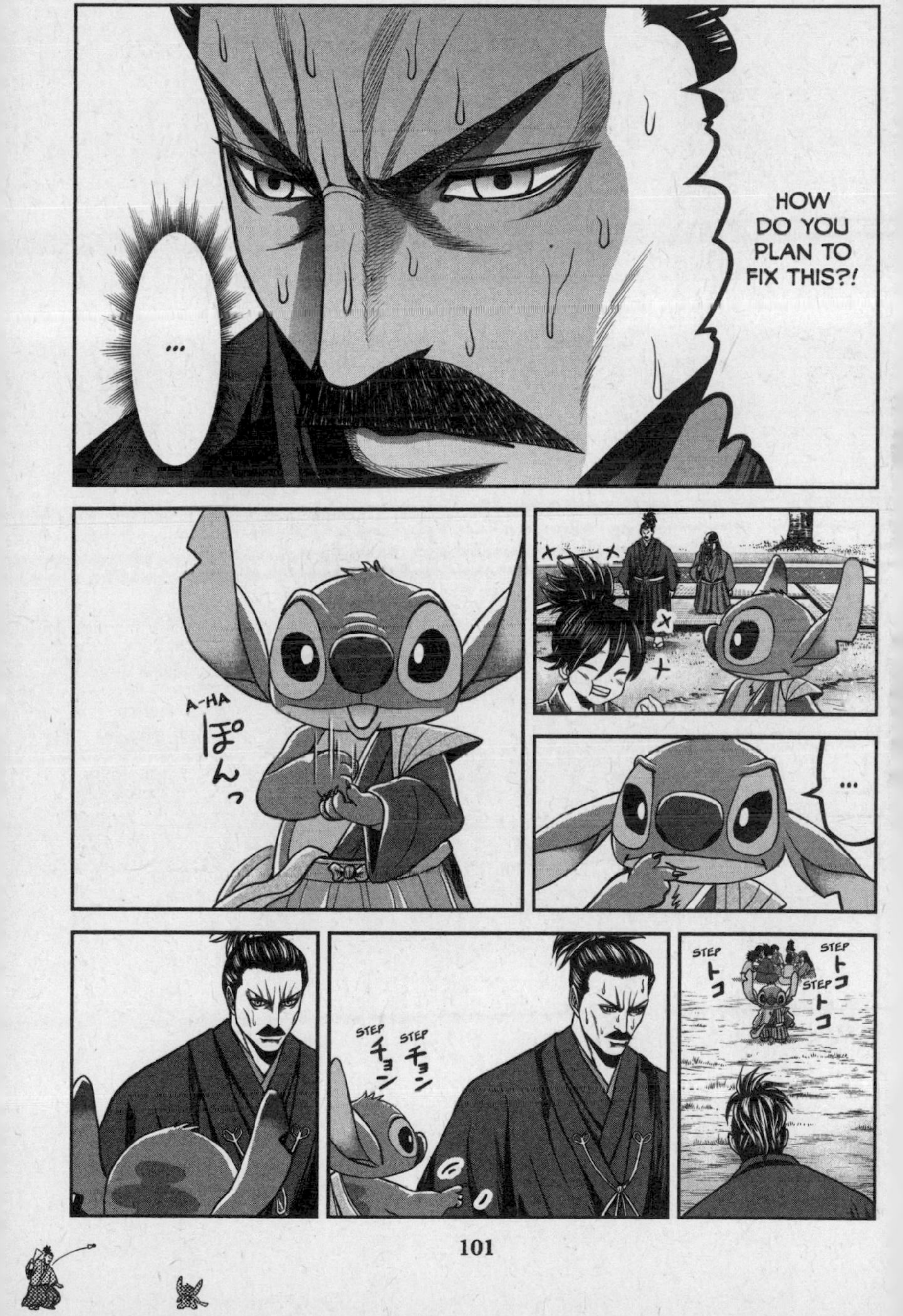
HOW DO YOU PLAN TO FIX THIS?!
...
...
A-HA
ぽんっ
STEP
トコ
STEP
トコ
STEP
トコ
STEP
チョン
STEP
チョン

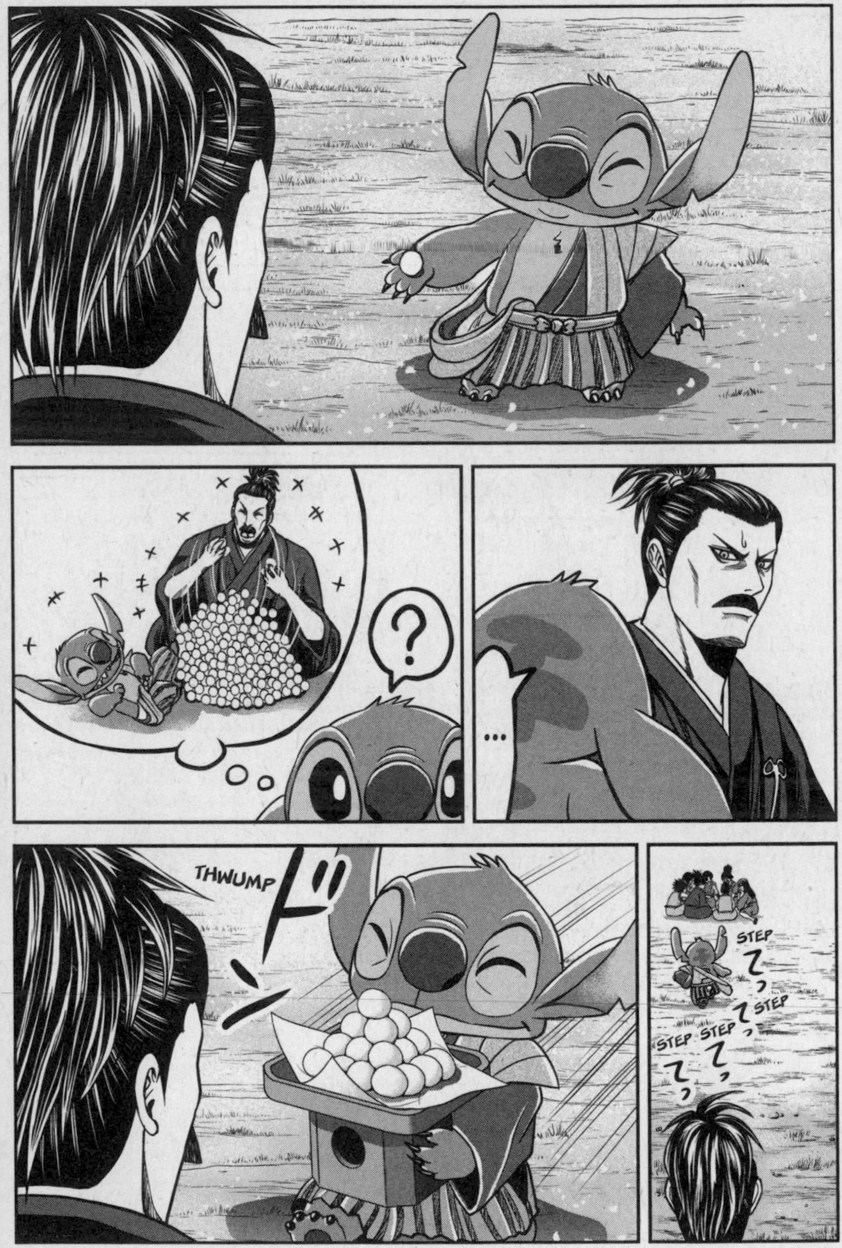
...
?
STEP
STEP
STEP
STEP
THWUMP

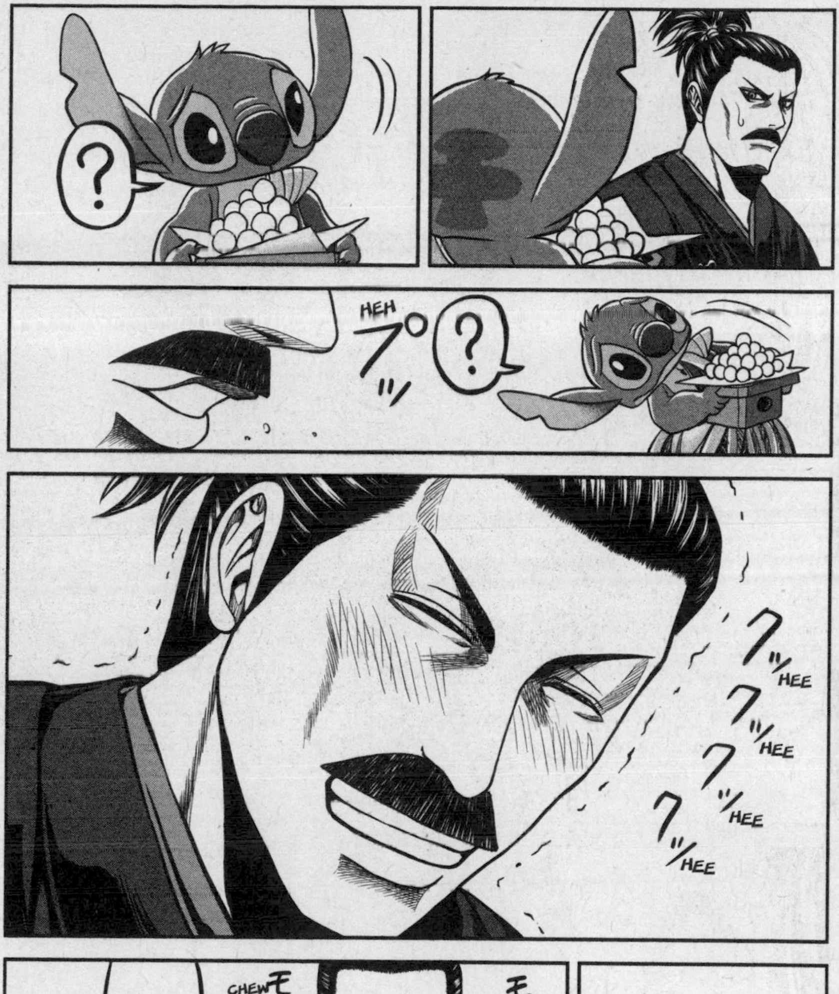
?
?
HEH プッ
クッ HEE
クッ HEE
クッ HEE
クッ HEE
モグ CHEW
モグ CHEW
DELICIOUS!
モグ CHEW
モグ CHEW

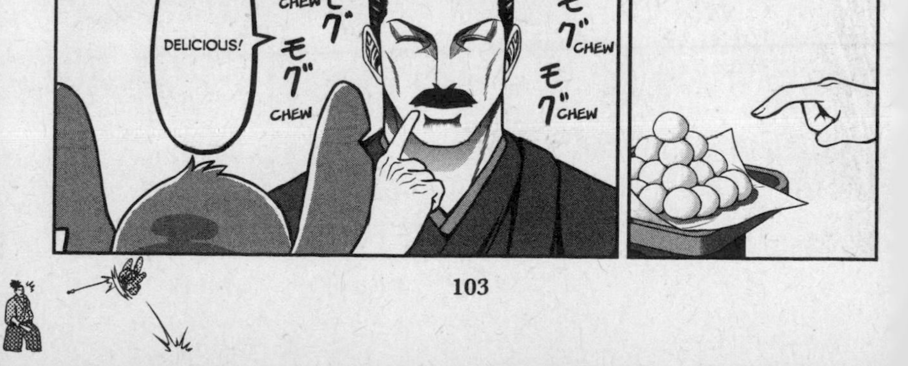

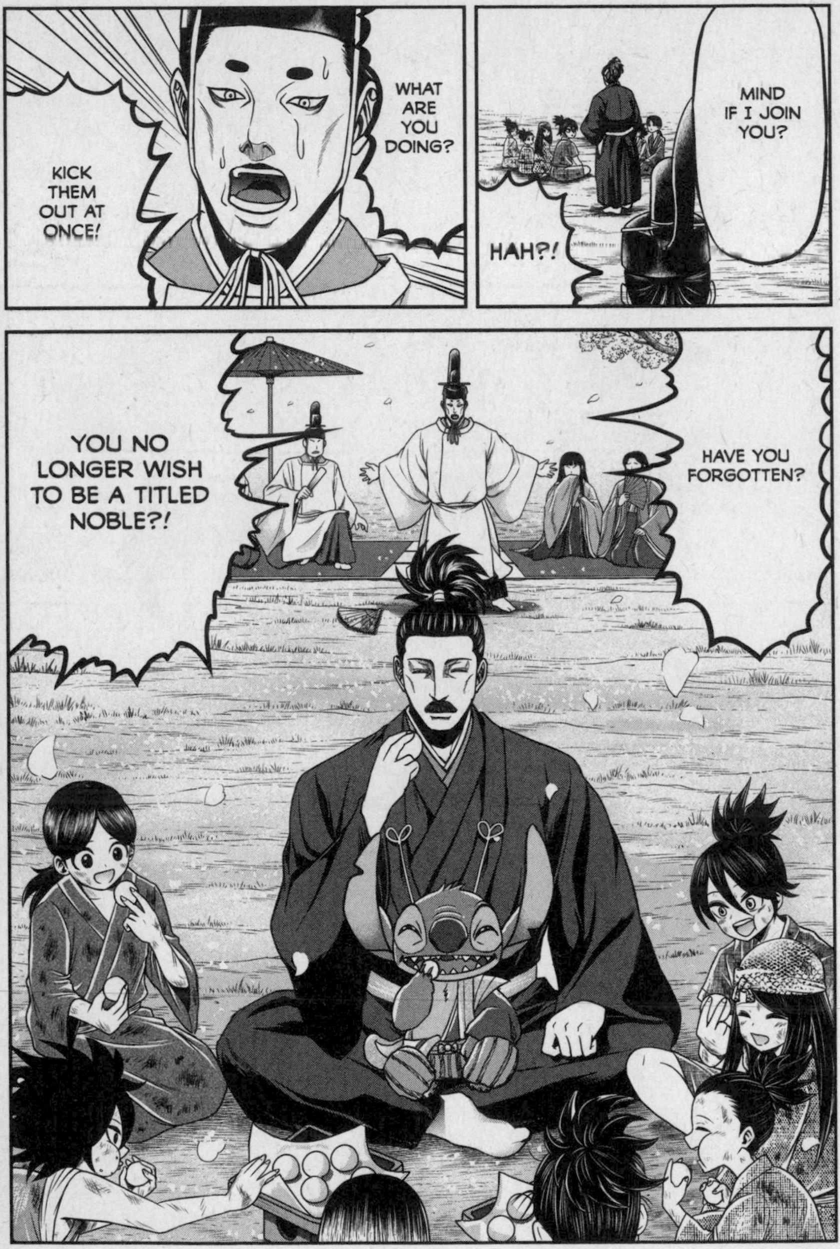
MIND IF I JOIN YOU?
HAH?!
WHAT ARE YOU DOING?
KICK THEM OUT AT ONCE!
HAVE YOU FORGOTTEN?
YOU NO LONGER WISH TO BE A TITLED NOBLE?!

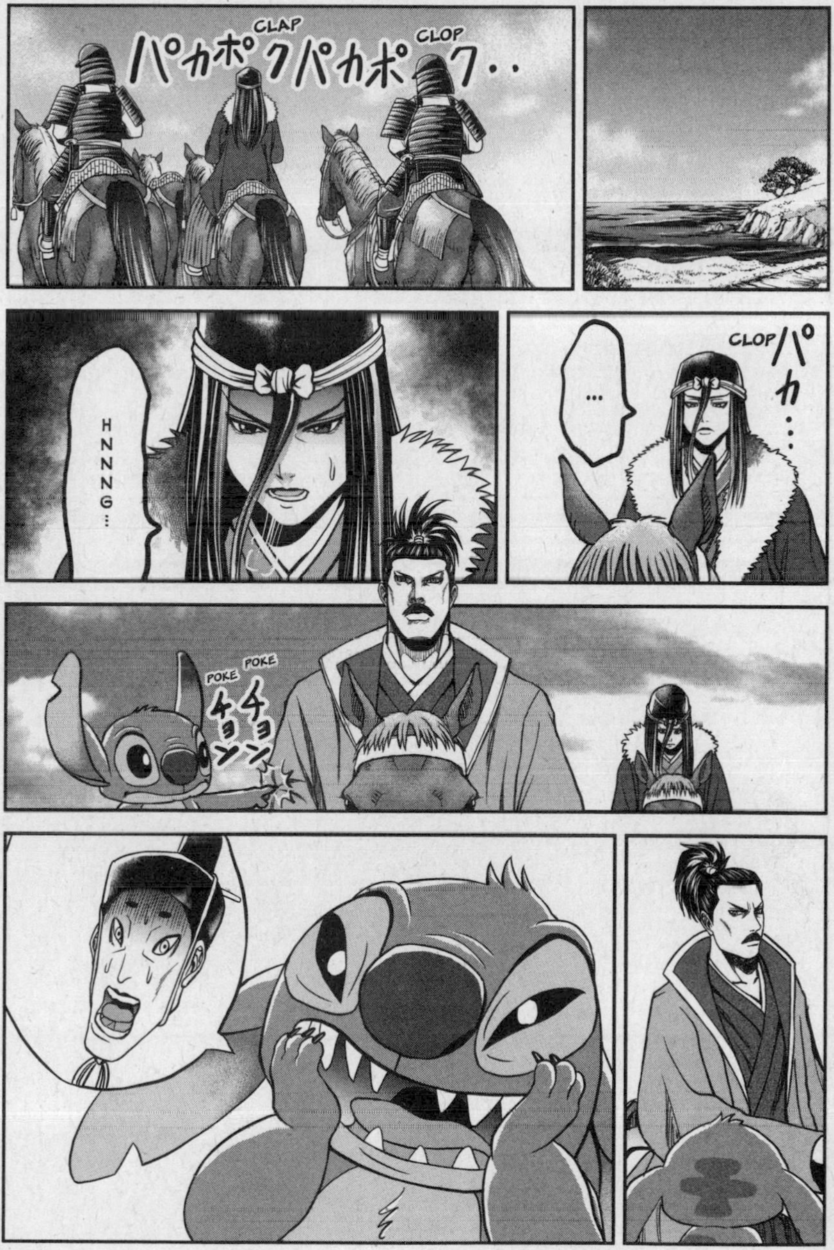
パカポクパカポク‥
CLAP
CLOP
…
CLOP
パカ…
HNNNG…
POKE POKE
チョンチョン

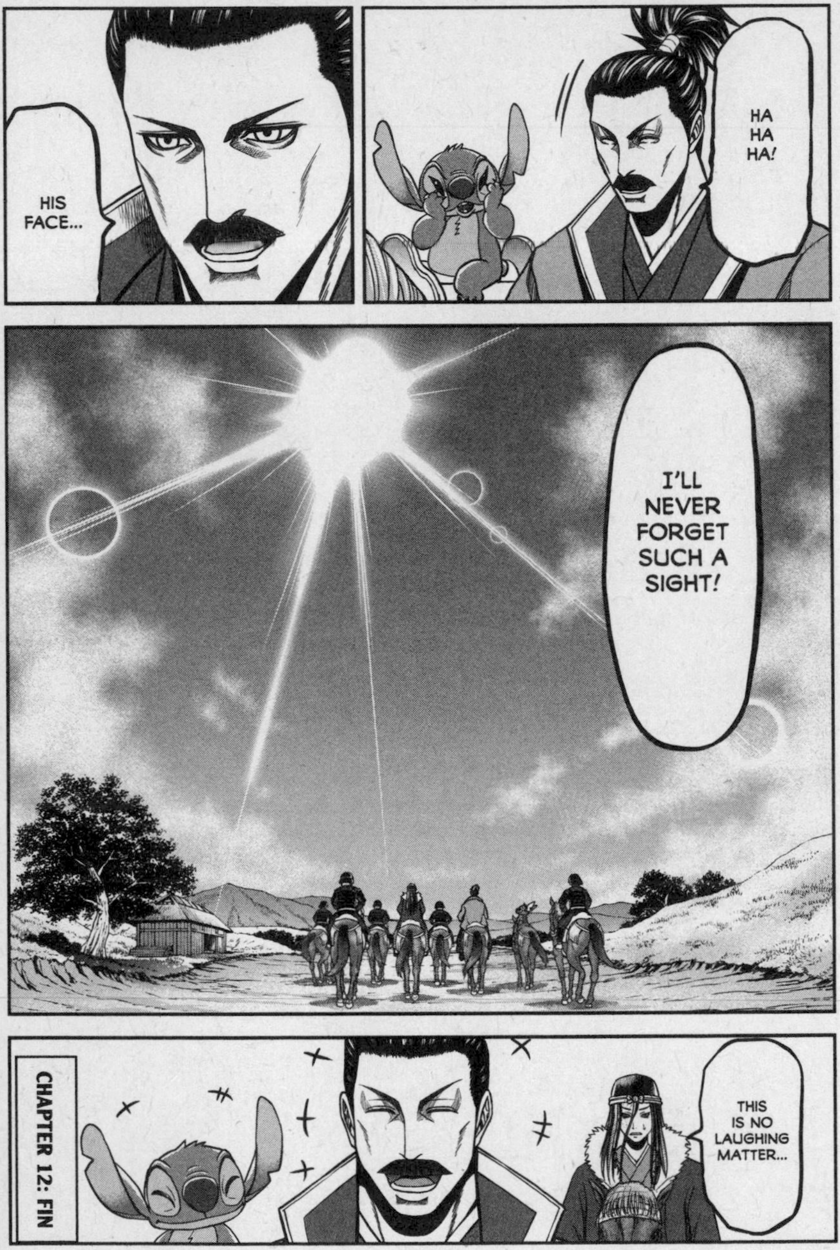
HA HA HA!
HIS FACE...
I'LL NEVER FORGET SUCH A SIGHT!
THIS IS NO LAUGHING MATTER...
CHAPTER 12: FIN

Disney

Stitch

STITCH & THE SAMURAI

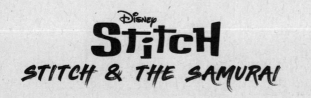

Disney

Stitch

STITCH & THE SAMURAI

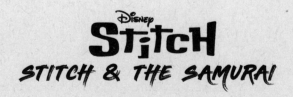

CHAPTER 13: LOVE CUPID ♡

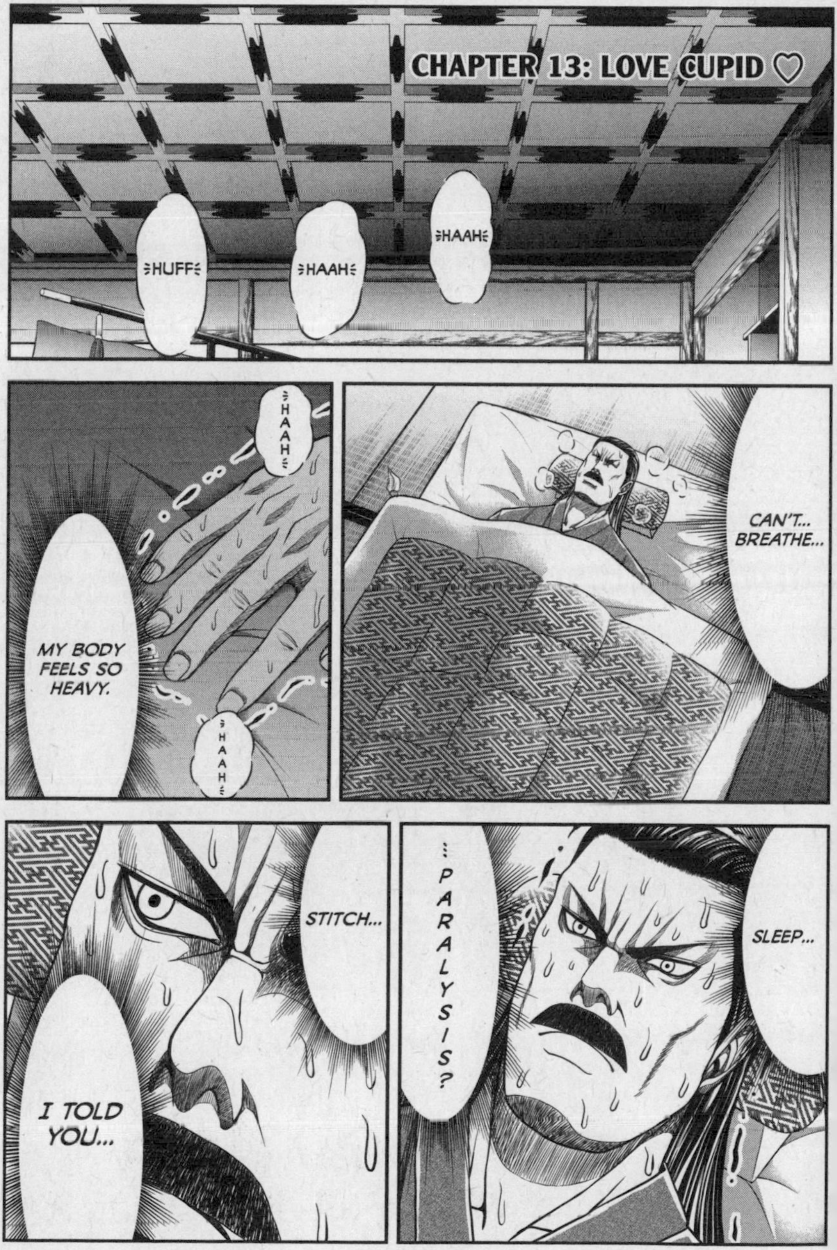
HAAH
HAAH
HUFF
CAN'T... BREATHE...
HAAH
MY BODY FEELS SO HEAVY.
HAAH
SLEEP...
...PARALYSIS?
STITCH...
I TOLD YOU...

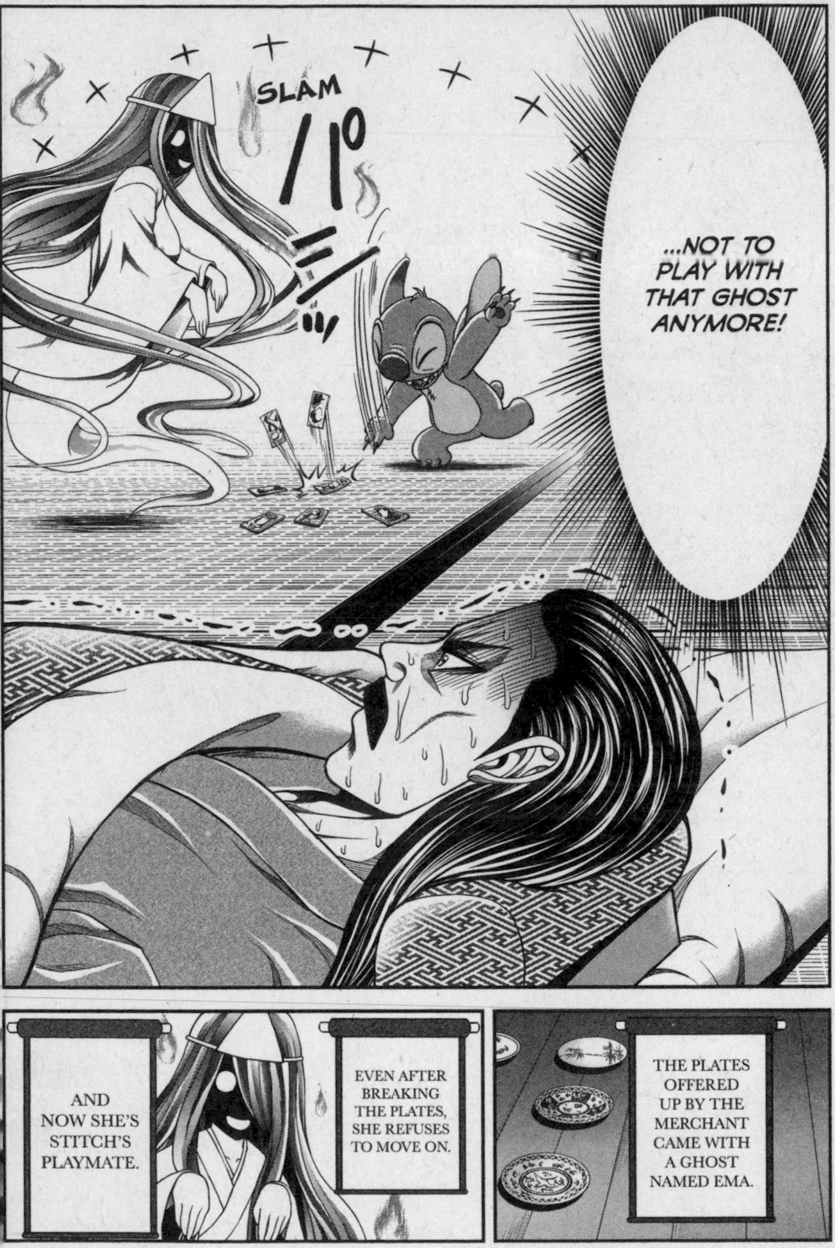
...NOT TO PLAY WITH THAT GHOST ANYMORE!
SLAM
THE PLATES OFFERED UP BY THE MERCHANT CAME WITH A GHOST NAMED EMA.
EVEN AFTER BREAKING THE PLATES, SHE REFUSES TO MOVE ON.
AND NOW SHE'S STITCH'S PLAYMATE.

♪
SIGH
TAP TAP
チョンチョン
HAAAAH
SIGH
HAAAH
SCOOT
スクッ
SIGH

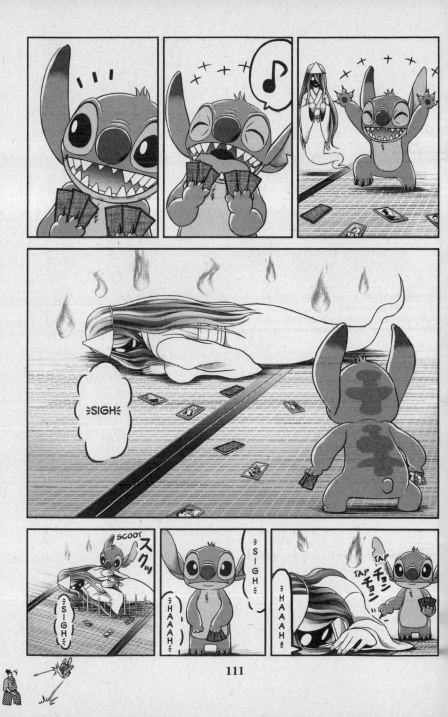

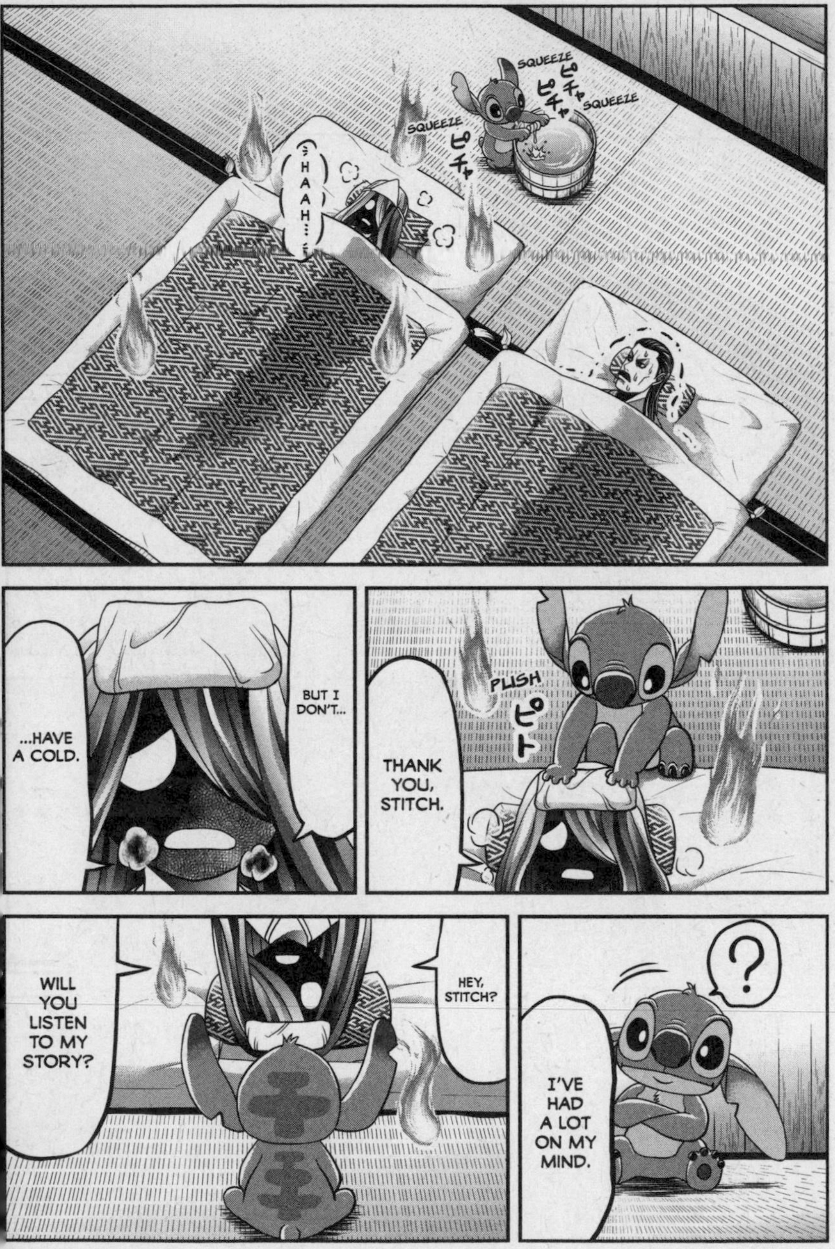
SQUEEZE
ピチャ
ピチャ
SQUEEZE
SQUEEZE
ピチャ
HAAH...
PUSH
ピト
THANK YOU, STITCH.
BUT I DON'T...
...HAVE A COLD.
?
I'VE HAD A LOT ON MY MIND.
HEY, STITCH?
WILL YOU LISTEN TO MY STORY?

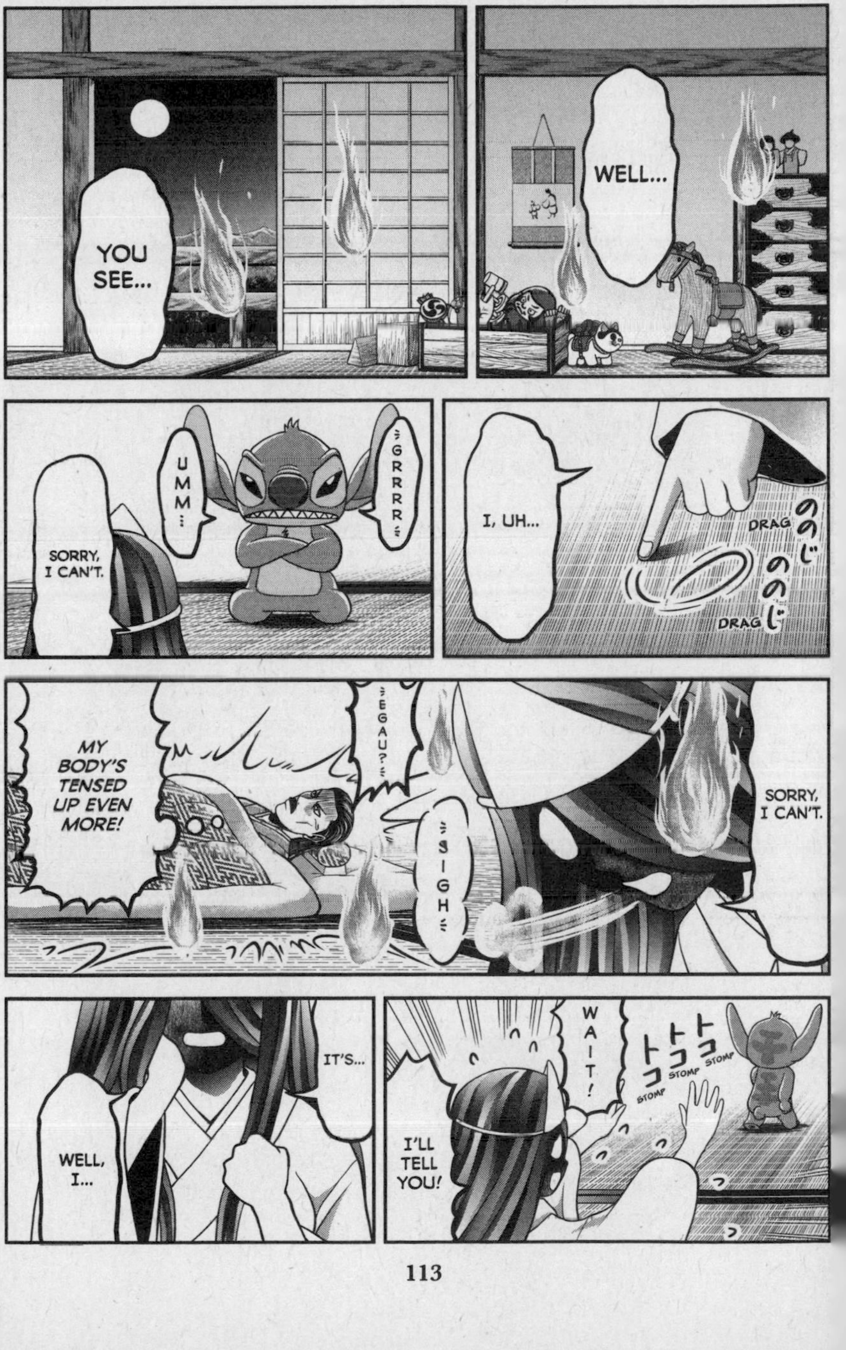

WELL...
YOU SEE...
I, UH...
DRAG のの じ
DRAG のの じ
GRRRR
UMM...
SORRY, I CAN'T.
SORRY, I CAN'T.
SIGH
EGAU?
MY BODY'S TENSED UP EVEN MORE!
トコトコ
STOMP STOMP STOMP
WAIT!
I'LL TELL YOU!
IT'S...
WELL, I...

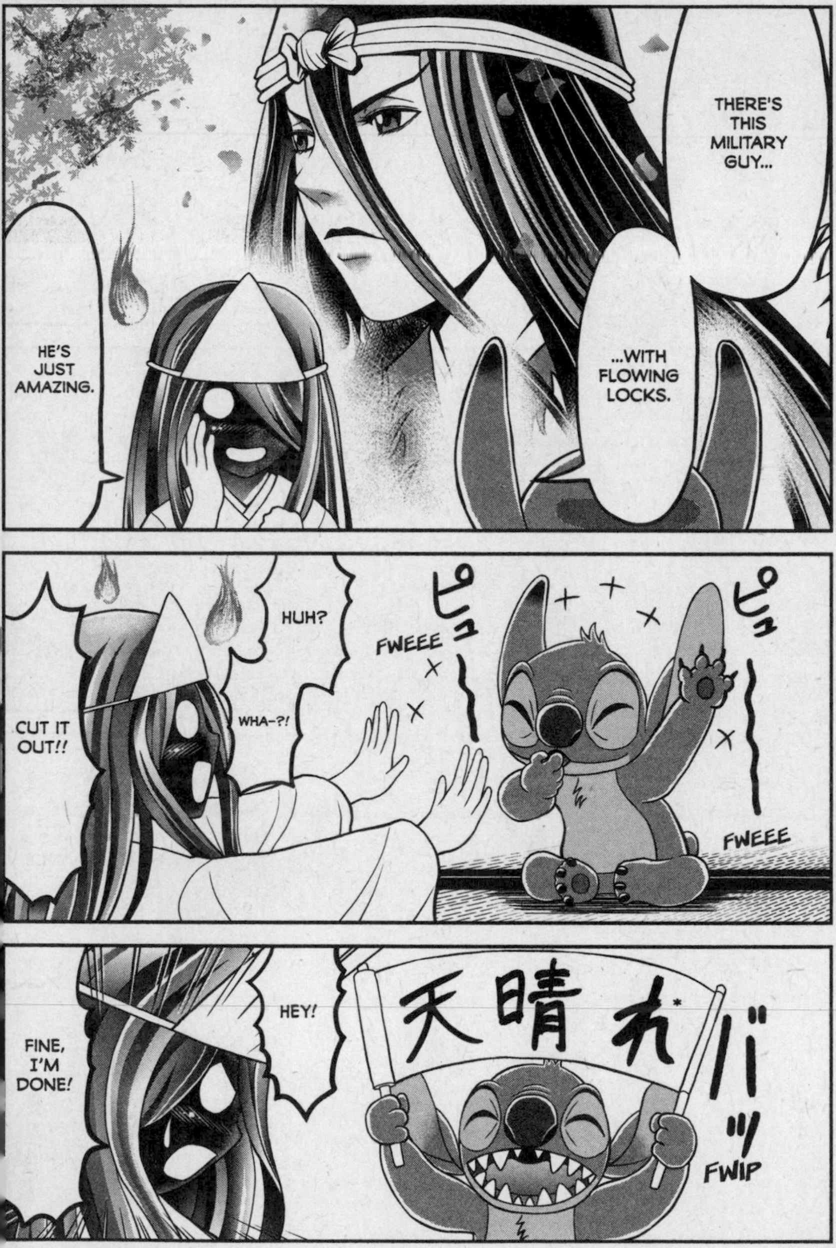
THERE'S THIS MILITARY GUY...
...WITH FLOWING LOCKS.
HE'S JUST AMAZING.
ピュ～～
FWEEE
ピュ～～
FWEEE
HUH?
WHA-?!
CUT IT OUT!!
天晴れ*
バッ
FWIP
HEY!
FINE, I'M DONE!

*GREAT!

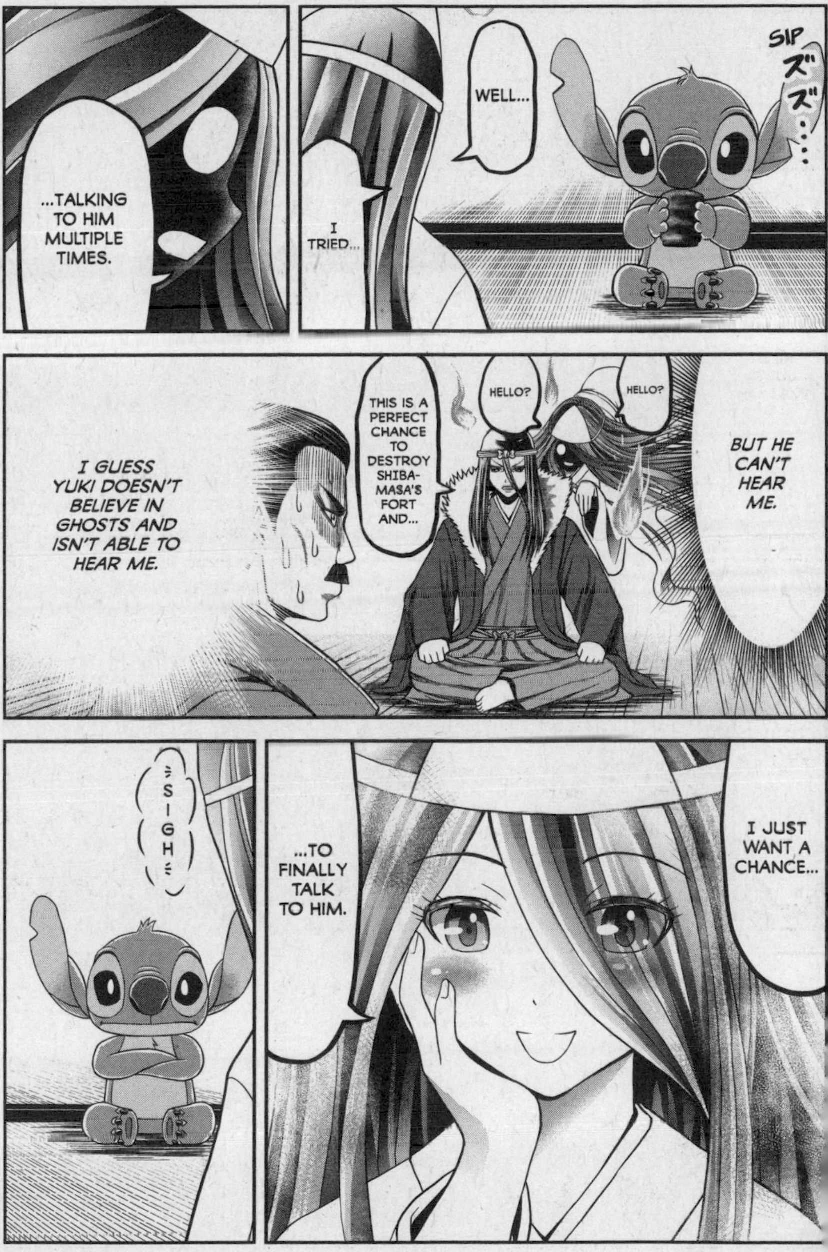
SIP
ズズ…
WELL...
I TRIED...
...TALKING TO HIM MULTIPLE TIMES.
BUT HE CAN'T HEAR ME.
HELLO?
HELLO?
THIS IS A PERFECT CHANCE TO DESTROY SHIBA-MASA'S FORT AND...
I GUESS YUKI DOESN'T BELIEVE IN GHOSTS AND ISN'T ABLE TO HEAR ME.
I JUST WANT A CHANCE...
...TO FINALLY TALK TO HIM.
SIGH

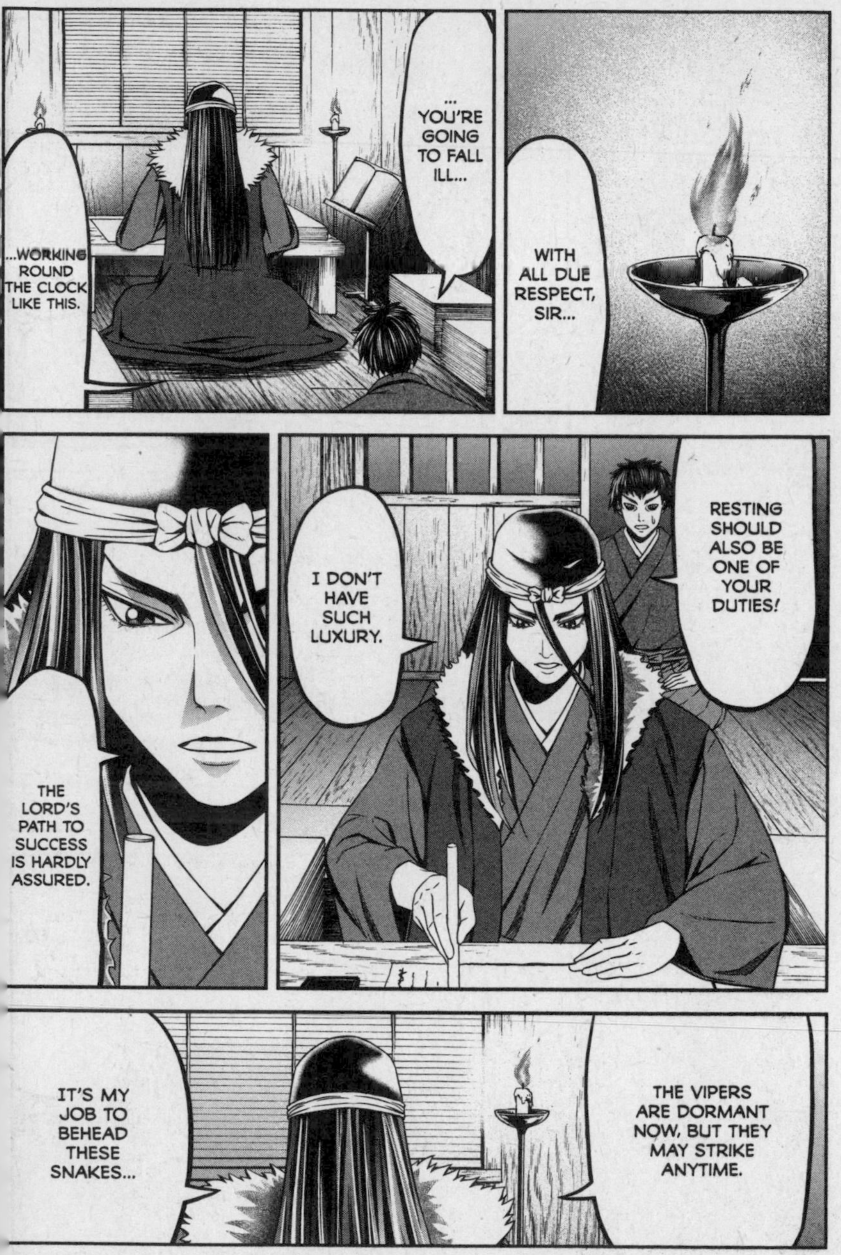
WITH ALL DUE RESPECT, SIR...
... YOU'RE GOING TO FALL ILL...
...WORKING ROUND THE CLOCK LIKE THIS.
RESTING SHOULD ALSO BE ONE OF YOUR DUTIES!
I DON'T HAVE SUCH LUXURY.
THE LORD'S PATH TO SUCCESS IS HARDLY ASSURED.
THE VIPERS ARE DORMANT NOW, BUT THEY MAY STRIKE ANYTIME.
IT'S MY JOB TO BEHEAD THESE SNAKES...

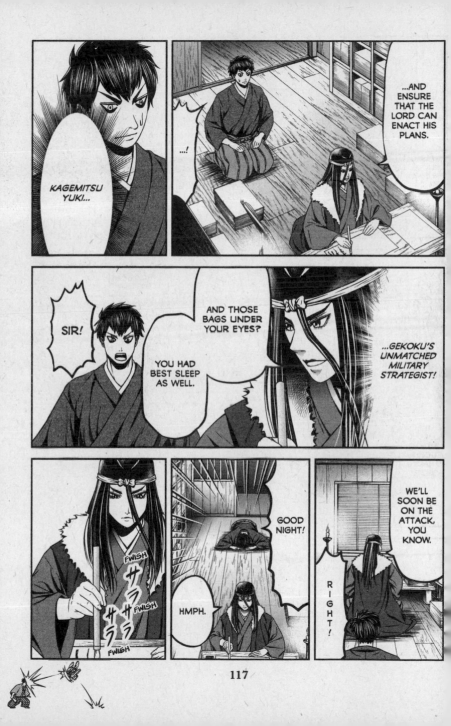

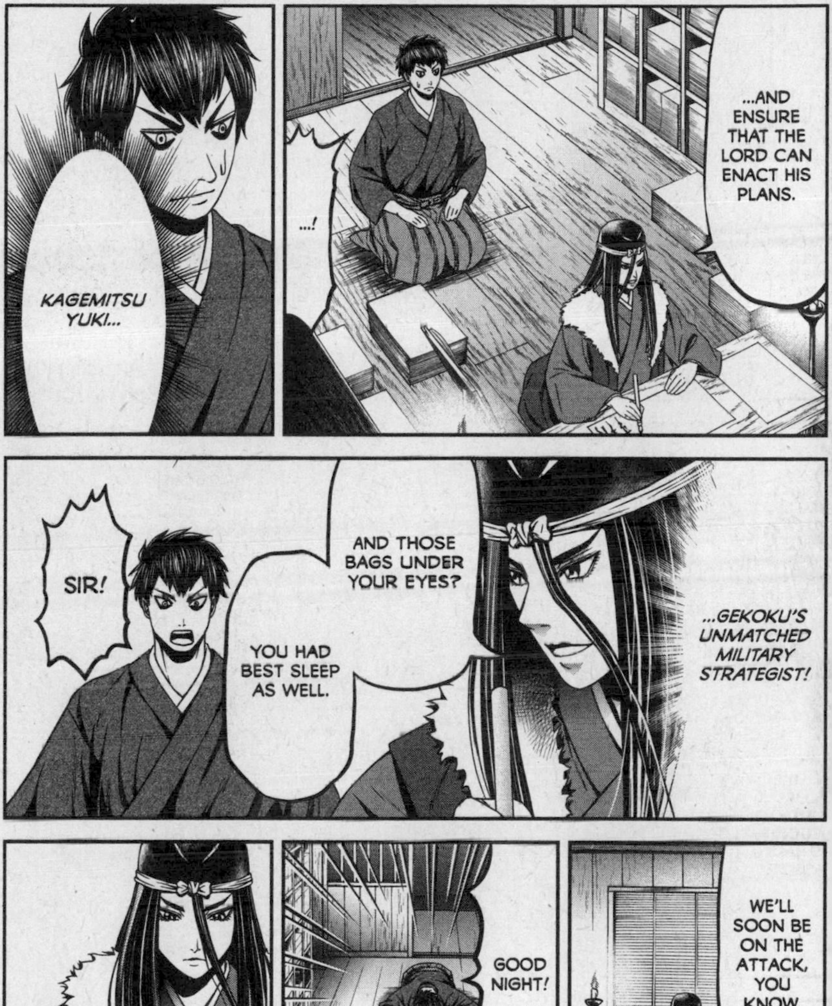
...AND ENSURE THAT THE LORD CAN ENACT HIS PLANS.
...!
KAGEMITSU YUKI...
...GEKOKU'S UNMATCHED MILITARY STRATEGIST!
AND THOSE BAGS UNDER YOUR EYES?
YOU HAD BEST SLEEP AS WELL.
SIR!
WE'LL SOON BE ON THE ATTACK, YOU KNOW.
RIGHT!
GOOD NIGHT!
HMPH.
FWISH
サラ
FWISH
サラ
サラ
FWISH

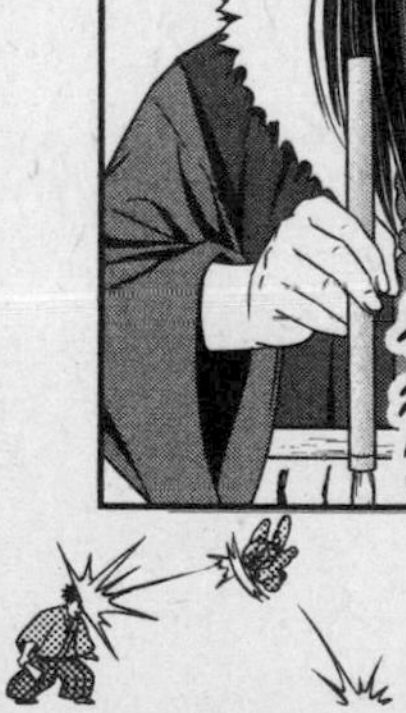

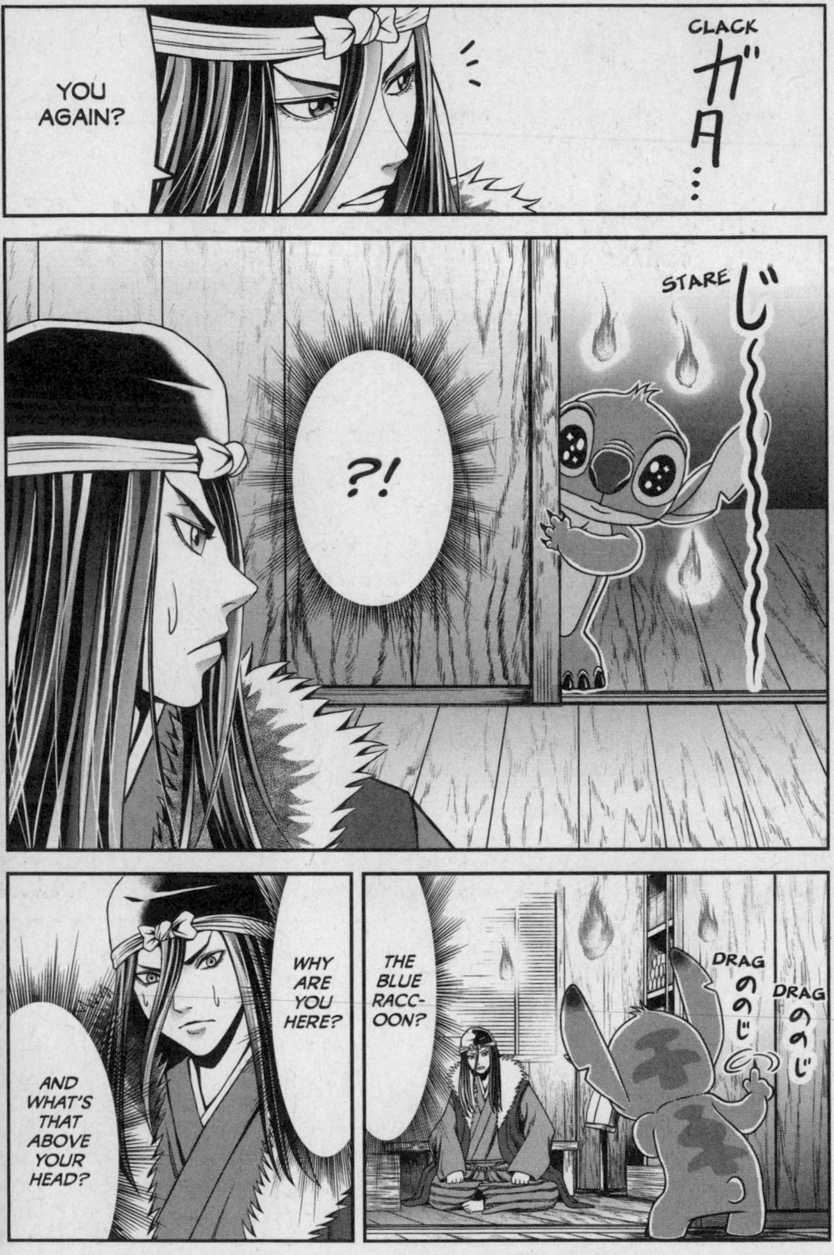
CLACK
ガタ…
YOU AGAIN?
STARE
じ～～
?!
DRAG
ののじ
DRAG
ののじ
THE BLUE RACCOON?
WHY ARE YOU HERE?
AND WHAT'S THAT ABOVE YOUR HEAD?

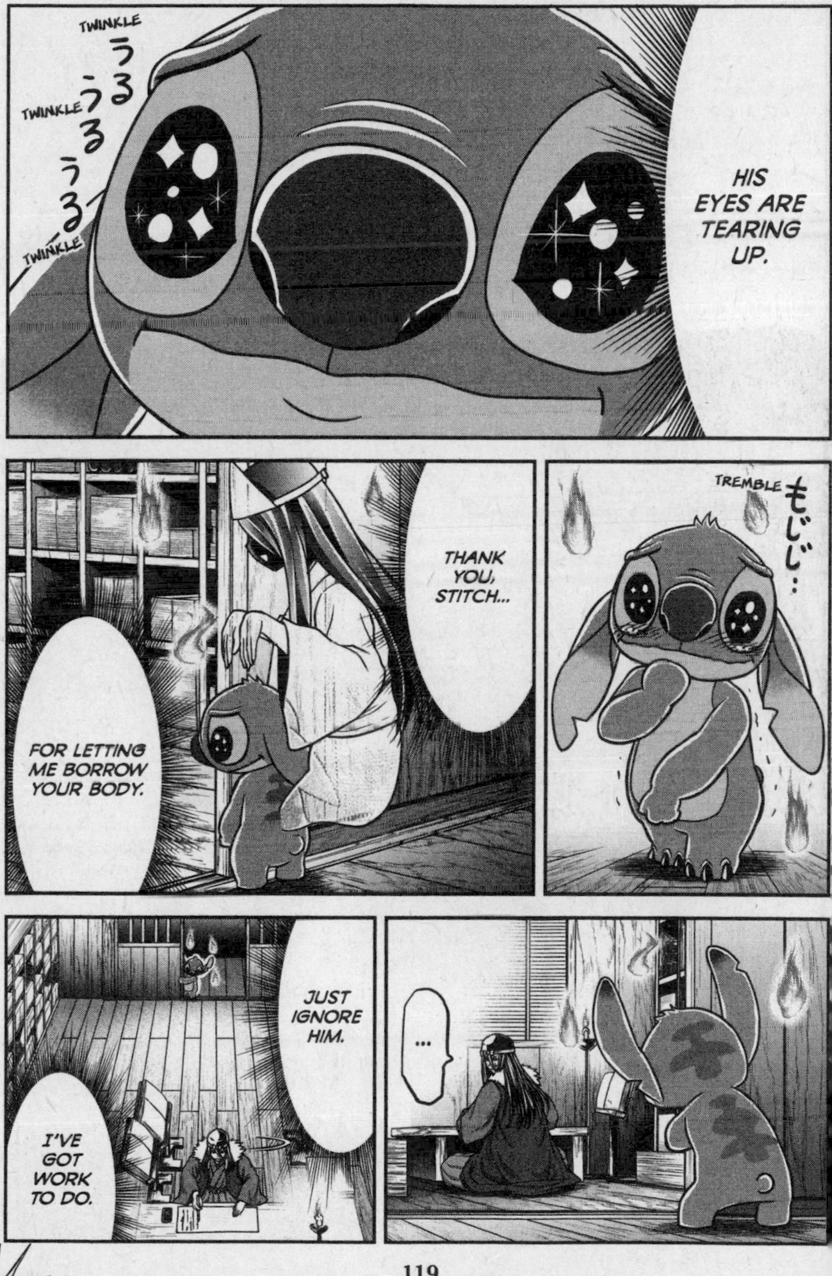
TWINKLE
TWINKLE
TWINKLE
うるうるうる
HIS EYES ARE TEARING UP.
TREMBLE
もじじ…
THANK YOU, STITCH...
FOR LETTING ME BORROW YOUR BODY.
...
JUST IGNORE HIM.
I'VE GOT WORK TO DO.

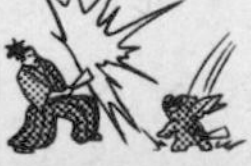

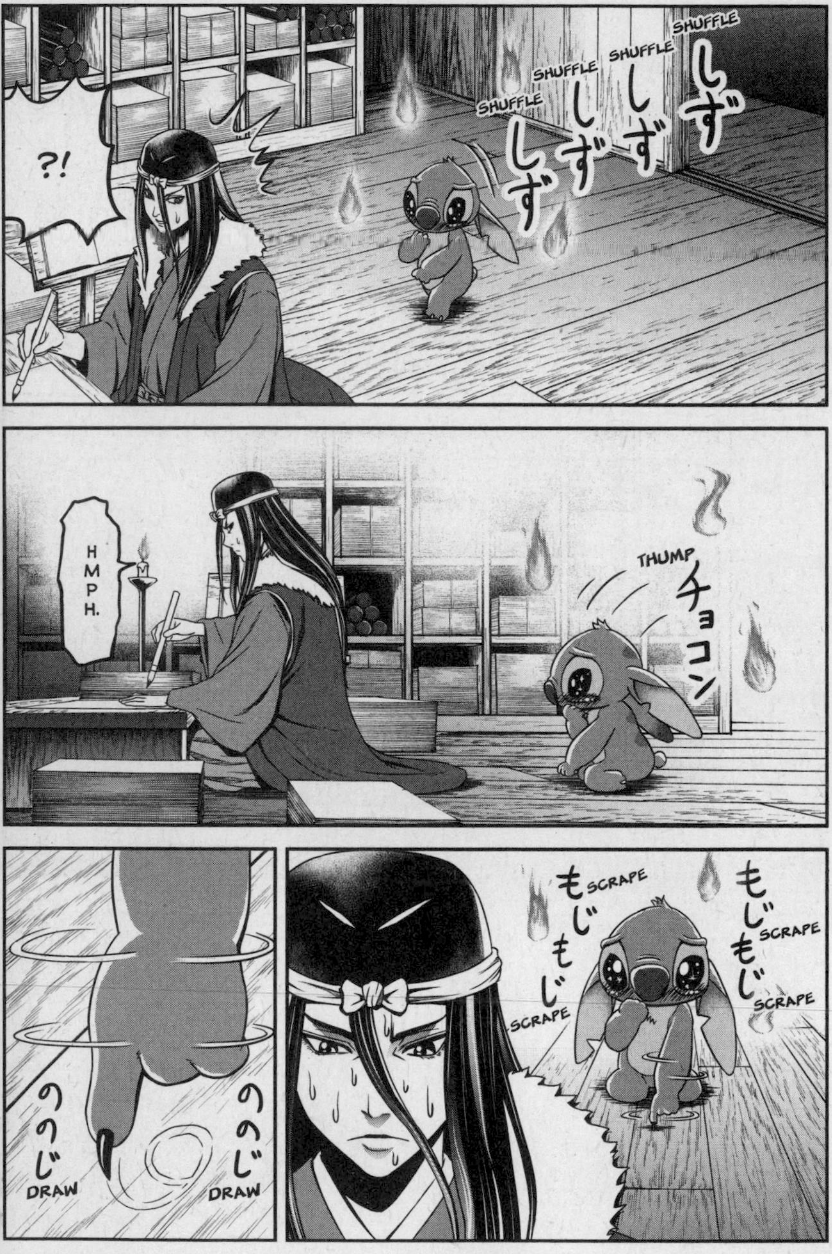

SHUFFLE
SHUFFLE
SHUFFLE
SHUFFLE
しず
しず
しず
しず
?!
THUMP
チョコン
HMPH.
もじ
SCRAPE
もじ
SCRAPE
もじ
SCRAPE
もじ
SCRAPE
ののじ
DRAW
ののじ
DRAW

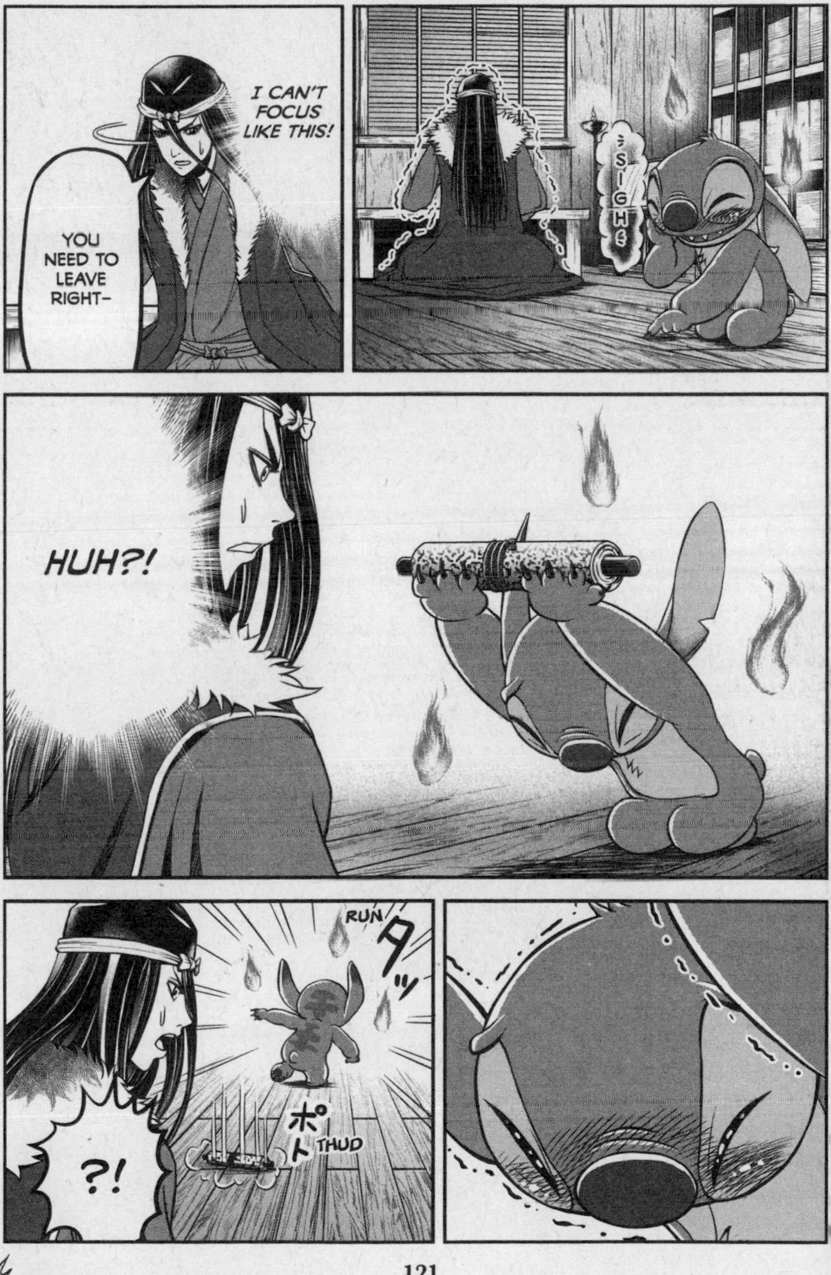
SIGH
I CAN'T FOCUS LIKE THIS!
YOU NEED TO LEAVE RIGHT-
HUH?!
RUN
タッ
ポト
THUD
?!

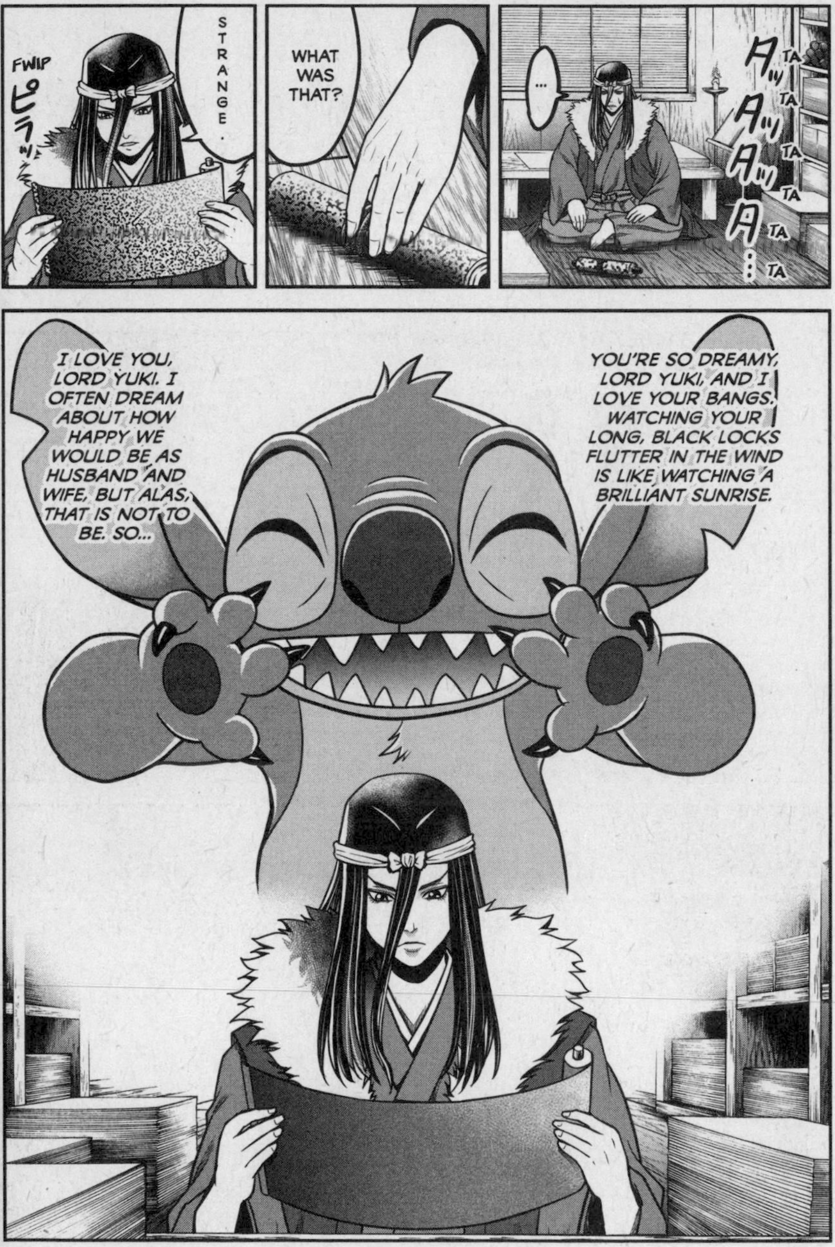
...
タッ タッ タッ タ…
TA TA TA TA TA TA
WHAT WAS THAT?
STRANGE.
FWIP
ピラッ
YOU'RE SO DREAMY, LORD YUKI, AND I LOVE YOUR BANGS. WATCHING YOUR LONG, BLACK LOCKS FLUTTER IN THE WIND IS LIKE WATCHING A BRILLIANT SUNRISE.
I LOVE YOU, LORD YUKI. I OFTEN DREAM ABOUT HOW HAPPY WE WOULD BE AS HUSBAND AND WIFE, BUT ALAS, THAT IS NOT TO BE. SO...

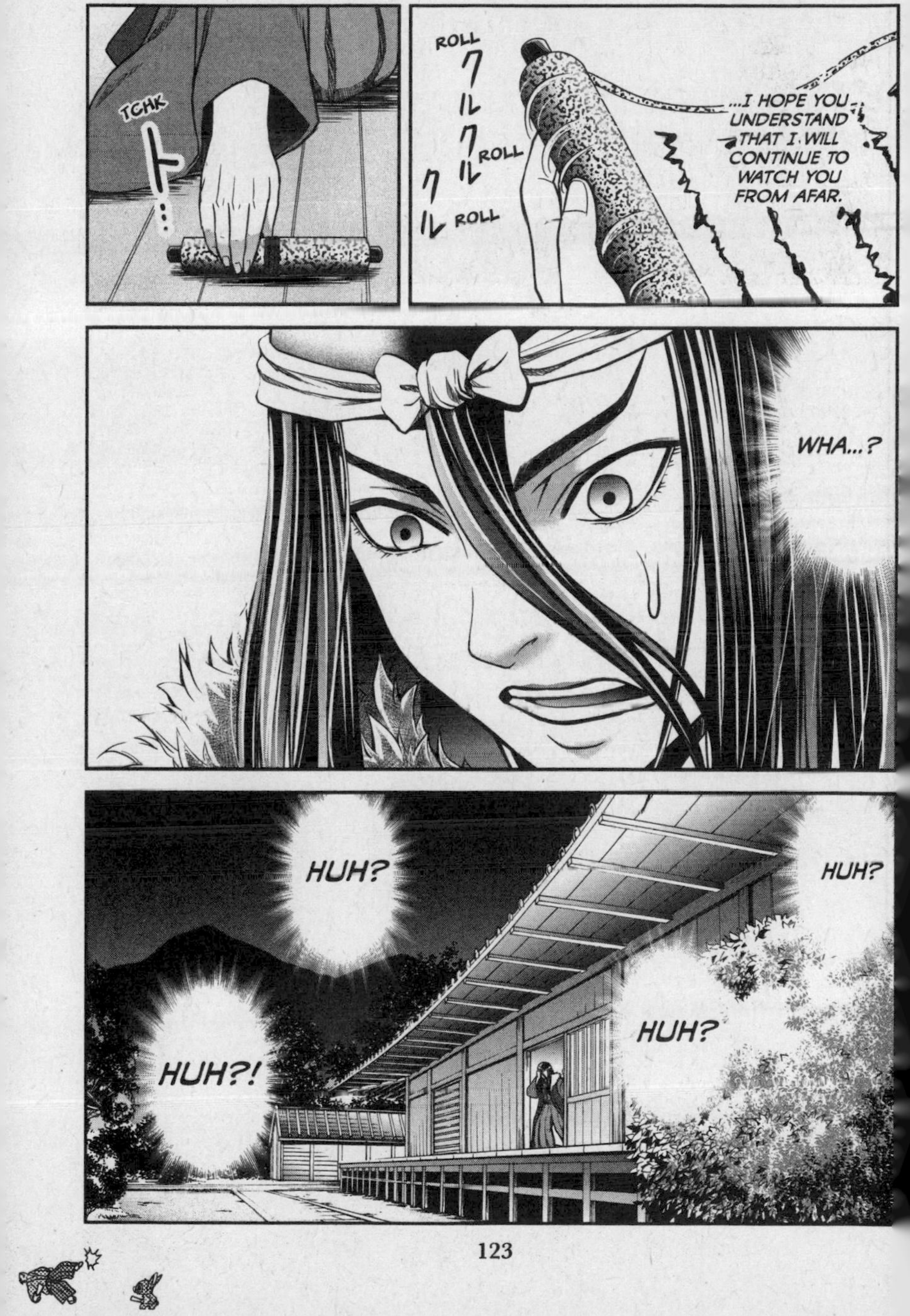
ROLL
クル
ROLL
クル
ROLL
クル
...I HOPE YOU UNDERSTAND THAT I WILL CONTINUE TO WATCH YOU FROM AFAR.
TCHK
ト...
WHA...?
HUH?
HUH?
HUH?
HUH?!

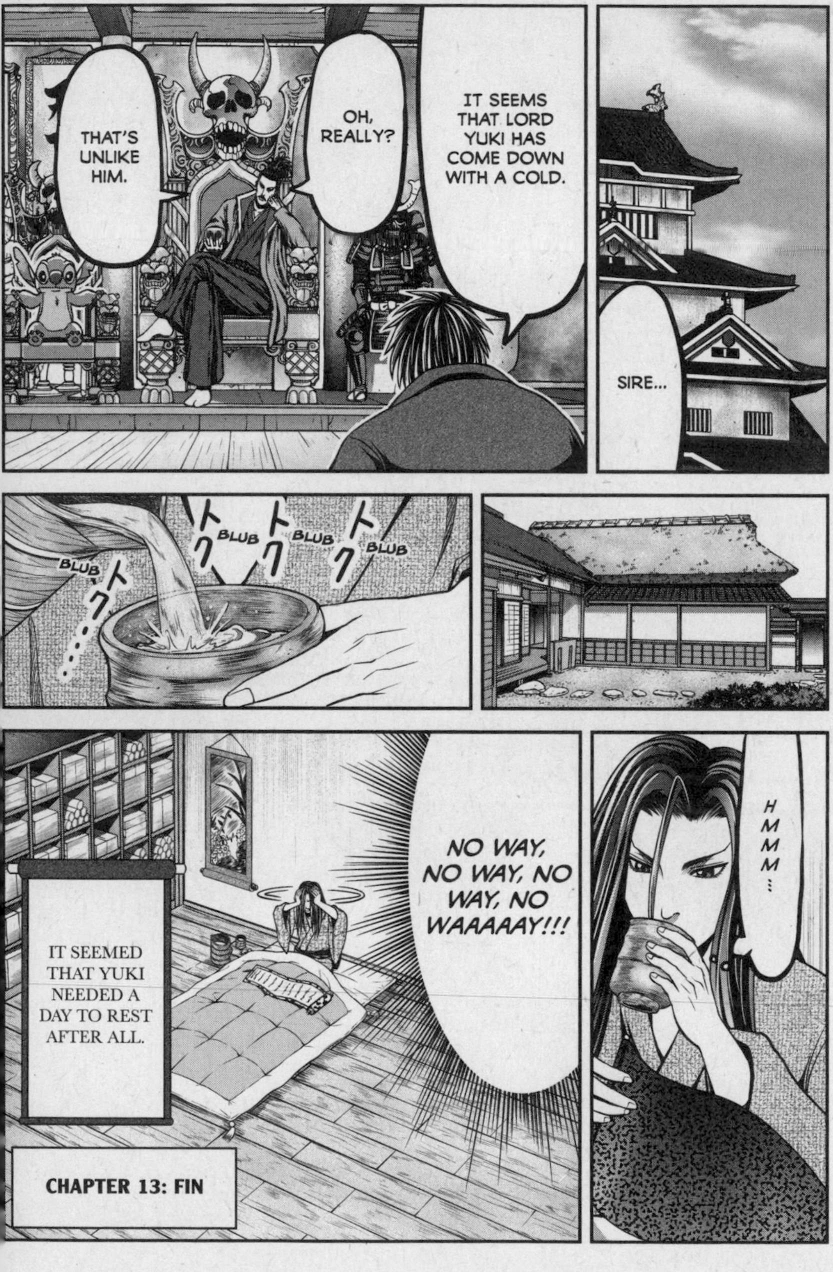
SIRE...
IT SEEMS THAT LORD YUKI HAS COME DOWN WITH A COLD.
OH, REALLY?
THAT'S UNLIKE HIM.
トク BLUB
トク BLUB
トク BLUB
トク… BLUB
HMMM...
NO WAY, NO WAY, NO WAY, NO WAAAAAY!!!
IT SEEMED THAT YUKI NEEDED A DAY TO REST AFTER ALL.
CHAPTER 13: FIN

Disney
STITCH
STITCH & THE SAMURAI

Disney

Stitch

STITCH & THE SAMURAI

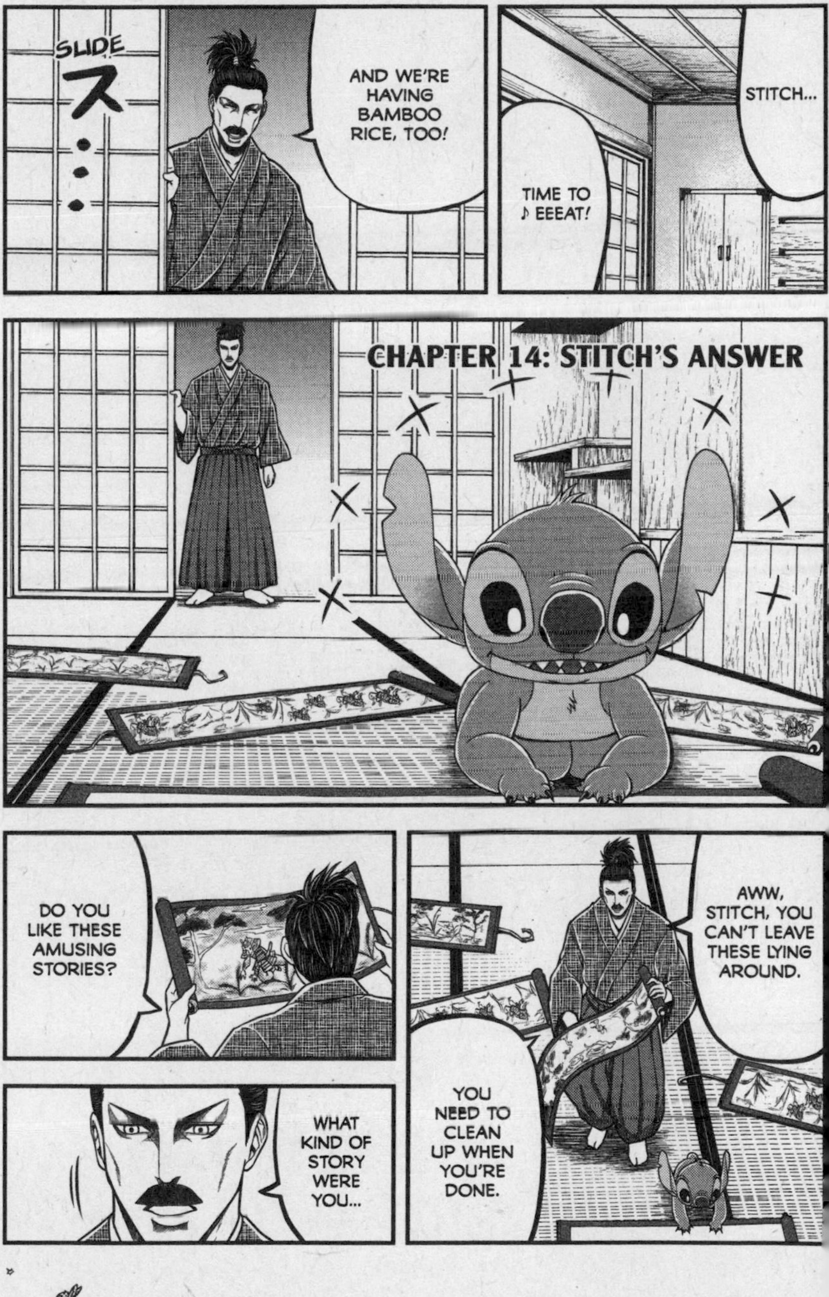
STITCH...
TIME TO ♪ EEEAT!
SLIDE
ス
AND WE'RE HAVING BAMBOO RICE, TOO!
CHAPTER 14: STITCH'S ANSWER
AWW, STITCH, YOU CAN'T LEAVE THESE LYING AROUND.
YOU NEED TO CLEAN UP WHEN YOU'RE DONE.
DO YOU LIKE THESE AMUSING STORIES?
WHAT KIND OF STORY WERE YOU...

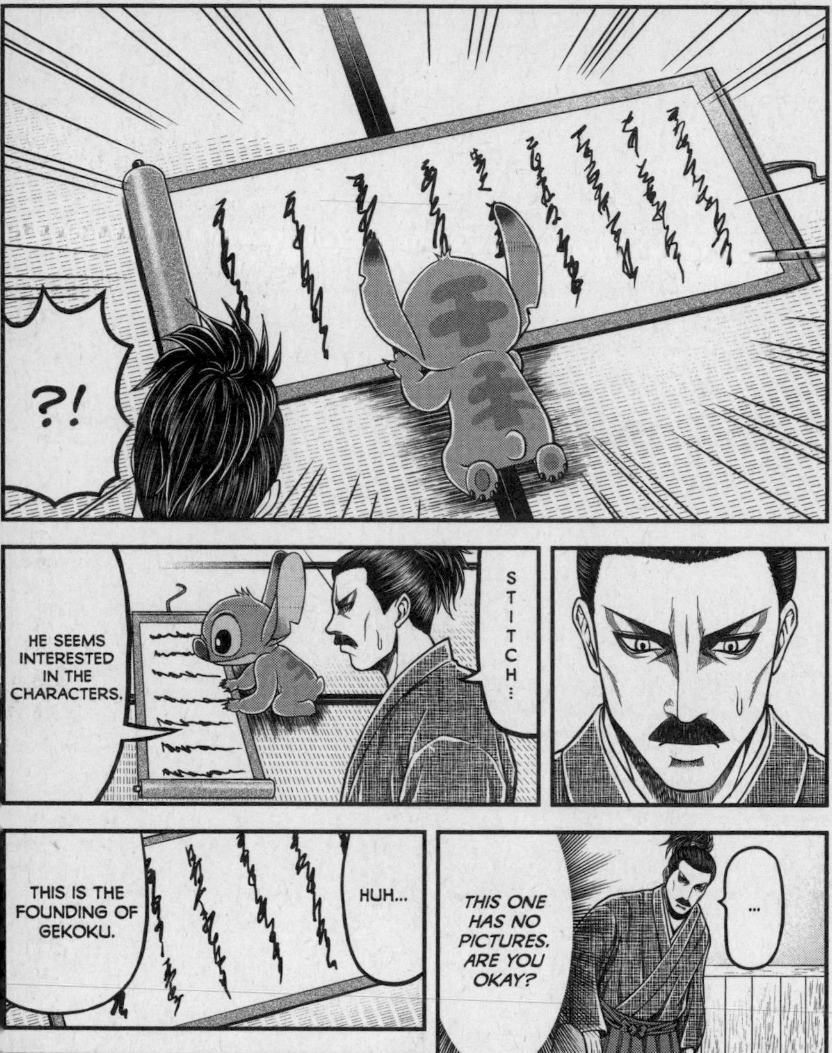
?!
STITCH...
HE SEEMS INTERESTED IN THE CHARACTERS.
...
THIS ONE HAS NO PICTURES. ARE YOU OKAY?
HUH...
THIS IS THE FOUNDING OF GEKOKU.
AND THE YEAR OUR COUNTRY WAS FOUNDED... YES.

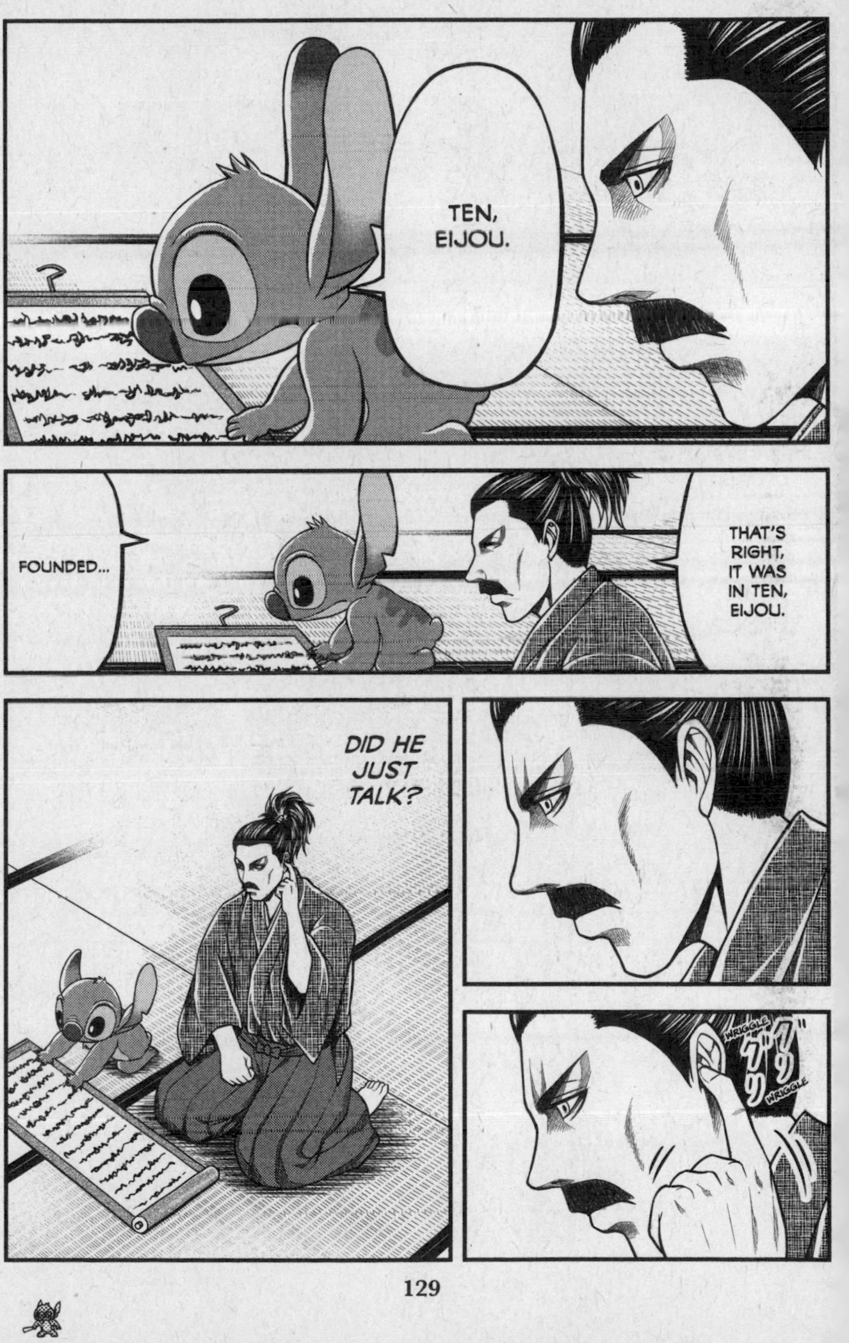
TEN, EIJOU.
THAT'S RIGHT, IT WAS IN TEN, EIJOU.
FOUNDED...
WRIGGLE
WRIGGLE
DID HE JUST TALK?

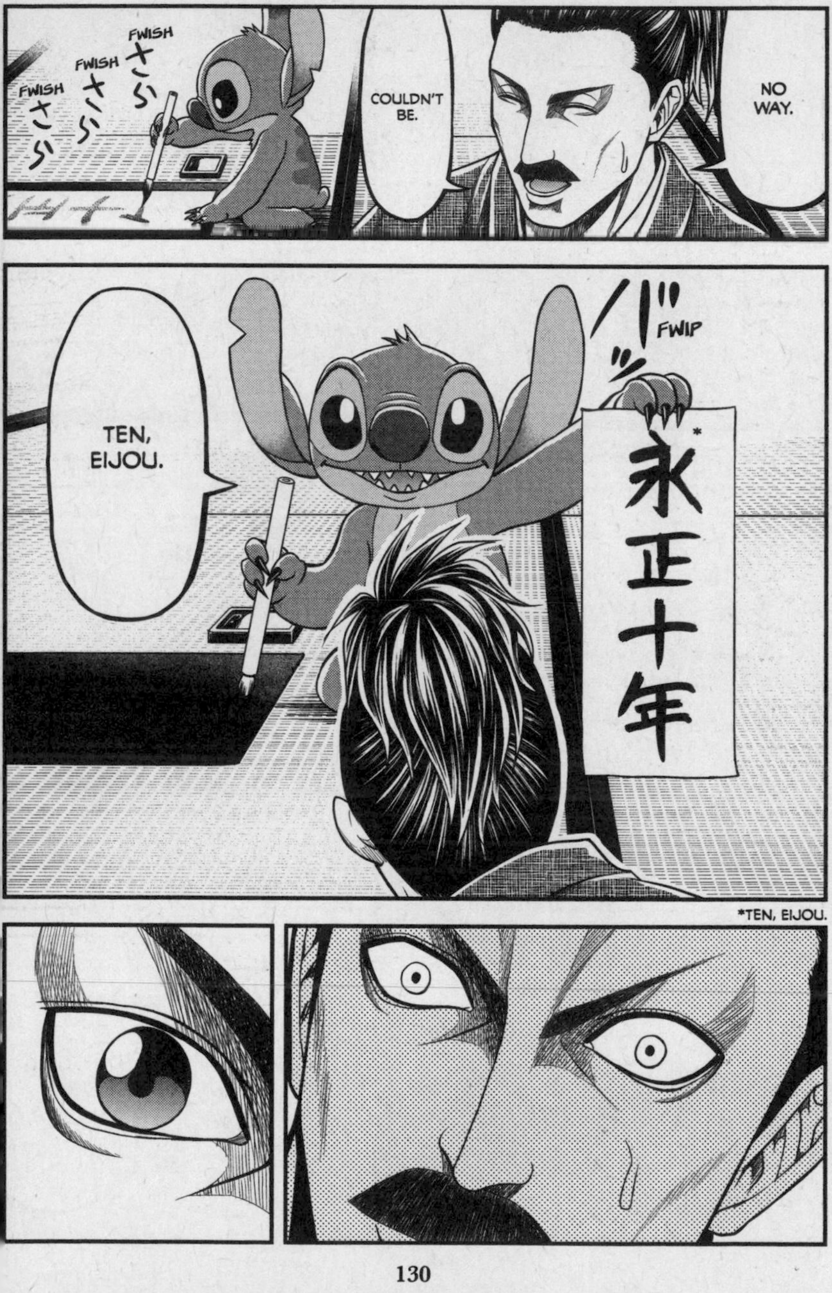
NO WAY.
COULDN'T BE.
FWISH さら
FWISH さら
FWISH さら
FWIP バ
永正十年*
TEN, EIJOU.
*TEN, EIJOU.

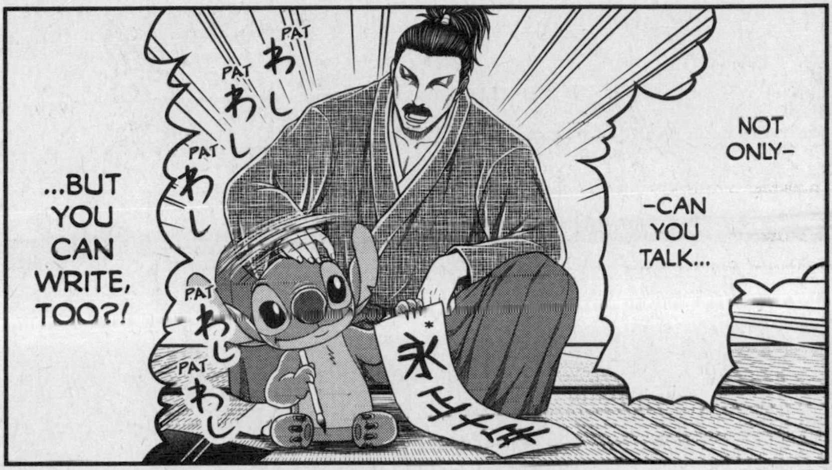
NOT ONLY-
-CAN YOU TALK...
...BUT YOU CAN WRITE, TOO?!
PAT わし
PAT わし
PAT わし
PAT わし
PAT わし

*TEN, EIJOU.

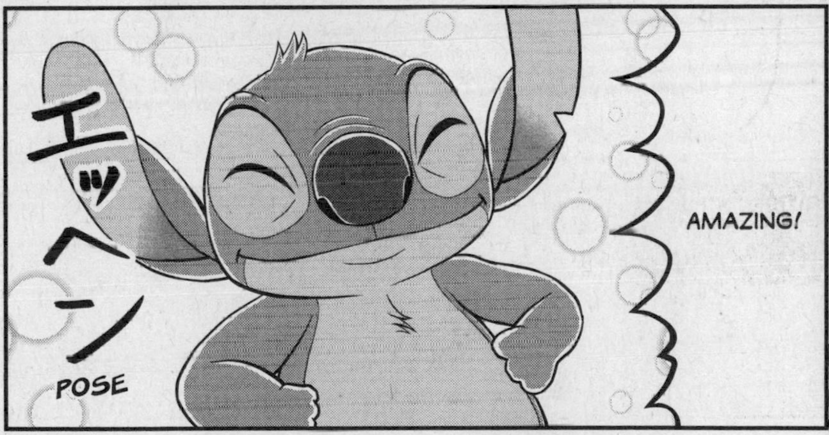
AMAZING!
エッヘン
POSE

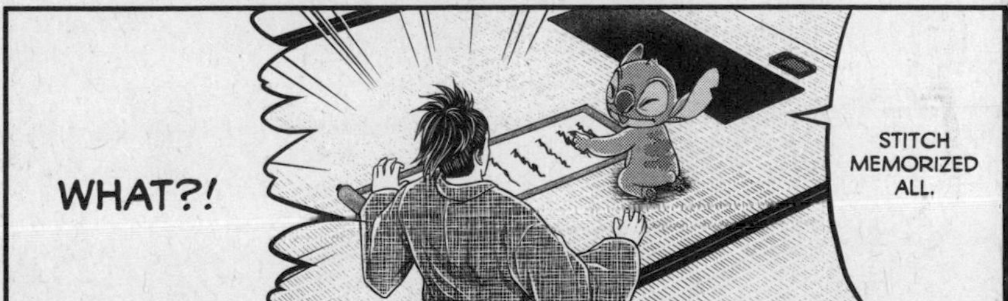
STITCH MEMORIZED ALL.
WHAT?!

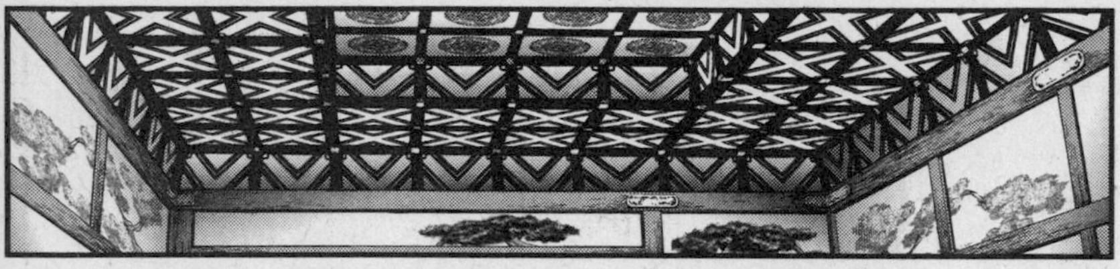

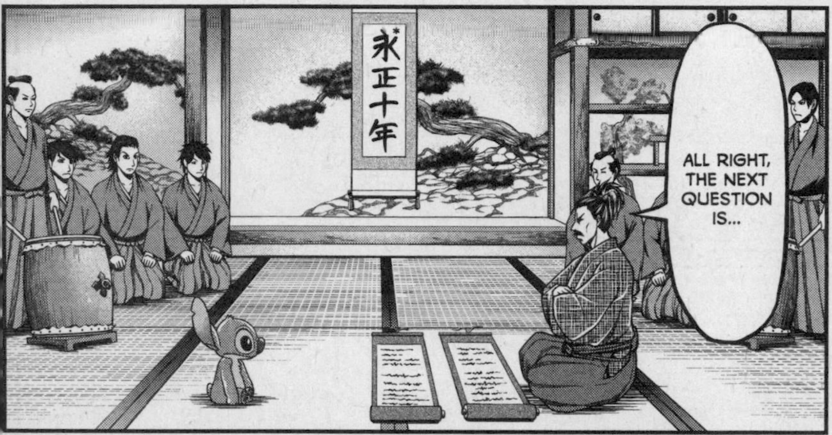
ALL RIGHT, THE NEXT QUESTION IS...
永正十年*

*TEN, EIJOU.

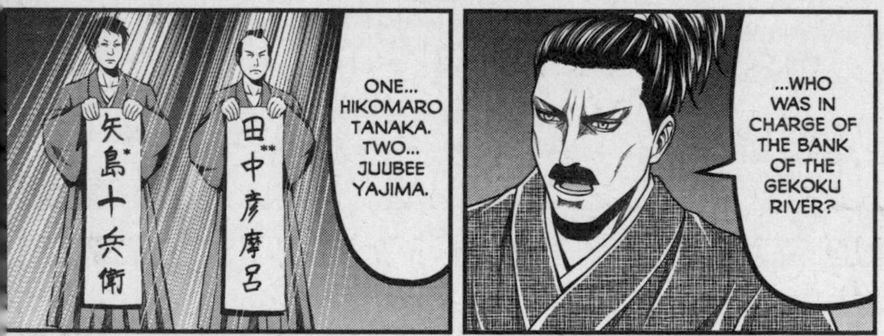
...WHO WAS IN CHARGE OF THE BANK OF THE GEKOKU RIVER?
ONE... HIKOMARO TANAKA. TWO... JUUBEE YAJIMA.
田中**彦摩呂
矢島*十兵衛

*JUUBEE YAJIMA **HIKOMARO TANAKA

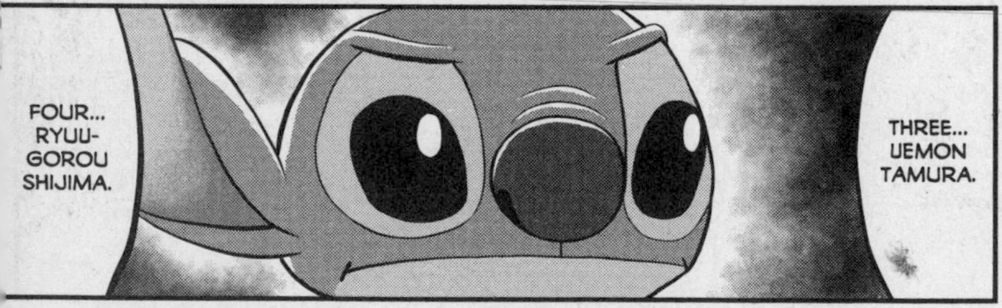
THREE... UEMON TAMURA.
FOUR... RYUU-GOROU SHIJIMA.

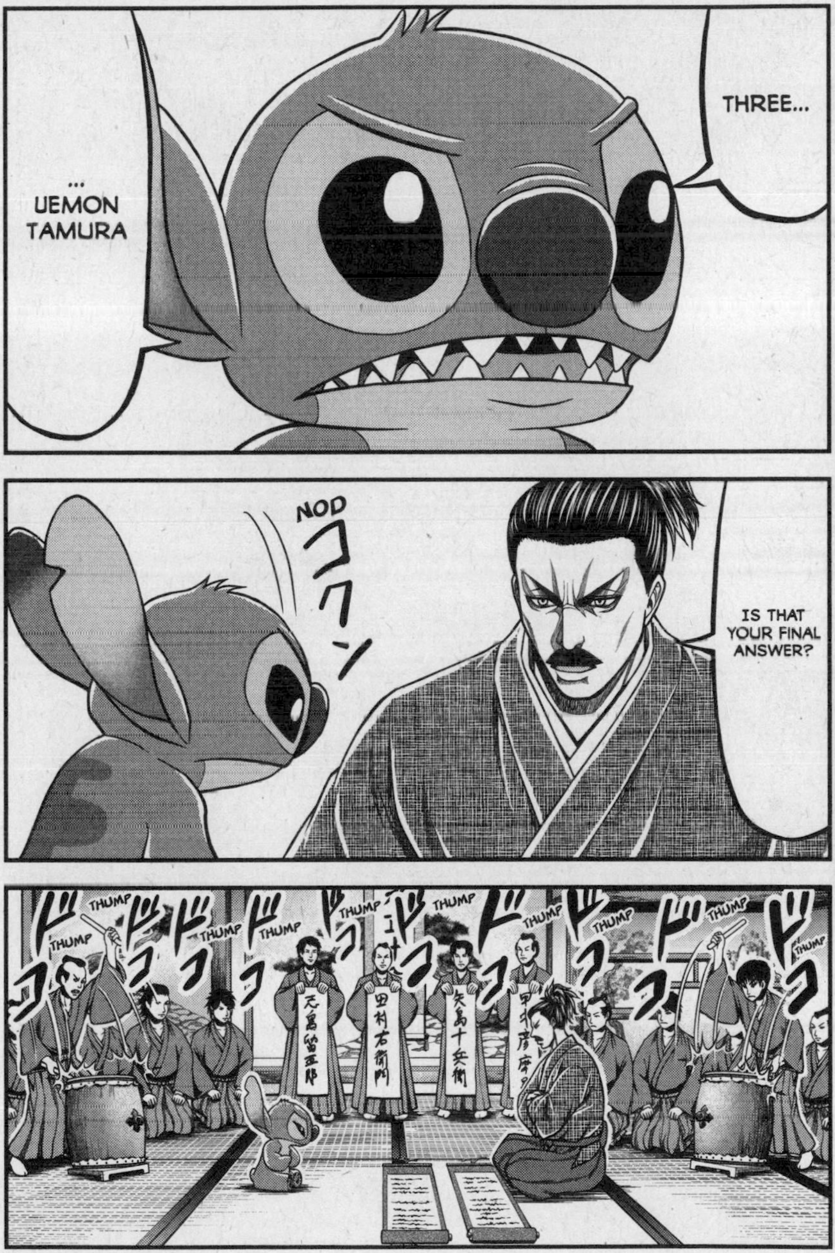
THREE...
...UEMON TAMURA
IS THAT YOUR FINAL ANSWER?
NOD
コクン
THUMP
ドコ
THUMP
ドコ
THUMP
ドコ
THUMP
ドコ
THUMP
ドコ
THUMP
ドコ
THUMP
ドコ
THUMP
ドコ
THUMP
ドコ
THUMP
ドコ
田村右衛門
矢島十兵衛

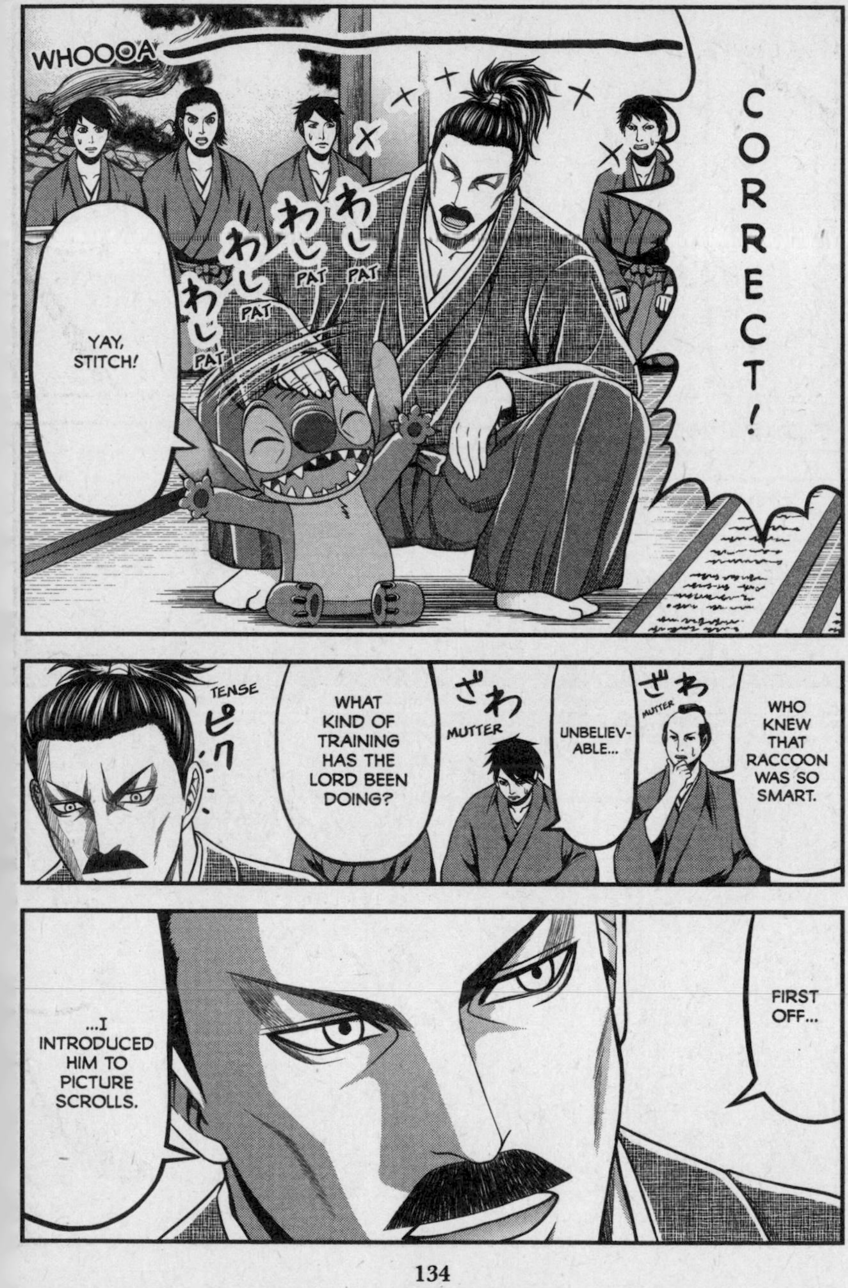
CORRECT!
WHOOOA
わしわしわしわし
PAT PAT PAT PAT
YAY, STITCH!
WHO KNEW THAT RACCOON WAS SO SMART.
ざわ
MUTTER
UNBELIEV-ABLE...
ざわ
MUTTER
WHAT KIND OF TRAINING HAS THE LORD BEEN DOING?
ピク
TENSE
FIRST OFF...
...I INTRODUCED HIM TO PICTURE SCROLLS.

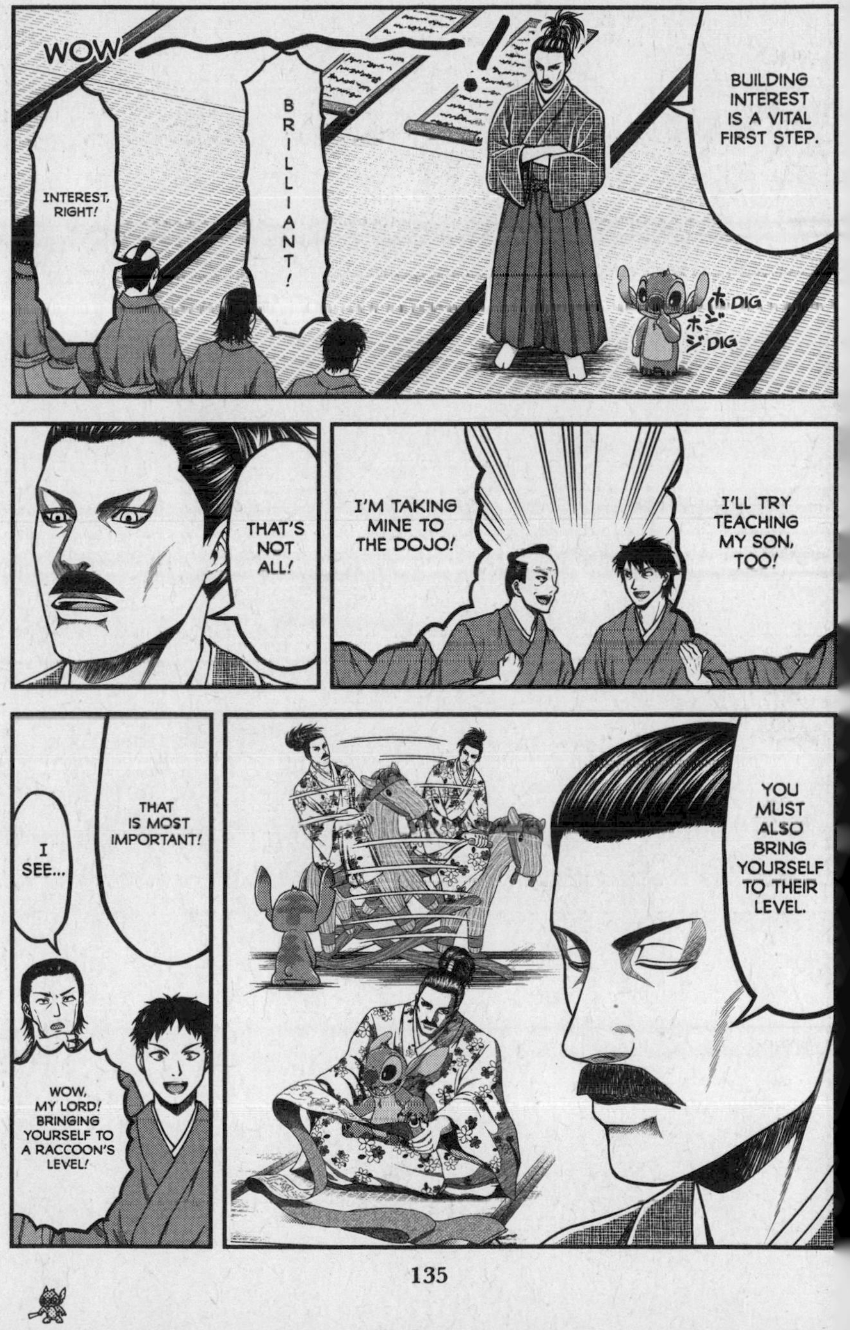
BUILDING INTEREST IS A VITAL FIRST STEP.
ホジ DIG
ホジ DIG
!
BRILLIANT!
WOW
INTEREST, RIGHT!
I'LL TRY TEACHING MY SON, TOO!
I'M TAKING MINE TO THE DOJO!
THAT'S NOT ALL!
YOU MUST ALSO BRING YOURSELF TO THEIR LEVEL.
THAT IS MOST IMPORTANT!
I SEE...
WOW, MY LORD! BRINGING YOURSELF TO A RACCOON'S LEVEL!

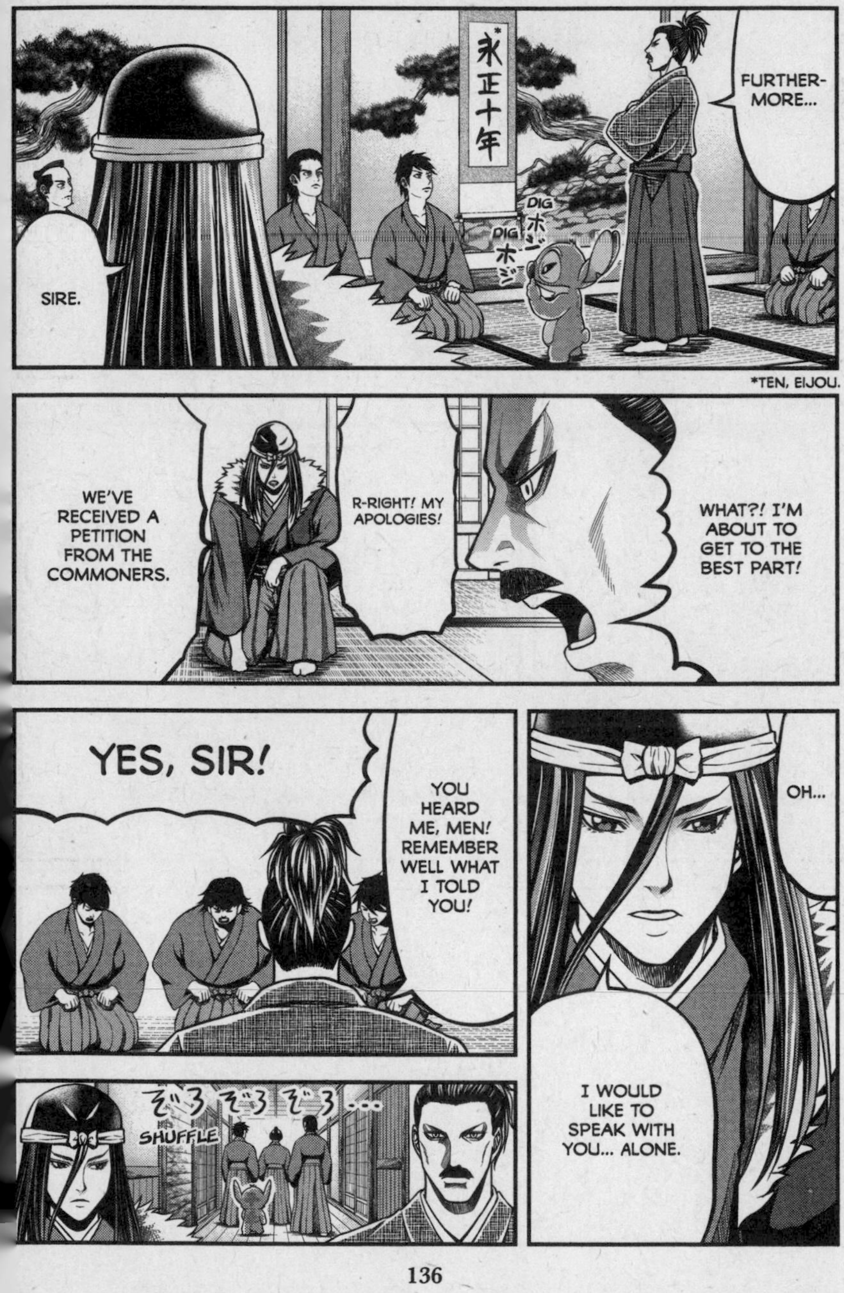
永正十年
FURTHER-MORE...
DIG ホジ
DIG ホジ
SIRE.
WHAT?! I'M ABOUT TO GET TO THE BEST PART!
R-RIGHT! MY APOLOGIES!
WE'VE RECEIVED A PETITION FROM THE COMMONERS.
OH...
I WOULD LIKE TO SPEAK WITH YOU... ALONE.
YOU HEARD ME, MEN! REMEMBER WELL WHAT I TOLD YOU!
YES, SIR!
ぞろぞろぞろ...
SHUFFLE

*TEN, EIJOU.

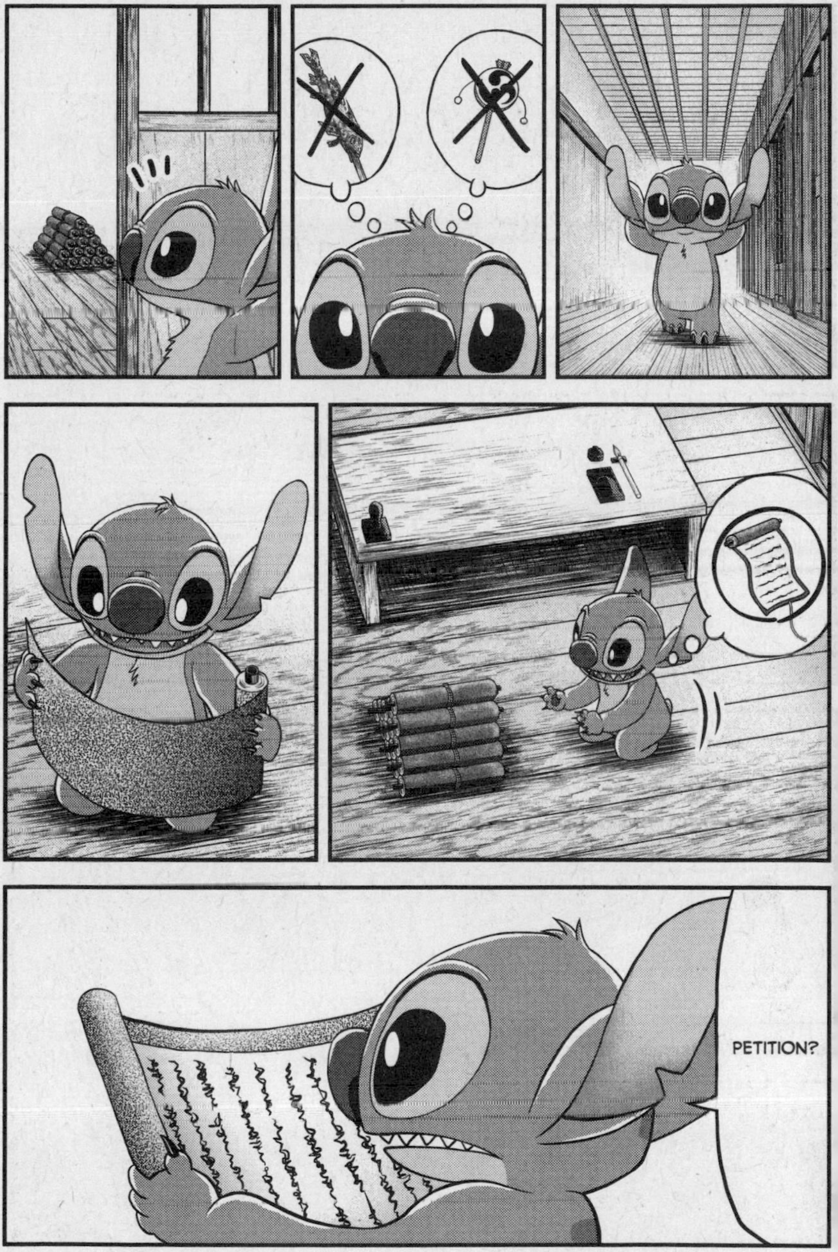
PETITION?

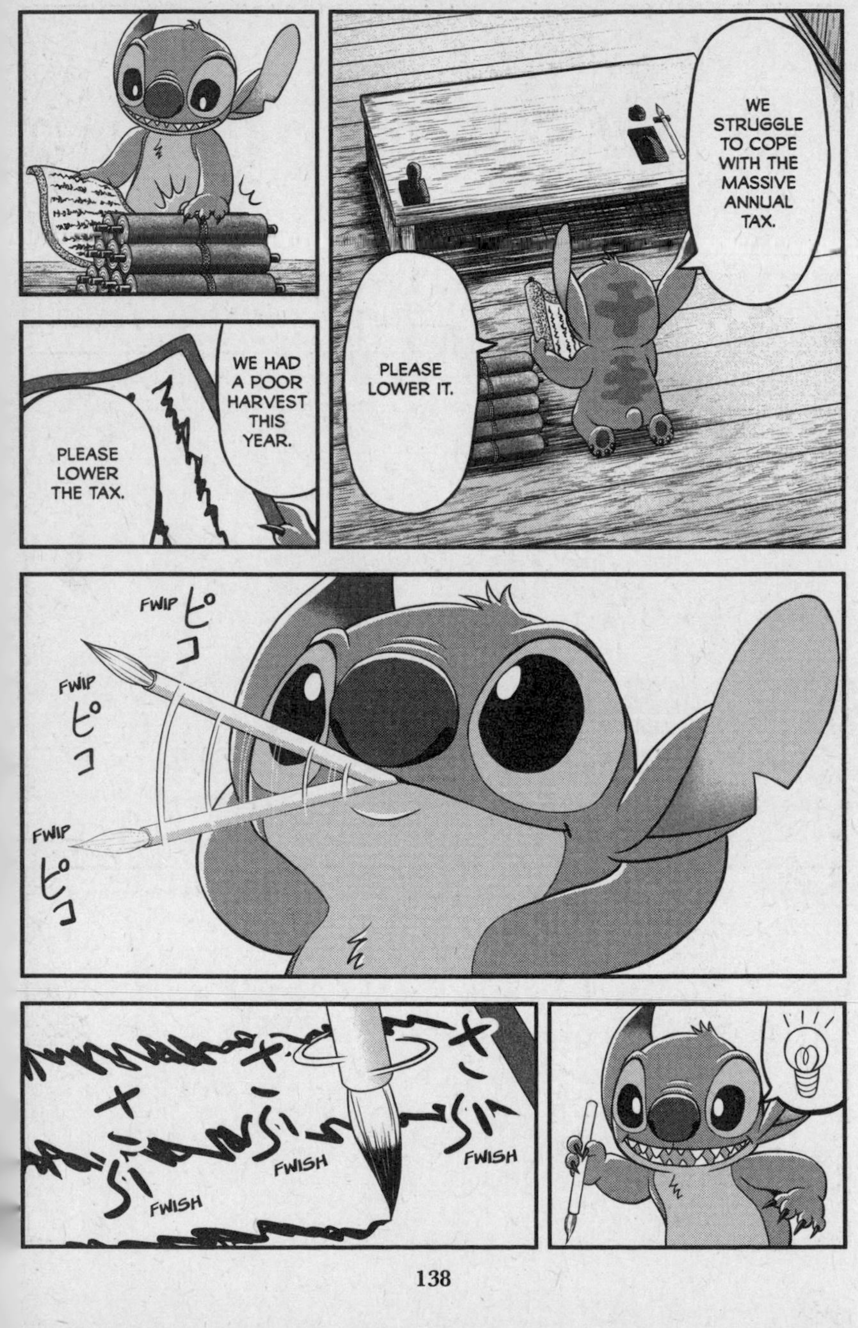
WE STRUGGLE TO COPE WITH THE MASSIVE ANNUAL TAX.
PLEASE LOWER IT.
WE HAD A POOR HARVEST THIS YEAR.
PLEASE LOWER THE TAX.
FWIP ピコ
FWIP ピコ
FWIP ピコ
FWISH
FWISH
FWISH

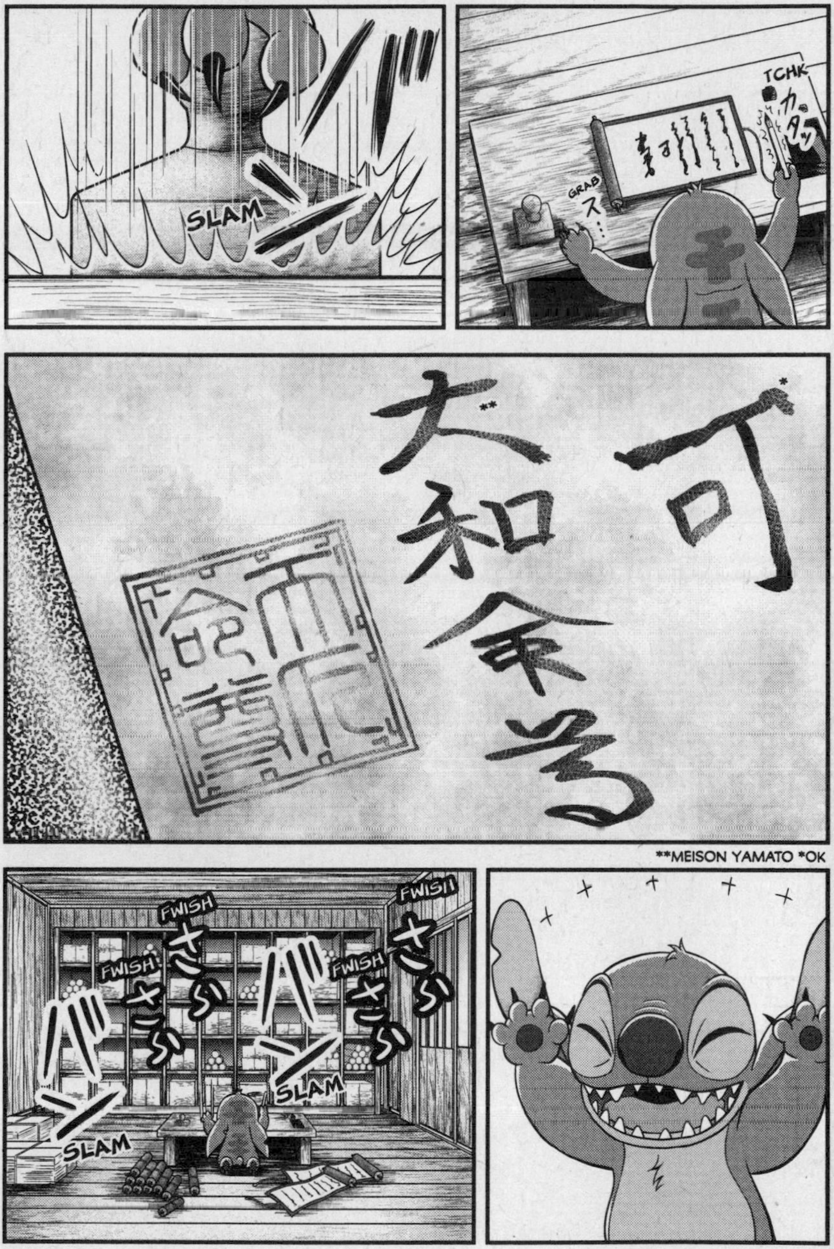
TCHK
カタッ
GRAB
ス…
SLAM
可
大和命名
**MEISON YAMATO *OK
FWISH
さらさら
FWISH
さらさら
バン
SLAM
FWISH
さらさら
バン
SLAM

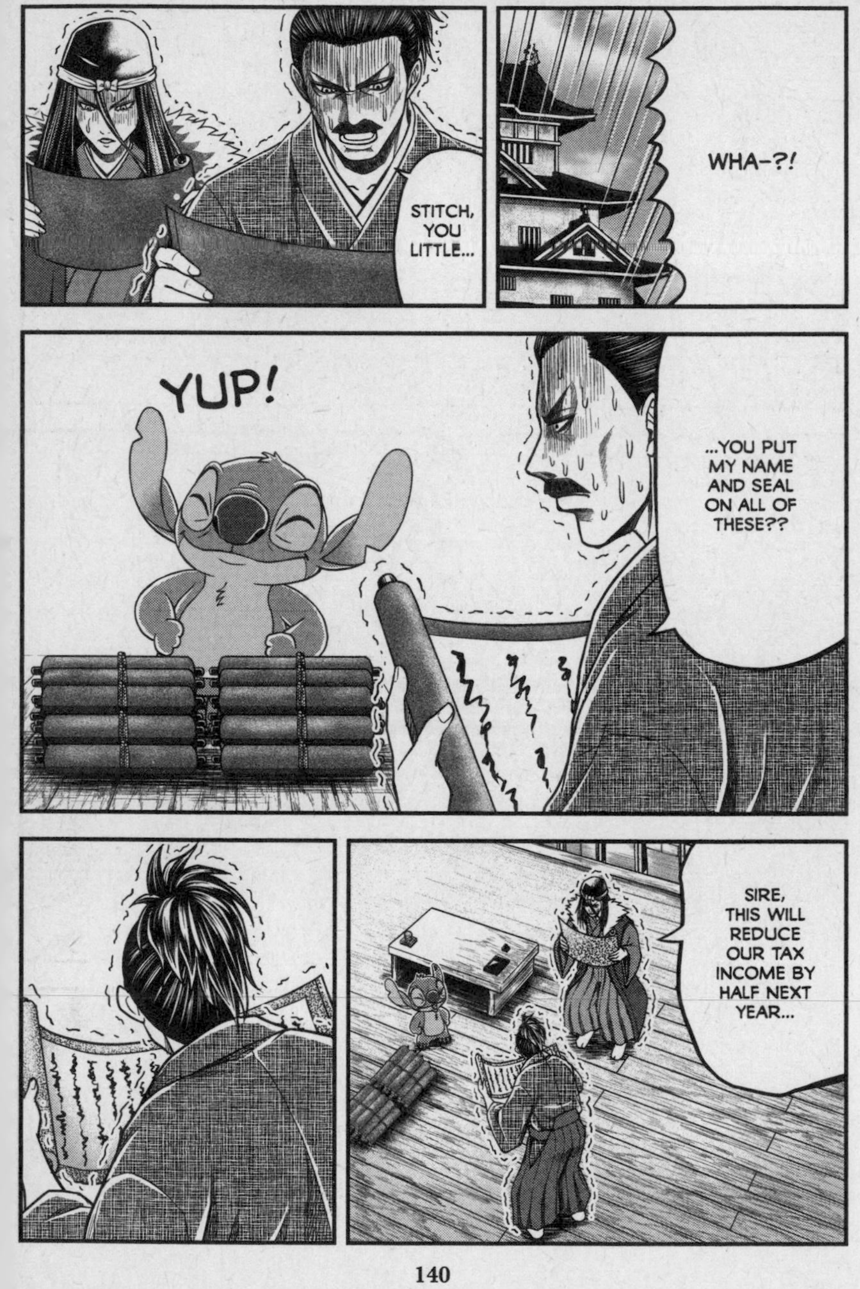
WHA-?!
STITCH, YOU LITTLE...
...YOU PUT MY NAME AND SEAL ON ALL OF THESE??
YUP!
SIRE, THIS WILL REDUCE OUR TAX INCOME BY HALF NEXT YEAR...

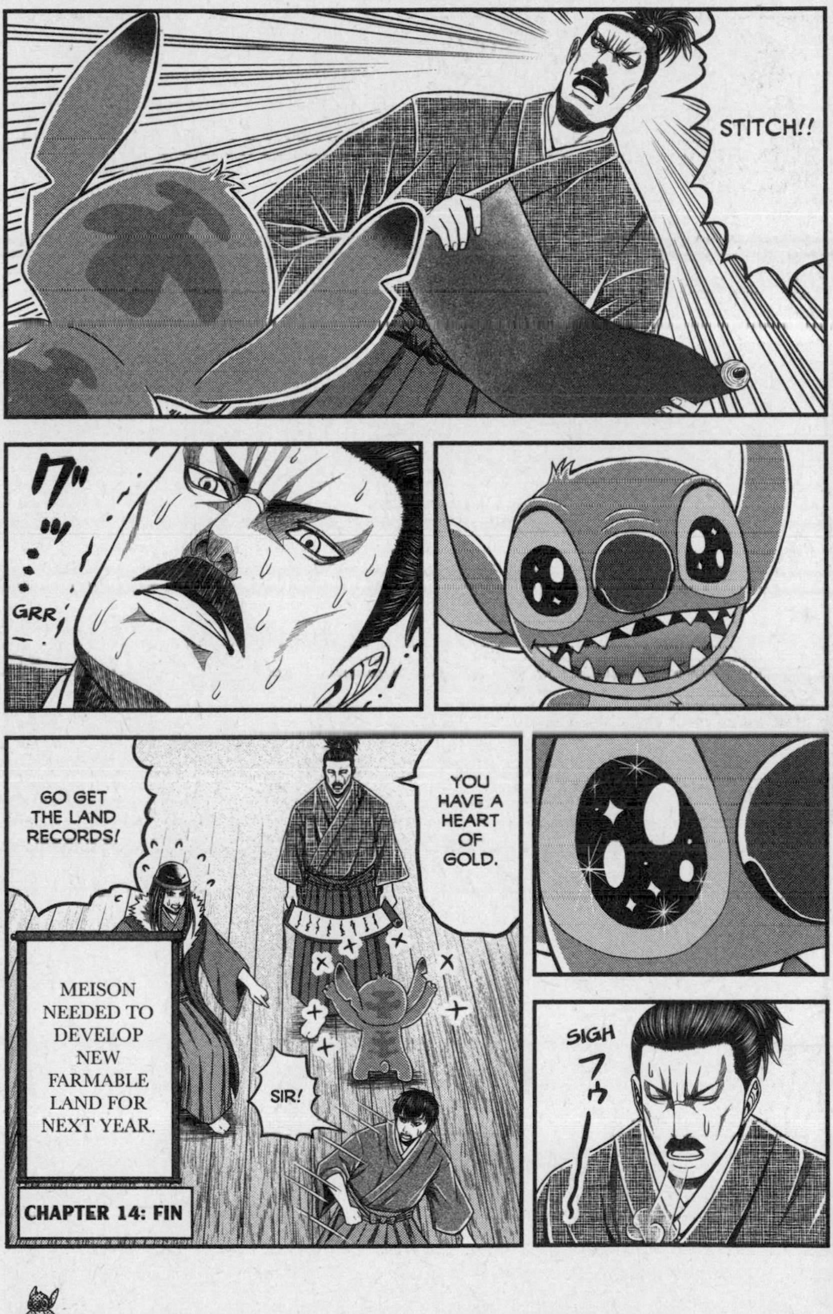
STITCH!!
GRR
SIGH
YOU HAVE A HEART OF GOLD.
GO GET THE LAND RECORDS!
SIR!
MEISON NEEDED TO DEVELOP NEW FARMABLE LAND FOR NEXT YEAR.
CHAPTER 14: FIN

Disney

STiTCH

STITCH & THE SAMURAI

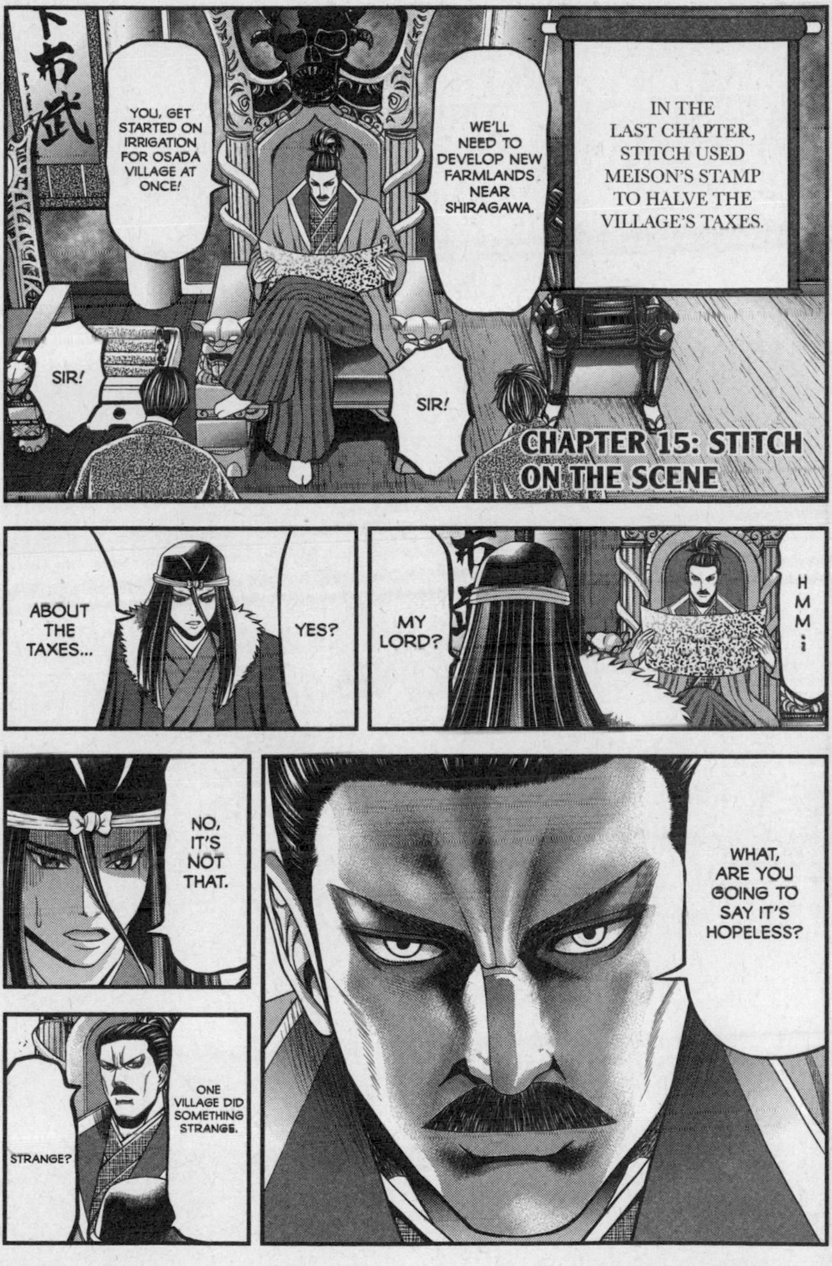
IN THE LAST CHAPTER, STITCH USED MEISON'S STAMP TO HALVE THE VILLAGE'S TAXES.
WE'LL NEED TO DEVELOP NEW FARMLANDS NEAR SHIRAGAWA.
SIR!
YOU, GET STARTED ON IRRIGATION FOR OSADA VILLAGE AT ONCE!
SIR!
CHAPTER 15: STITCH ON THE SCENE
HMM...
MY LORD?
YES?
ABOUT THE TAXES...
WHAT, ARE YOU GOING TO SAY IT'S HOPELESS?
NO, IT'S NOT THAT.
ONE VILLAGE DID SOMETHING STRANGE.
STRANGE?

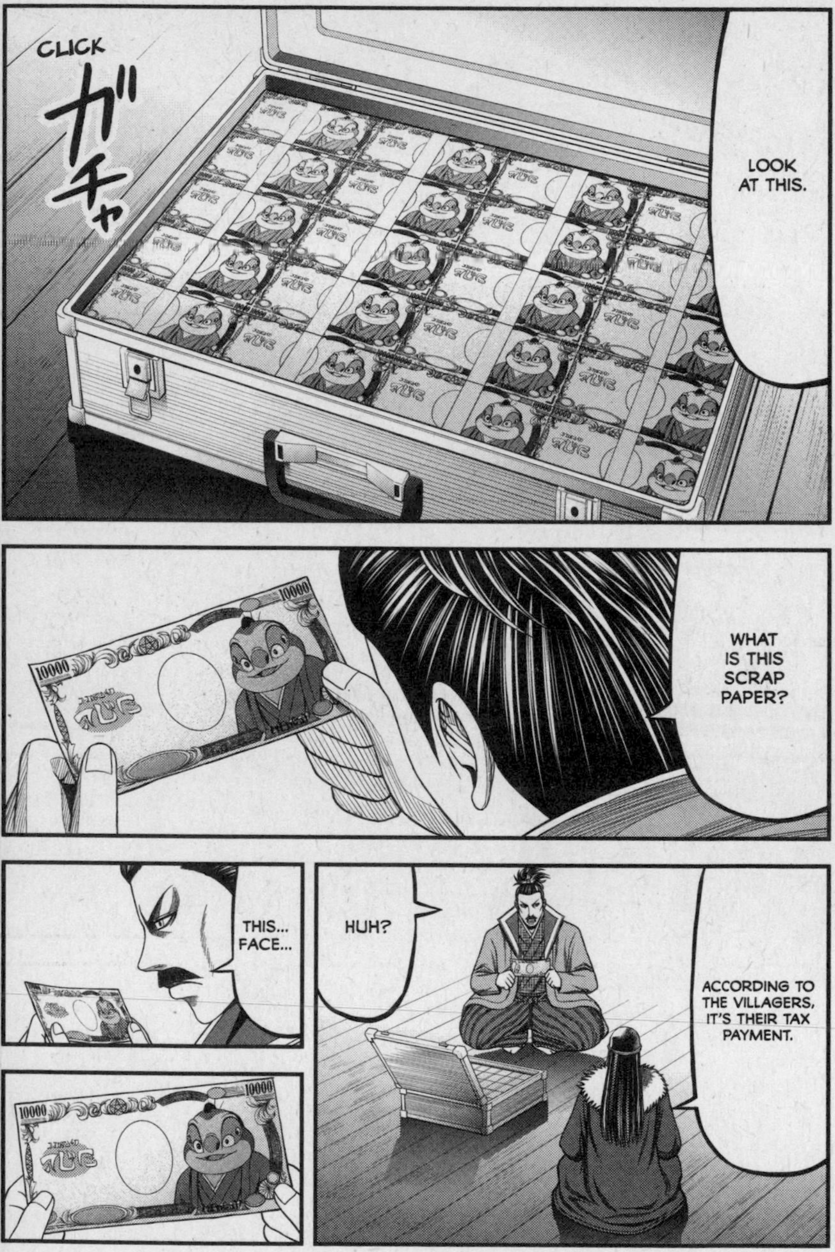
CLICK
ガチャ
LOOK AT THIS.
WHAT IS THIS SCRAP PAPER?
ACCORDING TO THE VILLAGERS, IT'S THEIR TAX PAYMENT.
HUH?
THIS... FACE...

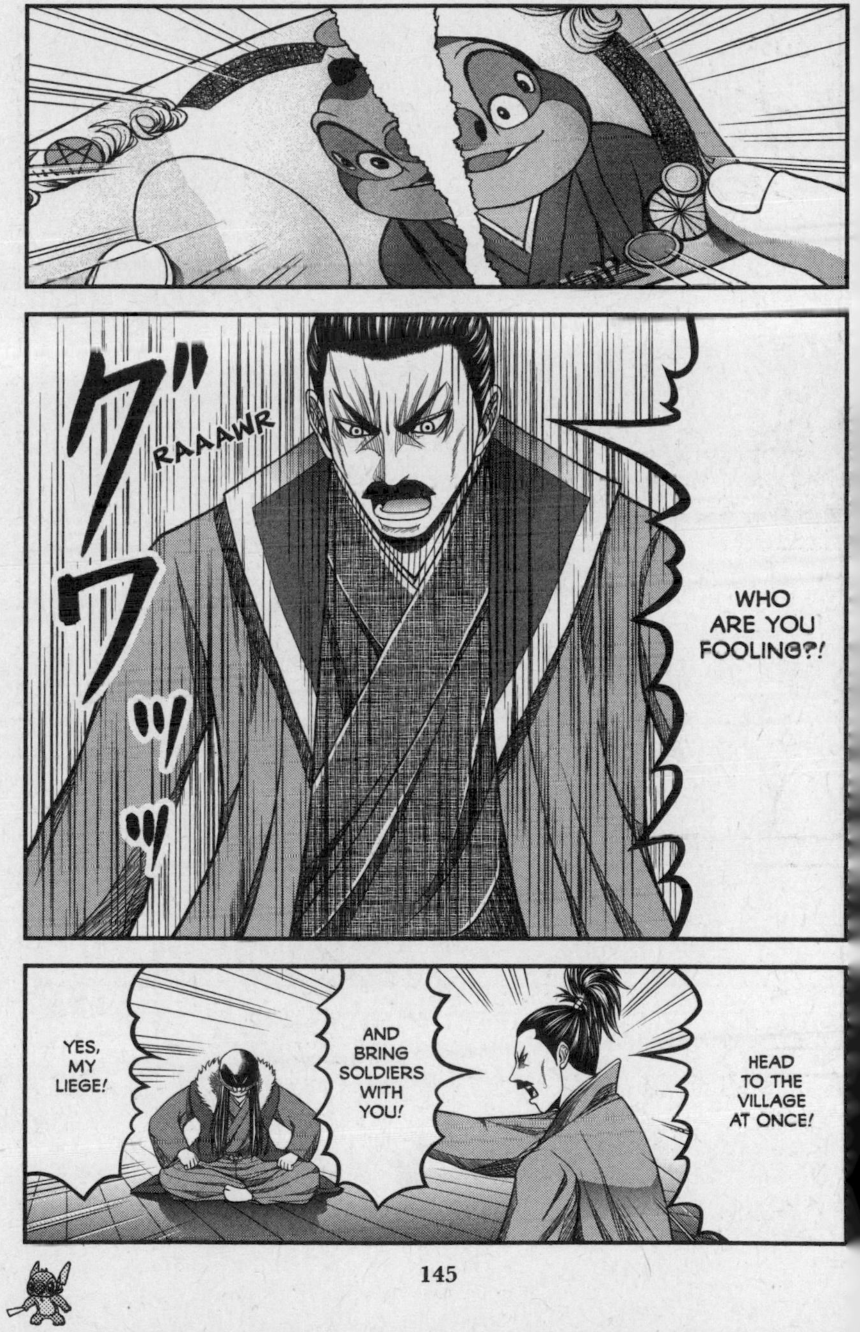
WHO ARE YOU FOOLING?!
RAAAWR
HEAD TO THE VILLAGE AT ONCE!
AND BRING SOLDIERS WITH YOU!
YES, MY LIEGE!

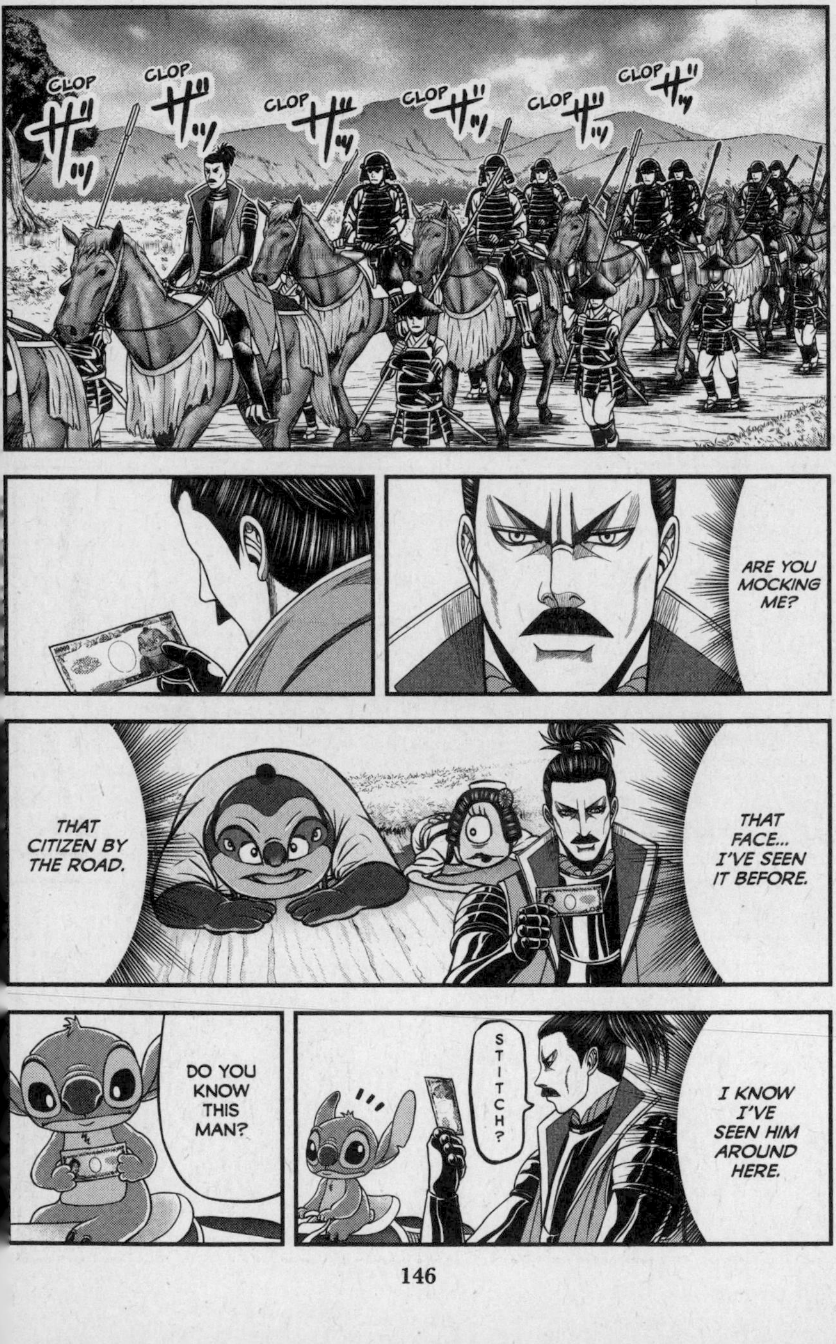
CLOP
ザッ
CLOP
ザッ
CLOP
ザッ
CLOP
ザッ
CLOP
ザッ
CLOP
ザッ
ARE YOU MOCKING ME?
THAT FACE... I'VE SEEN IT BEFORE.
THAT CITIZEN BY THE ROAD.
I KNOW I'VE SEEN HIM AROUND HERE.
STITCH?
DO YOU KNOW THIS MAN?

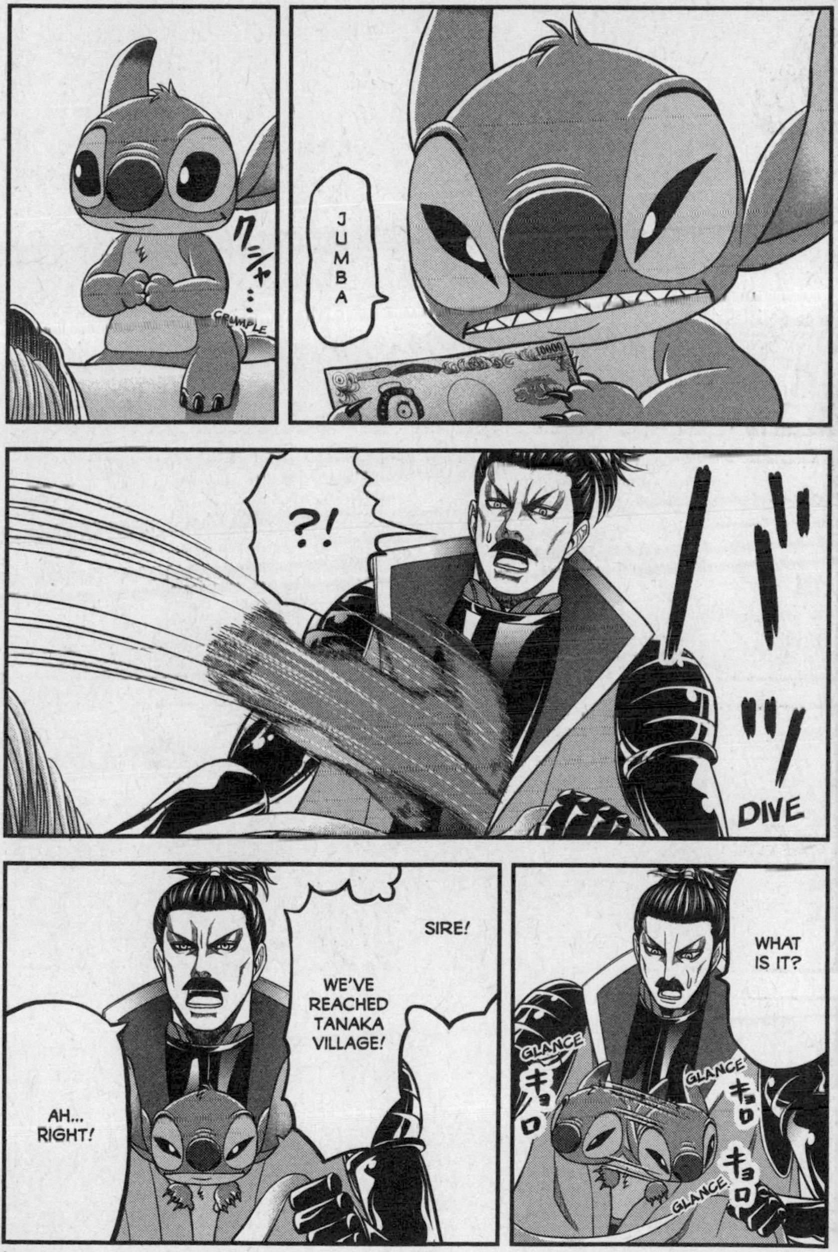
JUMBA
クシャ…
CRUMPLE
ドバッ
DIVE
?!
WHAT IS IT?
GLANCE
キョロ
GLANCE
キョロ
キョロ
GLANCE
SIRE!
WE'VE REACHED TANAKA VILLAGE!
AH... RIGHT!

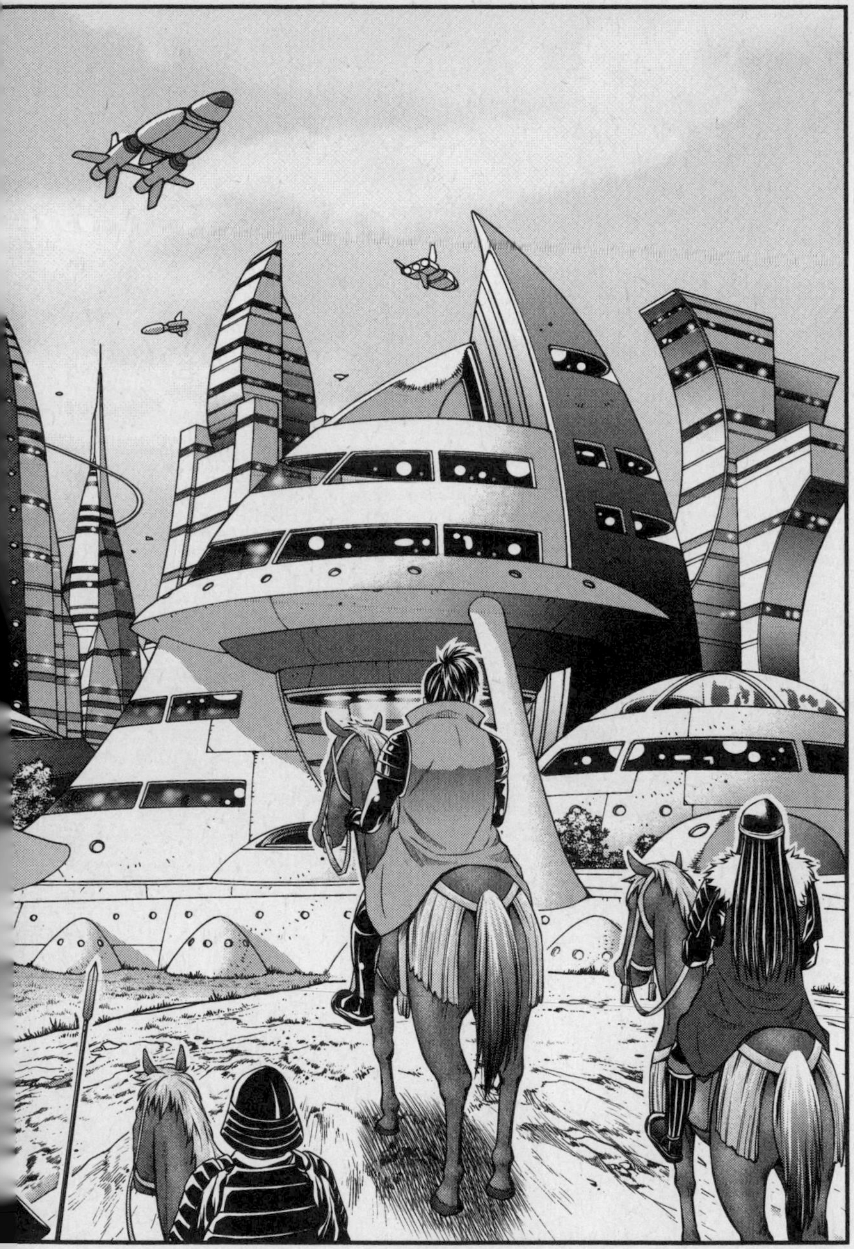

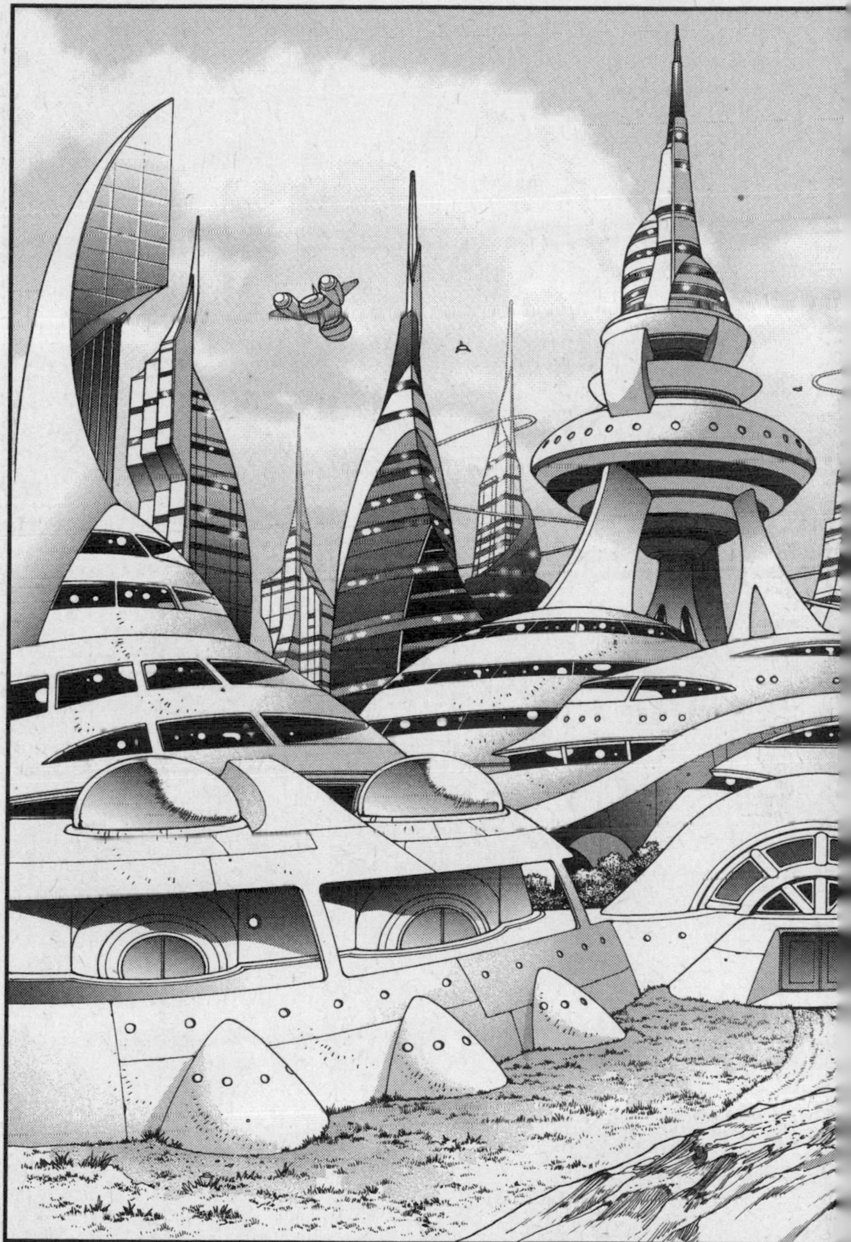

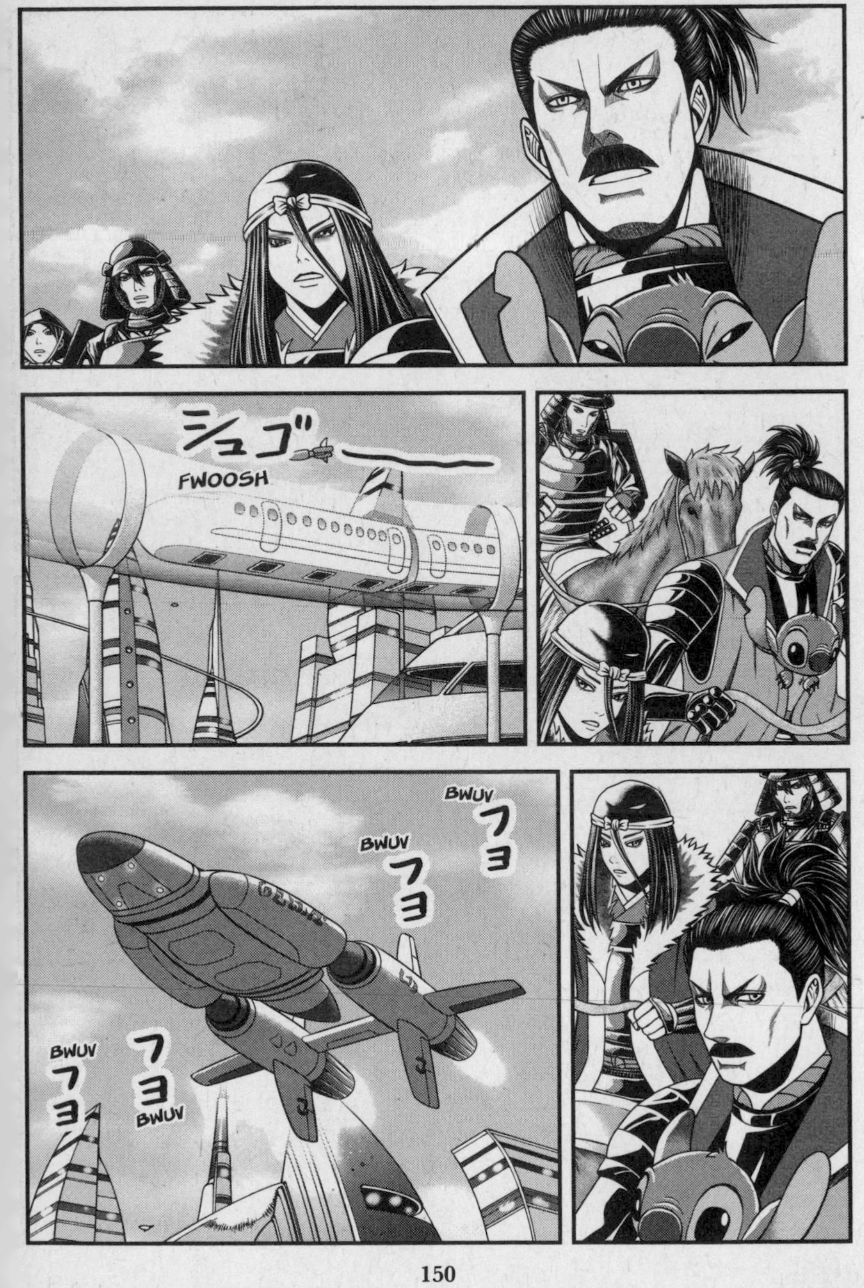
シュゴー
FWOOSH
BWUV
フヨ
BWUV
フヨ
BWUV
フヨ
フヨ
BWUV

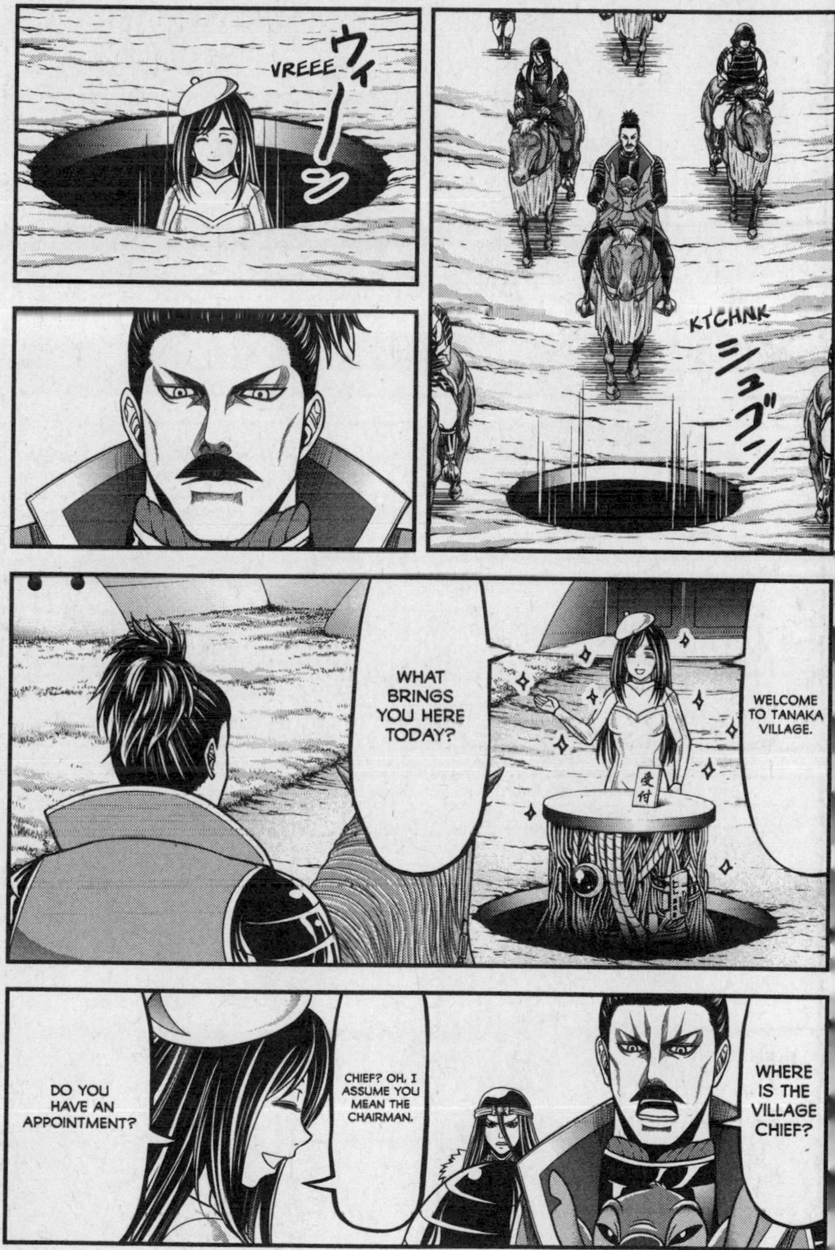
KTCHNK
シュゴン
VREEE
ウィーン
WELCOME TO TANAKA VILLAGE.
受付
WHAT BRINGS YOU HERE TODAY?
WHERE IS THE VILLAGE CHIEF?
CHIEF? OH, I ASSUME YOU MEAN THE CHAIRMAN.
DO YOU HAVE AN APPOINTMENT?

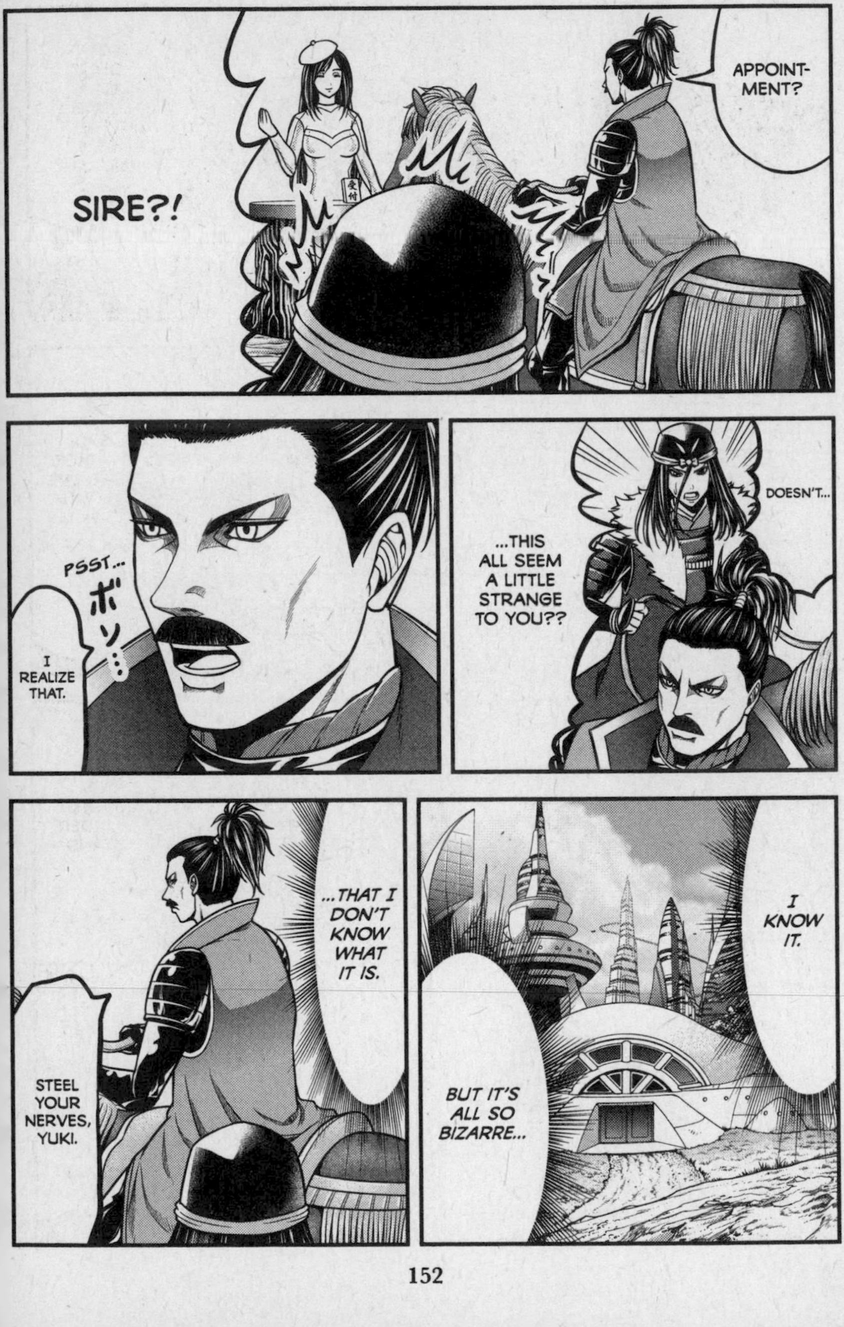
APPOINT-
MENT?
SIRE?!
DOESN'T...
...THIS ALL SEEM A LITTLE STRANGE TO YOU??
PSST... ボソ...
I REALIZE THAT.
I KNOW IT.
BUT IT'S ALL SO BIZARRE...
...THAT I DON'T KNOW WHAT IT IS.
STEEL YOUR NERVES, YUKI.

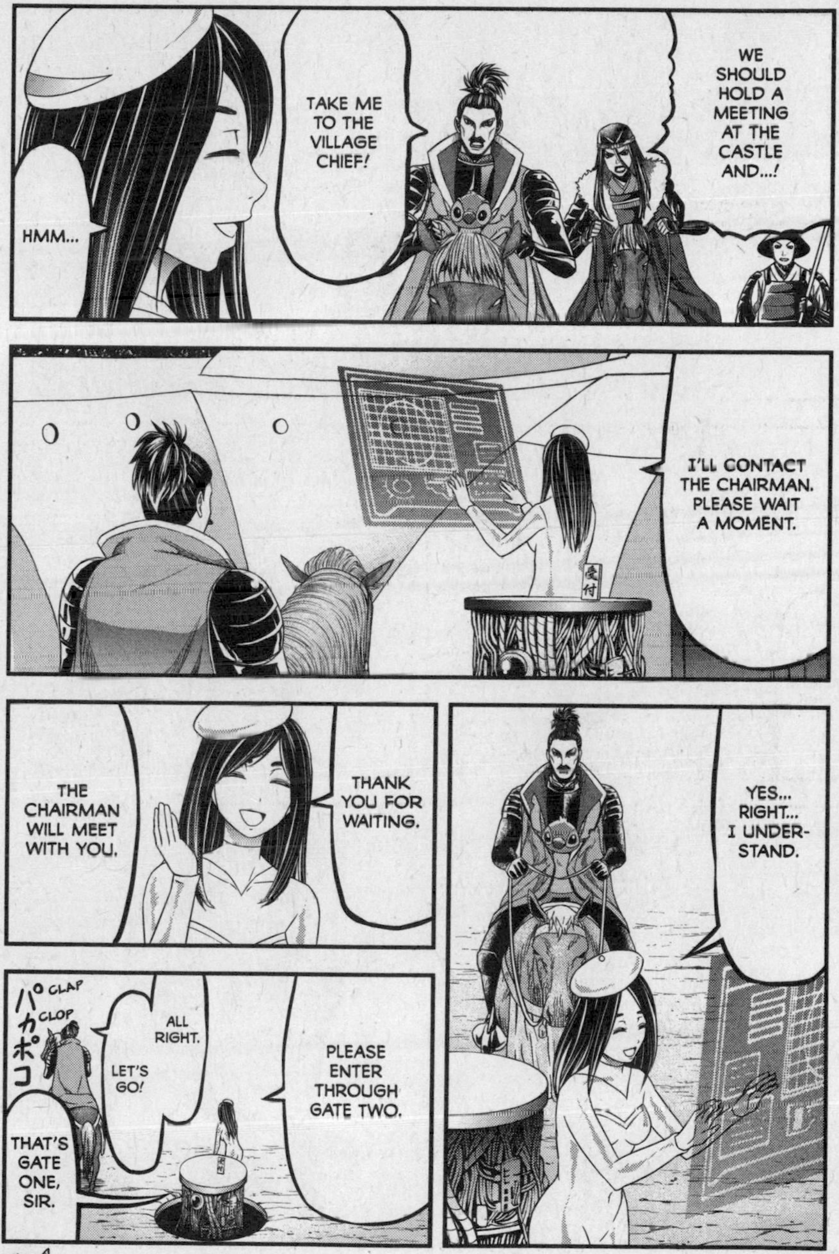
WE SHOULD HOLD A MEETING AT THE CASTLE AND...!
TAKE ME TO THE VILLAGE CHIEF!
HMM...
I'LL CONTACT THE CHAIRMAN. PLEASE WAIT A MOMENT.
YES... RIGHT... I UNDERSTAND.
THANK YOU FOR WAITING.
THE CHAIRMAN WILL MEET WITH YOU.
PLEASE ENTER THROUGH GATE TWO.
ALL RIGHT.
LET'S GO!
パカポコ CLAP CLOP
THAT'S GATE ONE, SIR.

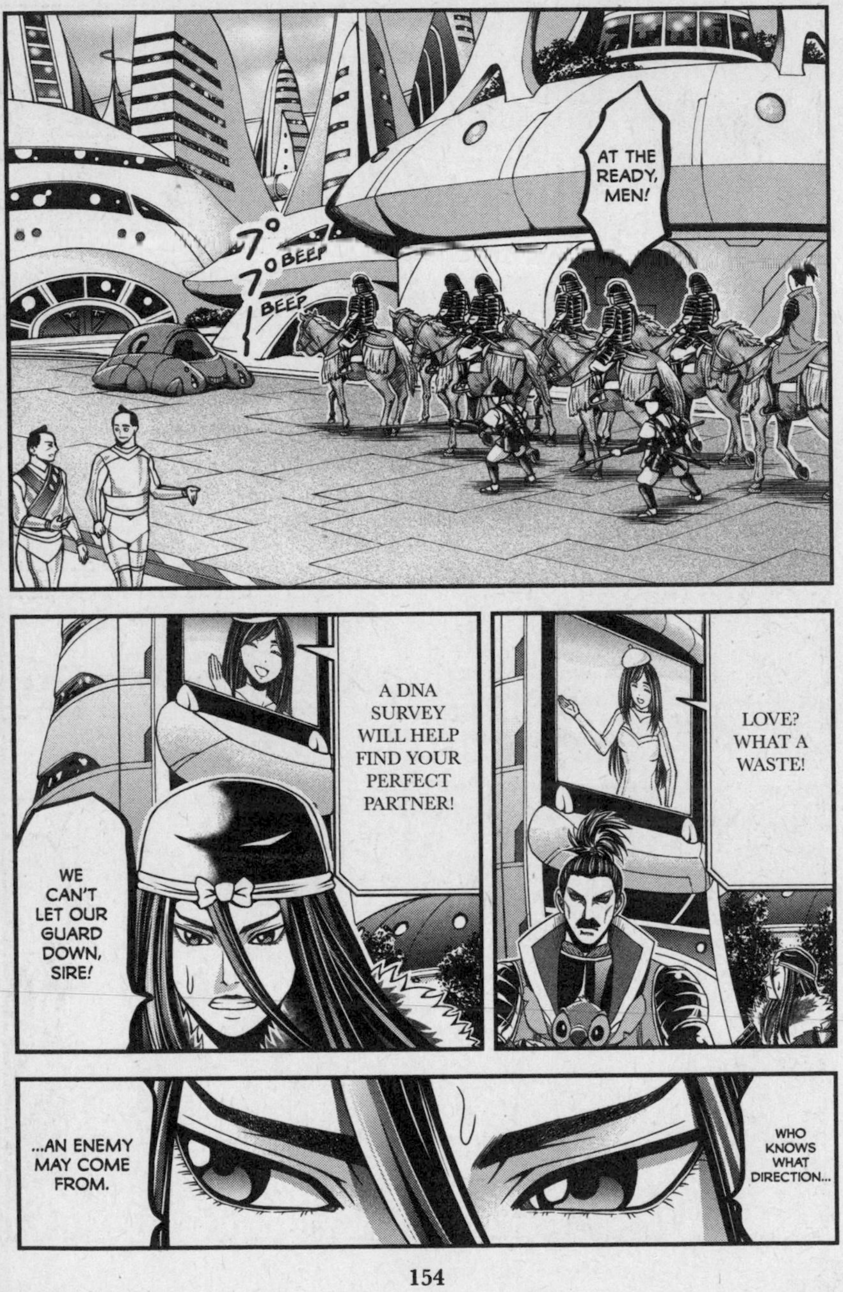
AT THE READY, MEN!
BEEP
BEEP
LOVE? WHAT A WASTE!
A DNA SURVEY WILL HELP FIND YOUR PERFECT PARTNER!
WE CAN'T LET OUR GUARD DOWN, SIRE!
WHO KNOWS WHAT DIRECTION...
...AN ENEMY MAY COME FROM.

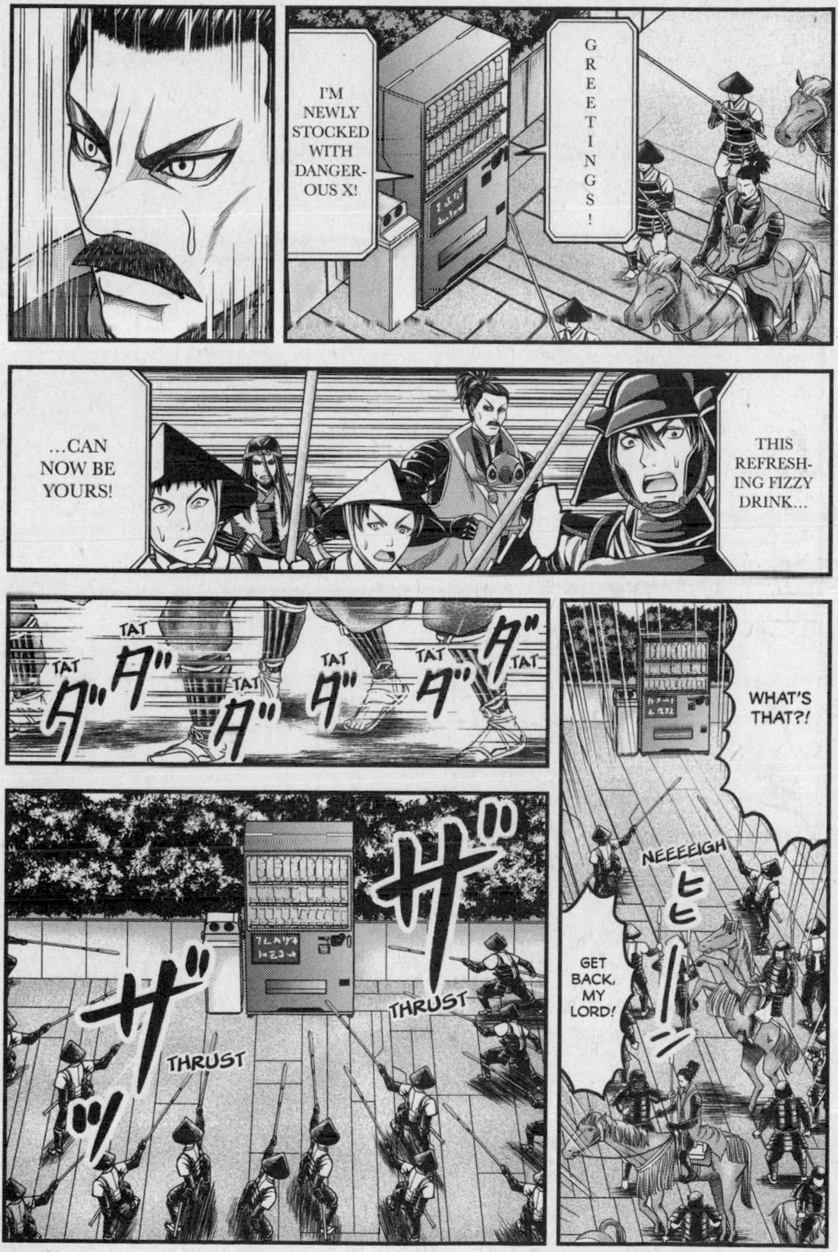
GREETINGS!
I'M NEWLY STOCKED WITH DANGEROUS X!
THIS REFRESHING FIZZY DRINK...
...CAN NOW BE YOURS!
WHAT'S THAT?!
NEEEEIGH
GET BACK, MY LORD!
TAT TAT TAT TAT TAT TAT
THRUST
THRUST

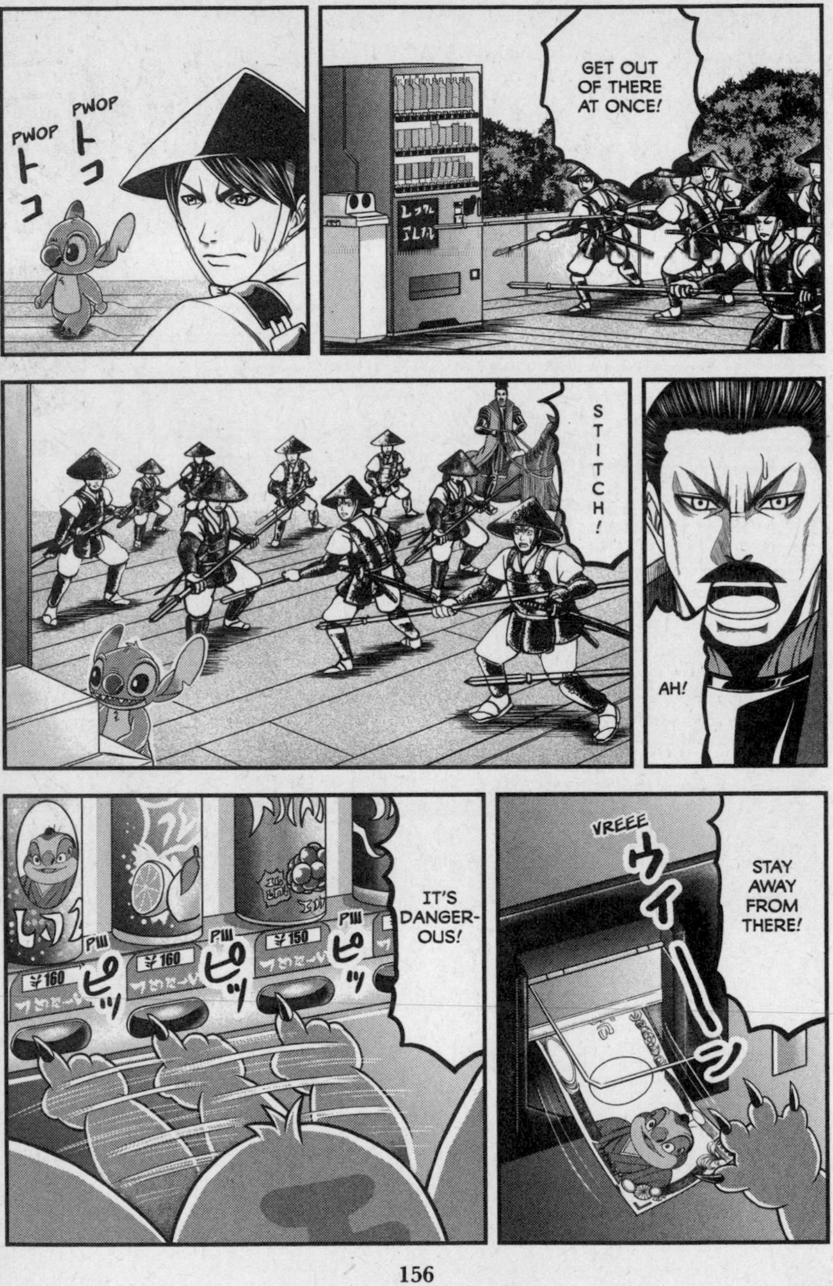
GET OUT OF THERE AT ONCE!
PWOP
トコ
PWOP
トコ
AH!
STITCH!
STAY AWAY FROM THERE!
VREEE
ウィーン
IT'S DANGER-OUS!
PIII
ピッ
¥150
PIII
ピッ
¥160
PIII
ピッ
¥160

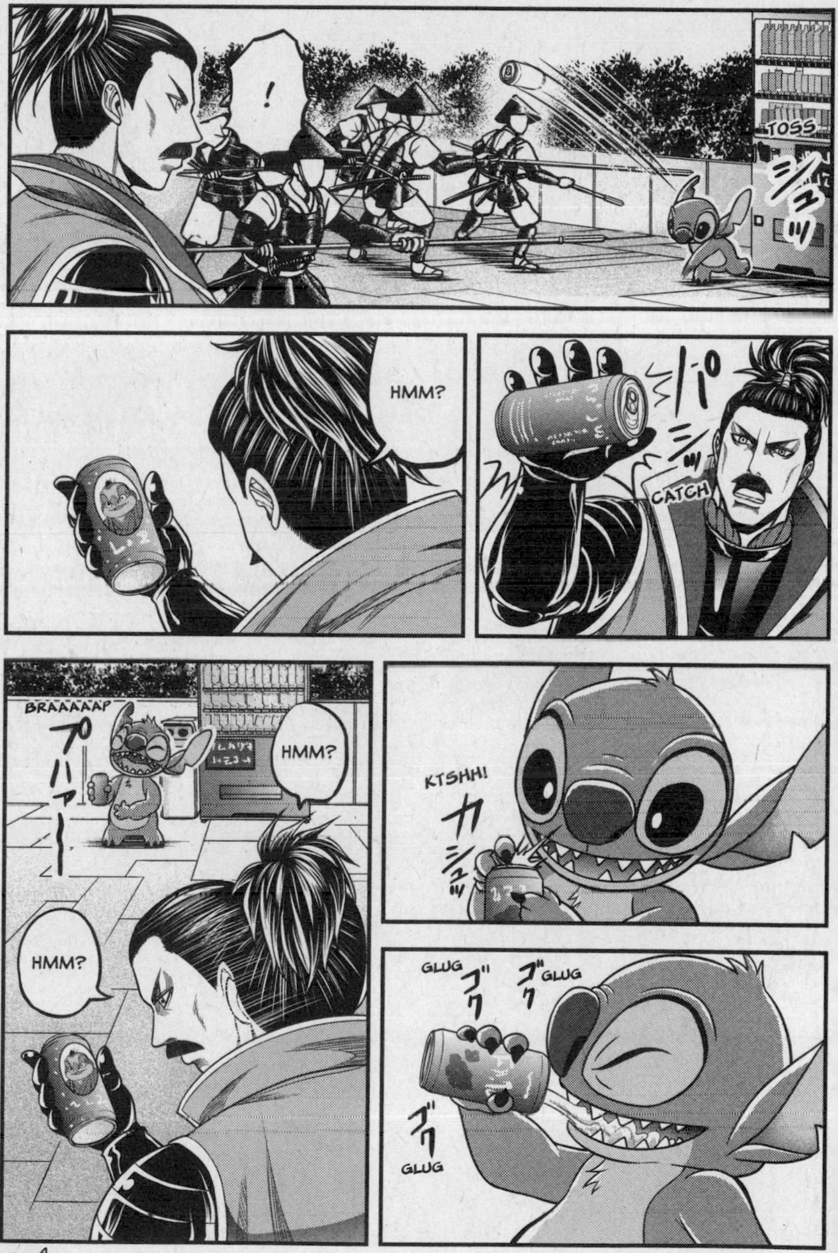
TOSS
シュッ
!
パシッ
CATCH
HMM?
KTSHH!
カシュッ
GLUG
ゴク
ゴク
GLUG
ゴク
GLUG
HMM?
BRAAAAAP
プハァー
HMM?

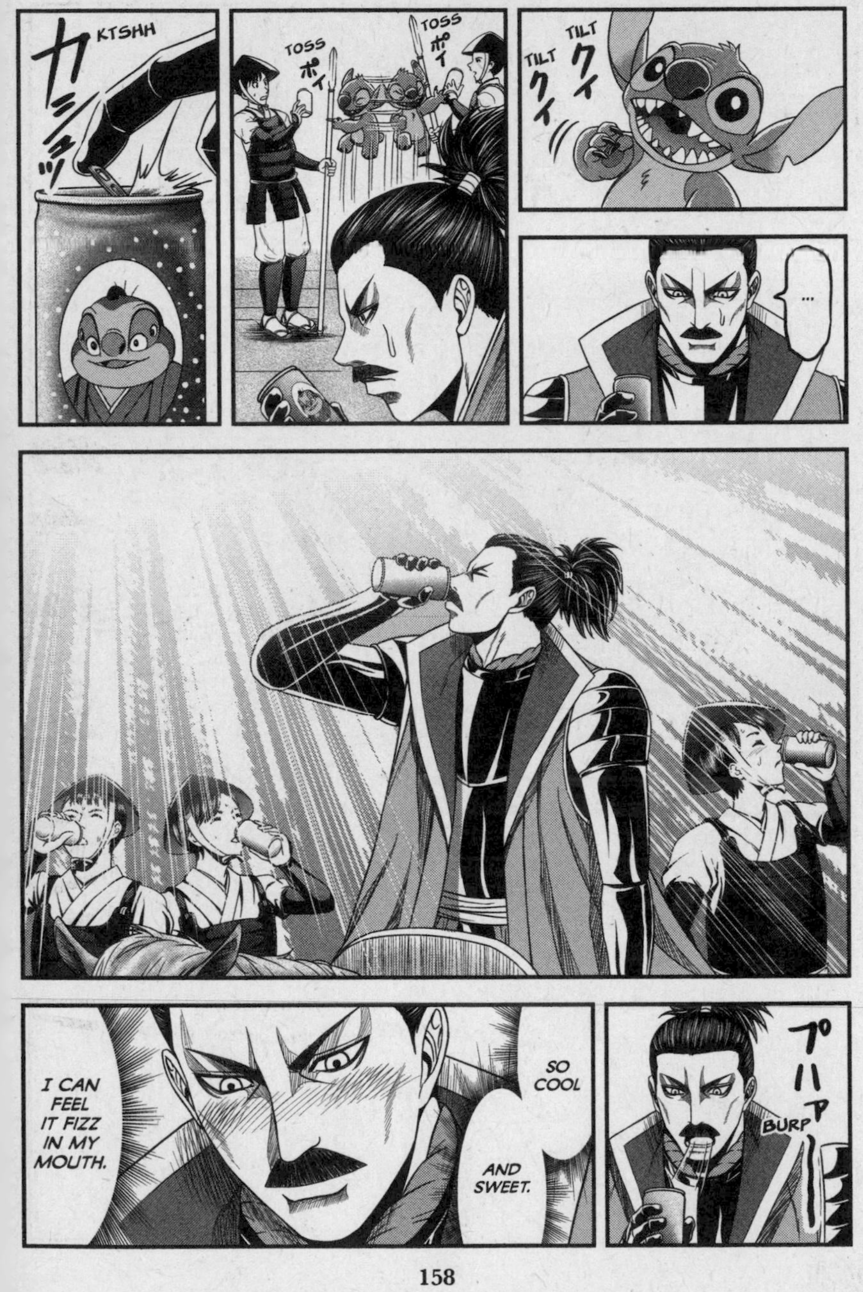

TILT クイ
TILT クイ
...
TOSS ポイ
TOSS ポイ
KTSHH カシュッ
BURP プハァ
SO COOL
AND SWEET.
I CAN FEEL IT FIZZ IN MY MOUTH.

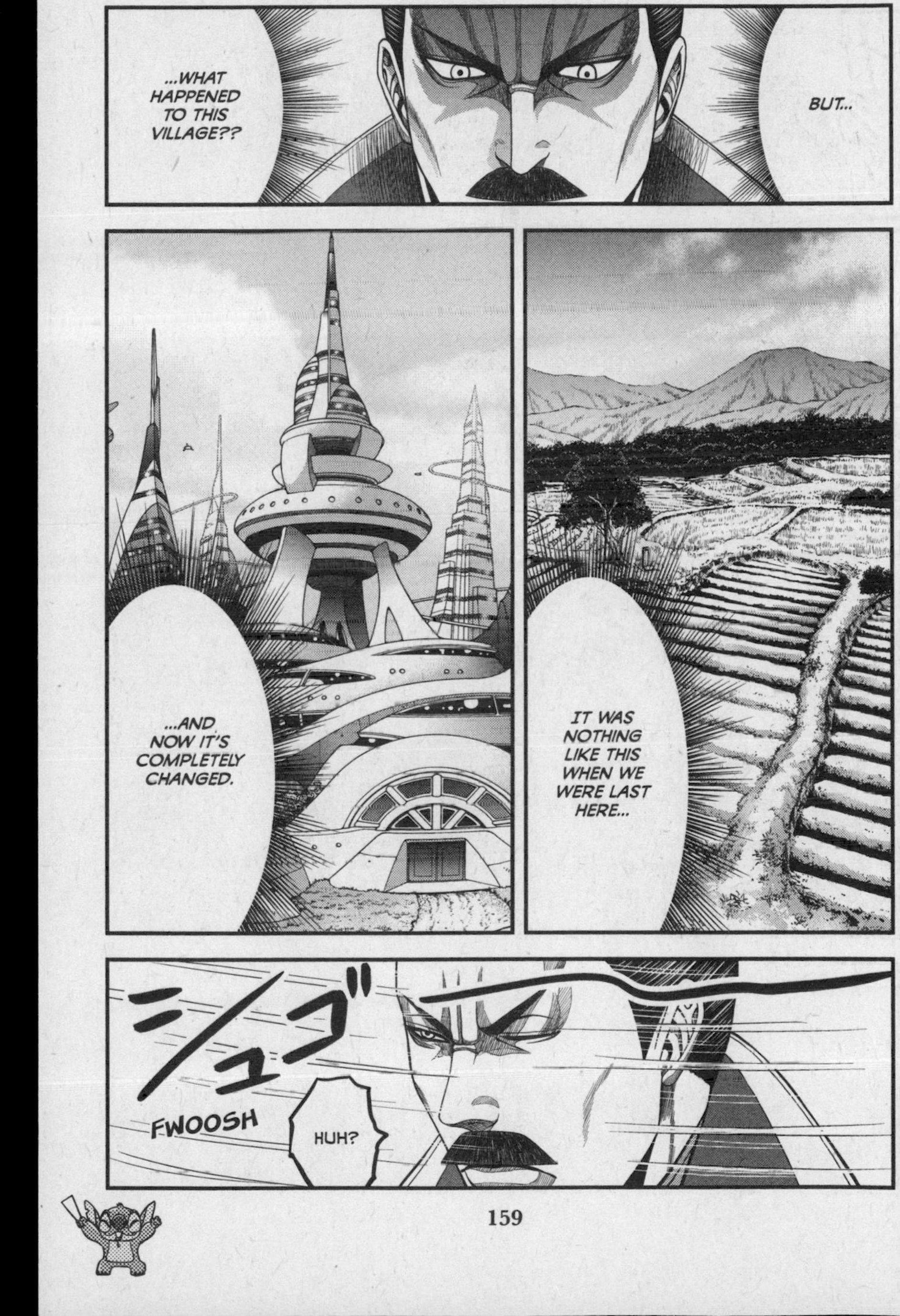
BUT...
...WHAT HAPPENED TO THIS VILLAGE??
IT WAS NOTHING LIKE THIS WHEN WE WERE LAST HERE...
...AND NOW IT'S COMPLETELY CHANGED.
シュゴ
FWOOSH
HUH?

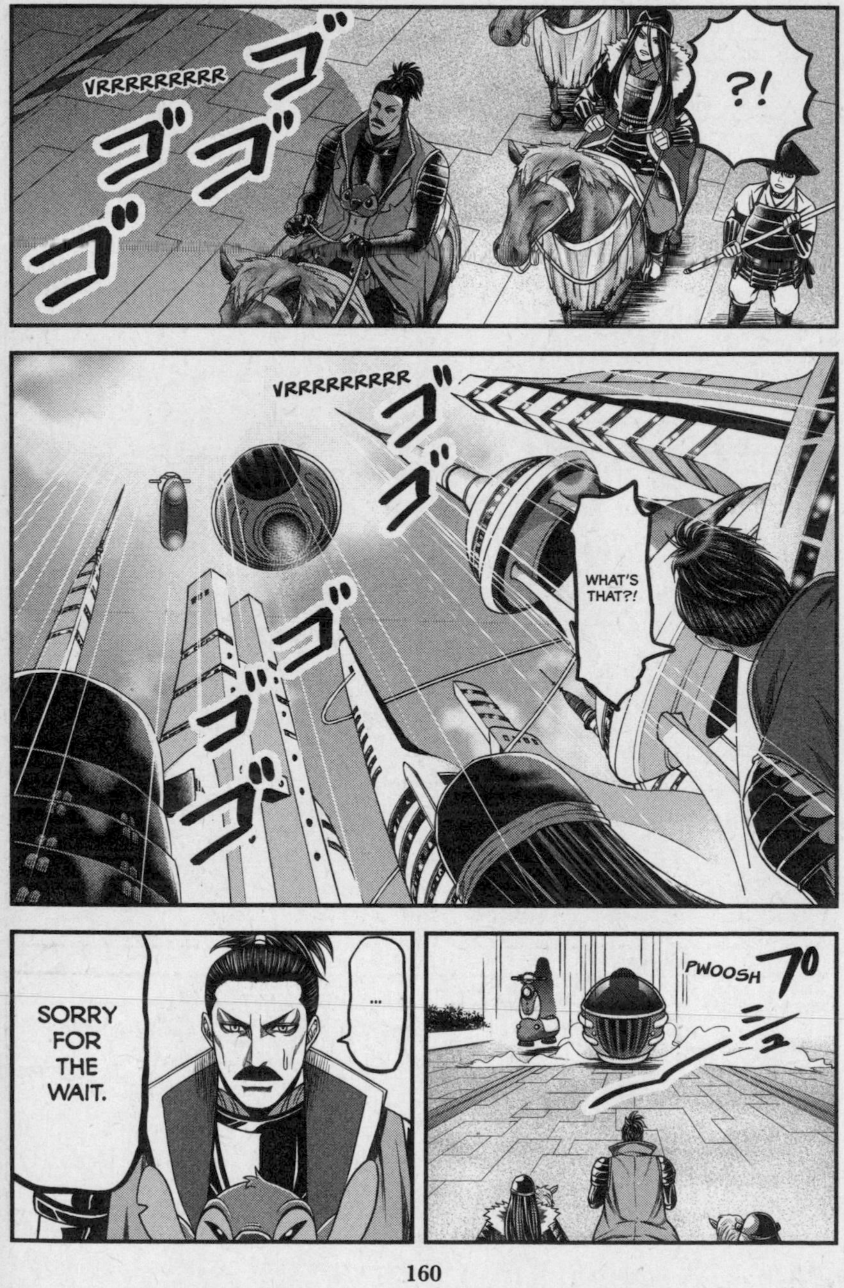
?!
VRRRRRRRRR
ゴゴゴゴ
VRRRRRRRRR
ゴゴ
WHAT'S THAT?!
ゴゴゴゴ
PWOOSH
…
SORRY FOR THE WAIT.

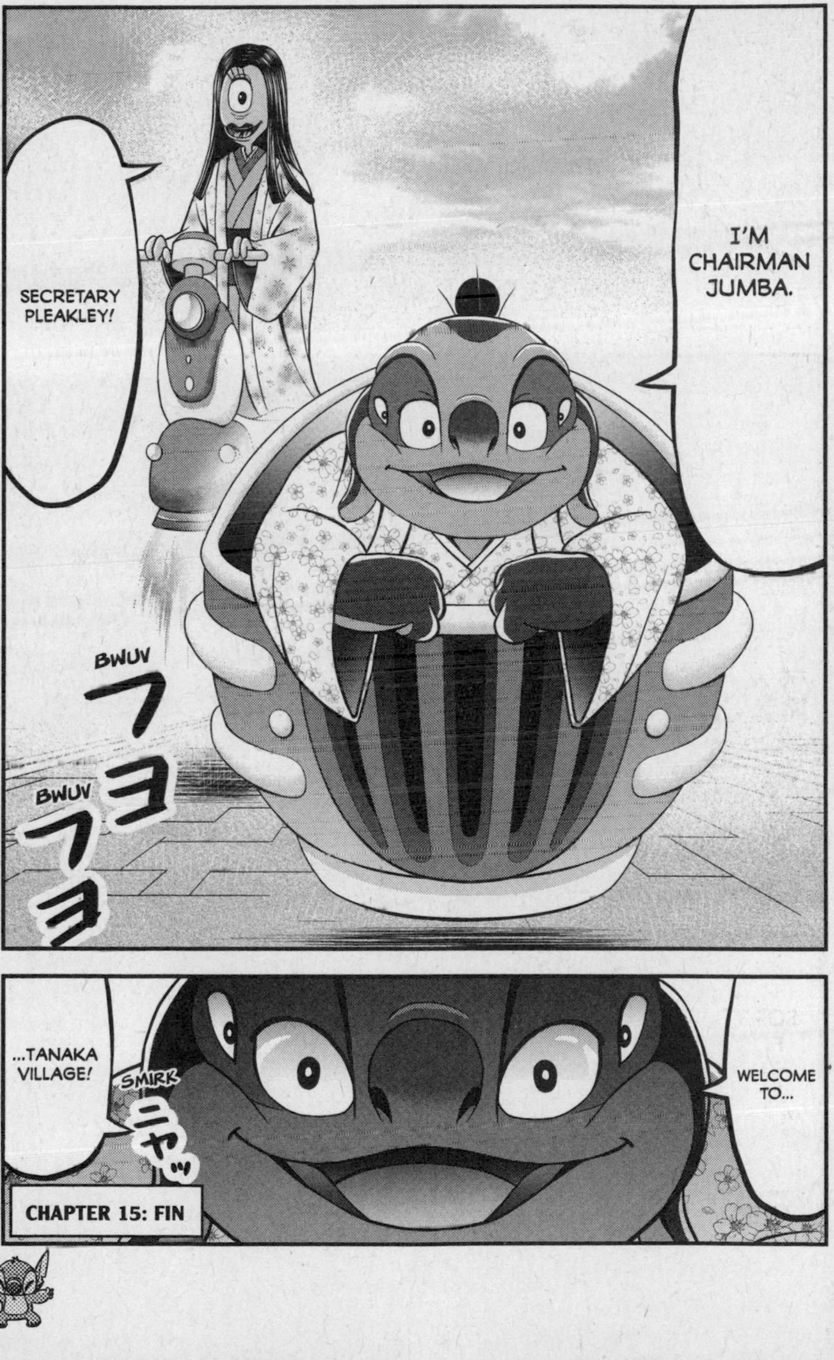
I'M CHAIRMAN JUMBA.
SECRETARY PLEAKLEY!
BWUV
フヨ
BWUV
フヨ
WELCOME TO...
SMIRK
ニヤッ
...TANAKA VILLAGE!
CHAPTER 15: FIN

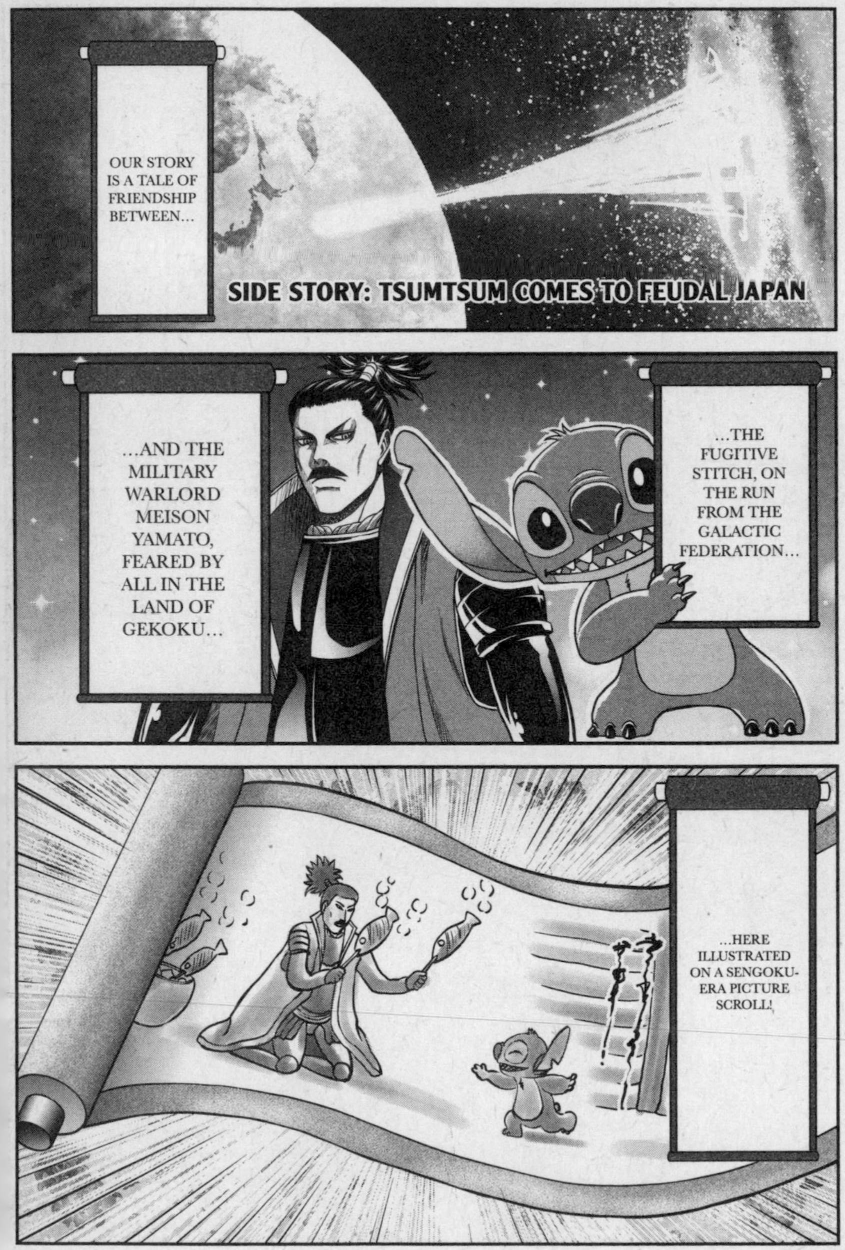
OUR STORY IS A TALE OF FRIENDSHIP BETWEEN…
SIDE STORY: TSUMTSUM COMES TO FEUDAL JAPAN
…THE FUGITIVE STITCH, ON THE RUN FROM THE GALACTIC FEDERATION…
…AND THE MILITARY WARLORD MEISON YAMATO, FEARED BY ALL IN THE LAND OF GEKOKU…
…HERE ILLUSTRATED ON A SENGOKU-ERA PICTURE SCROLL!

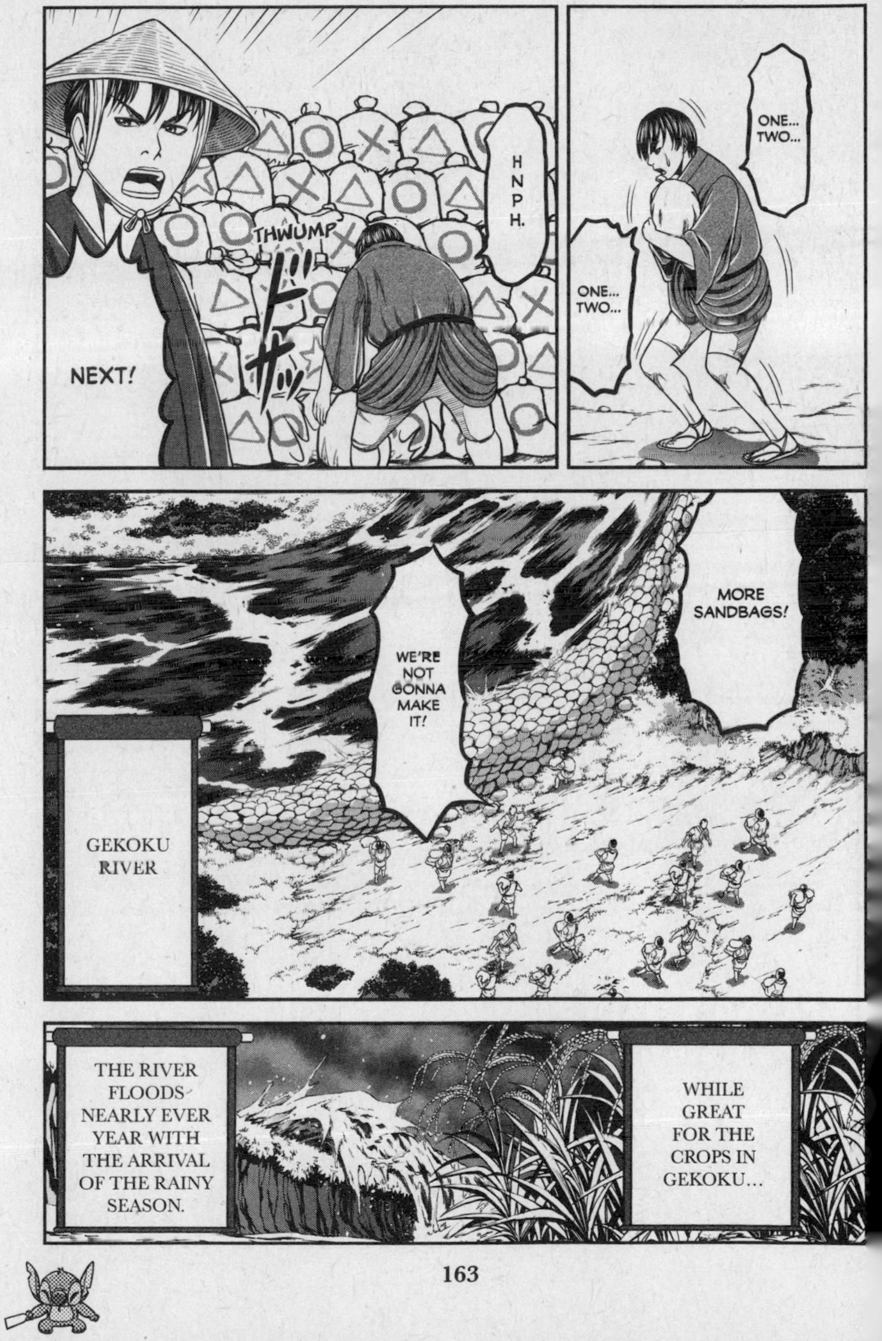
ONE... TWO...
ONE... TWO...
HNPH.
THWUMP
NEXT!
MORE SANDBAGS!
WE'RE NOT GONNA MAKE IT!
GEKOKU RIVER
THE RIVER FLOODS NEARLY EVER YEAR WITH THE ARRIVAL OF THE RAINY SEASON.
WHILE GREAT FOR THE CROPS IN GEKOKU...

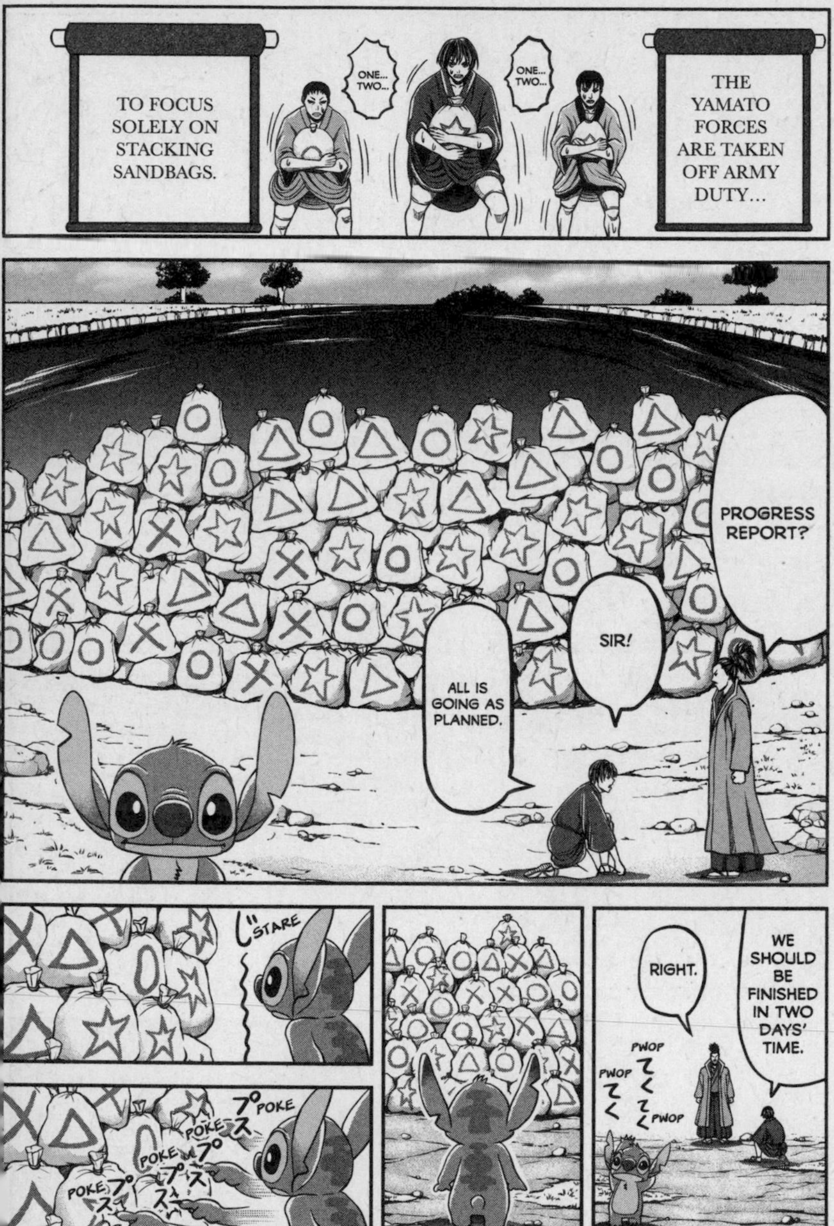
THE YAMATO FORCES ARE TAKEN OFF ARMY DUTY…
ONE… TWO…
ONE… TWO…
TO FOCUS SOLELY ON STACKING SANDBAGS.
PROGRESS REPORT?
SIR!
ALL IS GOING AS PLANNED.
WE SHOULD BE FINISHED IN TWO DAYS' TIME.
RIGHT.
てく PWOP
てく PWOP
てく PWOP
じ STARE
プス POKE
プス POKE
プス POKE
プス POKE

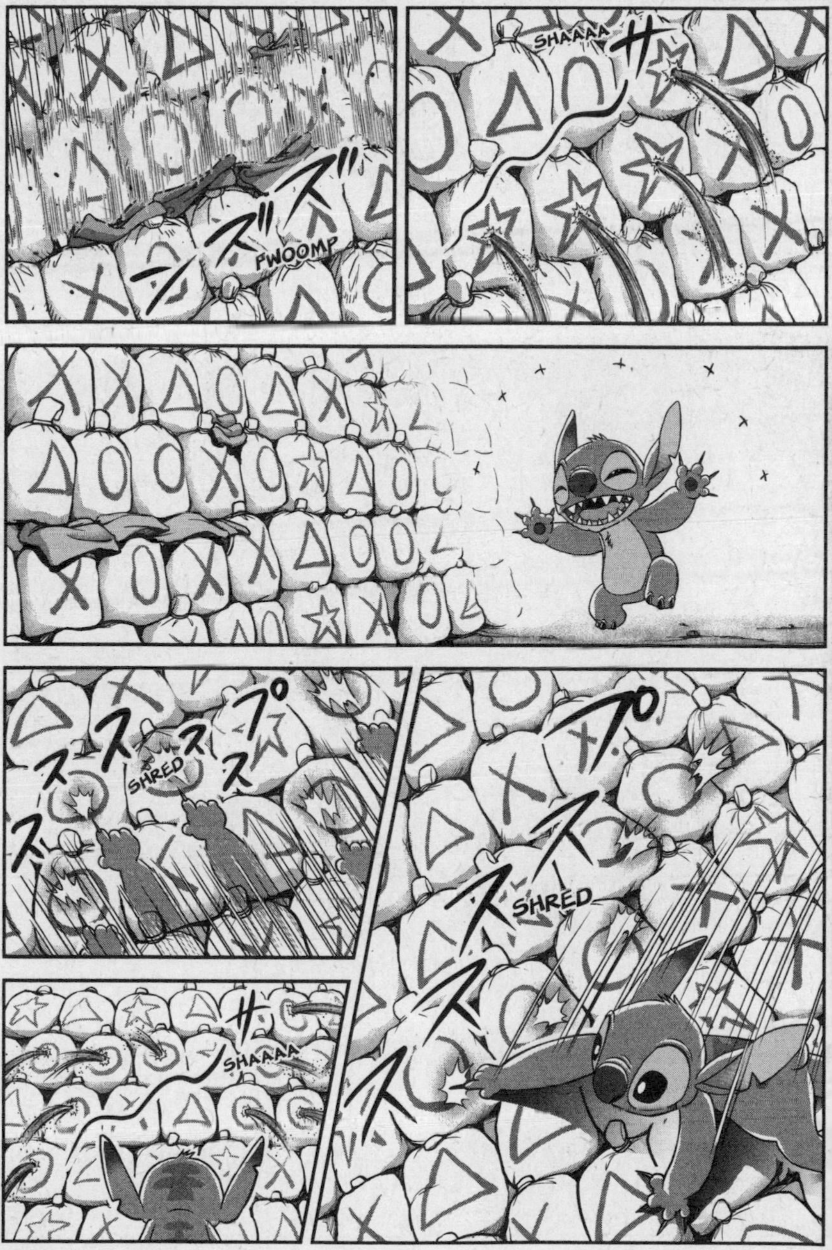
SHAAAA
FWOOMP
SHRED
SHRED
SHAAAA

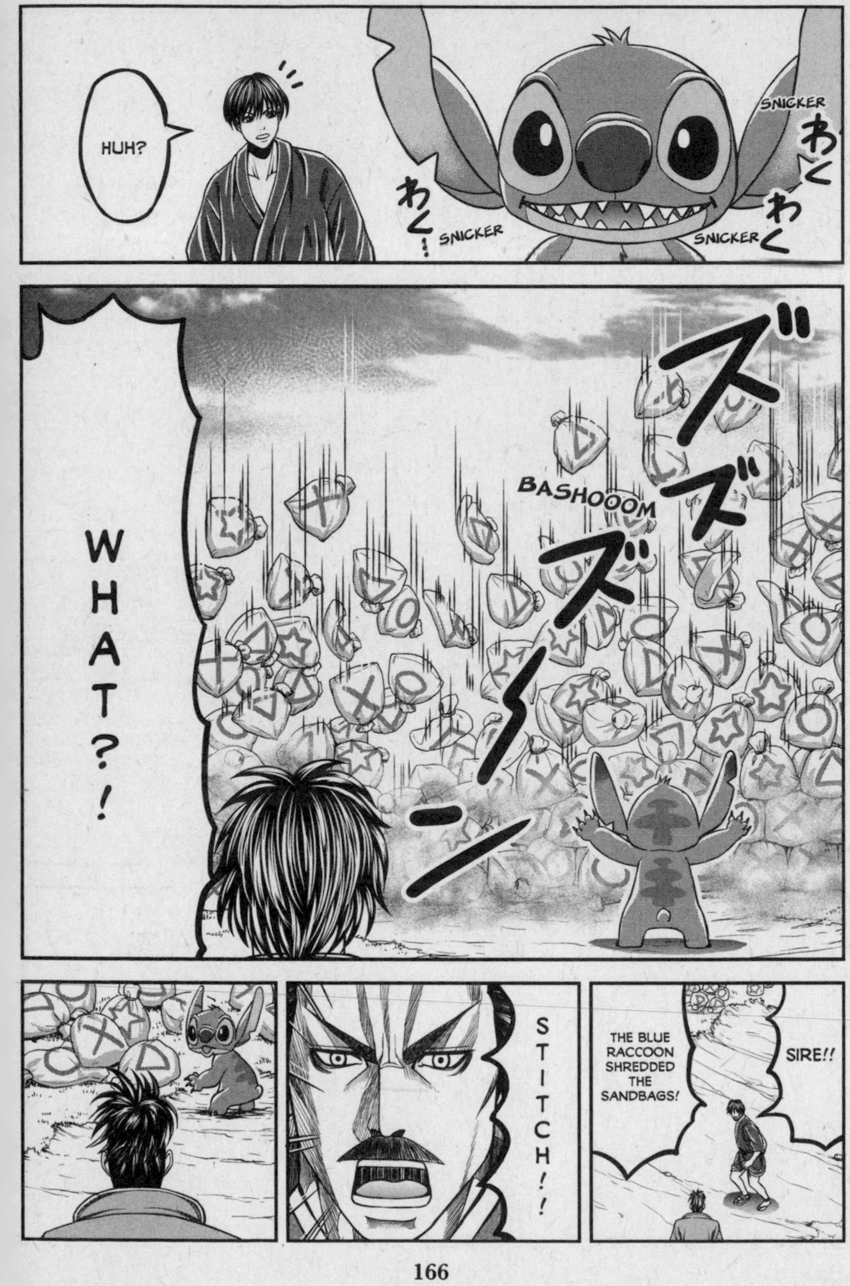
SNICKER
わく
わく
SNICKER
わく!
SNICKER
HUH?
ズズズーン
BASHOOOM
WHAT?!
SIRE!!
THE BLUE RACCOON SHREDDED THE SANDBAGS!
STITCH!!

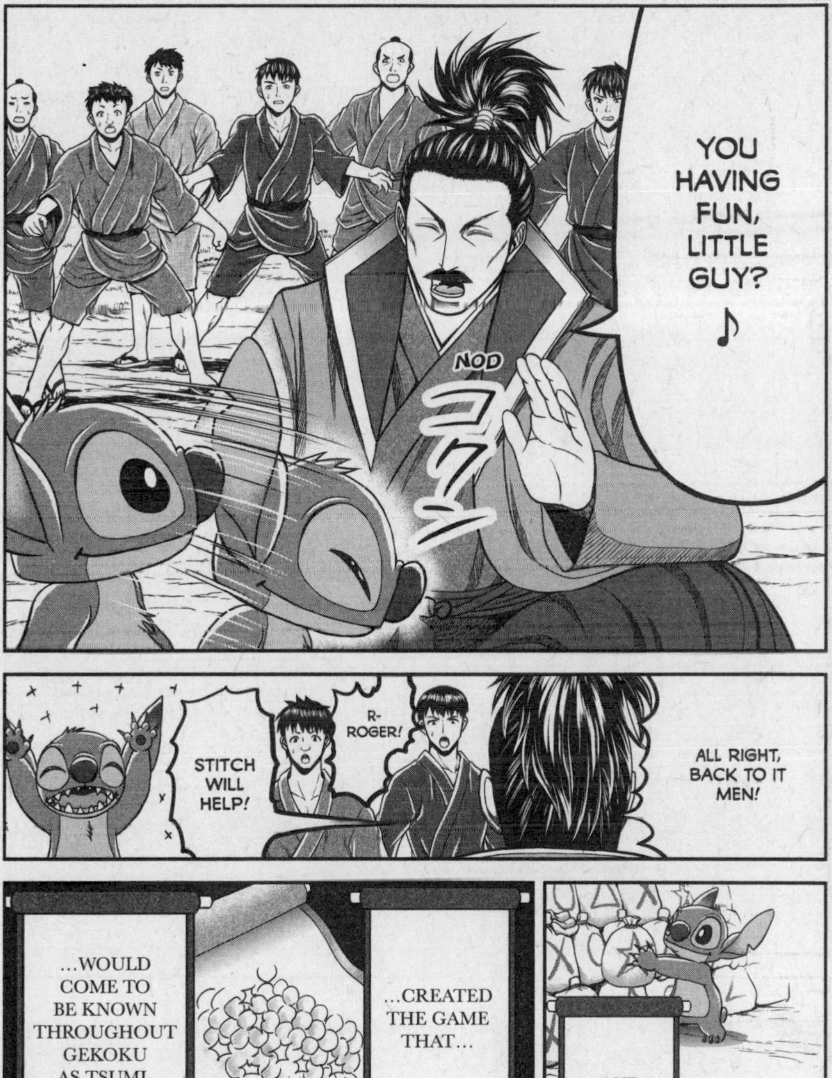
YOU HAVING FUN, LITTLE GUY? ♪
NOD
ALL RIGHT, BACK TO IT MEN!
R-ROGER!
STITCH WILL HELP!
AND THIS IS HOW STITCH…
…CREATED THE GAME THAT…
…WOULD COME TO BE KNOWN THROUGHOUT GEKOKU AS TSUMI-KASANERU!
FIN

AFTERWORD

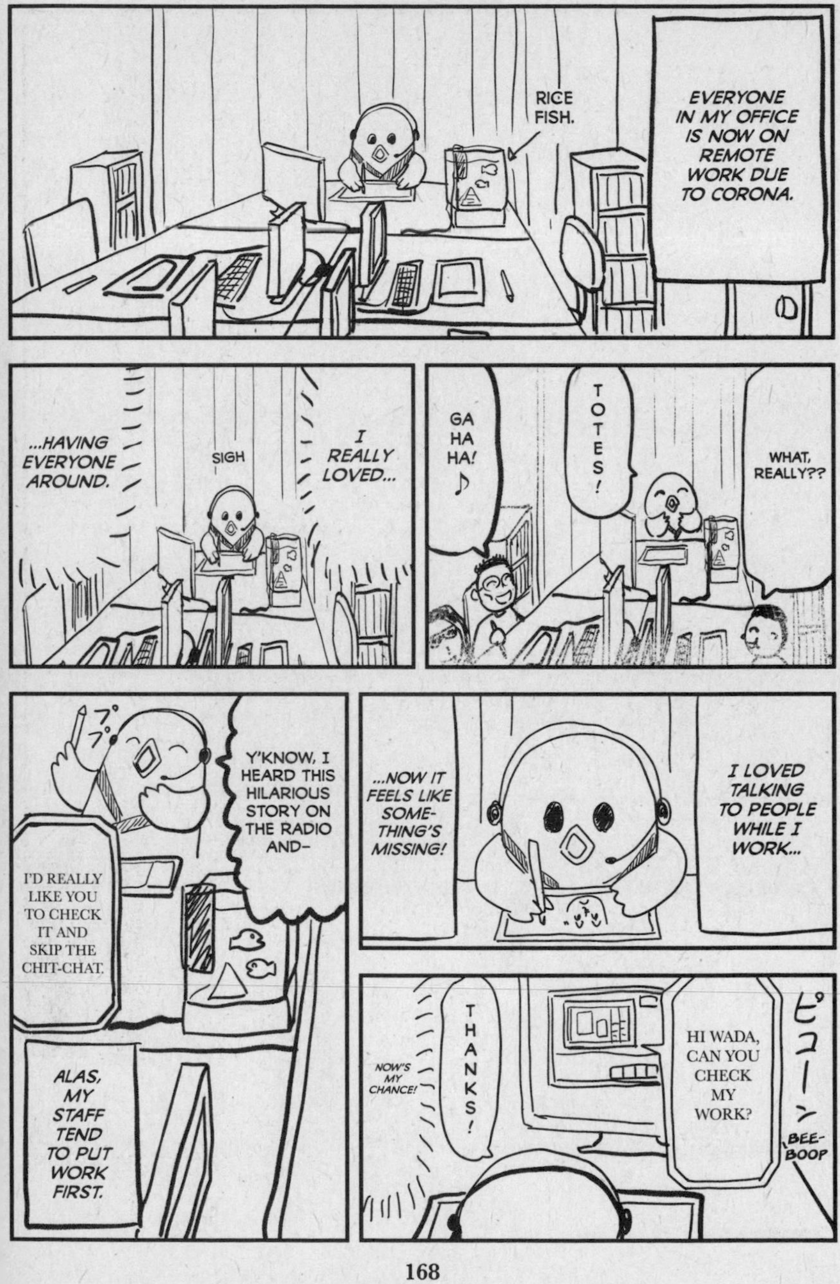

EVERYONE IN MY OFFICE IS NOW ON REMOTE WORK DUE TO CORONA.
RICE FISH.
WHAT, REALLY??
TOTES!
GA HA HA! ♪
I REALLY LOVED...
SIGH
...HAVING EVERYONE AROUND.
I LOVED TALKING TO PEOPLE WHILE I WORK...
...NOW IT FEELS LIKE SOME-THING'S MISSING!
ピコーン
BEE-BOOP
HI WADA, CAN YOU CHECK MY WORK?
THANKS!
NOW'S MY CHANCE!
ププ
Y'KNOW, I HEARD THIS HILARIOUS STORY ON THE RADIO AND–
I'D REALLY LIKE YOU TO CHECK IT AND SKIP THE CHIT-CHAT.
ALAS, MY STAFF TEND TO PUT WORK FIRST.

SPECIAL THANKS

NOBORU ROKUDA, HIDEKI MIYASHITA, TAKANORI YASAKA, DAIJU YANAUCHI, RYUUKI SATO, SHIHO ITO, PO

STAFF
SOUSHI ISHIKAWA, YUKI TAKO, NORIHISA OIDE

HELP STAFF
NORIYOSHI ISHIZAWA, T.T, TAKESHI HIRAI, TAKURO KAMIMURA

REFERENCE MATERIALS
HIDEKI MIYASHITA

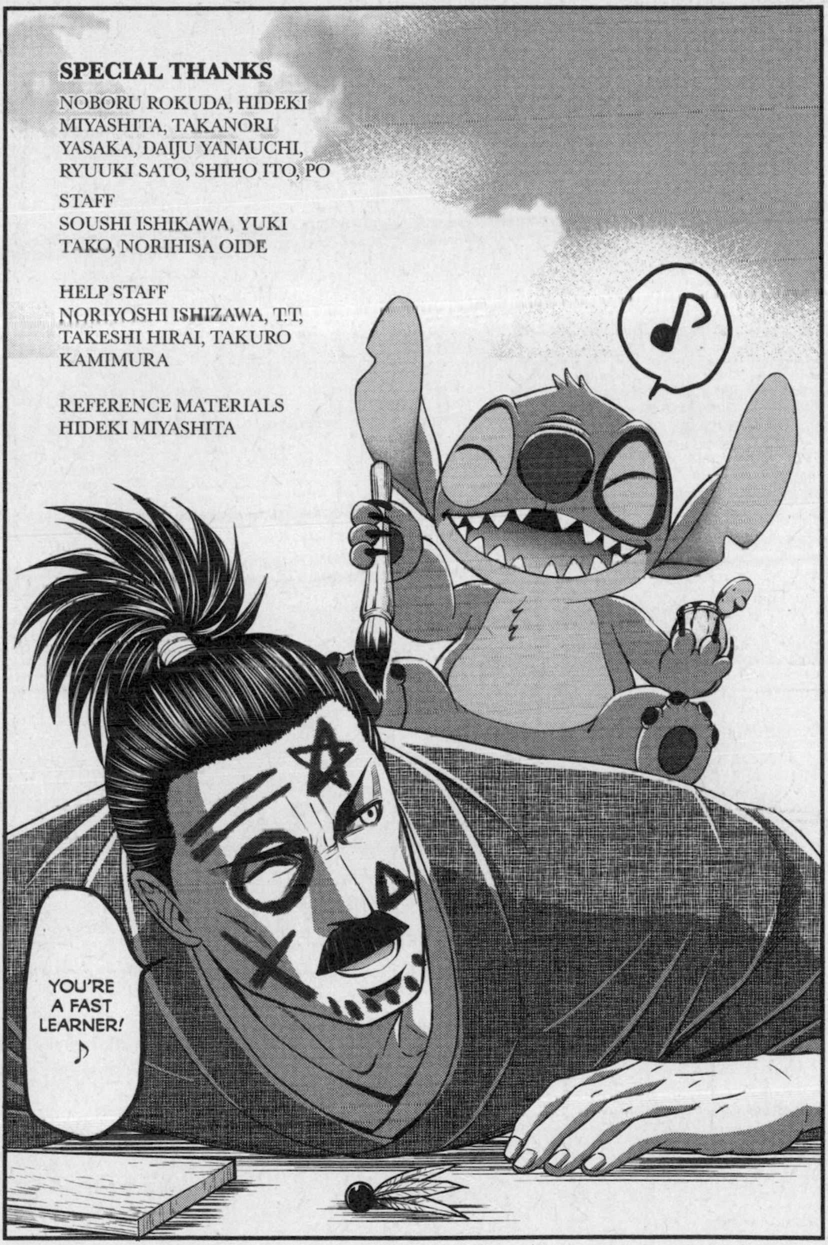
YOU'RE A FAST LEARNER!

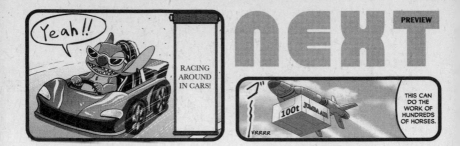

NEXT PREVIEW

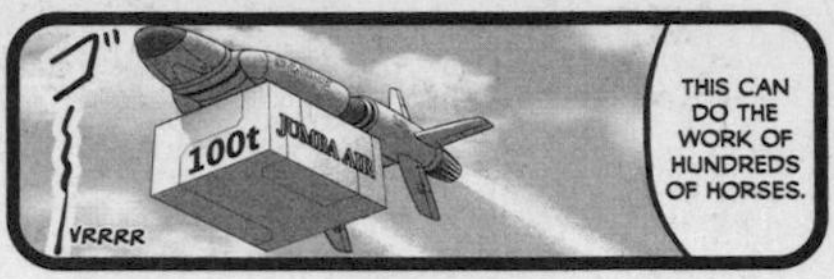
THIS CAN DO THE WORK OF HUNDREDS OF HORSES.
100t
JUMBA AIR
VRRRR

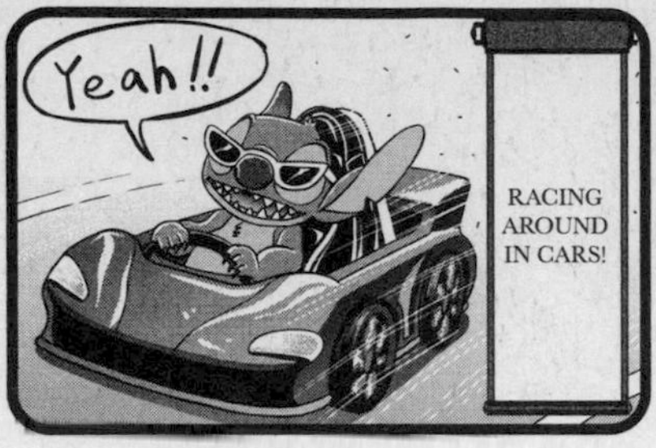
Yeah!!
RACING AROUND IN CARS!

WELCOME TO THE 'PERFECT" JUMBA VILLAGE

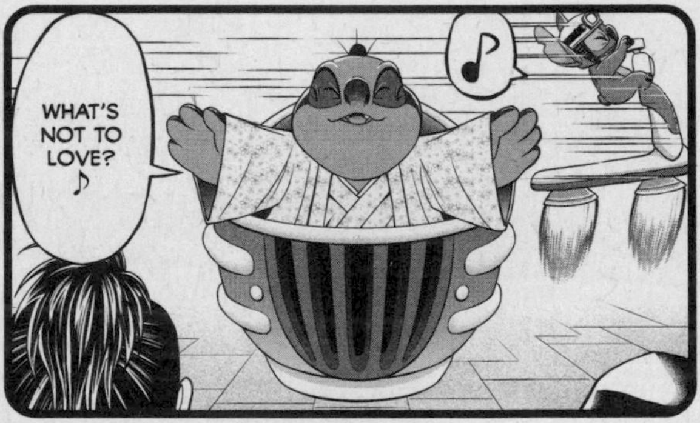
♪
WHAT'S NOT TO LOVE? ♪

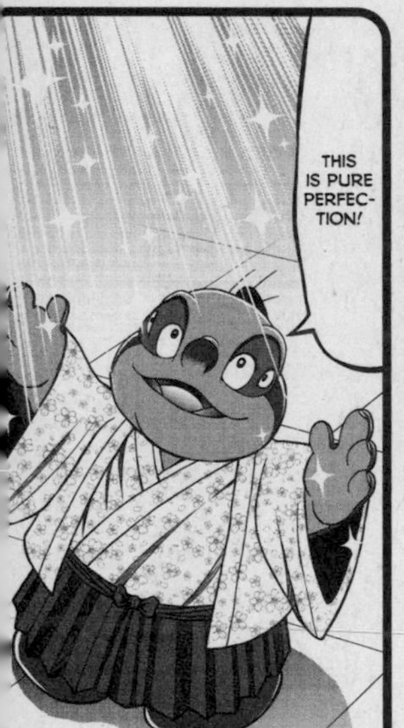
THIS IS PURE PERFEC-TION!

Disney
Stitch
STITCH & THE SAMURAI
HIROTO WADA

STAY TUNED!

COMING SOON!!

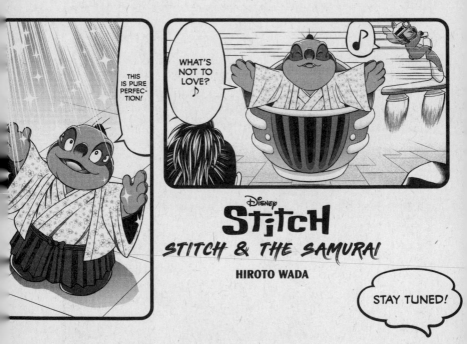

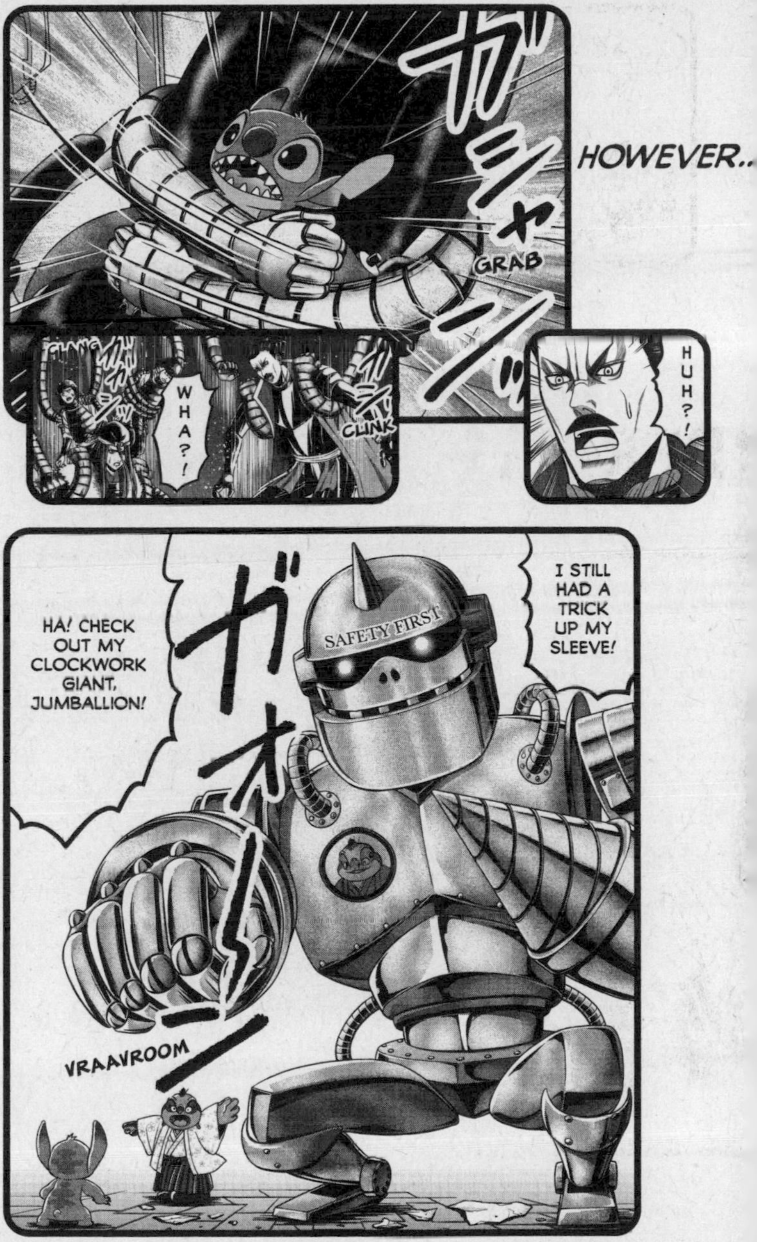
HOWEVER...
GRAB
HUH?!
WHA?!
CLANG
CLINK
I STILL HAD A TRICK UP MY SLEEVE!
HA! CHECK OUT MY CLOCKWORK GIANT, JUMBALLION!
SAFETY FIRST
VRAAVROOM

HOW WILL THEY GET OUT OF THIS ONE?!

VOLUME 3 WILL BE

LAUGHING UNDER THE CLOUDS, VOLUME 1

KarakaraKemuri

TOKYOPOP

Under the curse of Orochi, the great demon serpent reborn every 300 years, Japan has been shrouded in clouds for as long as anyone can remember... The era of the samurai is at an end, and carrying swords has been outlawed. To combat the rising crime rates, an inescapable prison was built in the middle of Lake Biwa. When brothers Tenka, Soramaru and Chutaro Kumo are hired to capture and transport offenders to their final lodgings in this prison, they unexpectedly find themselves faced with a greater destiny than any of them could have imagined.

© KarakaraKemuri 2011 / MAG Garden Corporation

THE FOX & LITTLE TANUKI, VOLUME 1
Mi Tagawa

1

The Fox & Little Tanuki
KORISENMAN

Mi Tagawa

TOKYOPOP®

TOKYOPOP

It is said that there are some special animals occasionally born with great powers. Senzou the black fox is one of those... but instead of using his powers for good, he abused his strength until the Sun Goddess imprisoned him for his bad behavior. Three hundred years later, he's finally been released, but only on one condition — he can't have any of his abilities back until he successfully helps a tanuki cub named Manpachi become an assistant to the gods. Unfortunately for Senzou, there's no cheating when it comes to completing his task! The magic beads around his neck make sure he can't wander too far from his charge or ignore his duties, and so... Senzou the once-great Fox Spirit must figure out how to be an actually-great babysitter to an innocent little tanuki or risk being stuck without his powers forever!

©2019 Mi Tagawa / MAG Garden

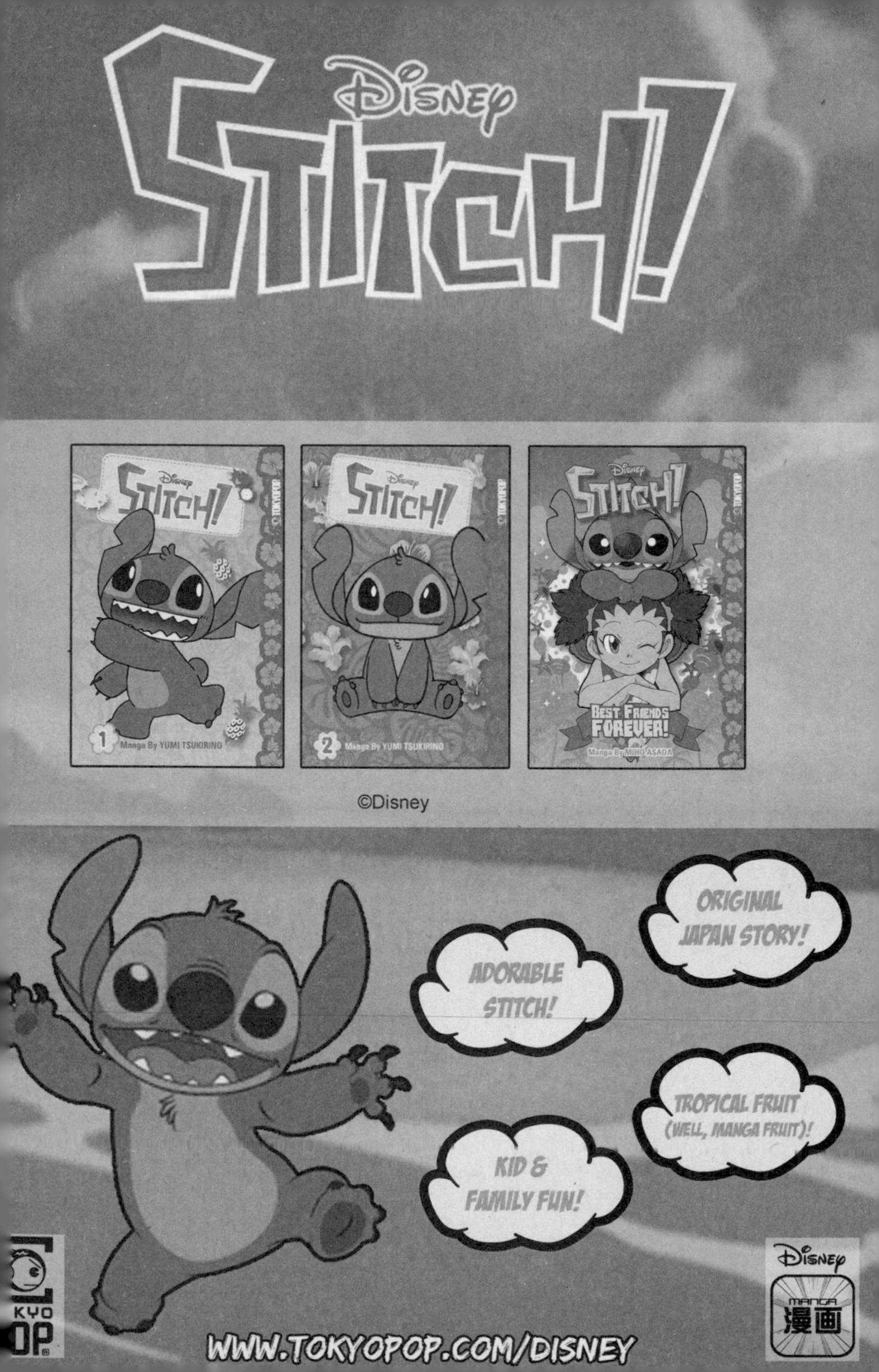
Disney
STITCH!
Disney STITCH!
1 Manga By YUMI TSUKIRINO
Disney STITCH!
2 Manga By YUMI TSUKIRINO
Disney STITCH!
BEST FRIENDS FOREVER!
Manga By MIHO ASADA
©Disney
ORIGINAL JAPAN STORY!
ADORABLE STITCH!
TROPICAL FRUIT (WELL, MANGA FRUIT)!
KID & FAMILY FUN!
WWW.TOKYOPOP.COM/DISNEY
Disney MANGA 漫画

Disney Stitch and the Samurai, Volume 2
Art by Hiroto Wada

Editorial Associate - Janae Young
Marketing Associate - Kae Winters
Translator - Jason Muell
Oopy Editor - Sean Doyle
Cover Colors - Sol DeLeo
Cover Designer - Sol DeLeo
Retouching and Lettering - Vibrraant Publishing Studio
Editor-in-Chief & Publisher - Stu Levy

A **TOKYOPOP**® Manga

TOKYOPOP and 🐢 are trademarks or registered trademarks of TOKYOPOP Inc.

TOKYOPOP Inc.
5200 W. Century Blvd. Suite 705
Los Angeles, 90045

E-mail: info@TOKYOPOP.com
Come visit us online at www.TOKYOPOP.com

f www.facebook.com/TOKYOPOP
🐦 www.twitter.com/TOKYOPOP
📌 www.pinterest.com/TOKYOPOP
📷 www.Instagram.com/TOKYOPOP

©2021 Disney
All Rights Reserved

All rights reserved. No portion of this book may be reproduced or transmitted in any form or by any means without written permission from the copyright holders. This manga is a work of fiction. Any resemblance to actual events or locales or persons, living or dead, is entirely coincidental.

ISBN: 978-1-4278-6806-0
First TOKYOPOP Printing: April 2021
10 9 8 7 6 5 4 3 2 1
Printed in CANADA

STOP

THIS IS THE BACK OF THE BOOK!

How do you read manga-style? It's simple! To learn, just start in the top right panel and follow the numbers:

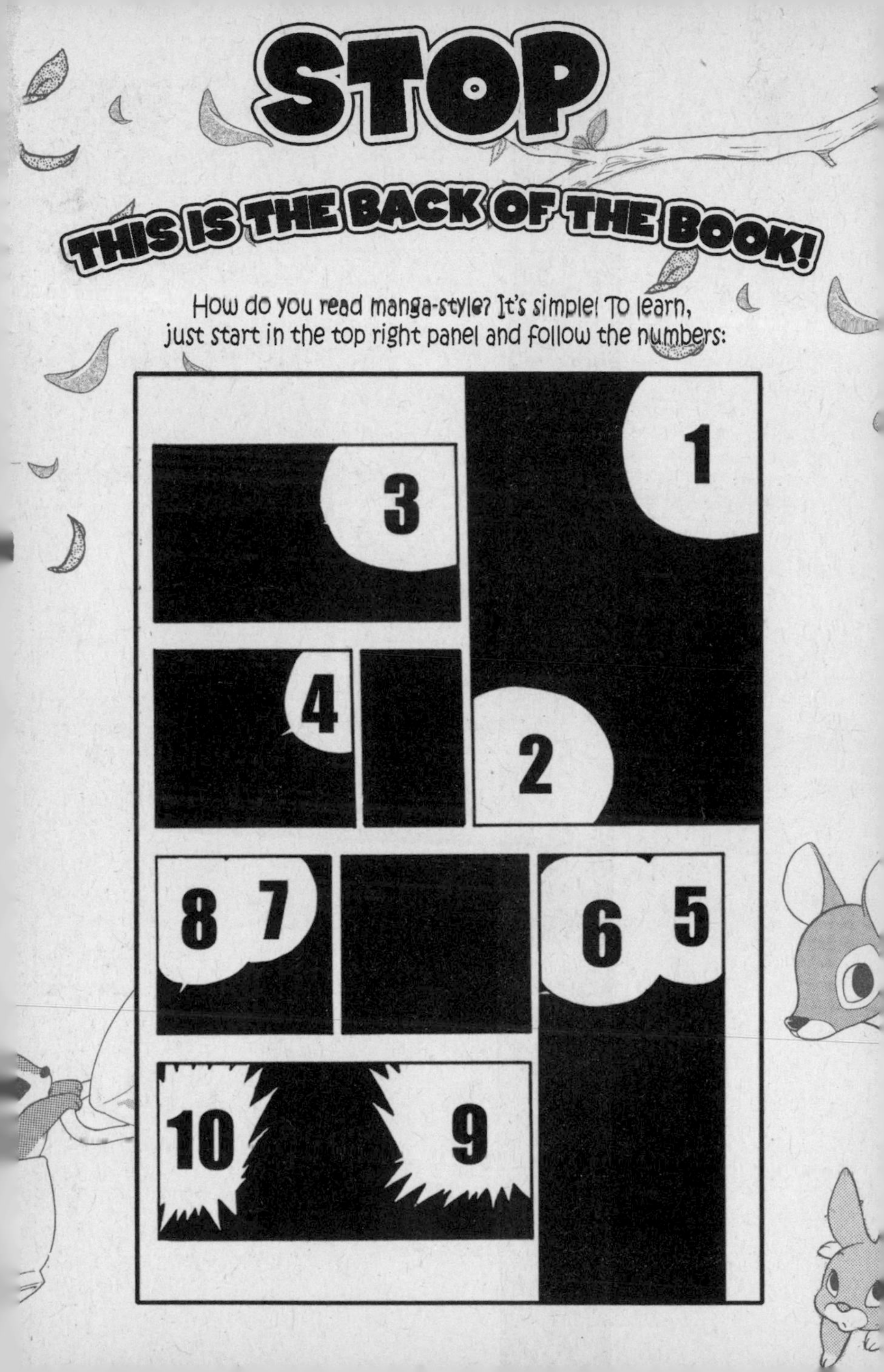
1
2
3
4
5
6
7
8
9
10